BLOOD OF THE RAVEN, BOOK 2

Ravenfall

ELIZABETH SCHECHTER

For more information contact:
Riverdale Avenue Books
5676 Riverdale Avenue
Riverdale, NY 10471

www.riverdaleavebooks.com
Cover design by Scott Carpenter
Design by www.formatting4U.com

First Edition, previously published as *Raven's Fall* February 2025
Second Edition, September 2025

Digital ISBN: 9781626017160
Paperback ISBN: 9781626017177
Hardcover: 9781626017184

Riverdale Avenue Books would like to thank you for purchasing book two of Blood of the Raven series, *Ravenfall*. Please, consider signing up to our newsletter where you can find the latest on us and your favorite authors, along with free copies of books from each of our imprints, at the link provided: https://preview. mailerlite.io/preview/1098983/sites/136486432257607665/0kJ9TD

If you are interested in being in our ARC reader/reviewer program, you can sign up here. Reviews are the life blood of the independent author and publisher and every single one counts to getting books into the hands of the right readers.

Chapter One

The *urla* in Dun Righ was the pride of High Queen Aideen. The ornamental lawn of smooth, even grass was usually kept immaculate, unmarred by weeds or blight. Today, however, there was a definite path being carved in the turf—the marks of a single man pacing back and forth through grass still kissed by frost. Diarmuid knew he might be courting the queen's wrath, but he simply could not stand still.

Six years. It had been six years since he'd married Grainne. Four times, her womb had quickened. Four times, the babe had died long before it had ever drawn breath. But this time, he'd dared to hope. At five months, Grainne had still been well, glowing in her joy. It had been the longest she'd ever carried a child, the first time she'd ever felt the babe move within her, and her hopes were high. High enough that she'd insisted on accompanying Diarmuid to the celebration of the birth of the High King's daughter. She would be fine, she assured Diarmuid. And so, they'd come to Dun Righ.

Only she hadn't been fine. She'd awakened him in the middle of the night in tears. She was bleeding. Frantic, he'd called for healers. Gormlaith, the queen's midwife, assured him that she would do all in her power to make certain that Grainne bore a healthy babe. Diarmuid had let her words wash over him—he'd heard the same too many times before. He'd sent the others back to Dun Morrigan, silently assuming that he and Grainne would be joining them before too long.

That had been three months ago. Gormlaith proved her words over and over. And finally, this morning, while Diarmuid had been breaking his fast with Eogan, the servant came with word from the midwife— Grainne was in labor. The baby would be born today. That had been hours ago, and Diarmuid had been forbidden to see his wife since then. So, he waited, and paced, watching the cold winter sun crawl toward the horizon as he silently traced the ruins of his despair into a narrow strip of frost-tipped grass on the High Queen's *urla*.

"Diarmuid."

The voice was familiar and unexpected. Diarmuid spun, shocked.

"Petran!" he looked at his brother, not quite believing what he was seeing. "What are you doing here?"

"Came to check on you. We miss you at home," Petran answered. "And honestly, I can count moons with the best of them. I know it'll be soon." He looked around. "Where's Grainne? What are you doing out here alone when everyone else is in the feast hall?"

"Is it that late?"

Petran nodded. "Diarmuid, what's going on? What's wrong? Where's Grainne?"

Diarmuid blinked. Where had his wits gone? "Are you alone?" Diarmuid looked around, half expecting to see the other sons of the Morrigan and their families appearing from the darkening sky.

"No. Turlach and Sorcha came with me. Sorcha wanted to see Cormac." Petran's smile faded, and he grabbed Diarmuid's arm. "You didn't answer me. Where's Grainne?"

Diarmuid turned to look at the house that he'd been doing his best to ignore. "There. They told me I can't see her. Not until—"

"She's giving birth?" Petran interrupted. "That's good, isn't it?"

Diarmuid turned back to Petran. He swallowed, meeting his brother's eyes. "You'll take care of them? The rest of the flock? If—"

Petran's jaw dropped. He looked horrified. He opened his mouth to protest, but Diarmuid shook his head and kept speaking, "You're the next oldest now. It's for you to do, if—"

"Don't *say* that!" Petran snapped. "She'll be fine! And the babe will be fine." He looked past Diarmuid, then stepped closer and pulled him into a tight embrace. "We've lost too many brothers. No more. You're not leaving us. And neither is she."

Diarmuid closed his eyes and rested his forehead on his brother's shoulder. "I never should have sent you home."

"No, you should have come with us," Petran murmured.

Diarmuid shook his head and straightened. "No. No, it was good that we stayed. Gormlaith… Petran, if I didn't know better, I'd swear that she's Aunt Brigid in disguise. I don't think Myrna could have done this."

Petran nodded. "Or she would have, with the others. How long has it been?"

Diarmuid closed his eyes and took a long breath. "Since dawn."

"And you've been here, killing the grass, since then?" Petran whistled. "Right. You need to get warm. You need a drink, something hot to eat, and someone else to take the watch for a bit. Tell Turlach where I am, will you?"

Diarmuid nodded past Petran. "You can tell him. And we'll all wait. I'm not leaving." He smiled at his brother's mate, who was limping toward them through the growing shadows.

"There you are," Turlach called. "What are we doing out here?"

"Waiting," Petran answered. "Where's Sorcha?"

Turlach shook his head. "On a tear." He glanced over his shoulder, then pitched his voice low. "I think we'll be taking Cormac home with us when we go. I know you think that the Queen is a lovely woman, and I know you think it's good for him to be part of the boys troop here—"

"He needs to learn to live alongside the mortals," Diarmuid said. "And it's good for him to be in a new place. The change—"

"Oh, I know that," Turlach agreed. "But he's learning more than that. Someone has put some funny ideas in the boy's head, and the healing we were hoping for doesn't seem to be happening here. Sorcha isn't happy, and I think the fostering ends tonight."

Diarmuid stared at Turlach. "Ideas? What sort of ideas?"

Turlach raised both hands. "Nothing I'll say aloud. But do you remember when we were coming to Dun Righ for the wedding? I told you about the girls that you'd find here? The ones that wanted a high-born husband?"

Diarmuid frowned, but he nodded. "That was a time ago. I do remember."

"Aideen was one of those. And I think she might be realizing that the high-born husband that she got isn't the one that she wanted. She isn't happy, and she's souring. And she's realizing that any sons of yours might have more claim to the throne than hers."

Diarmuid sniffed. "Hardly. There's not many that know that Eogan and I share a sire, and I've no claim nor desire to be High King." His eyes narrowed. "Turlach, are you telling me that the *Queen* is ill-wishing my child?"

Turlach coughed. "I never heard her say it, nor can I prove anything. But just now, I heard words from Cormac's mouth that I would never think to hear. Not from one that bore feathers. And he's been here long enough to pick up some habits that have made Sorcha ready to pull hair out by the roots, and she's not too picky about whose. Which is why I'm here and not there. I know better than to be between two she-cats when they fight, and one of them our Sorcha."

Diarmuid studied him for a moment, then looked up at the clouds painted scarlet and gray by the setting sun. "Spending the year here was supposed to help him. That's what Grainne thought. That new surroundings, new people, would bring him out of his pain. We'll bring the boy home. Niall will be glad of it. It's time Cormac started training with his father."

"True," Petran said. "He's grown taller. He'll be a big man, Cormac will. His namesake was a big man, too."

"Sorcha's father?" Turlach asked. Diarmuid nodded.

"Cormac probably massed the same as you both together," he said. "And none of it fat. But he was a merry man, for all of it."

"Our Cormac will be a merry one, too," Petran assured him. "We'll bring him home. He's been through a time of it, but we'll find a way to gentle him again. You'll see."

"It's simpler at home, on our mountain." Diarmuid turned back toward the house he'd been trying to ignore. "I want my son to see our mountain. My daughter."

A hand closed over his shoulder, and he turned to see Petran. "They'll be fine, Diarmuid. They'll both be fine."

Diarmuid nodded, looking back toward the house. It was far enough from the *urla* that he couldn't hear what was happening inside—that was why he'd chosen to wait here and not any closer. The waiting was torturous, but hearing Grainne calling for him had been worse.

"What are you all doing out here?"

Diarmuid smiled and turned toward the red-haired woman approaching them. "Sorcha. Waiting."

"Waiting?" Sorcha repeated. Her eyes widened. "Grainne's having the baby? What are you doing here?"

Diarmuid nodded toward the house. "Gormlaith wouldn't let me stay."

"Wouldn't—and you *listened*?" Sorcha gaped at him, then grabbed his arm and started to drag him toward the house. "Men!"

"What did I do wrong?" Diarmuid asked. "She told me I couldn't stay!"

"And what did Grainne want?" Sorcha asked. "You don't listen to the midwife for this. You listen to your wife, Diarmuid. Now you're going in there."

"But—"

She stopped and turned toward him. "Who knows more about this? You or me?"

"You do, but—"

"You were there when the pair of you started this road, no?"

Diarmuid blinked at her, realized what she was saying, then gasped, "Sorcha!"

She folded her arms over her chest. "You should be there at the end of the road, too. Myrna had Niall in for all of our children. You should be there for yours."

Diarmuid tried to think of an argument, but his brains seemed to be frozen. Silent, he nodded, and followed Sorcha back up to the door.

"I'll go in. Wait a moment," Sorcha said. She opened the door and slipped inside, leaving Diarmuid outside to fidget uncomfortably. He could hear voices inside, indistinct, and wondered what was happening. When Sorcha would come back, and if he'd be banished to the *urla* once more.

The door opened, and Sorcha looked out. She smiled. "Come inside. Grainne's been waiting for you."

* * *

At dawn, Petran sent Turlach back to Dun Morrigan to summon the others. Either they'd be here to welcome their oldest brother's child… or they'd be here to support Diarmuid and Grainne as they had before. Petran wasn't sure which it would be. He hoped not the latter. Not again. Alone, he wandered into the feast hall, thinking he might find a servant to bring him something to eat before he returned to his vigil. He wasn't expecting to find anyone but servants awake, so hearing voices made him stop and step back into shadows. He drew his cloak of feathers around himself, preparing to shift and fly.

"You're not going to be important anymore, Mama says!" a high voice exclaimed. 'And that's why they're taking you away. You can't stay here anymore. You can't sit at my table or share my lessons or be my foster brother anymore, because you're not important. Nobody is going to care about you anymore."

"I am so important! My father is the High King's own smith, and that's important!"

Petran moved through the shadows until he was behind a pillar and could see the two boys. One was his nephew, 11 year-old Cormac. The other, the one who was loudly declaring to his porridge that Cormac was no longer worthy, was the High King's seven-year-old son, Diarmuid. They were alone, which struck Petran as strange. Where were the rest of the boys being fostered at court? Or the man tasked with teaching them? Petran wasn't sure who that was, but these boys should have been breaking their fast with him and learning their morning lessons.

"You're not a smith, and you won't be for years and years. You're only here because you're Uncle Diarmuid's heir. Mama says that when Uncle Diarmuid's son is born, you won't be his heir anymore." The boy sniffed, then gestured with his spoon. "You'll go back to being a nobody that no one cares about."

Cormac frowned down at his own bowl. Then he raised his head. "Aunt Grainne's lost four babies. This baby is going to die, too, and good riddance."

"Cormac!" Petran snapped, stepping out into view. Cormac went white, staggering to his feet.

"Uncle Petran!"

"Shame on you," Petran growled. "Is this what fostering has taught you?" He heard giggling and turned on the younger boy. "And you! Don't think I won't be speaking to your father about this!" He turned back to Cormac. "Go to your mother, boy. And you'll tell her exactly what you just said, or I will, and it will be that much worse for you." He waited until Cormac had fled before turning to the other boy. "Your father is where?"

"Still abed," Diarmuid answered insolently.

"Then it looks like we'll be waking him," Petran said. "Up and march."

An hour later, Petran was fighting a headache, and to keep from swearing aloud as he crossed the *urla* toward the guesthouses. Eogan had been abed, all right. With Aideen, and she'd taken exception to Petran dragging her precious boy in by the ear. He hadn't realized that a woman could be quite that shrill—certainly none of his brother's wives ever were. But Eogan had made her be still once Petran told him the conversation he'd overheard. There would be some shaking up in the high king's household, Petran was certain. Now to see about his own kin—he whistled as he came to the door of the closest house, then peered inside. Empty. He hadn't seen Sorcha in the hall, nor had he seen Cormac since he'd sent the boy to find his mother. Not in the hall, not in the guesthouse. There was one other place he could check; he turned and started off toward the other guesthouse, the one where Diarmuid and Grainne were staying. The place where they were waiting. As he got closer, he heard it.

The wail of a baby's cry.

He stopped, his heart in his throat. He wasn't hearing things. That was a baby. And the sound was coming from in front of him. He staggered into a run, stopping only when he saw the door open. Sorcha came out, closing the door behind her. She saw him and smiled. She looked tired, but very pleased.

"And?" Petran demanded.

"And we're to send for the others," she answered. "Diarmuid wants to present the baby to them all."

"Already done," Petran said. "I sent Turlach an hour ago. *And?*"

Sorcha's smile broadened. "A boy." She glanced over her shoulder, and her smiled faded slightly.

"What?" Petran demanded. "What's wrong?"

"Nothing," Sorcha answered. "Just... no, nothing."

"Sorcha!"

"You'll see him when the others do," Sorcha said. "Now be still. Grainne needs to sleep."

"Looks as if you do, too," Petran said. He put his arm around Sorcha's shoulders. "Come on. Have you seen your boy?"

"Cormac? No. I've been here since before dawn. Why?"

Petran considered it. Then he shook his head. He'd tell her later. "Nothing. Come on. You need to sleep."

* * *

Petran was watching the skies from the *urla*, tracking the flock of ravens as they approached. Silently, he counted. Who had come? Who had stayed? The younger children had stayed behind, surely. They weren't ready for the all-day flight from Dun Morrigan. Who had stayed with them?

Turlach was the first to shed feathers, landing with a lightness that disguised his lame leg. He landed close enough to Petran that all the harper needed to do was close his arms to embrace his mate. The others shed their cloaks of feather around him, revealing that only the men had come, and then not even all of them.

"Fergus stayed behind?"

"Fergus stayed with the women, to help keep an eye on the littles," Cuanu answered. "What's the news, Petran?"

Petran grinned. "The news is that we're all to meet Diarmuid's son in the hall." He stressed the word, and saw smiles appear. "I haven't seen him yet. The only one who has is Sorcha."

Niall touched Petran's arm and arched a brow. Petran shook his head. "I haven't seen her since midday. I think she's been off with Grainne, teaching her to care for the baby. Don't be surprised if she wants another one after this, Niall."

Niall laughed silently, shaking his head. Petran grinned and gathered his brothers with a wave. "Come on. Eogan is waiting for us."

He waited, watching as they moved past him toward the hall. Cuanu was the next oldest after him, ever since his twin Ronan had died. Unmated still, and it looked as if he would always be so. Cathal and Maelan followed him, and silent Niall trailing after.

"What's wrong?" Turlach murmured.

"I don't know," Petran answered, keeping his voice low. "Sorcha's been very closed-mouthed about the babe. And I've not been allowed to see him."

"We'll see him now," Turlach said. He tucked his arm into Petran's. "Lead on, love. I'm tired."

Petran nodded and followed his brothers into the hall. Inside, the High King greeted them all, pouring mead with his own hands. The Queen was there, but her smile was brittle. Petran met her eyes, and she looked away before making a muffled excuse and leaving the hall.

"Something wrong with the Queen?" Cuanu asked Petran.

Petran considered, then shook his head. "She's had something stuck in her craw these past few days."

Cuanu looked puzzled. He arched a brow, glanced the way the Queen had gone, then narrowed his eyes at Petran. "Truly?"

"Something of the sort, yes," Petran answered mildly, ignoring Turlach's snickering.

"Strange." Cuanu moved away, and Turlach shifted closer.

"Does she now?" he whispered.

"I caught her boy and Cormac, and I perhaps heard what you heard, or worse," Petran whispered back. "And I brought it to Eogan. The queen will be taking the winter with her own kin, for her health. And we might have young Diarmuid to foster."

Turlach nodded. "That will be good for him. He'll learn."

Petran grinned. "He will, won't he?"

A quick flurry of movement, and Petran turned to see Niall heading toward the door. The reason was obvious—Sorcha had come into the hall. She kissed him, then drew him off to the side. A moment later, Diarmuid appeared in the door. He looked more tired than Petran could remember seeing him, but there was a light to him that was new. On his right arm was Grainne, still pale, leaning on her mate for support. And in the crook of Diarmuid's left arm....

"Oh, he's a tiny one!" Maelan said from behind Petran.

"Not surprising," Cathal added. "He's a month early."

"He cried well," Petran said. "Heard him from a good distance away."

"Good. Good lungs on him, then." Cathal said.

Diarmuid cleared his throat, and everyone fell silent. He glanced at Grainne, who smiled and nodded. Then he looked back at his brothers. "Brothers, come and meet our son."

Petran moved closer along with the others. From where he stood, the baby looked like a bundle of blankets. Then Diarmuid moved a fold of cloth, and Petran stopped. So did everyone else.

"Diarmuid?" Eogan finally broke the silence. "Are... are his feathers *white*?"

Diarmuid had been looking lovingly down at the baby in his arms. He glanced up, then back down. "Yes. So is his hair. What little he has."

"A white raven?" Petran murmured. "Is that because he was early, do you think? Will he get darker?"

"I don't know," Diarmuid answered. "Mother didn't answer when I asked her. It doesn't matter, Petran."

"Is he broken?" The voice was high, piping, and Cormac came closer, repeating himself. Petran hadn't even realized he was there. "Is he broken, like Fergus?"

"He is not," Grainne snapped. "He is perfect, and he is healthy." She reached out and rested her hand on the baby's chest. "He'll grow to be a fine man."

"Has there ever been a white raven before?" Maelan asked. "Cuanu, do you know?"

Cuanu scowled. Then he shook his head. "Not that I know of. Perhaps. If it happens now, it's likely happened before. I can find out, if you think it matters."

"It doesn't," Diarmuid said. "Not to us." He looked up, drew himself up to his full height, and announced, "I, Diarmuid, son of the Morrigan, called the Raven King, acknowledge this child as my son and heir." He glanced down again, and his smile softened his face. "His name is Lorcan."

Chapter Two

It was early enough on the late winter morning that there was still a sharp chill in the mountain air, still thin shreds of fog lingering over the *urla*. The figure moving through them was pale enough that he could have been made of fog, his white feather cloak and white hair making him look like a ghost. It was early enough that everyone was still abed, and it was still quiet within the walls. Lorcan liked the quiet and the early morning fog, the stillness that came before the world woke. He liked the way the cold air tasted, the way it smelled, before the silence was broken by the sounds of his family's voices and his uncle's forge.

Lorcan stopped in the center of the *urla* and closed his eyes. He wasn't sure what the difference was. He'd tried to explain it to his father, but the Raven King had listened, then shook his head. He didn't understand. It wasn't the first time—Lorcan knew he was different. Not just in looks, but something inside. He was different from the other ravens, and it changed the way he saw the world. This wonderfully rich silence, for example. It was something he had experienced nowhere else—not in the village of Scath, only a few miles away, not in the High King's *baile*, nor anywhere in the druid's college. It was a peace that he only knew in Dun Morrigan, and then only in the brief time between when the world woke and the family did. He couldn't explain it, so he savored it. This was his time. His alone.

He heard a crash of metal on metal, and a stream of profanity in a familiar, caustic voice. Lorcan sighed and opened his eyes. If Cormac was awake, and already in a foul mood, that was the end of peace for today. Briefly, he considered going down to Scath and spending the day with—no, he turned 19 today, and his mother would expect him to spend the day with the family. Even if some of the family would have preferred otherwise. Lorcan turned and headed toward the large hall. He wasn't sure why his older cousin seemed to dislike him so much. There was some reason, he knew, but no one would explain it to him. They would intercede, certainly. His father and Cormac's both had stepped in more than once over the years. But no one would ever explain.

More cursing from the forge. Some project of Cormac's must have gone terribly wrong, for that level of profanity this early in the morning. Lorcan shook his head and entered the cool, dark feast hall. No one else was there yet, and he crossed to the fire-pit and crouched down to stir up the coals. He tossed two logs and a handful of bark into the pit and watched as small flames appeared and started to lick the sides of the logs. He heard footsteps behind him and turned to see his father coming toward him.

"Good morning," Lorcan said, surprised. He rose and stepped easily into his father's embrace. He'd long since accepted that he'd never have his father's height, nor the breadth of his shoulders. His mother told him that he resembled her long-dead brother, which left him a full head shorter than his father, only a finger-width or two taller than his mother, and willowy instead of powerful. He was, according to his cousin, the runt of the flock. Lorcan grimaced at the thought and shoved Cormac's words away, stepping back. "You're awake early."

"And you're up with the dawn," Diarmuid said. "But then, you usually are." He reached out and ruffled Lorcan's hair. "Born with the dawn, you were."

Lorcan grinned. "So you've told me."

Diarmuid nodded, then gestured. "Come and fly with me."

Lorcan coughed. "Fly?"

"Not far. Just up to the perch," Diarmuid added.

"Oh. All right." He followed his father out of the hall and shifted, taking to the air as a white raven. He loved to fly, but he didn't fly well—whatever it was that made his feathers white also made them break easily. For short flights, he was fine, but longer flights didn't usually end well, and Lorcan was perhaps the only raven born to his feathers who knew of necessity both how to ride a horse and how to drive a chariot.

The perch was a ledge high up the mountain. It looked out over Dun Morrigan and the village and the road that led down to the sea. Lorcan wheeled over it as Diarmuid landed and changed, then joined his father. He looked around and laughed. "I don't remember it being this close up here."

"It's been a while since we've been here together," Diarmuid said. "Since we talked without other ears to hear."

Lorcan glanced at his father. "Is that why we're here?"

Diarmuid smiled, draping his arm over Lorcan's shoulders. "It could be. Or it could be that I don't spend nearly enough time with my son. You spend more time with your uncles, or down in the village."

Lorcan nodded. "And Mother. I spend time with Mother. She says I'll be a fine healer one day. Uncle Petran is teaching me harp and the bard songs. Uncle Turlach is teaching me about horses. Uncle Cuanu is teaching me history. He's given up on teaching me Latin and Greek, though. I've no talent for it. Uncle Niall has been teaching me to fight—"

"I know that. Niall says you're quite good. And the village?"

Lorcan licked his lip, then glanced at his father. "What of the village?"

"You spend a great deal of time there."

Lorcan felt his face growing warmer. "His name is Bran."

Diarmuid chuckled. "I'd wondered. You're young to mate—"

"He isn't," Lorcan said quickly. "Isn't mine, I mean. I know that. He knows that. It's just… I like him."

"That's not a bad thing, at 19," Diarmuid said. "Wait… Bran? Orla's Bran?"

"Yes, Da." Lorcan felt his face grow warm. "It's not like there are many others my age in the village. And through Aunt Orla and Aunt Caitilin, I'm kin to them all."

Diarmuid sniffed. "True. You could go spend time with Eogan—"

"I don't like it at Dun Righ, Da. It's too noisy, and too—I don't know."

"Too human?" Diarmuid asked. Lorcan considered, then nodded.

"Yes, I think that's it. They're always in a rush over something. They never slow down. It's never quiet. And… I don't know, they look at me oddly." Lorcan sat down and dangled his legs over the edge, looking down at his home. "Da, why am I different?"

Diarmuid whistled low, then sat down next to Lorcan. "Is this a 'why are my feathers white?' question or a 'why do other people look at me oddly?' question?"

"Both, I think."

"Other people look at you oddly because they can sense the godblood in you," Diarmuid said. "We're not like them, Lorcan. And we can't hide that."

Lorcan nodded. "And the other?" He reached out and touched his father's cloak of glossy, black feathers. "I'm the only white raven. That makes me odd. Odd even among the odd."

Diarmuid was quiet for a long time, and Lorcan watched clouds skate through the sky until he finally answered, "I don't know, Lorcan. I've never known. And I have never cared. You're my son."

Lorcan nodded. "Some care, though."

"Cormac? Has he been at you again?"

"I have to fight my own battles, Da. I'm not a child for you to protect anymore." Lorcan met his father's eyes. "And no, not recently. I avoid him, if I can. Da, why does he hate me?"

"A morning for big questions, hm?" Diarmuid said. He frowned slightly. "Did you know your uncle was married twice? That Caírech isn't Diarmuid and Siobhan's mother?"

"Uncle Eogan was married before he married Caírech?" Lorcan shook his head. "I didn't know."

"Her name was Aideen, and she had poison in her words. Unfortunately, that poison took root in Cormac when he fostered at Dun Righ. She taught him that because I had no son to follow me, that he was my heir, and that he would be the Raven King after me, and that his whole worth was tied into that. When you were born, and I named you my son—"

"He lost that worth," Lorcan finished. "Really? That's all? That doesn't make any sense, Da. To be Raven King, that means ruling this *baile* and the village. It's not much."

Diarmuid burst out laughing. "That's your birthright you're making light of, son."

"I know," Lorcan said. "But it's true. It's not as if he would be High King—" he stopped. Considered. "Unless she wanted him for Siobhan?"

"We never let it get that far," Diarmuid said. "She might have. It would have given her daughter immortality, if Cormac and Siobhan had mated. Not that it matters now, with Siobhan showing a preference for Ronan."

"But it mattered then. But then I was born, and he hates me for that." Lorcan shook his head. "I don't understand. He's a marvelous smith. Everyone says so. That's his gift. He can't be happy in that?"

"He will be, in time," Diarmuid said. "That's one thing we have in abundance. Time. Eventually, he'll heal—"

"Heal?" Lorcan frowned. "Did Aideen hurt him?"

"No, there was something else. Before you were born. There's none of us that like to talk about it, but Cormac came through it scarred. Scarred and scared. I wonder how much of the man he is now comes from the powerless child that couldn't stand and fight." Diarmuid shook his head. "He'll heal, eventually. I hope." He turned to Lorcan. "Have you considered what you want?"

Lorcan frowned, puzzled. "What I want? I don't understand. I don't want anything. I have my family. I have my studies with Mother and with my uncles. This is my place. My home. I'm happy. What else do I need?"

"A mate?" Diarmuid suggested. Lorcan rolled his eyes, making his father laugh. "You're 19. Niall was married at 19."

"I'm 19 today, and you just said I was young to mate!" Lorcan retorted with a laugh. "No, Da. I haven't yet met him. Her. I don't know." He shrugged. "Whoever my mate is, they're not in Dun Morrigan. Or in Scath. Or at Dun Righ. Or any of the places I've been. I haven't found them yet. Maybe I'm like Uncle Cuanu, and there's no one for me."

"That's a sad thought for a bright morning," Diarmuid chided. "None of that. You'll find them." He hummed softly, then rested his hand on Lorcan's shoulder. "Your mother told me the same as you've said, that you're coming along as a fair healer. Would you wish to go to the druid college to learn more?"

"She asked me the same question," Lorcan answered. "I may. I haven't yet learned everything that Mother has to teach me, though. I want to learn if I can use the healing chants. I know the words, and Mother thinks I will be able to use them the way she does. So perhaps next year."

"That's soon enough." Diarmuid stretched, wincing a little and working his left arm. He'd broken it years before, Lorcan knew, and it still troubled him.

"Should we go back?" he asked. "Mother will be waiting on us to eat."

"Then we should go back." Diarmuid grinned and launched himself from the ledge, changing forms in midair and spiraling down toward Dun Morrigan. Lorcan yelped in surprise and dove after him, letting the winds catch his wings and bear him up until he angled and followed his father back down to the ground.

From above, he watched as his father landed as a man, greeting the woman who stood waiting for him on the *urla*. He kissed her warmly and waited with his arm around her until Lorcan landed and came toward them.

"Good morning, Mother," Lorcan said, kissing her cheek.

"Good morning. Did you have a good talk?"

"How did you know?"

She smiled and glanced up. "You went to the perch. That's the talking spot. Come and eat."

"Lorcan!"

Lorcan turned at the sound of his name. "Uncle Turlach?"

The slightly built charioteer limped over and nodded to him. "If you've got a moment, I wanted to show you something. Diarmuid, Grainne, might I borrow him?"

"Go along," Grainne said. "We'll meet you inside."

"All right," Lorcan followed Turlach away from the hall and toward the far wall of the *baile*. "Are we going to the stables?"

"Yes. I wanted you to see something," Turlach repeated. He reached over and poked Lorcan in the arm. "The sword practice is paying off. You never got these muscles making poultices."

Lorcan grinned. "Uncle Niall says I'm getting good."

"Good. Pray to your grandmother you never see need to use it." Turlach stopped outside the stable door. "Petran? Bring her out."

Lorcan looked at Turlach, then at the stable door. His jaw dropped when he saw the delicately built mare that Petran led out into the sunlight. Her hide was as dark and glossy black as a raven wing, and there was strength and grace in her every movement.

"Turlach, she's beautiful," he breathed.

Turlach sniffed. "Told you, Pet."

"You did," Petran agreed. "So, Lorcan. What's her name?"

Lorcan went still. "What?" He looked from one laughing uncle to the other. "She's for me?"

"She's yours," Turlach said. "I saw her, and knew she belonged to you. I've been hiding her away while I trained her, but today it's time."

Lorcan stepped closer and took the rope harness from Petran, murmuring soft nonsense to the mare as he examined her from her nose to her tail and back. She nudged his shirt as he scratched her forehead. "You're a beauty," he murmured. "And that's your name. Beauty. I can't wait to take you out to run."

"She'll take harness, or you on her back. I trained her to do both," Turlach said.

"And she runs like the wind," Petran added.

Lorcan ran his fingers through the mare's mane. "I don't know what to say. Thank you. She's wonderful."

"I'll put her in her stall. Go have your meal," Turlach said. "Before the younger ones eat all the porridge. Go on."

Lorcan left them, and headed back into the hall, which was now bustling with noise and activity. Lorcan's younger cousins were arguing over their morning meal, about what he wasn't certain. He saw his parents sitting at the wide table at the head of the hall and had just started toward them when a voice cut through the din.

"Late again, Lachtna?" Cormac jeered.

"Lachtna?" Lorcan repeated. "That's new." He looked over at his cousin, noting the clenched fists. It was clear that Cormac wanted a fight. Lorcan wasn't going to give him what he wanted, though. Not today. Especially not over something that honestly amused him. "Lachtna. Milk-colored. That suits me. I like it. Thank you for the gift of a name, Cormac." He heard his father laugh, and resumed his walk toward the table.

"And he's so dim that he doesn't even notice he's being insulted!" Cormac snapped.

"Cormac, enough!" Sorcha hissed. Lorcan heard something heavy hit the ground, and footsteps behind him. He turned to face Cormac, whose face was crimson in his rage. What had brought this on?

"Milk-faced idiot," Cormac growled. "You're not a real raven, and you're not fit to follow the Raven King."

"That's not for you to say," Lorcan answered, keeping his voice low. "You're not the Raven King. Nor will you be."

Lorcan wasn't ready for the slap; he staggered back, more shocked than hurt. Cormac had never attacked him physically before. Now his ears rang, and he tasted blood. He heard his mother cry out, his father's angry bellow. Lorcan looked over his shoulder to see his father standing.

"I'm fine, Da," he called, and turned back toward Cormac. The smith looked both angry and unsatisfied, and Lorcan nodded before he asked. "Is that a challenge, cousin?"

"It is," Cormac snapped. "If you're man enough to accept it."

"A true challenge at the ford?" Lorcan asked. "Or settle this on the *urla* before the family?"

"And when I beat you, will you accept it?" Cormac asked in reply. "Will all of you accept it?" He turned to look around the room. Before anyone else could speak, Lorcan did.

"It's not theirs to say," he announced, pitching his voice to reach the entire hall. Not that he needed to do much—the hall was unusually silent. "This is my decision. And I say yes. If you beat me, then what I have is yours, and may it well become you. The ford, before the gods? Or here on the *urla*?"

"On the *urla*," Cormac answered. He turned and walked out of the hall. For a moment, no one moved. No one said anything. Then Diarmuid broke the silence.

"Niall, did you know your son was going to challenge mine?"

Niall stepped forward, his face flushed. He shook his head hard, then spat into the fire-pit, making his disgust plain. He reached into his pouch and drew out his wax tablet, scrawling something before handing it to Lorcan, gesturing for him to read it. Lorcan read the words silently, then stared at his uncle.

"Uncle—" Niall made an impatient gesture, and Lorcan shook his head. "No. This has been building for a long time, and maybe once I've beaten him, it'll be settled. But you can't do this. It will only make things worse."

"Can't what?" Diarmuid asked. He joined Lorcan and took the tablet. "Oh. Niall, I won't ask this of you."

Niall just pointed at the tablet.

"What does it say?" Sorcha demanded.

"It says that if Cormac does this, he's no son of Niall, nor of the raven. That if he goes through with this, he's disowned," Diarmuid answered. "But Lorcan is right. Let them settle this." He looked at Lorcan. "You can settle this?"

Lorcan nodded. "I can beat him, Da."

"Then let's go to the *urla*."

* * *

Lorcan went to his house to get his sword and his shield and was unsurprised to find his cousin Ronan waiting for him there. Cormac's younger brother, the two were as unalike as night and day, and Lorcan considered Ronan to be his closest friend.

"Did you know?" Lorcan asked.

"No," Ronan answered. "And before you ask, I don't know why, either."

"He was in a rare mood this morning. I heard him." Lorcan picked up his sword and turned. "Why?"

"Problems in the new iron," Ronan answered. "I think Cormac traded for inferior ore. He didn't let me help with the trading or inspect what he'd bought, so I'm not sure. But the entire batch is fouled. The sword he was working on for the king's youngest son shattered, and there's barely time to start over if we're to have it done before he comes of age. Father is going to have to take it on, and he's got no time as it is."

Lorcan grimaced, taking his shield from its peg on the wall. "Uncle Niall will be taking that out of his hide, I imagine?"

"He already did. My father is furious. And he doesn't have to yell to let you know it," Ronan said with a wry grin. "He's taught the both of us better than that. And Cormac knows better than that. But he was rushing, and you know he won't listen—"

"Because Cormac knows best," Lorcan finished. He bared his sword and ran his thumb over the edge, then slipped it back into the sheath. "So, should I be worried?"

"No," Ronan said, his voice firm. "I've sparred against you both. You're better than he is."

"Thank you." Lorcan sighed. "I wish it hadn't come to this. But I'm glad it has. Maybe this will end it."

Ronan snorted. "And if you believe that, then maybe all our feathers will turn as white as yours tomorrow. Cormac isn't going to change. He's only going to get worse." He glanced out the door. "Be careful, Lorcan."

"I will." Lorcan smiled at his cousin. "I'd ask you to walk out with me, but I don't want him to turn on you once this is done."

"More than he has already? Cormac's a bully, and we all know it. Nothing you nor I nor anyone else can do will change it. I've already decided to take myself off to Dun Righ for a space," Ronan answered. "Father says I might start my own forge there, if the High King is willing."

"I can't see why he wouldn't be. The son of the King's own Smith, and you as good as your father? And being at Dun Righ will let you see Siobhan more often," Lorcan murmured. Ronan blushed.

"I haven't spoken of that to my parents. Nor she to hers," he said.

"What are you waiting for?" Lorcan asked.

"Well, for one thing, my own forge," Ronan answered. "I want to be on my own before I take a mate. Once I've got the forge going at Dun Righ. That's what we decided."

"Congratulations, then," Lorcan said.

"Thank you. You should go on." Ronan looked out the door. "They'll come looking for you if you don't go."

"Right." Lorcan nodded and walked out of the house, blinking in the sunlight. His father was waiting for him just outside.

"You don't have to do this," Diarmuid said.

Lorcan looked up at his father and shook his head. "I do. I told you, Da. I need to fight my own battles. Maybe this will be the end of it." Diarmuid scowled, and Lorcan grinned. "I know. Probably not. But I can hope."

"I didn't think it would come to this," Diarmuid said. He fell in next to Lorcan, walking slowly toward the *urla*. Lorcan could see the others waiting. "I didn't think he was still so—" His voice trailed off. "Perhaps I should have paid more attention."

"And done what?" Lorcan asked. "You've tried to make him stop. Uncle Niall and Aunt Sorcha have tried. Everyone has tried. Cormac won't change. What could you have done different? What would have changed him?"

Diarmuid nodded. "True. Be careful, my son."

"I will, Da." At the edge of the *urla*, Lorcan stopped and handed his sheathed sword to his father, setting his shield on the ground as Grainne joined them. He hugged his mother tightly. She clung to him, cupping his face in her hands.

"My boy," she murmured. "How did you grow up so quickly? You're a man now. I can't hide you under my wings anymore."

"Will you hold my cloak for me, Mother?" he asked. He took the white feather cloak from his shoulders and passed it to her. She stroked it gently, then looked over her shoulder, across the *urla* to where Cormac was waiting, armed with a pair of iron-banded clubs. It was then that Lorcan noticed how people were standing—there was no one on the side of the *urla* where Cormac waited. The rest of the flock had ranged themselves around Diarmuid and Grainne, showing their support for Lorcan. Except for Cormac's own family—Niall and Sorcha, Niamh and Ronan were all nowhere to be seen. Lorcan frowned; Cormac had to have noticed that no one was supporting his challenge. Would that change his mind?

"Cormac," Lorcan called. "Have you changed your mind? Do you still want to do this?"

"Scared, you milk-faced fool?" Cormac jibed. "Come on and let me show you what a real man can do!"

Lorcan shook his head and looked up at his father. "I tried."

"You did," Diarmuid agreed. He picked up Lorcan's shield and held it out to Lorcan, then handed him his sword. "Now be careful."

Lorcan nodded again and stepped onto the *urla*. Cormac was bigger than he was, but Lorcan had seen him fight. He relied on that size, and on brute strength, which explained his choice of weapon. He was fast, but Lorcan knew that he was faster. That might be enough.

Lorcan licked his lips and waited. Cormac swaggered toward him, a smirk on his face.

"No boasting, Milk Boy?"

"I've no need to boast," Lorcan answered. "I know my worth. Unlike some."

Cormac's eyes widened, and he took a sharp breath. Then he roared and rushed Lorcan, his right-hand club raised high. Lorcan ducked, raising his shield and dodging to the side, feeling the bone-rattling impact of the club against the shield as the flat of his still-sheathed sword slammed into Cormac's gut. Cormac gasped and doubled over, stumbling forward; his movement carried Lorcan's sheath with him, leaving him with a bared blade. Lorcan skipped back, glancing at his shield and the fist-sized dent in the wood. Proof that Cormac meant to kill him—that would have shattered his skull. He needed to end this, and quickly. He rushed Cormac, slamming into him with the shield hard enough that Cormac yelled in pain, and his left-hand club ended up on the turf. He recovered quickly, pivoting and flailing with his other club, a blow that Lorcan barely blocked with his sword, and that left his hand tingling. He grimaced, taking a step back. Cormac glared at him and rushed him again. Again, Lorcan blocked the blow with his shield, hearing the wood shatter. He shook away the broken pieces as he slammed his shoulder into Cormac's side, knocking the bigger man off balance. Lorcan attacked again, kicking Cormac's knee until it buckled and he fell. As Cormac started to rise, Lorcan spun his sword, and brought the hilt down as hard as he could on the top of Cormac's head. It made a sickening, hollow sound, and Cormac fell like a downed tree, stretching his length on the grass. Lorcan backed away, breathing heavily and suddenly feeling ill.

A hand came down on his shoulder, making him jump. He turned and saw his father, looking stern and serious. Diarmuid's voice was quiet when he spoke, "Well done. Will you finish him? You were challenged. Mother will understand that."

"No," Lorcan croaked. He cleared his throat, seeing that Niall and Sorcha were behind his father, with Ronan and Niamh behind them. When had they arrived? They were watching him, and his aunt looked worried. "No," Lorcan repeated. "I'm not going to kill him. And not for fear of Grandmother's wrath. He's beaten. It's done. I'm satisfied."

"He won't be."

"Petran, hush."

"It's the truth."

Lorcan turned to face his uncles. "Perhaps. But I won't shed his blood."

Diarmuid nodded. "Well said. Grainne, take our son back to his house and see to him. Niall, Sorcha, see to your own."

Lorcan started to protest that he was fine when he realized that his shield arm ached. Quietly, he let his mother take his good arm and lead him away from the *urla*.

"He would have killed me," he said softly. "Mother, he was going to kill me."

"I know, Lorcan," Grainne said. "And you handled it beautifully."

"But I didn't. Not really," Lorcan protested. He looked back at the *urla*, at Niall, who was helping Cormac back to his feet. "He's still going to hate me. But now he'll hate me even more because he lost."

"Perhaps. Or perhaps you've knocked some sense into his head." Grainne led him into his house and gestured for him to sit down.

Lorcan perched on the edge of the bed, and only then realized that he was still holding his sword. He looked at it and sighed, setting it on the bed next to him.

"I didn't want to fight him."

"I know."

"Now what, Mother? What do I do now?"

Grainne took his arm and pushed his sleeve up, examining the bruise that was growing darker. "You leave it alone and let your father do what he needs to do."

"But—"

"Lorcan, you've satisfied the challenge. You beat him. There's nothing more for you to do. Now it's for him." She didn't say which him she meant, and Lorcan didn't have a chance to ask. She tsked and shook her head. "Lie down. I don't like the looks of this. Healing it will be easier if you sleep."

Lorcan looked at his mother and knew there would be no arguing with her. "Let me put my sword away," he said, standing up. He took the sword and hung it on its peg, then came back to sit back down. "I'll have to fetch my sheath later."

"Someone will bring it back," Grainne said. "Lie down."

Lorcan lay back on his bed, closing his eyes. He heard his mother start to sing the healing chants, and let her voice carry him into a dreamless slumber. When he woke, the bruise on his arm had faded to a dull purple and gold, his sword was once more in its sheath.

And Cormac was gone.

Chapter Three

Days passed. Lorcan slowly pieced together the story of what had happened while he'd been asleep. Cormac was unwilling to accept that he'd lost his challenge and had attempted to follow Lorcan and his mother. When Niall tried to stop him, Cormac turned on his own father, knocking him to the ground. The other ravens rose to defend their youngest brother, and Cormac fled Dun Morrigan rather than face his shame. By the time Lorcan awoke, Cormac was gone, and Cuanu had gone to Dun Righ to report what had happened to the High King.

"It's not your fault," Cormac's sister Niamh told Lorcan. "We all knew it was coming."

"But—"

"If it hadn't been you, it would have been Ronan," Niamh said. "He'd have challenged Ronan when Ronan took Siobhan as a mate. And Ronan wouldn't have been able to beat him. Not the way you did. Father knows. He's known for a long time, and he's been trying stop it. But you might as well try to stop a rockslide. He doesn't blame you."

Lorcan still had trouble facing his uncle and tried to find reasons to avoid the forge. Until Niall appeared in his doorway early one morning.

"Uncle," Lorcan stammered. "I—" Niall shook his head, gesturing for Lorcan to sit. Silently, Lorcan did as he was bid, wondering what Niall was going to do. His uncle dragged Lorcan's stool over and sat down facing Lorcan, taking out his wax tablet. He wrote and then passed it to Lorcan.

I'm not angry at you, the note read. *I'm sorry it came to this. I should have stopped him.*

"Could you have?" Lorcan asked. "Niamh says that you might as well have tried to stop a rockslide."

Niall snorted. He took the tablet back, wiped the words clean, then wrote again.

Perhaps. Perhaps he was cursed, and we just never knew. I don't know.

"Cursed?" Lorcan read the word aloud. Niall arched an eyebrow, and Lorcan shook his head. "Da said something happened before I was born. Something bad, and Cormac was involved. But he wouldn't tell me what."

Niall nodded. He gestured for Lorcan to wait, then got up and left. A few minutes later, he was back with Petran.

"You want me to what?" Petran said. Niall gestured to Lorcan. Petran frowned. "Lorcan, you don't know?"

"I don't know what?" Lorcan asked. Petran groaned.

"Diarmuid never told you. And you want *me* to do this?"

Niall made a graceful gesture, miming playing a harp. Lorcan grinned. "You're the harper, Uncle Petran."

"All right. Niall, you go get Diarmuid. I'm not doing this without his knowledge." Petran waited until Niall was gone, then took his place on the stool. "What do you know of a *deamhan aeir?* "

"Monsters," Lorcan answered. "From the old stories. I heard them in Dun Righ." He frowned. "Why don't you tell those stories?"

"Because there was a more recent *deamhan aeir.* One created out of revenge. It killed your uncle Ronan, my twin. And your uncle Oscar and your Aunt Muirenn, and their unborn child." Petran paused, then told Lorcan the story. Lorcan listened in horrified fascination, barely noticing when his parents came in with Uncle Niall.

"We killed it," Petran finished. "It died in fire, a long time ago. But we don't know what that thing did to Cormac while it had him. He wouldn't speak of it. He barely spoke at all for weeks after. And he would never tell us what happened. We could have had a druid come and see to him, but so many of them blamed us for the damned thing in the first place that we didn't know who to trust." He looked back over his shoulder at Diarmuid. "Anything to add?"

"Only that I didn't want to burden you with this," Diarmuid said. "Lorcan, it ended long before you were born."

"Except that it didn't, did it?" Petran said. "It's still going on, in Cormac's head. Did we fail him, Diarmuid? And did we fail him again, by letting it come to this?"

Niall handed his tablet to Diarmuid, who read aloud: *He wants to be the one in control of everything. In his work, in his life. He wants to be the one in power, so that he can't be hurt again.*

"If he stayed, he'd have killed someone," Petran said. "He's not seeing past the old hurt to know that it's not going to happen again."

"Will that change?" Lorcan asked. "Now that he's gone?"

Diarmuid sighed. "I don't know. That's why we haven't cast him out of the flock. The *ollamhs* will spread it from one coast to the other— he's welcome to come home, and we'll help him. But he has to be willing to take that help, and to give up this fantasy that he will take your place." He sighed. "Until he comes back, there's not much we can do. Except know that it's not your fault, Lorcan."

Lorcan nodded. "I wish you'd told me this before, Da. Maybe if I'd known, I could have done something different."

"Maybe. Or maybe nothing would have changed. There's no way to know now."

* * *

The days lengthened as winter fully gave way to spring. Lorcan spent his days working with his mother, learning the healing arts. He practiced sword and harp with his uncles, and learned the ways of his new mare, Beauty. He helped his cousin Ronan pack his tools for his move to Dun Righ and watched as his cousin flew off for the last time. He spent time in the village and rode over the mountain trails and down to the sea, taking his turn with the other men watching the coast for springtime raiders from the east. And everywhere he went, he listened for news of Cormac. It was as if he had vanished from Eire entirely.

"Lorcan!" His youngest cousin, Conor, poked his head into the stable. "Niamh is taking us foraging today for mushrooms and spider crabs. Come with us?"

"I promised Bran I'd help him today," Lorcan answered, not looking up from brushing. "He asked me to help him clean the tavern stables."

Conor laughed. "Oh, sure, you're going to swill the stables. What else is getting swilled today?"

"Conor!" Lorcan gasped. "Off with you! Before I tell your mother that it's your mouth that needs swilling out!"

Conor ran off laughing. Lorcan finished brushing the mare, then led her out into the sunshine. It was still early in the day, and it was promising to be a warm one. Probably not the best day to clean stables, but for other activities? Yes, it would be a good day. He twined his hands into Beauty's mane and leapt onto her back. As he rode toward the open gates, he saw his father. Diarmuid waved, and Lorcan drew Beauty up and waited. Diarmuid, Lorcan noticed, was armed.

"We've gotten word of raiders outside of Port Lairge," Diarmuid said without preamble. "We had a messenger as the sun rose. They need help, so we're flying out."

"Do you want me to come with you?" Lorcan asked, trying to hide his eagerness. He'd never flown out to actually fight raiders before.

"I want you to stay in Dun Morrigan, and stay alert," Diarmuid answered. "Oscar and Becc are coming with us. Turlach is staying here. He and Fergus will help your mother and the other women mind the younger children, but you're the next oldest, so I'm leaving you in charge—

"What?" Lorcan yelped. "Da!"

"You're ready for the responsibility," Diarmuid said. "I know you'll do fine. If anything, the men in the village know you, and will follow you."

"Yes, Da," Lorcan said. He rested his hand on Beauty's neck. "I was going down to Scath. Should I stay here instead?"

Diarmuid frowned, then shook his head. "Scath isn't too far. Just be sure your mother knows."

Lorcan smiled. "I told her over breakfast. Da, Niamh took Conor and some of the others out foraging. He mentioned spider crabs. That means the cove."

"When did you hear this?" Diarmuid asked.

"Only a little while ago. Conor wanted me to come with them."

"I'll stop them before they leave. They shouldn't be out to the cove when there are raiders about." Diarmuid nodded once. "I'll stop them. If you're going to Scath, go on. Warn the headman when you get there. I need to be off."

Lorcan watched Diarmuid walk off, and goaded Beauty through the open gates and onto the path down to the village. It was quicker to fly, but Lorcan had learned early that if he flew to the village and back, he would be grounded for days afterward until his broken primaries grew back in. Better to let the horse do the work, even if it did take a little longer. He heard ravens calling behind him, and looked over his shoulder to see his father, uncles and older cousins taking wing. As they flew out of sight, Lorcan realized a question he should have asked. Port Lairge was a fair distance away—at least an hour's flight, and longer by horse. The raid must have been very bad for a messenger to come this distance to ask for help. But when had the messenger set out, if he reached Dun Morrigan at dawn?

Something wasn't right. Lorcan gnawed at his lip, then growled softly. It was too late to do anything about it. He'd never be able to catch the others on the wing or following by horse. And he was the one entrusted with the safety of Dun Morrigan and Scath. He shook his head and looked back over his shoulder. The ravens were gone. Surely his father had asked the same questions? He had to have. Lorcan tried to reassure himself, then clucked to the mare and continued on toward the village.

Bran was waiting at the tavern gate for him. Taller than Lorcan by a hand and a half, he was heavy-set like his grandfather. His smile lit up the morning as he saw Lorcan riding toward him, and he came out to meet them in the road, walking at Lorcan's knee, his hand resting on Beauty's withers.

"I was starting to think you weren't coming," he said.

"There was an issue. I need to speak to your grandfather. Is he around?"

Bran looked up at him. "He's sweeping out the tavern. What's wrong?"

"I'm not sure." Lorcan rode into the tavern yard and swung down from Beauty's back.

"I'll see to her," Bran said. "She knows me. Go on. It sounds important."

Lorcan nodded. He paused, then stretched and kissed Bran's cheek. "I missed you."

"You saw me just three days ago!" Bran laughed.

"Still missed you," Lorcan answered. "I'll meet you in the stable." He hurried toward the tavern, stopping inside the door to let his eyes adjust to the dim light.

"Lorcan!" Bran's grandfather, Becc, called out. Lorcan smiled and greeted the stout older man with a warm embrace. Becc had been part of his life since he was a small child—Becc's older daughter, Caitilin, was married to Lorcan's uncle Maelan. Becc had assumed a grandfatherly role toward all the children in the flock. He'd been amused when Lorcan and Bran had started seeing each other; he seemed to know that it wasn't a true pairing, that Bran would never wear feathers as Lorcan's mate, but

28

it amused him all the same, and he teased them gently about it. "So, that grandson of mine convinced you to help him with his chores?"

"It didn't take much convincing," Lorcan said. "But I'm here for another reason, sir. There's a problem in Port Lairge, and the rest of the ravens have gone to deal with it. My father left me in charge."

"They went to Port Lairge?" Becc repeated. "Whatever for? Especially since there are *bailes* between here and there that have warbands."

Lorcan nodded. "I know. It doesn't make sense to me, especially since the messenger arrived at dawn. I'm hoping my father had the same thoughts before he left, but they still went. We're to stay near the *baile* today and be careful."

Becc nodded. "I'll spread the word. Do you think we should move up to the *baile* now?"

Lorcan frowned. "Perhaps tell people to prepare for a move. Just in case. But there's no signs of raiders on the coast or a warband in the area. Not that my father said. We're just to be ware."

"Then we'll be very ware," Becc agreed. "I'll spread the word. Are you still going to be helping Bran with cleaning the stable?"

"I asked my father if he thought I should stay in the *baile*, and he said that we're close enough here that it makes no difference. So yes, I'll be helping clean." Lorcan grinned. "It's better than waiting and fretting, after all."

"True," Becc agreed. He wiped his hands on a rag, then sighed. "I'm off. Go on then. You know where the tools are. You can leave your sword here."

"Yes, sir." Lorcan headed back out into the sunshine, turned around the corner of the tavern and headed behind the building to the stable. The inside of the stable was cool and dark, and Lorcan paused inside the door. He could hear horses moving but couldn't see anyone. "Bran?"

He heard a rustle, something moving quickly through straw. Then someone was on him, pushing him back against the wall, arms around his neck, lips against his. He grunted, wrapping one arm around Bran's waist, running the fingers of his other hand through Bran's tangled brown hair. They wrestled for a moment, pulling at each other's clothing, until Lorcan pulled back.

"Not here," he panted. "Not where anyone can walk in!"

"Up," Bran whispered, kissing him again. "In the loft."

Lorcan nodded and disentangled himself from Bran's grip, shifting and flying up into the loft. He dropped out of his raven form and landed lightly, taking his cloak off as he waited at the top of the ladder. Bran joined him, grinning widely.

"I love watching you do that," he said. "There are blankets. We can lay them out."

"Where?" Lorcan followed Bran and picked up one of the blankets, spreading it out over the hay. Bran knelt to lay his blanket on top, then turned on his knees and reached for Lorcan's belt. Lorcan laughed, stripping off his *leine* and tossing it on top of his cloak. He took off his shoes, then let Bran unfasten his trews, amused by his lover's unusual boldness. Usually, he was the one stripping Bran—this was new and novel. Then Bran looked up at him, and Lorcan saw a shadow in his face, something lurking behind the shy smile.

"Bran?" Lorcan asked, going to his knees. "Is something wrong?"

Bran blanched. He met Lorcan's eyes and sighed. "I'm not good at this."

"Good at what?" Lorcan asked. He reached out and rested his hands on Bran's shoulders. "Bran, what is it?"

Bran looked down, then shook his head. "Later. Now, there's just us." He reached out and tugged on the loosened waist of Lorcan's trews. "Take these off."

"Do I get to strip you?" Lorcan asked, sitting back on his heels. Bran blushed and nodded, and Lorcan rose. He slid his trews off and tossed them with his other clothes, then held his hand out to Bran, drawing him back to his feet. Gently, he slid his hands underneath Bran's *leine*. His skin was soft and warm, and he moaned softly as Lorcan trailed his fingers over his ribs. Lorcan grinned and pulled Bran closer, kissing him again and slipping one hand down the back of his trews, running his nails over Bran's arse. Bran's back arched, and he pulled away, fumbling at his own trews and shoving them down. He kicked them off, then reached for Lorcan's hand and drew him down to the blankets.

They lay facing each other, kissing and touching. It was something of a game between them—which of them would give in first and move beyond simple touches to something more? They never could decide if the person who gave in first lost the game or won it. Today, it was Bran who broke first, reaching between them and wrapping his hand around both of their cocks. Lorcan gasped and shuddered, his fingers digging into Bran's arse.

"Oh, no!" Bran groaned. "I forgot the oil!"

"What?" Lorcan asked. He blinked, then shook his head. "We'll manage." He smiled. "Turn around."

Bran looked at him, and his eyes sparkled. "Oh?"

"Yes. Come on. I want you." He slapped Bran's arse lightly. "So, get that arse up here."

Bran shifted up onto his knees. "Are you on your back, or am I?"

"Neither. The last time, you squashed me like a bug. On your side." Lorcan propped himself up on his elbow and watched as Bran twisted and rolled onto his side, facing Lorcan but with his head at Lorcan's feet. Lorcan reached out and ran his hand up Bran's thigh. "There. Now we're set."

His answer was Bran's mouth closing over his cock; he yelped, then leaned in and licked Bran's cock before swallowing him. He felt Bran's moan, and closed his eyes, focusing on his most pleasurable task. Bran smelled like soap, like the beer he helped his grandfather to brew, like musk and that something that was just Bran. Lorcan hummed softly and shifted, taking Bran deep enough that his nose brushed against Bran's bollocks, making Bran twitch. Amused, Lorcan shifted ever so slightly, enough so that he was just barely making contact between the tip of his nose and Bran's skin. Then he started moving his head. Slowly. Gently. Deliberately. Bran yowled, and Lorcan felt the scrape of teeth against the underside of his cock. He squawked with muffled indignation, and slapped Bran's arse. Bran responded by running fingers down the cleft of Lorcan's arse. It tickled, and Lorcan thrust forward to try and avoid the touch. Bran responded in kind, thrusting into Lorcan's mouth, seeming to lose all vestiges of control, dragging Lorcan over the edge into animal lust as they wrestled, thrusting and grunting. Lorcan wasn't sure which of them shot first. It didn't matter. He somehow ended up flat on his back, half on the blanket, half in the straw, and once more squashed like a bug.

A very satisfied bug.

He grunted and turned his head, releasing Bran as he opened and closed his mouth a few times, hearing his jaw crackle and pop. "No sleeping up there. Move."

Bran grunted and shifted, rolling to the side and turning around so that he could curl up against Lorcan. Lorcan closed his eyes, feeling sleep tugging at the edges of his mind. Bran hummed with pleasure and curled up with his head on Lorcan's chest.

"That was wonderful," Bran murmured.

31

"And… it was the last time, wasn't it?" Lorcan asked. "That's what you weren't going to say?"

Bran raised his head. "You can hear my thoughts now?"

"No, Bran. I can see it on your face." Lorcan smiled sadly. "May I ask why?"

"Because we're not going to be more than this, and you and I both know it," Bran answered. "You've got someone else to find, someone who'll wear your feathers. It's not me. So, you should go and find them." He shifted, and Lorcan rolled to face him. Bran leaned in closer and kissed him on the nose, then smiled. "Remember Caoimhe?"

Lorcan blinked. "Caoimhe? The potter's oldest daughter?"

"Yes."

"Of course, I remember her. It's been… what? Two years since her father died and her mother remarried? She lives on the coast now, I think. What about her?"

"She's coming back to Scath," Bran said. He paused, and his smile broadened. "I go see her occasionally. We buy fish from her village. And… she said yes."

"Said—" Lorcan sat up. "You asked Caoimhe to marry you? And you didn't tell me? Bran!"

"I didn't want you to be hurt by it."

"Hurt? Of course not!" Lorcan laughed. "Bran, you had to know I'd remember Caoimhe! She was my first lover!"

Bran sat up. He looked stunned. "She… she *was*?"

"You didn't know?" Lorcan smiled and rested his hand on Bran's knee. "It ended when she left Scath. Bran, if you two are happy together, that's fantastic. I'm happy for you! She's a wonderful girl."

Bran's head fell forward, and his shoulders shook. It took Lorcan a moment to realize that he was laughing. When he looked up, there were tears of mirth in his eyes. "I've been trying to figure out how to tell you for days!"

"Bran, you said it yourself. We've known since the beginning that we weren't forever," Lorcan said. He smiled and squeezed Bran's knee. "I'm happy for you. And thank you."

Bran looked puzzled. Then his eyes widened. "Oh." He blushed. "I thought it would make it… less painful. Or ease the blow. Or something."

Lorcan laughed. "It was a wonderful gift. Now, we have a stable to clean. Should we get to it?"

Bran groaned and reached for his clothes. "The sooner we get done, the sooner we can come back up here?"

Lorcan laughed. "If that's the incentive, then yes. Toss me my trews."

They dressed and climbed down from the loft. Bran brought out buckets, shovels and rakes while Lorcan led the horses out to the yard. Then they got to work, filling buckets with soiled straw and manure and carrying them to the midden, over and over until they were left with the bare earth floor. They were in the middle of spreading fresh straw when Lorcan heard the harsh cry of a raven, calling his name.

"What is it?" Bran asked. He wiped his sweaty brow with the back of his hand. "I heard it. Someone calling you?"

"Yes," Lorcan answered. He heard his name again and headed outside. Above, a raven was circling. He called back, and it dove as if it was hunting. His cousin Niamh landed in front of him, looking frightened.

"Niamh, what is it?"

"Conor. We can't find him. I think he might have slipped out to go hunting crabs after we told him that Uncle wanted us to stay home." She took a deep breath. "I flew out toward the caves to see if he'd gone after mushrooms. And I saw sails, out near the cove."

"If he's gone to the cove for crabs," Lorcan said. He swore, spinning and almost running down Bran.

"I'll get Beauty. Can she carry both of us?" Bran asked.

"You're not coming with me!"

"You're not going alone!" Bran retorted. "That's lunacy. I'm going with you. Now, I'll get her ready. Can she carry us both, or should I get Dust, too?"

Lorcan paused, then sighed. "Get Dust. We need to be fast. Niamh, go home. Tell Mother and Uncle Turlach where I've gone, and that Scath is coming. Tell her to put Rhys and the twins on guard and send whoever is fastest after Father." He turned to Bran. "Go tell your grandfather to have people start for the *baile*. And fetch my sword, will you? I left it in the tavern."

"You think we're going to be attacked?" Bran asked. He sounded horrified.

"I'm not taking chances. I thought there was something wrong with Port Lairge sending for help here. Now I'm sure of it—they wanted us undefended." He wiped his hands on his trews and pulled his hair back into a tail. "Go on!"

Niamh shifted and took to the air, and Bran ran off around the tavern. Lorcan went back into the stable, looking for Dust's bridle. He had just finished with Dust and was leading her and Beauty out when Bran came back, Lorcan's sword in his hands.

"You need a weapon," Lorcan said. "Just in case."

"I have my sling," Bran answered. "I'll keep guard from the cliff while you fly down to the cove. Let's go."

Lorcan nodded and leapt onto Beauty's back. Bran mounted Dust, and the two rode out of the tavern yard and east, toward the cove.

Chapter Four

Lorcan drew Beauty in and stroked her sweat-streaked neck, scanning the skies for a juvenile raven. Bran rode up next to him.

"Any signs?" he asked.

"Not in the sky." Lorcan slid from Beauty's back and passed the reins to Bran. "Keep an eye. I'm going to circle, then head down to the cove. If you see anything, shout."

Bran nodded, jumping to the ground. He touched Lorcan's arm. "Be careful, love."

"You, too." Lorcan kissed Bran's cheek, then shifted and took to the air, beating his wings hard to fly as high as he could. There, he soared, resting on thermals, and calling Conor's name. There was no sign of the younger raven, and he slowly spiraled down, making note of the ship anchored out in the deeper water. It was of a sort that he'd never seen before, a long vessel with multiple rows of oars and a painted sail. Lorcan had no idea where it had come from and he didn't want to know. He studied the cove below him, looking for signs that there had been someone here. There was no one on the trail, no signs of any person or raven that he could see, and he decided to land.

He dropped to the ground in human form and looked around. The shore was mixed sand and pebbles, wet where the tides had covered them, and there were no footprints. He looked up, saw Bran looking down at him, and waved. Then he whistled, a piercing sound that echoed off the rocks.

"Conor!" he called, moving toward the rocks along the waterline where they hunted crabs. "Conor, this isn't funny. We need to get home."

No answer. He growled softly in frustration. Was Conor even in the cove? With the tide out, you could walk along the cliff face for a good distance, and there were caves that could only be reached that way, where the crabs were larger and sweeter. He hadn't thought to check down the coast. He was about to take to the air again when he saw movement in

35

the shadows past the rocks. It looked too big to be a nine-year-old boy, and he was about to take to the wing when he heard Bran shout. He turned and saw a familiar raven swoop in to land on a nearby rock. Lorcan's hand went to his sword.

"Cormac, well-met," Lorcan greeted the raven. His cousin shifted human, and Lorcan stared at him. It had only been a few months, but Cormac had changed—his face was red and scarred, his nose had clearly been broken, and when he smiled at Lorcan, one of his front teeth was missing, and the other was chipped. "Cousin, it's good to see you," Lorcan said. "You've been missed at home."

"I'm sure I have," Cormac said, his voice dripping acid. "I'm sure that my mother wept with her grief at my going."

"She did, actually," Lorcan said. "Where have you been?"

"Making new friends," Cormac answered. His smile widened. "Making plans." He looked past Lorcan and nodded. Lorcan looked and saw men coming out of the shadows where he'd seen movement. Two of them were dragging a gagged and terrified-looking Conor between them. A third man carried Conor's cloak.

"Cormac!" Lorcan snapped. "Let him go!"

"Oh, we don't need him now," Cormac crooned. "He's served his purpose." He nodded again, and one of the men holding Conor drew his knife. Then he howled and fell, dropping the weapon and releasing the boy as a missile from above slammed into his face. Conor pulled away from the other man, running toward Lorcan. Lorcan shifted and dove at the man who held Conor's cloak, shifting back to human to draw his sword and cut the man down in a single movement. He grabbed the cloak and threw it at Conor, who snatched it out of the air, shifted, and took off.

"Get out of here!" Lorcan shouted after him. "Get back to the *baile* and warn them!" Then there was no time for anything else, as the men attacked, too many, and too quickly for him to shift and fly. More missiles rained down from above, and Lorcan glanced up to see Bran stooping to grab more rocks. He spun, shoved a man out of his way, and ran, starting to make the change… when something fluttered over him and dragged him to the ground. He swore, struggling in the net, shifting, then shifting back when he realized the spaces in the net were too small for him to slip through. He heard Bran shout, and a hail of more stones rained down. Cormac winced as one glanced off his arm, then he took to the skies.

"Cormac!" Lorcan screamed. "No!"

Bran saw the raven coming toward him and ran, disappearing from view. Cormac sailed after him. Lorcan heard a scream. Then nothing, until Cormac returned, coming over to crouch next to Lorcan. The sword in his hand dripped crimson.

"Well, now," he said with a laugh. "All that's left is the milk-faced mistake. Now what, Lachtna?"

Lorcan didn't answer, watching as the other men came toward him. They'd have to untangle him from the net. Then he'd shift and get away. Get help. Get revenge. Silently, he swore to his grandmother Morrigan that revenge for Bran would be his, and he could have sworn that he heard distant laughter. Then the men were on him, tugging the net and wrapping it even more tightly around him as they dragged him to his knees. He heard someone grunt behind him, and was starting to turn when something hit him hard on the side of the head. The world faded in a dull haze of pain where Lorcan somehow knew that he was being moved around and roughly handled but couldn't struggle or do anything to stop them. Then the world snapped back into place, and he groaned. There was something tight around his arms, around his body. He blinked and tried to move, then realized he was on the ground, his arms bound to his body, his wrists tied behind him.

"He's awake," someone called, his accent one that had never come from Eire. Lorcan shook his head and groaned again as everything spun around him.

"Good. If you'd killed him, we'd all be cursed. I told you. He and I, we're godbloods. Killing him brings the curse of our blood down on the killer." Cormac crouched in front of Lorcan. "You broke his skull."

"He'll live. Will killing him someplace else still bring down the curse?"

"I don't know. So don't kill him. Sell him. Sell him to someone you don't like. Let them kill him." Cormac reached out and shoved Lorcan onto his back. "Hear that, Lachtna?"

Lorcan blinked and looked at Cormac. "What? What have you done?" His breath caught in his throat as he realized that his cloak of white feathers was dangling from Cormac's hand. "Cormac, what have you done?"

"Taken back what was always supposed to be mine," Cormac answered. He held up the cloak. "Don't worry about this, Lachtna. I'll keep it in a place of honor—hanging on my wall as a trophy!" He laughed, then rose, taking a pouch from his belt and tossing it at one of the men; it jingled when the man caught it. "You've served me well. Give your master my regards and my thanks. And if you want more of this, once you get rid of this one, come back to where you first met me. We'll raise an army and take this whole kingdom."

"Cormac!" Lorcan gasped. "No!"

"And gag him, or he'll shout your ears off." Cormac gestured at Lorcan, then laughed. "Goodbye, Lachtna. Maybe you'll be luckier than the rest of the flock. Maybe whoever buys you will kill you quickly." He turned away and shifted, flying up and out of the cove.

"Cormac!" Lorcan shouted after him. The men dragged him to his feet and toward the waterline and the path along the cliffs.

His struggles only made them laugh.

* * *

Diarmuid landed at a run, shouting for his mate. Since the moment Cathal's daughter had caught up with them on the way to Port Lairge, bearing the news that her youngest brother was missing, and that Lorcan believed their summons to be a trick, he'd been terrified. He'd sent Cuanu, Maelan and Niall on to Port Lairge, and returned to Dun Morrigan with Cathal and Petran. Turlach met him in the door of the hall but looked past him.

"Conor is in your house with Grainne and Alis, Cathal. We haven't gotten much out of him. Poor thing is frightened out of his wits."

Cathal nodded, taking his daughter under his arm and leading her off. Only then did Turlach turn to Diarmuid. "Diarmuid, it's Cormac behind this. That's all Conor would say. I haven't gone. Maybe I should have, but I didn't want to leave the *baile*—"

"I understand," Diarmuid said. "Get your sword. You're with me."

"So am I." Diarmuid turned and saw Becc. The taverner looked stony. "Bran went with your boy. I'm coming with you."

"I'll prepare the chariot," Turlach said. "Becc, if you'll help me?"

The two headed for the stables, and Diarmuid looked around. The *baile* was filled with people. Normally, this wouldn't bother him—he was used to the people of Scath sheltering here. It was part of his duty to them as their king, and it had happened many times over the years, as the raiders from the seas grew bolder. But today it worried at him like a sore tooth.

"We'll be off in a minute," Petran murmured.

"It's been hours," Diarmuid answered. "And he hasn't come back. Conor says it was Cormac. How could we not have expected him to turn on the rest of us?"

"Diarmuid, we don't know what he's done. Other than frighten Conor."

Diarmuid turned. "Don't defend him, Petran. Not to me."

Petran held up both hands. "I wasn't. I'm saying we don't know." He sighed. "It's too convenient. Either nothing happened at Port Lairge, or they were attacked just to draw us off. Which means—" He let out a long breath. "He has allies. Oh, Mother, he's one of the raiders."

Diarmuid stared at his younger brother for a moment, then nodded. "You're right. You must be right. Which means— he's coming here. He won't stop until he has everything that should have been Lorcan's."

"Send the women and the children to Dun Righ?" Petran asked.

"Once we get back, we'll prepare everything. Grainne won't like it."

"Grainne has other things to worry her right now. Here comes Turlach. He'll follow us. Let's fly." Petran waved, then pointed. Turlach nodded and guided the chariot out the gates, goading the horses into a gallop as they passed out of the *baile*. Diarmuid was about to take flight when he heard his name. He turned and opened his arms to Grainne, pulling his mate close. She pressed her face into his chest and sobbed.

"I'll find him, *acushla*," he murmured into her hair. "I'll bring him home." He kissed her head and stepped back. "Be ready, Grainne. We've a lot to do once I get back."

"Be careful," she said. She wiped the tears from her face and drew herself up. Diarmuid kissed her and turned, taking wing and flying after the chariot.

The tides were coming in as Diarmuid landed in the cove. Petran landed next to him, with his sword bared.

"Good thing we got here when we did," he said. "Any later, and the tide would have washed everything away." He bended down and picked up a white feather. Then he shook his head and let it flutter to the ground. "Sea eagle. Not one of his."

Diarmuid nodded and walked down to the water's edge. The horizon was empty as far as he could see. How long had it been? How many hours?

"Diarmuid!" He turned and saw Petran taking something out of the shallows. "I saw it shining," Petran said slowly. "In the water. They must have thrown it away." He held Lorcan's sword out, hilt first. "You'll have to keep it for him."

"Is that all they threw in the water?" Diarmuid said softly.

"No," Petran said. "No, Diarmuid. No matter what else, Cormac wouldn't kill Lorcan and risk Mother's wrath. We've taught him that."

"We taught him a lot of things." Diarmuid spat. "But he's still done this! He's still turned on us!"

"He turned on us, but he won't risk himself," Petran said. He offered the sword again. "Take it. We'll give it back to him when we find him."

Diarmuid nodded, taking his son's sword in his hand. He looked around again. "I don't see anything."

"Nor do I. Maybe on the cliff—"

As Petran spoke, they heard a wail from above. They glanced at each other, then both of them shifted and took flight. As Diarmuid soared over the edge of the cliff, he saw the chariot. Then he saw what he'd missed when they'd flown into the cove. Becc was on his knees, cradling a body. Diarmuid landed and shifted back to human form, going to his knees next to the grieving man. He couldn't see how Bran had been killed, but it didn't matter. The boy was dead.

"He was going to marry," Becc said through his tears. "He was so happy."

"Marry?" Diarmuid repeated. Becc nodded, turning toward him.

"He told Lorcan today. He told me that Lorcan was happy for him." He shook his head. "What am I going to tell Caoimhe?"

"You'll tell her that he died a hero's death, one worthy of Cu Chulainn himself." Petran said. "And you can tell her that he'll be honored for the rest of time by the Morrigan's kin."

"That's a cold bed for a bride to lie in, love," Turlach said. "Becc, we'll bring him back. See him taken care of properly. Diarmuid, will you come? I want to show you something."

Diarmuid got to his feet and followed Turlach, who led him and Petran off a short distance. "Lorcan was on Beauty this morning. Becc said Bran took their Dust. Neither horse is here."

"They wandered off—" Petran started. Turlach shook his head.

"No, they didn't," Turlach said. "If Beauty had wandered off, she'd have found her way back to the *baile* and the stable. That's what horses do. No, someone took them."

Diarmuid sniffed. "Petran, you said it. Cormac wants everything that is Lorcan's. Including his horse. Turlach, can you find them?"

"Find the horses?" Turlach frowned. He crouched, wincing as it put strain on his old wound. "Maybe? It depends on the trail, on the ground. I could try."

Diarmuid nodded. For the first time in years, he missed Oscar. The sorcerer had been arrogant and annoying, but he would have found Lorcan in a heartbeat. He blinked.

"Turlach, do you think I can still drive a chariot?"

Turlach looked up, startled. "It's been years since our last lesson. I don't know. Why?"

"Because I was going to send you and Petran to the druid college while I took Becc home. But no. It's better that you two take Becc back to the *baile*. Handle anything that needs to be done for Bran, and have Grainne prepare the women and children to go to Dun Righ. I'm going to the druid college."

"Now?" Petran asked. "You won't get there before sunset. You'll end up sleeping in a tree somewhere."

"I know," Diarmuid answered. "But if I wait until tomorrow, then that's how many hours further away they've taken my boy. It's bad enough that I might fly in the dark, and even then, it will take me until long after dark to get there!"

Petran sighed and dragged his fingers through his hair. "I wish Oscar was here. He'd know what to do. He'd whistle, and Lorcan would appear. Poof."

Diarmuid snorted. "I was thinking about him. I wish he were here, too."

"What about your mother?" Turlach asked. "Have you asked her?"

Diarmuid stared at Turlach for a moment, then at Petran. Petran bit his lip.

"When's the last time she spoke to you?" he asked.

"Just after Lorcan was born, to congratulate us," Diarmuid answered. "She's never been communicative. You know that."

"I think it might be time for her to start," Petran answered. "See if she answers you."

Diarmuid frowned. He closed his eyes and silently called, *Mother? I need you.*

Almost immediately, he felt her overwhelming presence in his mind. *My darling. Even if I don't speak to you, I am always here.*

41

You know what happened?

I am aware. There is nothing more you can do.

Mother!

He is beyond your reach. He is no longer in Eire. His fate is in his own hands.

But he's only a boy!

He is a man, and he has a man's fate. He has a man's skill, and he has had your teachings and those of your brothers. They will serve him well.

You've looked into his future? Will he come home?

There are too many choices. Too many possible paths. I cannot see clearly where his road lies or if it returns to Eire. I can tell you that it will not be easy. But I have been watching this grandson of mine. He intrigues me.

You can't bring him home, Mother?

I heard Petran's comment about what Oscar could do. Tell him that Oscar could not have done that. Just as I cannot. No more than I could save my other sons. Especially since he is no longer under my wings. Outside of Eire, in the lands where I am not known, my powers are diminished. But I trust that he will survive his trials and return. And you must trust in him as well.

Diarmuid sighed. *Very well. And what of Cormac? What can be done?*

He has renounced his blood, save where it serves him to call himself a child of a goddess. Renounce him, call him outcast, and be free of him.

I meant what should I do about him?

As with Lorcan Lachtna, Cormac an Bratach has his own fate. He can still save himself, if he wishes. There is a chance that he will choose wisely. But I think not. So, guard yourself and your flock, my son. There is nothing more you can do. Her mental voice started to fade. *I will watch, my son. But I will not speak again. Not for some time. Trust me, and guard your flock.*

Yes, Mother. Diarmuid opened his eyes and found himself lying on the ground. Petran was standing over him, his face pale.

"You've been flat on your back for a while, Diarmuid," he said. "I sent Turlach and Becc back to the *baile* with Bran's body." He crouched down. "You talked to her. You've got that look on your face."

Diarmuid nodded and sat up. "I did. She says Lorcan is alive, but he isn't in Eire anymore. There must have been a ship. They've taken him away."

Petran frowned. "Raiders take captives and sell them as slaves," he said. "I've heard from traders that there's a slave market in Alba, in the Roman port."

"Then that's where you're going," Diarmuid said.

Petran gaped at him for a moment, then stammered, "I'm sorry?"

"You're going after him. Tomorrow morning, you and Turlach will go to Dun Righ. Tell Eogan his nephew has been taken by raiders. He'll send you with guards and funds. Find him and bring him home."

Petran looked skeptical. "Did Mother tell you to do that?"

"No. Mother told me that I should let Lorcan find his own fate. But I can't do that. I can't sit idly by when I could be doing something." He got to his feet and held his hand out to Petran, helping his brother to stand. "And when you get to Dun Righ, tell Eogan that I want it spread through the whole of Eire that Cormac is an outcast and an outlaw."

"Diarmuid!"

"On Mother's orders," Diarmuid added. "She called him Cormac the Betrayer and told me to renounce him and be done with it. I'll tell Niall and Sorcha myself."

"Better you than me." Petran grimaced and looked to the east and the sea. "I know you've traveled, but I've never been outside Eire. Ever. Never thought I would."

"I wouldn't ask this of you—"

"Hush. For Lorcan, I'd fly to the moon. Going to Alba is much closer." Petran reached out and clasped Diarmuid's shoulder, then shook his head. "We're in for interesting times, hm? Let's go home. We've a lot to do."

Chapter Five

A thump woke Lorcan. He shifted in the dark, making the chains on his wrists and ankles clank. He listened, but heard no creaking. That meant that the oars had stopped. They must have docked. He closed his eyes and drew his knees to his chest. How long had it been? He couldn't tell anymore. Days? Probably. He just wasn't sure how many, or even where he had ended up. He'd been locked in this dark little cell since he'd been taken on board this ship—the fourth one since he'd been taken from Eire. The only time he saw light, or another person, was when someone brought him a bowl of something to eat, and no one on either this ship or the last had spoken Gaeilge. He rested his forehead on his arms and waited. They'd come for him soon, he was certain. And then he would be sold again.

Alba had been the first stop, and the first time he'd been sold. He was certain that it had been Alba. They had only sailed a few hours, and the raiders hadn't even bothered taking him below decks. They had left him bound and struggling, laughing as he'd gotten sick to his stomach, but otherwise ignoring him. That had given him the idea—maybe he could escape them in Alba. With no one paying him any attention, he'd managed to loosen the bindings on his wrists until he could slip free of them. The raiders had never bothered to tie his ankles, and Lorcan waited. His chance came as they docked—two men had come to collect him, and neither looked very closely at him. Lorcan waited until they were close, then attacked, knocking the legs out from under one of the men, then attacking the other, grabbing him by the ears and twisting his head as hard as he could. He heard the crack and was fairly certain that the man was dead before he hit the ground. Lorcan didn't stop to check, scooping up the man's dagger and running for the dock.

He'd almost done it. Almost. He was almost to the rail, almost to the dock and the crowd where he might be able to hide, when something hit him from behind, knocking him down. He lashed out with the dagger, heard a scream, and tried to get back to his feet. But it was too late. The rest of the raiders were on him, pinning him down.

They used chains this time, manacles on his wrists and ankles. Then they picked him up and dragged him off the ship and through the muddy streets to a stone building. There, his wrists were unchained, and he was stripped of his armband and his torc before he was locked in and left alone. The room had a small window, placed up high, but there was no way for Lorcan to reach it. He paced, trying not to trip over his chains, listening to the voices outside the window. He didn't recognize anything that was being said—he'd been tutored in Latin and Greek as a child but his first teacher had pronounced him hopeless, and Uncle Cuanu hadn't pushed when Lorcan refused to try again. Now, he wondered if one of those languages was what he was hearing, or if it was whatever they spoke in Alba.

If he could find someone who spoke Gaeilge, maybe he could convince them to help him. He moved over under the window and raised his voice, "Can anyone hear me?" Outside, he heard laughter and shouting. He tried again. "Help me! I need help! Please!"

He heard more laughter. Then, something came flying through the window. Something liquid, and Lorcan ducked against the wall to avoid the spray. He didn't move; he could smell the stink of urine from where he stood. More laughter from outside, then the voices faded away.

He shuddered and moved away from the window and the puddles on the floor, skirting around the edge of the room until he was as far from the window as he could be. No help to be had. Not here. And even if he did get out, what then? Cormac had his cloak. He held Lorcan's life in his hands.

No matter. He needed to get free. He needed to get home. Whatever it took. He had to stop Cormac and avenge Bran. He slid down to sit with his back to the wall, closing his eyes. His throat felt tight, and he rubbed the skin where it had been scraped raw when they'd tugged his torc off. Bran. He'd been there the night that Diarmuid had presented Lorcan with that torc and called him a man grown. It had been their first night together.

The light coming through the window had faded quite a bit before the door opened again, and two new men came in. They grabbed Lorcan and dragged him out into the hallway. Two more men were waiting there.

One of them studied Lorcan for a moment, then nodded, said something that Lorcan didn't understand. He handed a pouch to the fourth man, who said something, nodded, and left. The men who held him forced Lorcan to walk, following the third man out of the stone house and back through the streets. Back to the docks, and onto another ship. That was when Lorcan finally understood that he'd been sold. That he was a slave.

From Alba, they'd sailed for a day and a night. Lorcan had been chained on the deck, part of a huddle of other chained men. Sails billowed above him, and the oars were still. He watched as the slavers worked at their tasks, always moving, every movement seeming to be with a purpose. He wondered about how he might be able to escape. When he would have another chance, chained as he was.

He tried once more when he was sold for the second time. His new owners removed his chains and stripped him of his ruined clothes. He'd fought them, but there were too many, and he was chained again before he knew it. There was no slipping these chains, nor enough play in them to continue to fight, and men had dragged him down below the decks and chained him in place on a bench. There he'd stayed, as other naked and chained men were brought in and treated similarly. Two men were crowded onto the bench next to Lorcan, so close that they were pressed into his sides. One of them, an older man that was chained on Lorcan's left, ignored him. The man on his right snarled at Lorcan. Lorcan just glared at him until he looked away. Then he closed his eyes. He could feel the ship moving up and down and knew that he'd be sick again before long.

The next days were hellish. They were never allowed to move, forced to sit in their own shit and piss and puke until the stench was appalling. Men screamed and cried and were sick as the ship was tossed on a storm that Lorcan was certain was going to kill them all. It was the first time he cried. Would the Morrigan avenge his death, if he died here, chained and afraid, and so far from home?

The man on his left nudged him and said something, his voice low and gentle. Lorcan looked at him, and he pointed to himself and shouted over the storm's fury, "Ivo!"

Lorcan blinked and sniffled. He pointed at the man and repeated what had to have been a name, "Ivo?"

The man nodded. He raised his eyebrows and nodded again. Lorcan bit his lip. "Lorcan. I am Lorcan."

"Lorcan," Ivo repeated. He nudged Lorcan's shoulder again and began to sing in a deep voice. Lorcan had no idea of the words, but the melody was sweet and soothing, and Lorcan found himself growing calmer. Uncle Petran used to sing to him the same way. The last thing he remembered before he fell asleep with his head on Ivo's shoulder was Ivo laughing.

Three meals after the storm, the ship docked, and they were herded up out of the dark. Lorcan blinked in the bright light, wondering where they were. The sky and the water both were different blues from what he was used to. It was hotter than he'd ever been, too, and the sun was somehow brighter. The slaves were crowded up against the rails, and Lorcan stared out at the port—he'd never seen so many buildings before, nor so many of stone! And the people! He had never known that people could have skin so dark. He turned, seeing a curved wall with a wide gap in it. A ship was sailing through it into another harbor. He wanted to keep watching, but one of the slavers grabbed his arm and herded him away from the rail with the other male slaves. In a line, they were marched off the ship and into a long building with small, high windows. There, they were fed and bathed, if stale bread and buckets of cold water could be considered a meal and a bath. Then they were left. Lorcan found a place to sit against the wall, wishing he could see out. They were going to be sold again. How many more times, and how much further from home would he be taken?

"Lorcan."

Lorcan looked up to see Ivo standing over him. "Ivo. Sit." He gestured to the floor next to him. Ivo shook his head, so Lorcan got up. He hadn't known until they were taken off the ship how much taller than he Ivo really was—Lorcan only came up to his shoulder. Ivo said something, then pointed, his movements short and jerky from the lack of play in the chains. He pointed at the door, then at Lorcan. Then at himself.

"We're going to be sold again. I know," Lorcan said. He nodded, and Ivo sighed.

The doors opened. Men came in, carrying short whips that they used to start the slaves moving out. Lorcan stepped forward, then stopped when Ivo stepped in front of him. Ivo met his eyes. He said something in his own tongue, then leaned forward and kissed Lorcan's forehead. Then he turned and walked away.

"Ivo!" Lorcan gasped. The taller man didn't turn, joining the line leaving the building. By the time Lorcan was outside in the sun, Ivo was gone. Lorcan stumbled along in the line, trying to find the other man. Then someone shoved him out of line, into a group of a handful of other men. They were taken into another building and locked in. When they were marched back out, and onto another ship, Lorcan searched the faces, but Ivo was nowhere to be seen.

Which brought him to where he was now, chained in the dark, about to be taken out and sold once more. He silently hoped there were no more journeys by ship to be had. He slowly got to his feet as he heard the lock on the door being worked, and let the men lead him out. Once more, he was taken from the ship. But this time, there was no line of slaves, no sign of the other men who'd been taken on this ship at the last port. This time, he was given a short tunic to wear, and he was taken off alone, accompanied by a stranger, and a man who Lorcan recognized from the last port. Once they were on land, he was pushed into the back of cart that looked like a hut on wheels. Once he was closed inside, the cart jerked into motion, and he sighed. Where was he?

They travelled for what seemed a long time. Through the gaps in the sides of the cart, Lorcan could see paved roads and buildings on either side that rose to touch the sky. He tried not to stare and failed.

It was close to sunset when they stopped outside a large building, and he was taken out of the cart and marched inside, down long corridors until they reached a door. When the door opened, Lorcan smelled water. The familiar man gestured for him to enter, and followed him inside, while the other closed and locked the door behind them. As soon as the lock was turned, the man with Lorcan struck his chains. He mimed that Lorcan should strip and handed him a thin robe. Confused, Lorcan put the robe on. It hung open in the front, and he wrapped it closed and held it that way. The man smiled, nodded and gestured for Lorcan to walk through another door. Lorcan hesitated for a moment, then nodded and went where he was bid. The next room was warm, warmer than Lorcan was used to, but he ignored it, staring in wonder at the elaborate decorations on the walls. He wandered over to one, examining the thousands of brilliantly colored tiles that made up the pictures. Laughter caught his attention, and he turned to see his escort smiling. He said something in that other language, then gestured. Two men in brief garments came forward. Lorcan's companion gestured to a place in front of him, then mimed taking off his robe. Lorcan looked at the other men, then back at his companion. He arched a brow, and his escort laughed and nodded. Lorcan shook his head, and his companion sighed, then left the room. He came back a few minutes later wearing a similar robe. He took his off and handed it to one of the attendants, then looked expectantly at Lorcan. Lorcan grimaced but took his robe off. One of the attendants took it and laid it on a bench, coming back with two jars. He handed one to the other attendant, then waited. Lorcan looked to his escort for guidance and remembered Ivo. He tapped his chest.

"Lorcan. I'm Lorcan," he said.

His escort smiled. "Felix," he said, repeating the gesture. Then he held his arms wide, and the attendant started rubbing something onto his skin. Lorcan blinked and looked at the man waiting next to him. He held his hand out, and the attendant opened the jar and handed it to him. Lorcan sniffed at the contents, then dipped a finger in to what appeared to be some kind of thick, heavily scented oil. He handed the jar back and held his arms out, the way that Felix had. His attendant started to smear the thick oil onto his skin, spreading it all over. Lorcan sneezed twice from the scent, and Felix laughed again. Then he frowned and said something to his attendant. The man left the room quickly, coming back leading an old man. He brought the man to Lorcan and said something.

"They tell me you're from Eire?" the old man said, his accent jarring in its familiarity. He tipped his head back; his eyes were milky white.

Lorcan gasped, then clasped the man's hand. "Yes! And you're the first person I've heard speak Gaeilge since I was taken from home." He looked around. "What's your name? And how long have you been here, Grandfather?"

The old man smiled. "I'm Ercc. And I've been here more years than you've been alive, I warrant. When I left Eire, Eochaid was still High King. Do you know from Eochaid?"

"I know his name, yes. His son Eogan is High King now," Lorcan refrained from adding that Eochaid was his grandfather. Better to leave that hidden for now.

Ercc nodded. "And, as to how I came here? I was a mercenary. Then I was a slave. Then a gladiator. Now, I tend the fires. Don't need to see to throw a log on, hm? What's your name, lad?"

"Lorcan mac Diarmuid mic Morrigan."

The effect on the old man was striking. He scuttled backwards and moaned, "The Battle Raven's own blood? Here?" One of the attendants grabbed him, and they chattered back and forth in that other language.

Then the attendant shoved Ercc forward, hard enough that he stumbled. Lorcan caught him before he fell.

"Peace, Grandfather," he said gently. "My grandmother's wrath is not for you. They wanted you to explain something to me?"

"Ahhh…" Ercc breathed. Then he swallowed. "The strigil. They wanted me to explain the strigil, because Felix worried you might kill the man who tried to scrape you."

"Scrape me?" Lorcan looked at Felix. He shook his head, and Felix nodded. He gestured to his attendant, who brought out a curved blade and started scraping it along Felix's skin, removing oil and dirt alike.

"Grandfather?" Lorcan asked softly. "What is this?"

"It's how Romans bathe, Lorcan."

"This is a bath?" Lorcan looked around. "Oil and a knife? Don't they have soap here?"

The old man cackled. "You sound like me, the first time I did it. Try it. Just don't kill Bruno here. He's a good boy."

"He pushed you!"

The old man shrugged. "He's better than most. Will you let them?"

Lorcan nodded, and held his arms out to his sides, letting Bruno come toward him with another curved blade. Without prompting, he held the blade out to Lorcan to examine.

"Grandfather, will you tell him thank you?" Lorcan asked as he took the blade. "It's not sharp?"

"You couldn't cut cheese with this. But it will get all the dirt off you. Let him work."

Lorcan handed the blade back and let Bruno work. The feeling was decidedly odd, and ticklish when Bruno went to work under Lorcan's arms. He tried to stay still, and mostly succeeded, although he was certain that Bruno was laughing at him by the time he reached Lorcan's legs. When he was done, he stood up and said something. Ercc smiled.

"He's asked me to explain to you how the rest will work. We'll go into the hot room now. You won't like it. I didn't, when I first tried it. You'll stay there for a bit and sweat. They'll pour cold water on you every so often. Let them. It feels good. There's a pool in there, too. Hottest bath you've ever taken. Then you go to the cold room to swim. You swim?"

"Yes," Lorcan answered, taking his robe from the attendant and putting it back on. "And this is all to take a bath? Does everyone do this here?"

"Men and women both. In the public baths, they even do business in there. Trading and whatnot. Since they spend so much time in there."

"Ercc, where are we?" Lorcan asked.

"They didn't tell you? Oh, of course. They couldn't tell you. We're in Rome, Lorcan. Did they give you sandals?"

"No."

Ercc said something, and Bruno left, coming back with wooden sandals. He handed them to Lorcan, who bent and put them on before taking Ercc's arm, leading him as they moved out of the warm room and into a hallway. There was a door at the other end; when Felix opened it, the wave of heavy, humid air hit Lorcan like a wet, wool blanket. He coughed. "Morrigan!"

The others hooted with laughter. Ercc patted his arm. "It's only for a short time. You can't stay in there long. Don't take your sandals off. The floor is hot."

Lorcan would rather not stay in there at all, but he knew there was no point in arguing. He followed the others into the long room. At one end of the room was a pool, at the other, a large stone basin. There were benches arranged between the two, but the room was otherwise empty. The air was so wet that there was water running down the tiles on the wall and dripping from the vaulted ceiling, and a thick haze of steam hung in the air. Lorcan could feel the sweat pouring off of him even before the door closed behind him.

"What now?" he asked.

"You could bathe in the pool, or go and pour cold water on yourself. I like the pool. Gets the last of the oil off," Ercc answered.

Lorcan left him and went to the edge of the pool, crouching down and dabbling his fingers in the water. "Is this for bathing or boiling?" he called over his shoulder, making Ercc laugh again. He took off his robe and started to take off his sandals, then remembered Ercc's admonition about the floor, and left them on as he got into the water. It wasn't very deep—only up to his hips, and it was hot enough to sting. He hissed as he ducked down so that the water washed over his chest and back. Bruno came toward him, carrying a bowl. The cold water, Lorcan assumed, and nodded. Bruno poured, and Lorcan yelped in shock as icy water cascaded over his head. He shook his now-wet hair, scrubbing his fingers against his itching scalp. Then he stopped. He was in a bath. He didn't have to itch anymore. He held his breath and dunked underneath the hot water, then rose and ran his fingers through his hair. Dirty hair clung to them, and he rinsed them off and dunked again and again, until he finally felt cleaner. Between dunkings, Bruno poured cold water over his head; Lorcan wasn't sure that it helped, but it did make him feel less like he was being cooked. Finally, he climbed out of the pool. He shook his head, spraying water around.

"Ercc, is there a comb, perhaps?" he asked as he put his robe back on.

"After the *frigidarium*," Ercc answered.

"Is that the cold room?"

"Yes."

Lorcan nodded and took Ercc's arm. "What else happens after that?"

Ercc hesitated for a moment. Then he answered, "Then you meet the Master."

"Your master?"

"Our master, Lorcan. He's the man who bought you. He ordered you cleaned up before he saw you himself." Ercc patted his arm. "He's a good man. Could have thrown me out in the streets when my eyes failed me, or put me down like a lame horse. He didn't. He'll do fine by you. You'll see."

They left the heat, and Lorcan gasped at the cooler air in the corridor. He wiped the sweat from his brow and looked around. "Is this the cold room?"

"It feels like it, doesn't it?" Ercc said. "No, there's a pool in the cold room. You can take your sandals off here. You won't need them again."

They kept walking, passing through an archway and into a room with a large, round pool of water in the center. Felix tapped Lorcan's arm and pointed. Then he went and jumped into the water, not even bothering to take his robe off. He disappeared under the surface for a moment and came up shaking himself like a dog. He splashed some water at Lorcan, who grinned.

"All right. I'm coming." He thought about taking off the robe, then decided against it. After all, Felix had left his on. He jumped in. The water was deeper than he thought, and he let himself sink for a moment before surfacing and tossing his hair back. He saw Felix in front of him and splashed him. Felix laughed. He looked up and said something, and Bruno and the other attendant turned to go. Bruno took Ercc's arm.

"Thank you, Ercc!" Lorcan called. "Will you tell Bruno I said thank you?"

"I will, Lorcan. And never you worry. She's still watching you, even this far from home."

Lorcan smiled. It was a comforting thought, that his grandmother could still watch over him. He swam to the edge of the pool and rested his forearms there. He heard Felix say something and looked over his shoulder to see him coming closer.

"I don't understand you," Lorcan said. "And you sent my translator away." He rested his forehead on his arms. Rome. He was in *Rome*. He might as well be in *Tír na nÓg*. How was he going to get back to Eire?

He felt Felix bump into him and was about to move when he felt a hand sliding over his arse. He jerked in surprise, looking at Felix. Felix smiled and squeezed, then bumped into Lorcan again. This time, Lorcan felt his erection. He shook his head, and pulled himself out of the pool, turning and sitting on the edge, wrapping the sodden, near-transparent robe around himself.

"No," he said. "Thank you, Felix, but no."

Felix just smiled. He rested one hand on Lorcan's thigh, pushing his legs apart. He reached with the other—

"Felix!" Another voice snapped, loud enough that it echoed from the walls. Felix jerked, pulling away from Lorcan as he stammered something. Lorcan turned and saw another door. There was an older man standing there, and he didn't look happy. He said something, and Felix quickly got out of the water and hurried out. Once he was gone, the newcomer turned to Lorcan.

"He tried to say that you invited it," he said in heavily accented Gaeilge. "But since you don't have a word of Latin, and he has no Gaeilge, I doubt that. Did he trespass too much?"

Lorcan gaped at him for a moment, remembering himself only when one eyebrow arched up. "No. No, sir. And if he'd forced it—"

"I've no doubt you'd have killed him. As much as he deserved it, he's too useful to me as an agent. Come along. We'll see you dressed and fed."

Lorcan got up from the pool's edge and followed the man out of the cold room and down the corridor. He felt completely off-balance. "Are you the man Ercc referred to as the master?"

"Is that what he called me?" He sounded amused. "Yes. My name is Manius Glabrio. I'll explain everything once you're dressed."

Lorcan bit his tongue on the stream of questions he desperately wanted to ask, starting with *Will you send me home?* This man reminded him of his own father, both in age and in attitude, and he knew well enough that if Diarmuid said answers would come after, then no amount of asking would get those answers one minute sooner. Manius led him into another room, one furnished with a table and chairs. Manius pointed to a folded piled of cloth on a chair.

"There's a tunic for you. Probably not what you're used to, but this isn't Hibernia anymore. Get dressed, and I'll have food brought in." He left the room, closing the door behind him. To Lorcan's surprise, there was no click of a lock. He was tempted to go and try the door. Then he looked down at himself, at the thin, wet robe that was all he wore. No, clothes first. Then try to escape. He'd get further if he wasn't conspicuously naked.

He had just slipped the clean tunic over his head when Manius returned, leading a line of men and women carrying trays and bowls that smelled incredible. Once the table was set, they left, and Manius closed the door again. He sat down, picked up an empty bowl, and held it out to Lorcan.

"Here. Sit. Eat. And tell me about yourself."

Lorcan smoothed the tunic over his chest, then combed his still-damp hair with his fingers. He felt more himself than he had in ages, and he sat down and took the bowl. "Thank you, sir. What do you want to know?"

"We can start with your name," Manius said.

"Lorcan mac Diarmuid mic Morrigan," Lorcan answered. "Sir, my father is a king among my people. He would pay a good reward for my return to him. So would my uncle."

"Your father is a king?" Manius arched an eyebrow. "And your uncle? Who might he be?"

"High King of Eire."

Manius looked shocked. "Your uncle is the High King. Your father is a king under him. And... mic Morrigan. Your grandmother is a goddess? Which makes your father the one they call the Raven King, I assume? I've heard tales of him. How did a prince and a *semideus* come to be a slave in Rome?"

Lorcan frowned. "I don't know what a *semideus* is, but I was betrayed by my cousin." As he ate, he told Manius everything — Cormac's jealousy and the challenge. How Cormac had left the *baile*. About his betrayal and murder of Bran, and about the long trip from Eire.

When he was done talking, and done eating, he rested his arms on the tabletop.

"I need to go home," he said. "I need to stop Cormac before he kills anyone else, before he turns on the rest of my family."

"But you say that he has allies among the raiders, and that he has some lever against you that you won't specify," Manius said. "Let me tell you what I think." He leaned back in his chair. "I am what is called a *lanista*. That's a teacher, a trainer of gladiators. This place is my gladiator school, the *Ludus Manius*. I started as a gladiator, and a slave. I earned my freedom through the strength of my arm, and I took over this school from the man who trained me. Do you follow me so far?"

"Yes, sir," Lorcan said. "Are you from Eire? Is that how you speak Gaeilge? And know of my father?"

"No, lad. I'm Roman, but my wife Dareen was a Hibernian slave. I learned the language from her. She told me of your people, too." Manius answered. He smiled. "Now, here's my thinking, lad. I could send you home, and accept that fine reward. But I bought you sight unseen, from the slave markets in Carthage, and I paid a high price for you, because the agents of every *lanista* in Rome heard tell of the white-haired Hibernian slave who fought like Mars incarnate. You killed five men, it's told. With your bare hands."

"Five?" Lorcan frowned. Then he shook his head. "Two. Maybe three."

Manius snorted. "Only two? But it doesn't matter. You're said to be a prodigious fighter. I can make you better. And if you want to take back your crown, Prince Raven, then you need that. So, I will give you your freedom. In one year."

"A year!" Lorcan gasped. "But—"

"The reward your father and the king would offer would only be a fraction of what I think you'll earn as a gladiator. You'll make us both very rich, Lorcan."

"I don't want to be rich," Lorcan said softly. "I want to go home."

"And I will send you home," Manius assured him. "In the spring. I will send you home with the money to hire mercenaries to fight in your name, and the skill in your arm to defeat your enemy."

"Do I have a choice?" Lorcan asked.

Manius shrugged. "Not really, no."

Lorcan leaned back in his chair. Something occurred to him, and he scowled. "I'm going to have to learn Latin, won't I?"

Manius laughed. "It would help. I'll arrange a teacher for you. I doubt you'll mind the lessons."

Lorcan sighed. Then he nodded. "Then I accept. Will you at least send a message? To let my father know I live, and that I will return? But that I must repay my debt to you first. That will keep him from sending anyone after me." He shook his head slightly. "My mother must be sick with worry."

Manius nodded. "I will send a message to your family. I cannot guarantee that it will reach them, but I will send someone. Now, come and get settled. It's late enough in the day that I'll just take you to your quarters. Tomorrow, you'll meet your new family. The *familia gladiatoria Manius.*"

Chapter Six

A cock crowing dragged Lorcan out of a deep sleep, and it took him several minutes to get his bearings. No, this wasn't his little house in Dun Morrigan. This was Rome, and he was on the straw-piled stone shelf that served as a bed in the narrow quarters he'd been given in the... what did Manius call it? The *Ludus Manius*. Yes. That was it. The gladiator school. And today, he was going to start his training to become a gladiator. Lorcan blinked, blinked again, and rolled onto his back to stare up at the ceiling.

A year. That wasn't too long. But what could Cormac do in a year? He'd told the raiders that they would rule Eire. Could he do that in a year? Maybe. Probably. Which meant that Manius was right. Even if he released Lorcan today and sent him home, it would be just as long before he got to Eire as it was for him to get to Rome. And when he got there, he'd be no better off than when he left. No, Lorcan needed more training, and possibly men to follow him into battle, if he wanted to beat Cormac and his allies once and for all. Which meant that he needed funds to hire men, and he needed to be able to challenge Cormac at the ford and win decisively.

He hoped his parents would understand. That they wouldn't worry too much. He reached up and rubbed the base of his throat, listening as the cock crowed outside once more. The window in the room was small, up high, and barred. He wasn't sure how he felt about that—he might still be a slave, but he'd given his word. Perhaps that wasn't enough in Rome, he thought, and got out of bed. He dressed in the tunic he'd been given the day before, grimacing at the lack of trews. Going bare from the waist down was exceedingly odd. He thought about braiding his hair, but decided against it when he realized he had nothing to tie off the end of the braid. He instead combed his hair with his fingers and went to the door. He expected it to be locked and was surprised when it opened easily. He stepped into the corridor and stopped. What now? What was he supposed to do? There were other doors on the hall, but they were all closed. He could hear shouting, though, and headed toward the sound.

The corridor branched, and Lorcan saw light at the end where the noise seemed to be coming from. Walking that way led him out into a large, round, sandy courtyard where there were four men fighting. No, Lorcan realized as he watched them. They were training. Each man had a different style of armor, and different weapons, and they seemed to be fighting in different manners. He studied them intently. This was what he was going to learn?

"Lorcan, there you are!" Manius called from behind him. "And you found your way to the arena. Good."

"I wasn't sure where to go," Lorcan admitted. "So I followed the sound. These are your gladiators?" He looked back out at the men on the sand. "Which will I learn?"

"That depends on what you have to show me today. What weapons do you have already?"

Lorcan nodded. "I can use a sword and a shield. Different shapes from what they have here, though. I can manage with those, I think."

"And I know you can fight bare-handed—" Manius started. Lorcan shook his head.

"If I could fight bare-handed as well as you seem to think, I'd have gotten away from them in Alba," he said wryly. "I was the smallest among my grown cousins. So, I learned early that when we brawled, I had to do whatever I was going to do fast, and do it as hard as I could. Then get out."

Manius laughed. "Fair enough. I don't think you have the build to be a *cestus*. Although you might surprise me. I'll have each of my men show you what they do in turn, and then you can try them. How does that sound?"

Lorcan smiled. "It sounds like you're the… *lanista*?"

Manius chuckled again. He turned back to the arena and whistled, an ear-piercing sound that made Lorcan jump. The men lowered their weapons and went to a rack along one wall, putting away swords and shields. One man put a long pole with three tines on the end into the rack, and draped a net over a box. Lorcan looked at the net and shuddered.

"Problem?" Manius asked.

"Not fond of nets," Lorcan answered. "That's how they brought me down."

"I see. We'll see how you do against one," Manius raised his voice and shouted in Latin. The men started moving faster, taking off helmets and trotting toward them. One of the men was tall, heavily built, and as dark as any of the people Lorcan had seen at the last port. Carthage, he remembered Manius saying. Felix had bought him in Carthage. The other three were all taller than Lorcan, but not as tall as the dark man. They all wore similar garments—an odd one that looked almost like very short trews, and that was held in place by a wide belt. And all four of them were tattooed on their right arms, a design that started on backs of their hands and extended up their arms to varying degrees. They all stared at him in open curiosity, and Manius spoke to them at length in Latin. Lorcan heard his name more than once.

"Now, Lorcan," Manius said. "These men will be your brothers from this day forward. I've told them who you are to us—our new *tiro*— and that they're to have the teaching of you. And that you speak no Latin."

"Tiro means what?"

"Gladiator in training."

"And you told them I have no Latin? That's going to make the teaching harder," Lorcan said. Manius smiled.

"If you get knocked down enough, you'll learn not to do whatever it was you were doing," he answered. He gestured to the dark man. "Now, this is Yaroah. He's from Carthage. Have you ever seen a Carthaginian?"

"When the ship was in Carthage, yes."

Manius chuckled. "Of course. He's a *murmillo*, and he fights with a *gladius* and a *scutum*."

"The sword and shield?" Lorcan asked. *"Gladius* and *scutum*. All right. But he had the same weapons, and different armor." He pointed at another man, one who was just the same height as Lorcan, but with dark hair cut very short. He grinned.

"This is Nona, and you're right. He is a *secutor*. He uses the same weapons, but his style of fighting is different, and so is his armor. You may benefit from this style, because he is especially trained to face a *retiarius*." Manius waited, and Lorcan realized why.

"Does that mean that he's a *retiarius*?" he asked, pointing at the taller, bald man who carried the net. "Nona fights against nets?"

"And wins," Manius said. "He's very good. So, you should learn from him. You'll also learn from Ennius how to use the net as a weapon, and how to use the trident." He turned to the other men and said something in Latin. Ennius looked thoughtful, and Nona grinned. He said something in rapid Latin, and Manius turned back to Lorcan.

"He says that you look like you'd make a good *secutor*. Because you're smaller. Being slight can be an advantage to a *secutor*." Manius turned to the last man, a stocky man who glowered at Lorcan, his arms folded over his barrel chest. His nose had clearly been broken at least twice, and his ears were oddly shaped. "This is Gnaeus. He's a *cestus*, and the *cestus* is also his weapon. He doesn't usually wear them for practice. Too much of a chance of his opponent getting hurt. But Yaroah is specially trained to face him." Manius gestured; Gnaeus rolled his eyes and held out one arm. His hand was wrapped in leather, and there was something else, covering the knuckles. Lorcan stepped forward and peered closer, then jumped back when Gnaeus jabbed at him. Gnaeus laughed, and it reminded Lorcan of Cormac.

"Those things, the wrappings have metal plates in them?" he asked Manius.

"Iron plates, yes," Manius said. "Some *cesti* might use spikes or hooks. Now that I think on it, this is not a style of fighting you will be training in. You don't have the stature. But you might spar against Gnaeus, so you know how to defend yourself."

Lorcan nodded, moving back to Manius' side. Manius nodded at him, then turned back to the others and said something. All four of them grinned and laughed, and Ennius said something before trotting off into the building.

"Lorcan, I want to see you fight. Ennius says you can you use his shield, and he's gone to fetch practice swords."

"Practice swords?" Lorcan said. "You mean wooden swords? I haven't used a wooden sword since I was 12!"

"I've never seen you fight," Manius pointed out. "I've only heard tell. And I'm not risking my gladiators on an untried slave. So, you'll use the wooden sword until I tell you otherwise. Is that clear?"

His words stung. Lorcan bit down on a retort. He had to remember that he was nothing more than a slave here, no matter what Manius said would happen in a year. He had to remember that this man was not his friend. Not his father. This man was his owner. He nodded. "Yes. Yes, sir."

"Good. Now go get the shield."

Lorcan nodded. "Who am I fighting?"

"Yaroah, to start."

Yaroah smiled and gestured for Lorcan to follow him, leading him toward the rack of weapons. He picked up his own shield, then waited as Lorcan took Ennius'. The shield was lighter than his own, and he wondered how much damage it would take. Would it protect him? He'd no idea. Only one way to find out. He hefted the shield, looked up at the big Carthaginian, and nodded. Yaroah smiled and led him to the center of the arena. Lorcan followed. He licked his lips and studied his opponent. He hadn't paid enough attention to the fighting he'd already watched, had no real idea of how Yaroah fought. But the man was bigger than he was, his arms longer. Whatever Lorcan did, he would have to do it both quickly and decisively.

Ennius came back, carrying a pair of wooden blades. He offered one first to Yaroah, the second to Lorcan. Then he grinned and reached out to ruffle Lorcan's hair.

"You do fine," he said in broken Gaeilge. Lorcan blinked and grinned. Ennius headed back to stand next to Manius.

Manius shouted something in Latin. Then he switched to Gaeilge, "This is just for sparring. First one on the sand ends it. Understood?"

"Yes, sir!" Lorcan called back. Yaroah looked at him expectantly, and Lorcan nodded and hefted his shield. He met Yaroah's eyes, watching. Yaroah's smile faded. He licked his lips, shifted his feet, then lunged. Lorcan blocked the overhand strike and went low, sweeping Yaroah's legs. The other man stumbled back, but Lorcan didn't give him a moment to recover, charging and crashing into him, shield to shield, then catching him in the middle while he was off balance. Yaroah grunted, recovering far faster than Lorcan would have thought. He struck again, and Lorcan just managed to block Yaroah's blow. It was hard enough that Lorcan felt the impact in his teeth. He gasped and skipped backward, out of range. Yaroah was going to be able to beat him easily if he didn't end this now. There was no way he would be able to get the upper hand—

The upper hand. Yaroah was tall enough that Lorcan guessed no one ever tried an overhand strike against him... and Lorcan couldn't do that anymore. He cursed under his breath. He'd lost a major part of his advantage in a battle against a mortal when Cormac had stolen his cloak. He couldn't change forms, couldn't disorient his opponent by becoming a raven.

Yaroah smiled and started forward, his shield raised. Lorcan reacted before he thought about it, rushing toward Yaroah, throwing himself down so he could strike up and under Yaroah's raised shield. He heard the bigger man grunt, then rolled and slashed sideways. He caught Yaroah behind the knees, and the big man howled and went down. Lorcan got to his feet slowly. First man in the sand ended it, Manius had said. But would Yaroah accept the defeat?

Yes, he would, Lorcan realized. Yaroah was laughing, one arm clasped around his gut. The others were laughing, too, and calling out in Latin. Whatever they said only made Yaroah laugh harder. He started to get up; Lorcan tucked his wooden sword under his arm and offered Yaroah his hand. The big man smiled broadly and let Lorcan help him up, then threw one arm around Lorcan's shoulder and called something to Manius. He gestured from Lorcan to himself and laughed with the others.

Manius came toward them, looking amused. "Unconventional," he said to Lorcan. "But effective."

Lorcan nodded, looked up at Yaroah. "What is he saying?" he asked Manius.

"Oh, Yaroah wants to be paired up with the ghost when he reaches the arena," Manius answered. "He means you, and for a spectacle."

"He thinks I'm a ghost?" Lorcan looked up at Yaroah. "I can't say I haven't heard that before. But what's a spectacle?"

"Occasionally, in the arena, there will be fights with a certain theme, or certain fighters. They're special things, made to draw a crowd, and usually for special events, like a feast day or a triumph. Having two fighters that are such opposites, and both skilled fighters… yes, that's something to consider." Manius nodded in thought. He looked impressed. "I think he's right. And I think you've proven yourself."

"I have?" Lorcan asked.

"I had you fight Yaroah because he's *primus palus* of the ludus. Do you know what that means?"

Lorcan shook his head. "No."

Manius smiled. "He's first among the fighters. And I'm not sure if it's your skill or that he underestimated you, but you beat him easily. Now, let's go down to the armory. You need a real sword."

Yaroah, Ennius and Nona trailed after Lorcan and Manius, each of them chattering in Latin and laughing. Gnaeus vanished before they went inside, and Lorcan wondered where he'd gone. Then he stopped thinking about it, as Manius unlocked a door and led them into a large room lined with racks of weapons of all types.

"Go and pick your sword, Lorcan," Manius said. He stepped back, and Lorcan started to look among the racks. He picked up the *gladius* similar to the one that Yaroah had used, then put it back down. It was too short, and too light for his hand. The others on the rack were the same. All of them short, all of them light. None of them right. He reached the end of one wall, and was about to go and look at the racks on the other side when something in the corner caught his eye. Another sword, yes, but it was longer than the swords on either side of it. He picked it up and unsheathed it, then smiled.

"Is this a *gladius*, too?" he asked. "It's longer."

Yaroah came over. He reached out and tapped the pommel. *"Spatha."*

"This sword is called a *spatha*?" Lorcan asked.

"It's a horseman's weapon," Manius called. "It's too long for foot combat."

"Not for me," Lorcan said. "I like it. Unless there's some reason for me not to choose this one?"

"None. It's yours. Now chose your shield."

Lorcan went to the racks of shields and studied them, finally picking one that felt good in his hand. "They all look the same."

"You can paint yours, if you wish," Manius told him. "When it's time for you to fight in the arena. Not before then." He said something to the men, who left the armory. Then he turned back to Lorcan. "Armor will wait until we know for certain what style you're fighting. I'll show you where to store your weapons. Then I'll take you to meet your language teacher."

Manius led him back toward the arena, and into another room where Lorcan left his sword and shield. Then they went back into the building, through other rooms and halls until they reached a colonnaded garden redolent with herbs. Lorcan stopped and took a deep breath.

"My mother would love this," he said. "Is it all medicinal plants?"

"How did you know that?" Manius asked.

"My mother is a healer," Lorcan answered. "And I was training to be one, too. I was to go to the druid college next year to finish my studies."

"And yet you fight like that?" Manius said, shaking his head. "You'd be wasted as a healer, Lorcan."

"I can fight, then I can put them back together," Lorcan replied, and Manius laughed.

"True enough." They walked around the garden. As they turned a corner, Lorcan saw Gnaeus come out of a room. His face looked oddly red on one side. He looked at them, then hurried the other way. Manius growled softly.

"Gnaeus!" he snapped. Then he continued in Latin, sounding angry. Gnaeus seemed to shrink, muttering in reply. He glared at Lorcan, no doubt furious that Lorcan was a witness, even though Lorcan had no idea what was happening or why Gnaeus was in trouble. Manius went silent, and Gnaeus fled. Once he was gone, Manius turned to Lorcan.

"Do you want to know?" he asked.

"No," Lorcan replied, his voice firm. "You're the *lanista*. That means you're in charge. If he's in trouble, that's between you and him. Unless it's a rule I need to know, so I don't have you yell at me the same way?"

"That depends. Do you understand what the word 'no' means?"

Lorcan blinked. "Of course!"

"Then I doubt we'll have an issue. Come inside." He headed for the door that Gnaeus had come from. Lorcan followed and was struck by a wave of recognition. This room—it could have been his mother's. Bundles of drying herbs hung from the ceiling, and the shelves and tables were covered with the paraphernalia of the healer's arts. Lorcan stopped and closed his eyes, a pang of homesickness piercing him like a dart.

"Father?" A woman's voice, speaking Gaeilge with a slight accent. "I heard you with Gnaeus. If you're not going to sell him, then tell him that if he comes here again and he isn't bleeding, that he will be. And that if he doesn't leave me alone, I'm going to put *koneion* into his beer. I'm tired of him." Lorcan opened his eyes, but didn't see who was speaking. Then she came into view, saw him, and gasped. "Oh. You should have said—"

"Livia, this is Lorcan," Manius said in Gaeilge. "And he understands every word you just said."

"Oh," Livia murmured. She turned slightly pink. "I—"

"It's a pleasure to meet you," Lorcan said softly, and bowed. He met her eyes, her dark blue eyes, and *knew* her. Knew her and knew without

64

a shadow of a doubt that she was the one. No wonder he hadn't been able to find a mate in Eire.

She'd been in Rome the entire time.

"Lorcan has no Latin. At all," Manius said, pulling Lorcan out of his stunned reverie.

"And you want me to teach him, the way I did with the Saxon last year?" Livia said. She picked up a cloth from the table and wiped her hands, allowing Lorcan a moment to shake off the shock of recognition and really look at her. She was almost of a height with him, perhaps a finger or two shorter, and her hair was dark brown, braided, and wrapped around her head like a crown. Strands had escaped to frame her face, making her look sweetly disheveled. She wore a draped gown that did nothing to hide her generous curves. She noticed him looking at her and raised her chin in challenge. "Will you be a good student?" she asked him.

"I'll try," he answered. "I've tried to learn before, though. It didn't go well."

"We'll try again. You've got more incentive to learn." She smiled. "Where are you from, Lorcan? Hibernia?"

"Eire," he answered, and she laughed.

"Same place. Hibernia is what we call it. Mother called it Eire. Come and sit. We'll start now." She looked at Manius. "Unless you have other plans?"

"None. Get him started. I want him fluent as soon as he can be." Manius waved and left, and Livia gestured to a chair.

"Sit. Tell me about yourself while I finish." She picked up a mortar and pestle. "That oaf interrupted me in my work."

"I could help?" Lorcan offered. "I was training to be a healer at home."

She looked at him, surprised, and Lorcan noticed the spray of golden freckles across her cheeks. "You're a healer? Then how did you come to be a gladiator?"

"That's part of telling you about myself, I suppose," Lorcan answered. "What can I do to help?"

She handed him the mortar, and he ground herbs into powder as they talked. He told her of his training in Eire, about his parents and about Dun Morrigan. He told her about Cormac, and about being kidnapped and sold.

"Your father told me that if I give him a year, he'll see me freed.

65

And by that time, I'll be trained properly, and I'll have earned the money to hire men, if I need them," he finished. He tipped the powder in the mortar into a jar. "You speak Gaeilge with him. Why?"

"Because the gladiators don't. Well, not much," Livia answered. "It keeps our conversations private." She took the jar from him. "Do you know how to make salves?"

"Yes."

"Tomorrow, then. It's getting late, and you'll want to eat."

Lorcan nodded. "I never did stop to eat earlier. I'm starving." He picked up a cloth and wiped his hands. "Livia, is Gnaeus bothering you?"

"He's an idiot. I wish my father would sell him," Livia said. She looked over her shoulder, then shook her head. "It's none of your concern, Lorcan." She turned back to him and smiled. "But thank you. What's your full name? You didn't say."

"Didn't I?" Lorcan thought back and grinned. "I suppose I didn't. Lorcan mac Diarmuid mic Morrigan."

To his shock, Livia's eyes widened. "Mic Morrigan? You... you're one of the Raven's kin? My mother told me stories about them! About you, I mean. She said that they could change shapes, become ravens. I thought it was just a tale!"

Lorcan nodded. "We can. I can't. Not now. But when I was home—" he stopped. "It's not a tale."

"How, though?" She studied him. "There's a lot of you, and not a lot to a raven. How do you change?"

Lorcan shook his head.. "That's a secret. We have to keep that secret, you understand. Someone found out once, and it went very badly for all of Eire."

Livia frowned, sitting down across the table from him. "That... I think I know what you're talking about. A spirit? An evil spirit? I can't remember what Mother called it."

"She told you about the *deamhan aeir?*" Lorcan asked, stunned.

"That's it, yes. She and her brother left Hibernia for safety. Only their ship was taken by pirates, and she ended up here as a slave." She leaned forward. "I won't tell. How do you do it?"

Lorcan grinned at her. If he had his way, eventually, she'd have her own cloak of feathers. "My grandmother the Morrigan gave us the gift of the change. It's tied into our cloaks of feathers. Mine was stolen by my cousin when he betrayed me."

66

"And without it, you can't change," Livia murmured. "Thank you for trusting me. I've always wanted to know."

"You're welcome. I'll admit, I'm not very good at flying, though. My feathers are white, and they break."

She nodded, then looked thoughtful. "Apollo has a sacred raven, you know. A white one."

"Really?" Lorcan laughed. "I've never seen another one. Will you show me?"

"If Father says I might. And then only after you have your tattoo."

"I have to be tattooed, like the others?"

"The mark of the gladiator. Once Father says you're ready for it, I'll start working on it. Lorcan, if you can change, if you can fly, how did you get caught? Couldn't you just fly away?"

"I tried," Lorcan admitted. "They used a net, and the holes were too small for me to get through." Lorcan sighed, folded his hands on the table. "I'll get back there. I'll get my cloak back. And I'll make sure that my cousin can't hurt anyone again."

"Then I wish you luck of it," Livia said. She got to her feet and held her hand out to him. "But first, let's get you fed, and we'll start your lessons. You've got a year of training, and it'll go faster if you understand what's going on around you."

Chapter Seven

Over the next few weeks, Lorcan's lessons began in earnest. He spent his mornings in the arena, sparring with Yaroah under Manius' watchful eye. At the hands of the experienced gladiators, he learned that he wasn't as skilled a fighter as he'd thought—he spent a good portion of every morning on his back in the sand as first Yaroah, then Nona disarmed him and knocked him flat. After a few weeks of that, Ennius showed him that he had no idea how to defend himself against a man wielding a net. Not that he needed the reminder, he thought sourly as he hung his weapons on their pegs in the armory.

"Don't take it so hard," Manius said from behind him. "These men have been fighting for years, all of them. You're... what? Twenty?"

"Nineteen," Lorcan answered. "I've been training since I was 10. I'm supposed to be good at this. I feel like I've never held a blade before when I face them."

"Only nine years? Yaroah has been a gladiator for that long," Manius told him. He came over to stand next to Lorcan. "Who have you fought? Really fought, not just trained with."

"Raiders," Lorcan answered. "And only once, when I was taken. The years before that, my father didn't think I was old enough to go out with them when the raiders came in the spring."

"Ah. So, you've been studying fighting, but you've not really fought," Manius said. He rubbed his chin. "All that training has never been put to a real use. Do you understand the difference?"

"I think so," Lorcan said. "Like learning healing. I've studied how to sew a wound, but never done it myself."

"Exactly. We'll take what you've learned now, and we'll hone it. You're getting better. You almost took Nona down today."

Lorcan grimaced. "But I haven't won a fight since that first day. And I beat Yaroah!"

"Do you know why?" Manius asked. He grinned. "It's very simple. You did something that Yaroah wasn't expecting. Because you have skill, and training, but no experience. What you did on that first day was something that an experienced fighter would not have done."

"I surprised him?" Lorcan considered it. "And that works?"

"Clearly, it did."

"Then… would that work in the arena?" Lorcan leaned against the wall. "Once I have the experience, if I kept doing things that aren't expected?"

"I wouldn't try to make a fighting style of doing the unexpected," Manius said. "But keeping it as a tactic, perhaps. We'll see how it works as you continue your training. Now go bathe, and go to Livia for your lessons."

The lessons with Livia were no less frustrating, for all that they were less painful. She would tell him what she was teaching him for the day, giving him the names in Latin, then she would speak only Latin to him. He bumbled through his lessons, feeling singularly stupid and clumsy as he tried to make sense of what she was telling him. It helped that she started in her workroom, teaching him the Latin words for the tools he'd been using since he could see over his mother's worktable. But the language still made no sense to him, and he struggled with unfamiliar words and phrases that he could barely manage to remember.

"Why can't I make sense of this?" he snapped one evening as they worked in the garden. The days had gotten unbearably hot, so working in the garden was done at twilight, when it was cooler. Livia was sitting on a bench, tying herbs into bundles for drying, while he knelt in the garden bed behind her, weeding. She looked at him over her shoulder, amusement dancing in her eyes.

"Because you're convinced you can't?" she offered. "Because someone let you give up when it got hard the first time you tried?" She switched to Latin as she turned back to her work and said something that Lorcan didn't catch.

"I missed that. Turn around?"

"In Latin, Lorcan," she chided without turning.

Lorcan growled and tried to remember how to say it. "*Da… da mihi…oscula? Da mihi oscula.*" He looked up to see Livia looking at him. She smiled, laying aside the bundle that she was working with—an herb he knew as *Lus na gCnámh mBriste,* but that she called *solidago.* She got up from her bench, came to kneel in front of him, took his face in her hands, and kissed him.

"Since you asked so nicely," she whispered against his lips, and kissed him again. Lorcan forgot trying to figure out what it was that he'd said. He wrapped his arms around Livia and held her tightly. For weeks, he hadn't dare do more than admire her, hadn't dared breathe a word of how much he wanted her. She'd told him of Gnaeus' unwanted advances, and he didn't want her to think he was trying the same thing. But to have her in his arms, kissing him? He whimpered softly as she pulled away.

"Livia," he whispered. "What did I say?"

She laughed, running one finger over his upper lip. "What were you trying to say?"

"I wanted you to look at me."

"And?"

"And I couldn't remember how to ask you to turn around. So, I put it together from what I did remember. Give me eyes, I think?" He smiled. "What did I really say?"

"You asked me to give you a kiss," Livia said. "Really, Lorcan, I was starting to wonder if you were ever going to ask!"

"Ask… you were waiting for me?" Lorcan ran his hand down her back. "I was waiting for you. I didn't want to push."

"Because of—" She looked thoughtful. "Thank you."

"Well, I've no wish for you to put… what did you say? *Koneion*? What is that?

"You would call it fealla bog."

He coughed. "Really? I don't want to find poison in my beer, my Livia," Lorcan teased, and she laughed. "So, you tell me, lovely Livia, what do you want us to do now?"

She smiled. "My bedroom is off the workroom. It's closer than yours. And more private."

"Then by all means." Lorcan got to his feet and helped Livia to rise. He heard her gasp, and turned to see Manius standing on the walkway.

"I was wondering when you two would finally take the next step," he said.

"You knew?" Livia blurted. "Father—"

"You know I've no objections," Manius interrupted. "And Lorcan is a fine man. The usual instructions, Livia."

"Yes, sir."

Manius turned, then stopped. "How go the lessons?"

"Slowly," Lorcan answered in Latin. He frowned, then haltingly added, "I am not good."

Manius sniffed and answered in Gaeilge. "You're better than you were."

Lorcan switched back to Gaeilge. "It would be hard for me not to be," he said. "And Livia is a good teacher." He turned to her and smiled, taking her hand. "I'll keep trying."

"Good. Oh, and Livia? Start his tattoo."

Lorcan coughed. "I'm ready?"

"I think you are, yes." Manius smiled. "The Taurian Games are coming, and the Circus Maximus, and there's a spectacle for the Emperor's birthday in the fall. You're far enough along that I think you'll be ready to debut at the Games, and I want to pair you with Yaroah for the spectacle, for that contrasts fight he keeps proposing. So tomorrow, we'll measure you for armor, and you'll start training two on two against Nona and Ennius."

"Yes, sir," Lorcan said. "Thank you."

Manius waved and walked away, and Livia tugged Lorcan's hand. "This way." She pulled him out of the garden and through the doorway into the workroom. Lorcan had never been further than the workroom, although he had seen the inner door. Now Livia led him into that room and closed the door behind them. She turned to face him.

"Before we begin," she said. "I'm no blushing virgin. I enjoy men, and you won't be my first. Does that matter to you?"

Lorcan blinked. "Should it? I mean, does it matter to Roman men? It doesn't matter to me, but I'm not Roman."

Livia sighed. "I'm the daughter of a slave and of a former slave. I don't have any family status to speak of, and I'm already looked at as little more than a prostitute. I have no dowry, and no status, and am unlikely to ever marry, unless it's to a gladiator. You, on the other hand, are a prince in your own land—"

"And right now, I'm a slave," Lorcan interrupted. "And in my own land, a woman's worth is more than her chastity. I don't care that you've loved other men. I care that you want me, enough to welcome me to your bed." He stepped closer. "And if you come back to Eire with me, then you'll be a princess in our land."

Her eyes opened wide. "I haven't even slept with you yet, and you're talking about marriage?"

"I shouldn't," Lorcan said. "I shouldn't think of more than this. Right now. Nothing is certain for tomorrow. But I am thinking about it. Since the moment I first saw you, Livia, I've wanted you by my side. So, if—" He took her hand. "If it comes to that, to me going home, will you consider coming with me? As my mate?"

"Lorcan," she murmured. She licked her lips, then smiled. "Yes."

Relief flooded through him, and he laughed and scooped her up, hugging her tightly as he carried her to the bed in the corner. "My Livia. My beauty."

She twined her arms around his neck. "My Lorcan. You're not the only one, you know."

"The only what?"

"That first day, I came out and saw you with my father, and I wanted to put you on the floor and have you right then." She leaned closer and nipped his earlobe. "I don't know how I've managed to be so patient for so long."

Lorcan couldn't think of anything else to say. He set Livia down on her bed and knelt in front of her. "I didn't want to push—"

"If you don't push now, I'll be very disappointed," Livia murmured. She leaned forward and down, tugging Lorcan's tunic up and over his head. She tossed it to the side and ran her hands over his shoulders. Her palms were warm against his skin. "I want you to push. I want you to push hard, and fast, and until I'm screaming."

Lorcan coughed. "Livia!"

"Too forward?" She laughed. "Stand up, Lorcan. I'll teach you all my wanton ways. I'm not your first, am I?"

"No," Lorcan said, standing up. "I've been with a woman before. And a man. You said you enjoy men? So do I. And I enjoy women, too."

She giggled. "Good. If you've done that before, I won't have as much to teach you. And if we see a pretty boy, we can share. I had one lover who liked that."

"Thankfully, I'm not slow in that regard," Lorcan said. He helped her unwrap the loincloth that he wore under his tunic, then pulled her to her feet. "Except for this. How do I undo this?" he asked, tugging at her gown.

She answered by untying the cords that made up her belt. "The fibulae hold the whole thing up," she said, touching one of the pins at her shoulder.

"Oh?" Lorcan unfastened one of the pins, watching in amusement as the loose garment slipped down and bared one ample breast. "That's very convenient." He unfastened the other pin, and let the gown fall to the ground, then stepped back to admire her. The loose gown had only hinted at the treasure hidden beneath woolen folds. "You're so beautiful."

She blushed, color spreading down past her collarbone. "I'm not. I know what I look like."

"You don't know what I see," Lorcan said. "I see beauty." He moved in close and slid his arm around her, pulling her against him. "I see the only woman I will ever want, or need, or desire. I see my Livia."

"Lorcan—"

He leaned down and kissed her, feeling her arms around his neck again, her body warm against his. He wanted to explore her, learn her every freckle and eyelash until he could draw them from memory. But they had time for that. All the time in forever once he had his cloak back. He refused to consider any other alternative. He would regain his cloak, and his Livia would wear feathers and be at his side forever. For now, though. For now, he had to live in the moment. This moment, with her lips on his, her breasts against his chest, and the scent of her arousal rising like the headiest Egyptian perfume. She nibbled on his lower lip, and he shivered.

"Why are we still standing?" she whispered. Lorcan smiled and turned them, sitting down and pulling Livia into his lap, his cock trapped between their bodies.

"Better?" he asked.

"No," she answered, and pushed him backwards. He laughed, shifting around until he was stretched out on the bed. She straddled his legs, running her hands over his stomach, down his hips, over his sides. Her hands were warm and soft on his skin, and he reached down to run his hands up and down her thighs. She hummed, then stretched out on top of him, resting her hands flat on his chest, and her chin on her hands. She smiled at him. "Now that I have you here, I'm not sure what to do with you first."

He ran his hands up and down her back. "So long as you do something, or I'll do something."

Her laughter was deep and full, and as heady as mead. "Oh? What will you do, my Lorcan?"

He grinned and rolled onto his side, only to find himself once more on his back as Livia pushed him back down. She stretched up and kissed him, then pushed herself up. "No more wasting time," she said, shifting until she was straddling his hips. She started to move against him, grinding against him, her hands braced on his belly. Lorcan groaned, running his hands up her thighs, thrusting up gently against her.

"I thought you said no more wasting time," he asked.

"I'm not," she answered. "I'm enjoying you." She reached out and scratched her fingernails over his nipples; he gasped and arched his back, startled by the sudden shock of pleasure. Neither Bran nor Caoimhe had ever done that to him. He heard Livia laugh, and then he looked up at her.

"So, not as experienced as you thought?" she teased. "You look so confused!"

"I'm learning that I don't know as much as I thought about a great many things," he answered. "What else do you have to show me?"

"Don't move," she said. "Stay absolutely still." She smiled and raised herself up, reaching down and steadying Lorcan's cock as she slowly lowered herself down onto him, taking him into her heat with an aching slowness. Lorcan gripped her legs, closing his eyes and fighting to obey her words and not his instincts. He wanted to push up against her, wanted to roll her onto her back and drive into her until they both came. Instead, he did his best to hold perfectly still, even though he was certain that he was going to die before she was done. He heard her laughing again, as she raised herself up once more, then lowered herself again, taking him deeper. She stopped, and raised herself once more; Lorcan heard himself whine, a high pitched, tortured sound that seemed to come from both the back of his throat and the depths of his being.

As if she'd been waiting for that, Livia lowered herself completely onto him, until there was no space between them. She ran her hands over his belly, then braced herself and started moving against him, making little, throaty groans in time with the motion. It felt as if his heart was going to burst from the sheer want of her, and Lorcan reached up and cupped her ample breasts in his hands, running his thumbs over her nipples. She gasped, and her smooth movements stuttered. She ran her hands up his arms, taking his hands and lacing her fingers into his, using him for leverage as she started moving faster, more erratically, her breath and her moans coming louder and louder. It was too much—Lorcan braced his heels and thrust upwards, grunting and moaning his need. She squealed, stilled, then started moving with him, her moans mingling with his, turning to full-throated cries as he crested, and she followed. Their movement slowed, stilled, and she stretched out with him once more, curled half-on, half-off of him, her head pillowed on his shoulder. Lorcan closed his eyes, listening to his heartbeat slowing.

All at once, he heard something rustling in the outer room. He raised his head. "Did you hear that?"

Livia hummed but didn't move. "The cats, more than likely. We have awful troubles with mice."

Lorcan frowned. He wasn't all that familiar with cats—he knew that they were useful creatures to keep against mice, but it was the foolish mouse indeed that invaded a *baile* inhabited by 24 ravens. But it didn't sound small enough to be a cat.

"You said something before," Livia murmured. "I didn't understand it."

"I did?" Lorcan asked, distracted from the sounds. "What did I say? I'll explain if I can."

"You asked me to be your mate." Livia raised her head. "Not your wife."

"Ah. Yes," Lorcan said. "Livia, I'm not used to thinking of it in human terms. One of the things my grandmother gave to us was the ability to recognize our mates. Ravens mate once, you know. And that once is forever." He ran the tip of his finger over her lips. "I knew you from the moment I first saw you."

Her eyes widened. "You weren't just trying to get me to your bed, then? When you told me you'd bring me back to Eire and marry me?"

"No, my Livia." Lorcan rested his hand on her bare back. "I meant every word. And if it never happens, and I stay in Rome for the rest of my days, I still mean every word."

Her smile was brilliant. "But we're not staying in Rome. We're going to Eire. I know we are."

"In the spring," Lorcan said. "I promised your father a year." He smiled. "And I'm promising you forever."

* * *

"Good. Very good. Much better," Yaroah said. "You do well, Ghost."

Lorcan grinned. His pallor seemed to amuse the big Carthaginian, who would not be broken of his habit of calling Lorcan 'Ghost.'

"Thank you," he answered in Latin. "I try."

"You do well," Yaroah repeated. "How is the hand?"

Lorcan grimaced, flexing the fingers of his right hand. The new tattoo hurt, and his hand was stiff and a little swollen. But he liked the stylized raven that Livia had inscribed on the back of his hand, and the bands around his wrist. There would be more, she had told him. For each arena win, she'd add more to his arm. Knowing that, Yaroah's full arm tattoo was both impressive and daunting. "Hurts," he told Yaroah.

"I remember. We fight again later. Come to soak?"

"Soon," Lorcan answered. "I..." he frowned, then held his sheathed sword up. "Put in?"

"Put away," Yaroah answered.

"Put away. Yes. I come soon," Lorcan answered. Yaroah nodded and left the arena, and Lorcan turned and headed down the corridor toward the room where their weapons were stored. He'd added a long dagger to his kit, for the spectacle fight with Yaroah—the both of them would be armed with swords and daggers. It was a combination that Lorcan had never tried before, and he felt more than a little awkward and exposed without a shield in his left hand. But Manius said he was doing well, and so did Yaroah. He hung his spatha and dagger on their pegs next to his shield and walked out into the arena. He trotted toward the passage that led to the baths, and nearly bumped into Gnaeus, who was standing just inside, in the shadows where Lorcan didn't see him.

"Gnaeus," Lorcan said, and nodded his head politely. He didn't train with Gnaeus, and didn't have enough Latin to really converse, so he'd not had any real contact with the man apart from passing in the corridors and sitting at the same table at meals. He frowned slightly, then asked, "You come bathe?"

"No," Gnaeus said. He gestured Lorcan closer. "You fight with me."

"Not cestus," Lorcan protested. He raised both hands, realizing that Gnaeus had left him barely any room to pass. "Manius says no."

"Yes." Gnaeus stepped closer, and Lorcan noticed that his hands were wrapped as if he was going into the arena.

Gnaeus didn't wear his cestus for practice against anyone but Yaroah.

Lorcan stepped back, into the arena, feeling the sand underneath his bare feet. He had no weapons, no armor. He wore nothing but a wrapped loincloth, the *subligaculum* that all the gladiators wore. Clearly, Gnaeus had been waiting for just this opportunity. But *why*?

"Gnaeus, no," he said. "No fight."

"She is mine," Gnaeus snapped. "Mine!"

Lorcan gaped at him, remembering the noises he'd heard outside Livia's bedroom. It must have been Gnaeus. And now…

Now, Gnaeus would kill him, if he let the man get close or if he didn't end this. He'd brawled with the other boys, at home, but he already knew that his experiences at home meant nothing here. His playful wrestling matches among his cousins were no use to him against a trained fighter who was going to kill him if he failed. Or maybe it could be.

He backed up again, tensing. Watching. Gnaeus stepped forward, raised his fists… and Lorcan charged. He came in low and fast, slamming his shoulder into Gnaeus' midsection and driving the bigger man down onto the sand. Gnaeus recovered faster than Lorcan expected, his left fist slamming into Lorcan's jaw, knocking him sideways. Lorcan tasted blood; he rolled away and up onto his knees, spitting and seeing red on the sand. No, that wasn't going to work. He needed to get out of the arena. Gnaeus was already up, already advancing. Lorcan launched himself at Gnaeus' legs, knocking him down again. This time, before Gnaeus could recover, Lorcan was up and running, heading for the door that led into the building. How had they gotten so far?

"Manius!" he shouted.

Before Lorcan reached the door, Gnaeus hit him from behind, landing on him and knocking the breath out of him. Lorcan twisted, then howled as what felt like his uncle's anvil connected with the back of his right shoulder. Pain raced up and down his arm, and it didn't want to move when Gnaeus dragged him over so that he was lying on his back. Then Gnaeus straddled him, pinning him in place. Lorcan dug his heels into the sand, trying to throw Gnaeus off of him, but he had no leverage against Gnaeus' greater weight. Desperate, he grabbed a handful of sand and threw it into Gnaeus' face; Gnaeus screeched, then caught Lorcan around the throat with one big hand. He squeezed, growling and sputtering, his other fist raised. Lorcan heard a shout. Then the world exploded. To his distant surprise, he didn't black out. He was aware of Yaroah, practically screaming in his own language, and the sudden disappearance of Gnaeus' weight from his hips as the Carthaginian physically dragged the cestus away. Manius was there, trying to help Lorcan sit up, asking him questions that he couldn't understand and couldn't answer. Then Livia appeared, peering into his eyes, wiping away blood, giving orders. Lorcan tried to tell them that he was fine. He was just dizzy. But his words didn't seem to want to work together, and he felt suddenly sick.

"Lorcan," Livia switched from Latin to Gaeilge. "Lorcan, can you hear me? Don't try to move."

Not moving sounded wonderful. If only the arena would listen to her. He wanted to tell her that the arena was dancing around her and had just managed to make his eyes focus when he saw movement behind her. The world snapped back into focus, and he saw Gnaeus, rising from Yaroah's still form, coming toward them. His eyes were on Livia, and he had Yaroah's sword raised...

"Liv'a!" Lorcan croaked, pushing himself forward, trying to make his right arm move. He grabbed her arm with his left hand, pulled her behind him, and raised his right arm to defend himself. He heard Manius' roar of rage, saw the older man move, but it was too late. Lorcan heard the snap as the flat of the blade hit his forearm. At first, he thought it was the sword that had broken. Then he saw the blood, and a new wave of pain joined the rest. Lorcan crumpled, clutching his injured arm to his chest, hearing the commotion around him without knowing what was happening. Someone grabbed his shoulders, and he heard Livia shouting *Hold him! Lorcan, drink this!*

A thick, honey-sweet syrup was poured into his mouth. He gagged and swallowed, coughing. Nona's face swam in front of him—he was saying something, but Lorcan had no idea what. Then it didn't matter, as whatever Livia had made him drink took hold and he faded into a painless darkness.

He woke in his own bed, soaked in sweat, and with everything aching. He blinked, looking up at the shadowed ceiling, and wondered how he'd gotten here.

"Ghost?" Yaroah sat down on the edge of the narrow bed. There was a large knot on his forehead, and his eye was swollen almost closed. "I must stop calling you that. You nearly were one."

"What?" Lorcan repeated. "How much I hurt?"

"Wait. I will get Livia," Yaroah said. He got up and went to the door, calling out into the corridor. A few minutes later, Livia came in. She looked pale, and her hair was falling out of its usual braid. There was a smudge of dirt on her face, and the tracks of tears.

"Thank you, Yaroah," she said. He nodded and left, closing the door behind him. She came over and sat down on the edge of the bed. In Gaeilge, she asked. "What's your name? And your mother's name?"

Lorcan blinked, then remembered his training. "Oh. Because of my head. Lorcan Lachtna. And my mother's name is Grainne. And you are my Livia. I'm sorry I frightened you." He looked at the door. "Was I truly almost a ghost? How badly am I hurt?"

Livia snorted. "Not as badly as Yaroah thinks. Do you want a list?"

"Other than my broken head, what?" Lorcan asked. He blinked again, and noticed his right arm felt heavy, and was tucked underneath the blanket. "My arm?"

"Your arm is broken," Livia said simply. "Both bones of the arm, and about halfway between the wrist and elbow. If he hadn't hit you with the flat of the blade, then Yaroah might not have been wrong. As it was, you'll have scars on your arm from where the edges of the blade cut you. You'll also have a scar here, from the cestus." She reached out and trailed a finger gently over Lorcan's cheek. "You've a host of nasty bruises, and you cut the inside of your mouth rather badly. I thought at first that he'd knocked teeth out, but it seems not." She sighed. "He attacked you over me?"

"He must have been listening to us. What I heard in the workroom," Lorcan said. "Where is he?"

"You needn't worry about him," Livia said. She sounded satisfied and annoyed in equal measure. "Apparently, losing his chance to debut you in the spectacle was enough to convince Father that Gnaeus really was the problem I've been complaining about for almost a year."

"What?"

"He's gone. Father sold him. By now, Gnaeus is on his way to the iron mines of Elba, and good riddance to him." She rested her hand on Lorcan's chest. "Don't worry about him. Now, our only priority is to see you healed."

Lorcan closed his eyes. "The Morrigan's blood heal quickly."

"Good. Father wants you back on the sands as soon as you can be." She leaned down and kissed him. "And I want you back in my bed as soon as you can be."

Chapter Eight

The *spatha* felt odd in his left hand, but not as odd as it had when he had first started. It had been two weeks since he'd been allowed to start sparring against the battered, straw-filled armor that they used as a practice dummy, trying to build up the muscles in what should have been his shield-arm. It had been a month since Gnaeus had attacked him, and Lorcan's right arm was still splinted and uncomfortable. It always seemed to be damp from sweat, due to what Lorcan thought ridiculous temperatures, but what Livia assured him was mild summer heat. He'd wear the splints for another month, she said. Less if he listened to her, did the gentle exercises that she had instructed him to do, and for the love of Apollo, Lorcan, don't rush it! But it was frustrating to not be able to train, to not be able to even really be any help in the workroom. So, he'd asked permission to work his left arm, something that Manius had laughingly granted. Lorcan wasn't sure why Manius had laughed, but he hadn't laughed when he'd seen Lorcan this morning, instead offering instruction on his posture and his stance, wondering aloud at the idea of having Lorcan fight with two swords instead of a sword and shield. It would increase his flexibility as a gladiator, his winnings in the arena, and his worth as a slave.

That last had made Lorcan's blood run cold. "But only until spring," he said.

"Of course, only until spring!" Manius had laughed again, then continued in Gaeilge. "If I even thought about selling you, my daughter might poison me. Keep working on your guard. You're too used to fighting with a shield, and you're not protecting your right side."

"I'm backwards," Lorcan answered. "I'm still learning how to reverse it."

"Reverse it but remember your guard." Manius stepped back to watch Lorcan spar. "And keep practicing your Latin."

Another source of frustration, and Lorcan took it out on the dummy.

His language lessons weren't going well at all—he understood many of the words, but he couldn't translate them fast enough in his head to follow in a full conversation, nor could he remember how to put his own sentences together properly. If he tried to speak in Latin, he stammered and chose the wrong words, sounding as if his head had been broken more seriously than his arm. He managed in the ludus with a mix of half-Latin, half-Gaeilge, and none of the rest of the *familia* laughed at him. Not anymore, anyway. Not since he'd lost his temper at Nona and set the other man on his arse in the sands. But the one time he'd left the ludus with Livia and gone to the temple of Apollo to see the white raven... Lorcan grunted and swung, and his spatha lodged in the armor at the dummy's neck. He growled and tugged the sword free. No more leaving the ludus for him. Not until he could speak properly.

It hadn't even been a real raven. Apollo's worth the frustration. The white raven in Apollo's temple was only a statue. It wasn't a real raven at all.

"Lorcan!" Nona called from the other side of the arena. "Lorcan, come and see!"

Lorcan turned, seeing the other gladiators clustered around a section of the wall underneath a small ledge. "What?" Lorcan called back. He sheathed his spatha and crossed the sand. "What, Nona?"

Yaroah pointed. "Something is up there. A bird, I think."

Lorcan frowned. He was about to say that there had been birds in the arena before when he heard it—the raspy croak of a raven. His eyes widened.

"That's why we called you," Nona said. He tapped Lorcan's right hand, and the raven tattooed there. "Raven?"

"Yes." Lorcan looked around. "How do I get up there?"

Yaroah blinked and looked surprised. Then he cupped his hands. "Nona, Ennius, steady him."

Yaroah lifted Lorcan high enough that he could see over the edge of the ledge. There was a raven there, an older female. One of her wings drooped lower than the other. Lorcan croaked in the back of his throat, and she looked at him, dark eyes blinking.

"Raven?" Nona called.

"Yes. Wing hurt." Lorcan braced himself on the wall with his good hand, then reached for the raven with the other, calling softly. A nest call, the one he remembered calling to his own mother. The raven skipped closer, then lowered her head and pecked the back of his hand. He clicked at her, the closest he could come to snapping his beak, and she looked at him again.

"Come on, love," he said softly in Gaeilge. "Let me help you."

To his surprise, the raven came to him, climbing to perch on his wrist as if she were a hunting hawk. He drew his arm close to his chest and was about to tell the others to put him down when he heard Livia's voice, "What are you doing? Yaroah, put him down!"

Yaroah lowered Lorcan to the sand immediately. Lorcan turned to face his clearly angry lover, clasping the raven to his chest. "Are you trying to break the other one?" she demanded. Then she saw the raven. "Where did that come from?"

"She," Lorcan answered. "She's hurt. She was up on the ledge."

Livia blinked and *looked* at him for a moment. Then she looked back at the raven. "She was? And she's hurt? How did she get there?"

"Yes. She's broken, just like I am. I don't know how she got up there, but I know how to help her," Lorcan said. "But I need you to do it. It will take two hands. Maybe more than two hands."

"Oh… of course," Livia said slowly. "Let's take her to the workroom. What will I need?"

"Bandaging," Lorcan answered. He ducked his head and blew gently on the raven's head. "We need to hold the wing still."

"I see." Livia led the way down the corridors, and the other gladiators followed. Lorcan ignored them. He set the raven down on the worktable and croaked at her. The raven croaked back, but didn't fight as Lorcan gently moved her wing, folding it against her body.

"Wrap the bandaging around her," Lorcan said. "Not too tight. Just to hold the wing in place."

Following his instructions, Livia wound bandaging around the injured wing, binding it to the raven's body. "She's very tame," she murmured. "Someone's pet, do you think?"

"I don't know," Lorcan answered. He didn't look up, watching the raven's reactions. "I don't think so. But I've never met a tame raven before. I don't know how one would act."

"She's not attacking you," Ennius said.

"I think she knows I'm another raven," Lorcan answered. "Just a funny looking one."

That drew a laugh from Yaroah. "Then perhaps we named you wrong. You're not Ghost. You are Raven!"

Lorcan looked up and grinned. "What's that in Latin?" he asked. He was met with stunned looks. "What?"

"Lorcan, you've been speaking Latin. Since the moment Yaroah put you down, you haven't said a single word in Gaeilge," Livia answered. "You've been so distracted by the raven that you didn't even notice."

"I have?" Lorcan gasped. He looked around, saw the other men nodding. "I speak right?"

"And now he's lost it," Nona said with a laugh. "Now he's thinking about it."

"What's all this?" Manius said from the doorway. "Did I hear Lorcan?"

"Apparently, if he's not thinking about speaking Latin, he does quite well," Livia said. "And he's been distracted."

"Distracted how?" Manius came in and saw the raven on the table. He arched an eyebrow and looked at Lorcan. "Visiting relative?"

Lorcan smiled. "I don't think so." He let the raven perch on his wrist, drew her to his chest. "She needed help. We help."

"Don't let her distract you from your training, Lorcan," Manius said. He looked thoughtful. "The Emperor's feast day games. Livia, will he be ready?"

"If he does what he's supposed to do, then the bones should be whole by then," Livia answered. "We'll have to brace the arm to protect the bones, though. So they don't break again." She looked over at Nona. "Any ideas? You're our tinkerer."

"Some sort of leather bracer, maybe?" Nona answered. "Wood or metal plates inside to keep it solid. Let me work on it."

"Thank you, Nona," Lorcan said. He looked up as he realized something. "How you all know?" he asked. "About ravens? About me? I not tell you."

"I did," Manius said. "There are no secrets in a *familia*. They know, and knowing, they will guard your back."

Lorcan smiled. He looked around at the others, realizing that *familia* had become family. "So, what name her?"

"You're certain it is female?" Yaroah asked. Lorcan arched an eyebrow, and Yaroah laughed. "Fair enough. You would know. Call her Corvina."

Lorcan nodded, his head lowered, ruffling the feathers of the raven's breast with his fingers. "Corvina. Welcome to the family."

* * *

Corvina seemed to take her role in the family seriously, refusing to be separated from Lorcan. She would reluctantly perch on a bench near the arena door, or on top of the practice dummy if no one was using it, but as soon as Lorcan sheathed his sword, she would scream at him until he came and got her. In the workroom, she would sit on the table, or stalk around and explore the room and terrorize the cat. She even accompanied Lorcan into the baths, splashing in the puddles around the plunge in the *frigidarium*. The only place she didn't go was the bedroom that Lorcan and Livia now shared.

"Is she jealous of me, do you think?" Livia asked early one morning, after a few weeks of having Corvina around.

"Hmm?" Lorcan, half-asleep, yawned and wiped sweat from his face. How could people live in this heat all the time? It was barely past dawn, and he was already drenched in sweat. "Why do you say that?"

"She doesn't come in here." Livia drew a ticklish design on his chest with her nails, making Lorcan grimace. He swatted at her hand and considered.

"If she was jealous, or trying to claim me as her mate, she'd have attacked you. I think she knows you're my mate."

"And she's giving us privacy?" Livia chuckled. "She's very smart. Are all ravens so smart?"

"I only know the smart ones, so I can't answer that," Lorcan answered. He ran his left hand up Livia's back, considered the splint on his right arm. He raised it. "It's been how long now?"

"You both should be out of your splints soon." Livia curled up with her head on his chest. "Will she fly away, do you think?"

"I'd be surprised if she doesn't," Lorcan answered. "She might stay, though. She lives easy with us."

"Of course she lives easy with us. You feed her cheese," Livia teased. "Is that even good for ravens?"

"I don't know. I mean, I like it," Lorcan said. "Is it good for me?"

"Silly bird."

Lorcan laughed, tightening his arm around Livia. "Your silly bird. There might be another reason she stays outside, you know." He rolled, shifting so that he and Livia were face to face, and ran one hand down her side. "We make an awful lot of noise in here."

Livia chuckled, reaching between them and wrapping her hand around his erect cock. "Are we going to be making more noise?"

"I thought we might," Lorcan murmured. He kissed her, letting her push him onto his back. She seemed to enjoy being the one on top, and Lorcan had discovered that he loved being able to watch her, being able to touch her as she moved over him. She giggled as she straddled his hips, running her nails down his chest and over his nipples, making Lorcan gasp and squirm.

"How much noise?" she whispered. "Do we want everyone to know how we spent our morning?"

"Do you think they don't know already? They knew before I moved into your room!" Lorcan answered. "If you don't get on with it, there won't be a morning. Someone will come fetch me for training soon."

"Oh, we can't have that." Livia laughed. She raised herself up, reaching down to hold Lorcan's cock steady as she lowered herself onto him. Lorcan closed his eyes and moaned softly. They moved together now, familiar with each other—Lorcan knew her reactions, could feel her breathing, her very heart beating in time with his own. He surged up against her, feeling her body responding to him, feeling his body responding to hers. When he was sure she was about to peak, he pulled her down to him, wrapping his arms around her and kissing her, muffling her cries. Then he rolled until they were both on their sides, until he could move more freely, thrusting hard, feeling her building to a second climax as he reached his own. She whimpered as he let her go, flopping back onto his back, panting as the sweat pooled and dried on his skin.

"I liked that," Livia murmured, taking her usual position with her head pillowed on his shoulder. "All the fun, none of the noise."

Lorcan chuckled, then sat up as he heard someone calling his name and Livia's. Livia got out of bed and went to the closed door.

"What is it?"

"Excuse me, but Lorcan has a visitor in the garden."

* * *

Curious, Lorcan followed Livia out into her garden. A visitor? Who would know to visit him here? And why?

Lorcan knew that he'd had never before seen dark-haired man standing in the center of the garden before. He also knew that he'd have known this man anywhere. He stopped, startled. He knew this man in his bones, the same way he knew Livia. This man was his *mate*. But that was impossible.

Wasn't it?

No, it was impossible. He had his mate already. Ravens only mated once. He couldn't have two.

But Morrigan's bones, he wanted this man! No, that wasn't right. He *needed* this man. And he didn't even know his name!

The newcomer was tall, and very thin, looking as if he was all bones, angles, and whipcord muscle. His dark hair curled close to his head, and his skin was the color of burnished oak. He wore a toga, but looked uncomfortable and out of place in it, as if he wasn't used to wearing it. He turned toward them as they came out from under the colonnade, and Livia stopped in her tracks.

"Tavi?" she gasped. Then she squealed, "Tavi!" and ran to him, throwing her arms around him. He laughed and accepted her enthusiastic embrace. "Look at you!" she babbled as she stepped back. "You got so tall! How could you get so tall in two years? When did you get back?"

"A few days ago," Tavi answered. "Uncle thought it would be a nice surprise for grandfather if Father was here for the celebration, and Father asked me to come with him. You look wonderful, Livia." He looked up at Lorcan, and to Lorcan's surprise, he started speaking in Gaeilge, "You must be Lorcan?"

"Yes," Lorcan said. He walked closer, trying not to stare. Who was this man? "You know me?"

"I know of you. Manius asked me to come meet you," Tavi answered. "He heard we were back in Rome. He hoped that I might be able to help you with your Latin." He smiled, his teeth very white against his dark skin. "I study and teach languages."

"Which explains how you speak Gaeilge?" Lorcan asked.

Tavi's grin grew broader. "That and I've lived most of my life in Britannia. What you would know as Alba. I'm my father's chief translator. But I've also lived in Rome, visiting my grandfather. And for the year or two we lived here, Manius taught me. He was my first arms instructor—"

"And his last," Livia interrupted. "Tavi is an excellent language teacher, but he's hopeless with a blade."

"Hush, woman," Tavi answered, grinning. "Yes, my last instructor.

But he's my father's friend, so when he asked, I agreed to come. And I'll admit that I was interested. Your name is familiar to me for some reason. I can't remember why though. So, shall we begin?"

Lorcan frowned. "I thought I was training this morning."

Tavi nodded. "All right. I'll watch you train, then we can go to the baths together and start lessons there."

Livia took Lorcan's arm. "I'll be in my workroom. Do you want me to finish that tonic?"

"Yes, please," Lorcan answered. He leaned down and kissed her, then gestured out of the garden.

"You trained with Manius?" he asked as Tavi fell in next to him.

"My brothers and I all did. My father and my uncle were both gladiators for a while. They were *auctorati*."

"I don't know what that is," Lorcan admitted.

"A free man, fighting as a gladiator," Tavi answered. "When my father gave it up to marry, Manius promised that he'd train Father's sons. Which are my brothers and me."

"How many brothers?" Lorcan asked.

"Seven. Well… six still living. I'm the eight son, and the 11th child, and the youngest." Tavi said. "And I'm the hopeless one. I trip on my own feet whenever I get on the sand. Father sends me out with a guard when we're in Alba."

Lorcan nodded. They walked out into the arena, and Lorcan left Tavi to go get his weapons. He picked up his *spatha* and set Corvina in her place on the bench. The raven scolded him, and he laughed and rubbed her under her chin until her eyes closed. Then he tapped her beak and headed toward the practice dummy. He could see Yaroah standing with Tavi, and they appeared to be talking in another language.

"Lorcan!" Nona called. He came out into the sunlight, and Lorcan could see that he was carrying something. "Come try these."

Lorcan met Nona near the dummy. "You finished the brace?"

"Yes. I made two, so you'll match." Nona held one up. "Give me your good arm. We'll try it."

Lorcan held his left arm out and let Nona lace up the leather sleeve. It covered him from the knuckles to the elbow, and he could feel the rigidity in the leather.

"I used a mix of reeds and iron rods. Reeds to keep it light, and rods to keep it strong. They all start over the wrist," Nona said as he tightened the sleeve. "So you can bend." He stepped back. "Let's see how you move."

Lorcan nodded, flexing his left wrist. The leather was stiff, but that would change the more he worked it. Slowly, he started to run through his initial exercises, the gentle, graceful movements that warmed his muscles and that required more control than sparring. He paid attention to his stance, to the problems with his guard, tapping the armored dummy just enough to feel the contact.

"It's like watching a dancer."

Lorcan heard the unfamiliar voice as he pulled his sword back. He turned and smiled at Tavi, whose eyes widened. His cheeks colored slightly.

"Lorcan is quite good," Manius agreed. He was standing with Tavi and Yaroah, and he nodded. "How is your arm today?"

"Good, I think," Lorcan answered. "The splint go soon, Livia says."

"How did you break it?" Tavi asked. "In practice? And answer in Latin."

Lorcan frowned, thinking about the words. "I was attack. Attack? No. Attacked. I was attacked." He paused, looking for the next word. "Gnaeus. He did not want me."

Tavi arched a brow. "He didn't want you?"

"Was wrong?" Lorcan looked at Manius.

"Gnaeus didn't like you, Lorcan."

"Ah. He did not like me." Lorcan shrugged. "Because of Livia."

Tavi looked at Manius. "One of your gladiators attacked another because of Livia?"

"Unfortunately, yes," Manius said. He turned back to Lorcan. "Do you think you're ready for a bout?"

Lorcan looked down at his splinted right arm. "Will Livia yell?"

Manius and Tavi both laughed. "Perhaps she will. But you're a gladiator, Lorcan. Not a healer. Not here. Go fetch your shield. And bring the wooden swords. This is just for practice."

Lorcan nodded and went to get his shield. When he came back, Yaroah was waiting for him, carrying his own shield. He took the wooden gladius that Lorcan offered

"Take it easy. Yaroah, you're not allowed to break him anymore," Manius said.

Yaroah laughed. "I will not break him. He must not break me!"

"I won't," Lorcan assured him. He met Yaroah's eyes, licked his lips, and waited. He'd noticed that Yaroah usually started his fights with an overhand strike, the better to take advantage of his height. Today was no exception—Yaroah yelled and lunged, then yelped as Lorcan moved under his swing and struck, driving his sword across Yaroah's ribs. He spun as Yaroah moved through the space where Lorcan had been standing, then struck again, going low and knocking Yaroah's legs out from under him. Just as in their first fight, Yaroah fell to his knees, then got back up, laughing.

"You knew what I would do!" he accused. Lorcan grinned.

"You always try to take their head off," Lorcan answered. "We all know it."

"He has a point, Yaroah," Manius said. "And I've told you that more than once."

"Another reason we will pair well together. Lorcan goes low, I go high. We will win every battle." Yaroah nodded, then stuck his practice sword under his arm and clapped Lorcan on the shoulder. "You have gotten faster. Faster than when we first fought. Very good, Raven."

Lorcan grinned. He jumped in surprise when Tavi spoke—he'd forgotten the man was there. "Raven? Because of your pet?"

Yaroah glanced at Lorcan, who shook his head slightly. Yaroah smiled. "Just so. Before the raven, I called him Ghost."

"I can see why," Tavi agreed. "Lorcan is really quite good. Has he debuted yet?"

"He was going to debut at the Taurian Games. Then his arm was broken," Manius answered. "Now, it will be at the Circus Maximus, I think. Or the Ludi Romani"

"Oh, then I'll see him there." Tavi smiled. "Will he be fighting in the birthday games?"

"Don't tell him, Manius!" Yaroah said. "Let him be surprised."

Manius laughed. "Come and talk with me, Tavi. Tell me how Arcus is doing, and those brothers of yours. I know Antius is here, and Galius is in Thracia. Young Decus is still in Alba, no? What about the twins?"

The two left, talking animatedly. Lorcan looked up at Yaroah once they were gone. "Thank you."

"The *familia* keeps its secrets, Raven," Yaroah said. "Now, Tavi is one of us. But I will not tell him if you do not want me to."

"Not yet," Lorcan said. "I don't know him enough. When I'm ready, I'll tell him myself."

"That is fair. Now, shall we spar?" Yaroah took his sword out from under his arm. "Or do you wish to beat the dummy again, so you can use your proper sword?"

"Spar. I am bored with fighting armor." Lorcan raised his wooden spatha. "I will not get better if I do not get hit back."

Yaroah crowed with laughter. "I will not hit hard. Livia will hurt me if I break you again."

* * *

Lorcan ran his fingers through his sweat-soaked hair and sighed. He was tired, but it was a good tired—he'd sparred with Yaroah for what seemed like ages, then they teamed up against Ennius and Nona. It had been more like playtime than practice and had gone on until Manius had returned to the sand and called an end to the day, sending them off to the baths. As a group, they had visited the *natatio* first, a small, open-air pool that Lorcan hadn't known existed until Yaroah had shown him weeks after he had first arrived. He'd left Corvina there when they went on to the *tepidarium*, where Lorcan sent his greetings to Ercc, via the bath slave Bruno. Oiled and scraped, the gladiators stayed and lounged on the benches.

"You're getting better, Raven," Ennius said. "You're almost as good as Yaroah."

"Thank you," Lorcan answered. He picked up a flagon of watered wine that Bruno had left and sipped it. "I have to be better, for when I go home." He didn't miss the glance that Ennius shared with Yaroah, and sat up. "What?"

Nona reached over and smacked Ennius on the back of the head. "Idiot!"

"What?"

Yaroah silenced them both with a look, then came over to sit on Lorcan's bench, one set in the corner of the room, where Lorcan could see everything. "What was it he told you? Manius, I mean."

Lorcan frowned. "That I give him a year. Then, he send me home. Why?"

Yaroah sighed. "Because he made me the same promise. I was sold here as a prize of war a long time ago. And…" he paused. Then shook his head, seeming to change his mind about what he was going to say. "Not important. Manius made me that same promise," he repeated. "Years ago. But now? I think I will not see Carthage again. Not so long as Manius owns me. I think you will not see Eire again. Not so long as Manius owns you. He will say in the spring, no. It is the wrong time. You are not ready. The weather does not permit. The augury is poor. We will wait, and you will go next year. And so it goes. We make him rich, and he makes us promises he does not keep."

Lorcan stared at him, suddenly frozen despite the heat of the room. "You… the same he tells you?"

Yaroah nodded slowly. "He told me the same. I no longer believe him. Perhaps he will keep his word to you. But I do not think so. You are my brother, and I do not wish to see you hurt. But we all of us—" he gestured to the other men. "We belong to him. There is no way we can fight him. We have no right to say no, and there is no law that says he must speak truth to slaves."

Lorcan nodded slowly. Yaroah patted his leg and rose. "We go to the *caldarium*. Will you come?"

Lorcan shook his head. "Not yet. Later."

Yaroah touched Lorcan's shoulder, then led the other men out of the *tepidarium*. Alone, Lorcan shifted on the bench, pulling his legs up and sitting with his back against the wall.

He should have known that Manius would never let him go, he thought miserably. He should never have set his heart on going home. The message Manius had assured him would be sent had probably never happened, either. His father would never know where he was, and no one would ever come for him. Now… what was he going to do now?

"Lorcan?"

Lorcan looked up to see Tavi, clothed only in the thin bathing robe. He looked worried. "What's wrong? Are you in pain?"

Lorcan shook his head. "No, I am fine."

Tavi frowned and switched from Latin to Gaeilge. "You're not fine. What's wrong? Should I go get Livia?"

"No. Thank you, but no," Lorcan answered. He swung his legs down and gestured. "Sit down?"

"Thank you," Tavi came and sat next to Lorcan. Very close to Lorcan, his leg close enough to touch. "You don't look like you're in the mood to have a lesson."

"I'm not."

"Tell me about the trouble you're having in speaking, at least?" Tavi asked. "That will help me learn what I need to do to teach you."

Lorcan frowned. "Apparently, if I'm not thinking about it, or if I'm distracted, I can have whole conversations. If I am paying attention, I can't think fast enough to translate, or remember any of the right words."

Tavi nodded. "And you've tried to learn before? It sounds like you have."

"My cousin Siobhan had a language tutor. She's not much older than I, so we shared lessons when I fostered with my uncle. When I went home, I tried to continue. I have an uncle who is a *brehon*. He tried, but I'm hopeless."

Tavi smiled. "I don't think so. Not hopeless like I am with a blade. Not if you can have full conversations when you're not thinking about it. Tell me about the tutor?"

Lorcan blinked. "I can't tell you much. I barely remember him."

"Was he mean? Did he punish you for getting things wrong?"

Lorcan frowned, thinking for the first time in years about the shrill little *brehon* who had seemed to delight in reducing two children to tears. "I… yes. Yes, he was. And yes, he did. It was the first time in my life I'd ever been strapped. He seemed to especially like making Siobhan cry. My uncle sent him away."

"Right," Tavi said, nodding. "Then that's where the problem is." He smiled and put his hand on Lorcan's knee. "I'm not going to punish you for not getting it right the first time, or for needing more help. I'm definitely not going to try and make you cry."

Lorcan wasn't sure if it was the heat of the room, or if Tavi's hand was just that warm, but it felt as if he was in the *caldarium*. He licked his lips and looked for his cup. "Wine?" he croaked, then cursed silently. He stooped and picked up the flagon, offered it to Tavi.

Tavi just smiled. "Thank you." He took the flagon with his other hand and sipped, his eyes never leaving Lorcan's. His eyes, Lorcan noticed, were a curious shade of coppery brown, almost the same shade as amber. "What did Livia tell you about me?" he asked as he set the wine down.

"Nothing," Lorcan answered. "There was no time."

Tavi nodded. His hand never moved from Lorcan's knee. "We were lovers once, before I left for Alba. And we would occasionally share—"

"Oh, was that you?" Lorcan interrupted. "She told me that she'd shared pretty boys with one of her lovers."

He laughed. "Yes, that was me. And you, Lorcan, are a very pretty boy," he murmured.

"Are… are you asking me to share your bed?" For a moment, he thought of Livia. What would she say? No. No, she was his mate. Tavi couldn't be. Having two mates… it just wasn't possible. No matter how much he wanted this man.

"I'm asking you to share yourself. I know Livia won't mind because we've done this before," Tavi answered. "Have you ever been with another man?"

"Yes." Lorcan answered. "You think she won't mind?"

"No. You can ask her, if you want. I'm certain of her answer."

Lorcan licked his lips again. "I don't know. I barely know you."

Tavi smiled. "Of course. I can wait until you know me better. And I assure you, I cannot wait to know you better."

.

Chapter Nine

The next morning, Tavi was on a couch in the *triclinium* for the morning meal before Lorcan was. He dressed in a plain tunic and looked like any of the other men on their couches, except for his lack of tattoos. He shared Lorcan's couch, and encouraged him to answer questions in Latin, prompting him gently with hints when he forgot the words. The pattern of the days that followed was set then—Tavi would observe in the arena while the gladiators practiced. It seemed to Lorcan as if every time he looked at Tavi, Tavi was watching him. Intently, as if he was trying to memorize every movement Lorcan made. It was distracting to be under such scrutiny. Lorcan tried to sneak another look and got whacked on the thigh.

"You're not paying attention, Raven!" Yaroah scolded. "That gets you killed in the arena!"

Lorcan blushed. "Sorry. I do better."

Yaroah grinned, looked sidelong at Tavi, then laughed. He reached out and tapped Lorcan on the top of his head with the wooden practice blade. In a low voice, he said, "Use this head, not the other one."

"Yaroah!"

Yaroah hooted with laughter, then attacked, forcing Lorcan to pay attention.

Once practice was over, Tavi would join the gladiators in the bath. In the *tepidarium*, he would continue Lorcan's lessons, with help around the edges from Yaroah, Nona, and Ennius. After a few weeks, Lorcan felt as if he were making progress. He no longer felt tongue tied and stilted when he had to speak Latin and said so to Livia as they sat in her workroom.

"Your accent is getting better, too," she confirmed. She set aside the mortar and pestle that she'd been working with. "Let me see your arm."

It was a common request, one that Livia had made at least once a day since Lorcan had started sparring against the others. Lorcan held his splinted arm out to Livia, and they ran through the usual exercises. She nodded and reached for a small knife.

"It's time, I think," she said, cutting the linen straps that held the splints in place. The skin underneath the splints and bandages was pale and sickly looking, and the arm felt weak. Lorcan grimaced as he massaged his forearm.

"You'll need to build the strength back up," Livia said. "I wonder… do you think it's time for Corvina, too?"

Lorcan considered it, then nodded. "Bird bones knit quickly. It may be past time. We should do this outside." He called Corvina out from under a table, picking her up. Then he and Livia walked out into the garden. Lorcan sat down on the bench there, guided Corvina down to his lap, and held her as Livia unwound the bandages keeping the raven's wing in place.

"Time to see if she's well?"

Lorcan looked up to see Tavi standing nearby. "It's time for both of us to fly, I think." He glanced at Livia, who drew her hands back. Then Lorcan let Corvina go. She shifted for a moment, hopped down onto the bench, and from there onto the ground. She pecked at something, shook all of her feathers, then flapped her wings and took to the air. She landed on the edge of the roof and croaked at them.

"You're welcome, Corvina!" Livia called back. Lorcan laughed and got up, brushing feathers off his tunic.

"We should go tell Manius that I've got both arms again," he said. "Come with me?"

Livia took his hand, and they walked out of the garden and along the colonnade. Tavi fell in on Livia's other side; he turned, clearing his throat intending to say something, then yelped. Something solid landed on Lorcan's shoulder, and he heard a gurgling croak in his ear. He laughed.

"Staying?" he asked, reaching up to ruffle Corvina's feathers. She hopped onto his hand and he brought her down to rest against his chest. "I'm glad you are."

"She'd be a fool not to stay," Livia said. "You feed her cheese."

Tavi laughed, then cleared his throat. "I had an idea, and I spoke to Manius about it. He's willing if you agree. How would you feel about trading teaching for teaching?"

Lorcan frowned. "You speak Gaeilge like you were born to it."

"But I'm hopeless with a sword," Tavi replied. "I'll teach you Latin. You teach me how not to kill myself."

"If you're at risk of killing yourself when you fight, you're holding the wrong end of the blade," Lorcan said archly. Livia hooted, and Tavi burst into peals of giggles.

"That's the deal," Tavi said once he'd wiped his eyes. "On the sand, you can only tell me what to do in Latin."

Lorcan considered it, then nodded. "When do we start?"

"Tomorrow."

* * *

Tavi was in the *triclinium* the next morning, the same as every other morning. He smiled his greetings to Lorcan but didn't turn from his conversation with Yaroah. They were speaking in that other language—whatever they spoke in Carthage, Lorcan guessed. Lorcan ignored them, taking one of the light, flat bread rounds from the communal platter at the center of the table. He tore off a piece and offered it to Corvina, then ate a second piece himself. A piece of cheese was placed onto his plate, and he turned and nodded at Nona. Nona smiled in response and offered a tidbit of cheese to Corvina. Her talons pricked Lorcan's shoulder through his tunic as she shifted from foot to foot, and he clicked at her until she settled.

"Will we be sparring again today?" Nona asked. "Yaroah?"

"Not today," Yaroah answered. "Lorcan is going to try and teach our fish to fly."

"What?" Lorcan asked. "What does that mean?"

"He means me," Tavi said. "Manius used to say that teaching me to fight was like teaching a fish to fly."

Lorcan reached for a boiled egg and took a bite, considering. "What have you tried?" he asked.

"Sword and shield," Tavi answered. "My father thought I might become a soldier, since I'm the youngest and I won't inherit much of anything. My next two older brothers are centurions. And centurions use sword and shield."

Lorcan nodded. He offered a piece of egg to Corvina, then finished his own. "What are the other options? What other weapons do you have here?"

"Wrong question. What weapons could you teach me to use?" Tavi asked in response. Lorcan grinned.

"You've already tried sword and shield. So, swords are out," he answered., switching t0 Gaeilge "I learned to use a club, but I was never good at it. I don't have the right build for it. Neither do you. You need bulk to use one in battle. Spear. Sling." He frowned, thinking of Bran. Then he swallowed and continued, "Axes. Have you used an axe?"

"To cut wood," Tavi answered. "But to fight? No."

"If it cuts wood, it will cut men. Anything can be a weapon, after all. Is an axe a Roman weapon?" He looked around the table. Manius, lounging silent on his couch, shook his head slowly.

"Not really," he answered in Latin. "They're part of the centurion's equipment, but they're not really weapons."

"But you could still use one as a weapon? It's not forbidden?" Lorcan persisted.

"It's not, but these axes aren't what you're used to, Lorcan. They're different from Hibernian war-axes. They're called *dolabra*. I have a pair. I'll bring them to the arena."

Lorcan rose from his couch with the others, but his mind was elsewhere. He was already thinking about war axes and teaching Tavi to use them. In the arena, he stripped off his tunic and left it on the bench. Corvina settled into it as she would settle into a nest, not protesting that Lorcan had put her down. That was unusual for her, but Lorcan didn't have a chance to think on it; when Manius brought the pair of *dolabra* to the arena, they were nothing like the axes that Lorcan was familiar with.

"This is an axe?" Lorcan asked, picking up one of the weapons. It had an axe head similar to what he was used to, but instead of ending at the handle, the axe head tapered off into a long, narrow point. He studied it for a moment, feeling the weight of it. The handle was worn smooth and felt good in his hand. "I've never seen one like this before."

"It's part of a common centurion's standard equipment," Manius said in Gaeilge. "A rather common one, actually. But it is not, technically, a weapon. It's a tool. It's used for cutting timber and digging latrines more than it's used as a weapon. And besides, Tavi wouldn't be a common centurion," Manius said. He didn't explain further, and Lorcan frowned.

"Latin, Lorcan," Tavi called. "On the sands, you speak Latin." Lorcan nodded. "Let me try," he said. "It can be thrown?"

"Thrown?" Nona gasped. "You throw axes?"

"I've seen Pictish warriors fighting with axes. It's impressive," Tavi said. "And scary."

Lorcan looked up. Tavi had stripped, the same as the other men. Lorcan had seen him in the bath every day for weeks, had admired the long lengths of him when they were in the *caldarium* pool, but the sight of Tavi standing there, wearing only a *subligaculum,* was incredibly enticing. Lorcan bit his lip and turned toward the practice dummy. "Stand back," he called.

Then there was only the axe and the armored straw dummy. Lorcan took a test swing, checking the weight and the feel of the axe in his hand. It was much heavier than the axes Ronan made, most likely from the longer head. Lorcan grinned as he realized that spike gave a second weapon. He spun and buried the point in the dummy's neck.

"Oh, I like this," he said. He pulled the *dolabra* free, backed up, and threw it the way he would throw one of Ronan's axes. It hit the armor and fell to the sand. "Too heavy to throw," he proclaimed. "My cousin is a smith. His axes are perfectly balanced to throw and are in high demand among the High Kings warriors."

He picked it up and turned, seeing Tavi nodding. Only then did he realize he'd done it again.

"That's interesting," Tavi said. "I think that's the first time I've seen what you described to me. You've gotten better since we started working together, but this… this was different. You went from broken Latin to flawless, and the only difference was that you stopped paying attention to what you were saying. How long did you learn from this horrible teacher in Hibernia?"

Lorcan answered in Gaeilge, "The better part of two years, I think. That's how long I was fostering."

Tavi nodded again. "So, is this the weapon for me? And do I have to throw it?"

Lorcan looked at the *dolabra* and shook his head. "You'd need to be much bigger and stronger to throw this effectively. Yaroah might be able to do it." He glanced over at the big Carthaginian and changed back to Latin. "Want to try?"

Yaroah shook his head. "I like my sword. I am a fighter, not a wood chopper."

Lorcan laughed. "All right. Tavi, come here. See how it feels." He handed the *dolabra* to Tavi, who grunted slightly.

"It's heavy. Heavier than a sword." He looked at Lorcan. "What do I do? I don't think I can move like you did."

"You don't have to," Lorcan said. "Remember, I'm used to axes as weapons. Take it to the dummy and attack it."

Tavi paled. "What?"

"As if it was someone attacking you," Lorcan explained. "Ah... you said Picts? Pretend it's a Pict coming at you. This is your only weapon. Stop him."

Tavi's jaw dropped. He looked at the dummy, then at Lorcan. "Really?"

"Go on. Try it. If it doesn't work, then we'll find something else."

Tavi swallowed, then hefted the *dolabra* and moved toward the dummy. Lorcan studied him as he moved. Tavi was taller than Yaroah, but he lacked the gladiator's grace. His walk was closer to a stumble, and his movements were choppy.

"Manius?" Lorcan called, trying to keep his voice low. "Was Tavi always so tall?"

"No. He was actually small for his age when I met him, but after he started training with me, every few months, he'd take pains in his limbs, and then he'd grow." Manius frowned. "What are you thinking?"

"Livia said he's grown more in the past two years. I think that he might not have had a chance to get used to how his body changed before it changed again," Lorcan answered. "If he grew that much that fast."

"I see. You're thinking that by the time he knew where his body was—"

"It wasn't there anymore," Lorcan finished. "But he's probably stopped growing now, if he's as old as I am?"

"He's a bit older," Manius agreed. "And I agree with you. I should have thought of it myself. Go on then. Teach him where he is."

Lorcan glanced at the *lanista*, then moved over to stand near Tavi. "Think of it as part of your arm," he said.

"No part of my arm was ever this heavy," Tavi grumbled.

"Yes, but you want it to move with you," Lorcan frowned. "I'm doing this wrong. Put it down and close your eyes."

"What?"

"Just trust me," Lorcan said. He moved the *dolabra* out of the way, then went to stand in front of Tavi, who hadn't yet closed his eyes. "Ready?"

"What am I doing?" Tavi asked.

"Listening to me. You see where I am. Now close your eyes." He waited until Tavi huffed and closed his eyes before continuing, "Think about where you are. How you're standing. How your weight is balanced. Now twist from side to side." He watched as Tavi twisted at the waist, his arms held loose at his sides. "Good. Now, you know where you are. And you know how close I am?"

"Yes."

"I'm going to try to hit you in the chest. Stop me." Without waiting, he threw the punch. If he connected, Tavi would end up with a bruise. But Tavi twisted, bringing one arm up knocking Lorcan's fist out of the way. His eyes flew open, and he gaped at Lorcan.

"How did you do that?" he demanded.

Lorcan grinned. "My problem is that I think too much about the words that come out. Your problem is that you've not been thinking about the space you take up."

Tavi blinked. He looked thoughtful, then grinned. "I see. I think I see. Manius?"

"He's right, Tavi," Manius answered. "Lorcan, how did you know?"

Lorcan picked up the *dolabra*. "I learned to fight from my uncle. So did most of my cousins. My cousin Becc is a year old than I am, and tall like Tavi here. Maybe a little taller. He grew so fast that he never knew where his feet were. And every time he grew, Uncle Niall had to stop and show him how to move again." He grinned. "Which was interesting, since Uncle Niall is mute."

Tavi's eyes widened. "You're making that up!"

"I'm not!" Lorcan laughed. "Now come on. Ah... Manius, do we have a club? A stick? Something about the same size as the *dolabra* handle?"

From behind him, Yaroah said something in his own language. Tavi looked up sharply. He nodded, then grinned. "Looks like this fish is going to fly after all."

Lorcan worked with Tavi for most of the morning, teaching him to move and how to hold the pair of long clubs that Manius produced. Then he turned to his own practice, pairing with Yaroah to spar against Nona and Ennius. For the first time since his arm had been broken, Lorcan held his sword in his right hand, and lifted his shield.

"It feels odd," he said. "I've been fighting left for weeks now."

"You'll be a two-handed fighter, and that much more dangerous. And that much more valuable," Yaroah said.

Lorcan glanced over his shoulder, saw that Manius was out of earshot, and lowered his voice. "What was it that you said to Tavi?"

"He will tell you," Yaroah murmured back. "Just... do you remember what I told you? In the bath, the day that Tavi returned?"

Lorcan nodded. "I remember. You think my teaching will make it worse?"

"I think so. And I think we should not let Manius think we discuss anything more serious than the weather and pretty girls?" He looked over at Tavi, who was sitting on the bench with Corvina. "Or pretty boys, hm?"

Lorcan felt his face grow warm. "Am I being obvious?"

"Not so much, no. He is. He is very attracted to you."

"I know," Lorcan nodded. "And I am to him. But Livia—" He shook his head. "I'm not choosing him over Livia. I love her."

"Now that, we all know," Yaroah said with a smile. "You wear her love for her like a cloak, and she wears her love for you like a jewel around her throat. Now come. Let's go break some heads."

Lorcan laughed and followed Yaroah out onto the sand.

* * *

"So, what did Yaroah say?" Lorcan asked, keeping his voice low. He had lingered in the *apodyterium,* waiting until the other gladiators had dressed and gone and he was alone with Tavi. He held his tunic in his hands, watching as Tavi scrubbed at his curly hair with a cloth.

Tavi looked up. "He said that you were locking your own chains. And he told me that I should pretend to not learn from you. If you can fight and teach, that makes you even more valuable a slave."

Lorcan blinked. "He told me the day I met you that Manius promised him the same thing that he promised me. That he'd free me after a year."

"Yaroah has been here since I was a boy," Tavi said. "He told me once that if he ever won his freedom, he'd leave Rome so fast that the dust wouldn't have time to cling to his sandals." He shook his head. "Why did Manius make that promise to you?"

"Because I told him how I was captured, and what's going to happen at home if I don't return," Lorcan answered. "My cousin betrayed us, and he has allies among the raiders. He intends to overthrow my father, and possibly try to take all of Eire for himself." He slipped his tunic on over his head, then went to pick Corvina up so she could take her accustomed perch on his shoulder. To his surprise, she pecked at him, and sidled away on the bench. "Corvina, what are you doing?"

"Helping me?" Tavi said from behind Lorcan. Lorcan turned to find that Tavi was standing right there. Close enough to touch. He hadn't yet dressed, and he still looked every bit as enticing as he had in the arena. "Thank you, Corvina."

"Helping you how?" Lorcan asked.

"By not being in the way when I do this?" Tavi answered in Gaeilge. Then he leaned down and kissed Lorcan, his lips barely brushing against Lorcan's. He pulled back slightly, met Lorcan's eyes, then dove in again, this time kissing Lorcan with a passion born from what must have been weeks of pure frustration. He pushed Lorcan so that his back was against the wall, and tugged Lorcan's tunic up so that skin met skin. Lorcan whimpered as Tavi's thigh pressed between his legs, up against his bollocks.

"If you say stop, I will. If you don't want this, tell me," Tavi whispered into his ear.

Lorcan looked up at him, at those deep amber eyes, and lost himself in them. "Don't stop," he whispered, and surrendered his mouth once more. Tavi's hands on his skin burned, and they seemed to be everywhere underneath Lorcan's tunic. Lorcan wrapped his hands around Tavi's waist, pulling him closer. He shouldn't want this. He *shouldn't*. But sweet Morrigan, he wanted this man. But that was impossible! He couldn't take two mates! That wasn't how the magic worked!

But he was a freak. Not a real raven. Maybe… maybe it wasn't the same for him. He dismissed his doubts as he ground his crotch against Tavi's thigh, wanting more, needing more. It had been so long since he'd last laid with a man.

Tavi pulled back slightly, reaching between their bodies to wrap one big hand around Lorcan's cock. "I want this. I want to bend you over a bench," Tavi growled. "I want to take your ass and make you scream. I've been dreaming of it since I first saw you."

Lorcan closed his eyes, unable to catch his breath. "Yes," he whispered, barely making a sound. "Here?"

"Oh, yes. Here and now. On your knees."

"Lorcan?" Livia called. "Are you in here? Father wants you to come meet him so he can pick out your armor— oh"

Lorcan pulled away from Tavi, feeling as if he'd been struck. Livia. How could he have gotten so carried away as to have forgotten his mate? He looked from Tavi to Livia. Tavi didn't seem at all bothered by being caught, standing an arm-length away from Lorcan in all his naked glory, his cock still erect. And Livia didn't seem angry at all, for all that she had to know what was about to happen. She actually looked... pleased?

Confused, Lorcan paced the length of the room, tugging his tunic back into place. As he passed the bench, he held his hand out to Corvina. She clambered up his arm to her usual place in his shoulder, preening his hair gently. He reached up and ran his fingers over Corvina's breast feathers, trying to make sense of his own emotions. She clicked and rubbed her beak on his cheek, gurgling softly in his ear. The comforting, familiar sound seemed to help; he went to Livia's side and took her hand. Then he turned to Tavi.

"Tavi, would you excuse us for a moment?"

"Oh, of course. I'll be here. Somewhere. Not here in the changing room, but here. And dressed. I'll be dressed." Tavi's smile faltered slightly, but he didn't follow them as Lorcan led Livia out of the *apodyterium*. Outside, he stopped. Where? Livia answered by taking over, tugging his hand and almost dragging him through the halls to her workroom. Once inside, she pushed him into a chair and took out a flask of wine. She poured a measure for him, then waited for him to drink.

"Out with it," she said. "What's wrong?"

Lorcan met her eyes. "Ravens mate once. For a lifetime. Did you know that? I don't remember if I told you." He looked down at his cup. "I was always told that I'd know my mate the moment I saw them. And I did. I knew you. I knew I'd been waiting my whole life for you. Morrigan's feathers, Livia, I love you!"

"I know that. And I love you." Livia took the cup and set it down, then took Lorcan's hand. "And now?"

"I knew him, Livia. The same way I knew you. I love him. The same way I love you." Lorcan looked at her. "And that's not possible. I can't have two mates."

To his shock, Livia laughed. "Is that all? Lorcan, why can't you have two mates?"

Lorcan blinked. "What?"

Livia shook her head and slipped onto his lap, sliding one arm around him and cupping his cheek with the other hand. "You're not all raven. You're a man, too. Doesn't that mean anything? Lorcan, why can't you love more than one person? It's not as if you can run out of love, after all."

Lorcan licked his lips. "Livia, I didn't explain everything. There's one more part to my grandmother's gift, one more thing tied into my cloak." He met her eyes. "My family, the Morrigan's kin, we're immortal. And I can share that with my mate."

"Oh," Livia breathed. "Oh, and if you're only supposed to have one mate—"

"I'd have to choose between the two of you. You're my mate... and so is he. He doesn't even know it yet. So... I don't know. He's my lover. Or he wants to be." He sighed. "And I want him to be, too. But—"

"You haven't had him yet? I didn't realize I was interrupting your first time!" Livia interrupted. "Lorcan, I thought you had had him already. In the baths, during your lessons. I was hoping you had, really. He's lovely, and I knew you'd enjoy him... oh. Oh, I see." She laughed. "That was why you jumped the way you did? Did you think I would be upset?"

"I did, yes." Lorcan looked at her. "I don't want you to think that I've betrayed you."

"Oh, my love. I know you won't. I know you can't," Livia murmured, and kissed him. "Lorcan, Tavi is a darling. I don't mind. Why should I worry that you love each other? I know you'll always come back to me."

Lorcan met her eyes. "He told me you were lovers once."

She smiled softly. "We were. I still do love him. As much as I love you, my silly bird, so we have that in common. The only reason it ended between us was that he went back to Alba. He wanted me to come with him, but I was studying with the healers, and I didn't want to give that up and leave my father just to be someone's mistress. He can't marry me. I don't have the status he needs." She kissed him gently, then cocked her head to the side. "Does it help if I give you permission?"

"Permission to... to sleep with him?" Lorcan asked. "Livia, why would I want to?"

"Because we might both enjoy it?" Tavi said from the doorway. He spoke quietly, and in Gaeilge. "Because Livia likes watching, or at least she used to like it. May I come in?"

"Do you always listen at doors?" Lorcan demanded. He shifted Livia from his lap and got to his feet. "This was supposed to be a private conversation."

"I was worried I'd upset you. And when you didn't come back—" He stopped. Blinked. "Silly *bird*? She called you silly bird. And Yaroah calls you Raven. Lorcan... Oh, Minerva, I'm an idiot! I should have made the connection already! *You're* the Raven Prince! That's what I was missing! That's where I heard your name before!"

Lorcan stared at Tavi in shock. "What? What are you talking about?"

"Two men came to my father in Alba. Months ago. They came from Eire, telling us that the nephew of the High King had been kidnapped. They were sent to find him. But we missed you. You were already gone."

Lorcan sat down, stunned. "I... I was only in Alba a few hours."

"And they told us it had been three days since you were taken." Tavi started to pace.

"Who went?" Lorcan asked.

"Who... oh, in Alba? Two men. Ah... Petrus?"

"Petran!" Lorcan gasped. "My uncle Petran! And the other must have been Turlach!"

"That's the name," Tavi agreed. "Does Manius know who you are? Did you tell him?"

"Of course I told him!" Lorcan snapped. "It doesn't seem to make a difference. He's not going to let me go or give me my freedom. He was supposed to have sent a message to my father, but I doubt that he ever did." He deliberately didn't look at Livia. Had she known her father wouldn't keep his promise?

"Livia, did you know about that?" Tavi asked.

"I knew about the promise," Livia said. "I didn't know about the message. And I thought he'd keep his word this time. With who Lorcan is... I didn't think he'd lie. And now... Tavi, what do we do?"

"We have to get you out of here." Tavi scowled and dragged his fingers through his hair. "Wait. Just wait. I'll be back." He turned and hurried out. Lorcan looked at Livia, who shook her head.

"I don't know."

A few minutes later, Manius stormed into the workroom, with Tavi on his heels. "Lorcan! Did you put Tavi up to this?"

Lorcan's jaw dropped. "Up to what?" he asked. "I've no idea what he did!"

105

"Father, Tavi told us to wait here, that he'd be right back," Livia added. "Tavi, what did you do?"

"I offered to buy Lorcan," Tavi admitted, his face coloring. "Whatever the price. I said that I would speak to my father. Or I could pay Manius myself—"

"You can't. Manius told me that any ransom my father and my uncle would pay would pale in comparison to what I could earn him in the arena," Lorcan said. "Yaroah and Nona agreed with him when I told them. Where would you find that much money?"

Manius looked at him and burst out laughing. Then he turned and left. In the silence that he left behind, Livia and Tavi both stared at him, then at each other. Tavi cleared his throat. "Livia, you didn't tell him?"

"I thought you'd told him!" Livia answered. "I mean, it's not mine to tell!"

"But—"

"Tell me what?" Lorcan asked.

Livia stepped in front of him. "Who Tavi is. We've never told you his full name, or who he is."

"Because my full name is a mouthful and no one calls me by it except my grandfather," Tavi answered. "Lucanus Decius Octavius."

Lorcan frowned. He'd learned a little about how names were put together in Latin, but learning that Tavi was a use-name, and that his tutor was really Lucanus son of Decus, and something about eight? Why was that important?

"He's not understanding, Tavi," Livia said. "He doesn't know."

"Oh. I suppose not." Tavi ran his fingers through his tousled hair, this time from what looked more like embarrassment than frustration. "Lorcan, I was named Lucanus for my grandfather. My father Decus is the youngest son, and I'm—"

"The youngest of 11. And you have seven brothers. You told me that."

"I didn't tell you that my grandfather Lucanus is the Emperor," Tavi said.

Chapter Ten

Lorcan stared at Tavi. "The Emperor?"

Tavi nodded. "I'm sorry. I thought you knew."

"And what are you doing here?" Lorcan demanded. "Surely the Emperor can afford real swordsmen to teach his family?"

Livia snorted. "You're better than any swordman they could hire."

"Livia, that's not helping," Tavi said. "I'm here because I've known Manius since I was a boy. My father and my uncle both fought as gladiators. I told you that. They fought with Manius, and they've been friends ever since. Now my father is the provincial governor of Alba. My mother was his third wife, and the daughter of a Numidian general." He looked down at his hands. "That's why I'm darker than the rest of my family."

Despite himself, Lorcan snorted with mirth. "Oh, I'd know nothing about that."

Tavi smiled slightly. "Manius refused to sell you to me. Complete, outright refusal. So now, I have to go to my grandfather and my father, tell them that I found you. Father already made his report to Grandfather about the visitors from Eire—"

"And then what?" Lorcan asked. "If you go to your family, what then?"

Tavi blinked. He looked at Livia, then back at Lorcan. "I... don't understand. Grandfather will order you freed. And he'll send you home."

Lorcan stared at him for a moment. Home? That easily? But...

"I'm not ready," he said softly. "If I go back as I am now, Cormac will kill me."

"You can train as a free man, Lorcan," Livia said.

"Not here," Lorcan answered. "For all that your father may have lied to me, he's taught me a lot. And he has more to teach me. So does the rest of the *familia*. I need to stay. I need to learn."

Tavi frowned. He hitched one hip on the edge of the worktable and folded his arms on his chest. "You're serious?"

"Yes. I need to stay. So, thank you, Tavi. I appreciate what you want to do for me. But I'm not ready to fly free yet."

Without warning, Corvina squawked and snapped her beak in a warning. Lorcan stepped in front of Livia and looked at the open door. "Who's there?"

Manius stepped back into view, his arms folded over his chest. "Lucanus Decius Octavius, you are no longer welcome in my *ludus*."

"What?" Lorcan gasped. "Manius, no!"

"You are not the *lanista* here," Manius snapped. "This is my *ludus*, and my word is law here. You are a slave. And you are my slave. Remember that, Lorcan."

Lorcan swallowed. "I remember." He looked up at Tavi. "I'm sorry."

Tavi shook his head. "Not your fault. Mine. I should have checked to make sure we were alone. Be well, Lorcan. I'll see you when you fight." He smiled at Livia. "You're very lucky, Livia. Be happy." With that, he turned and walked out of the workroom. Manius stepped into the doorway, blocking it.

"I see I've given you too much freedom," he said, his voice low. "You forget your place and your purpose. You say you have a lot to learn? Then you're going to. Without distraction. Livia, he's no longer to sleep in your bed or work in your workroom. His place is in the arena, and in his cell down with the other gladiators. That's all."

"Father!"

"And if I have to put him in chains at night to see him stay there, and bar the door to see that you stay out, I will!" He pointed at Livia. "Do not defy me in this, or I'll take a strap to you."

Lorcan growled at the threat, and Corvina snapped her beak. "Livia had nothing to do with this," Lorcan said.

Manius sniffed. "I am the *lanista* here. You will both do as I say." He paused. "You're valuable to me, Lorcan. But not indispensable. Do you understand me?"

Lorcan licked his lips. "Yes, sir."

"Then off to your cell and stay there."

* * *

Training, the baths, then back to his cell. Manius barred Lorcan from eating in the *triclinium*, having the house slaves bring his meals to him in his cell. He held to his word and refused Lorcan access to the workroom and his work with Livia. Refused to allow him to speak openly to the other gladiators, or to Livia, even to the point of joining them in the baths. Anything that might have been mistaken for a liberty was stripped from him. Lorcan wondered if Manius was trying to break him, trying to force him to accept his place as a slave.

It wasn't going to work. Lorcan wasn't a slave. He was a raven, the Morrigan's own kin, and he would fly free again. He just needed to be patient. But as the days dragged on, patience began to turn to anger, and that anger frequently boiled over onto the sands of the arena.

"Lorcan, you're fighting as a *secutor* today," Manius ordered. "Ennius, prepare yourself."

Lorcan scowled, but said nothing, going to get his arms and armor ready. He hadn't fought as a *murmillo* since the day that Tavi had tried to buy him. Instead, he'd been made to fight as a *secutor*, a role he despised. He purely hated the close-fitting helmet that *secutores* wore—it was heavy, hot, and while he wore it, it was hard to breathe or to see. And he still had not gotten the knack of fighting against an opponent with a net— Ennius had won every bout they'd fought. It was humiliating, and he was sure that was the point of the exercise. He picked up his shield, studied the painted white raven on its surface, then put on the hated helmet and picked up the *gladius* that Manius insisted he use. His world narrowed to the tiny eye-slit, Lorcan immediately started to sweat. Across the arena, Ennius was twirling his net in the air, his trident held low. Lorcan licked his lips and advanced.

Ennius struck immediately, throwing the net and trying to entangle Lorcan's *gladius*. Lorcan twisted his sword, twining the net around the blade, and pulled—to his shock, the net flew out of Ennius' hands. Lorcan backed up, shaking the sword until the net slid free. He kicked it away, then considered. The net was no longer a problem, but Ennius had a longer reach with his trident, and now he could use his dagger. Unless…

Lorcan started forward at a trot, and saw Ennius raise the trident, exactly as he hoped. He raised his shield in response… and at the last moment, tossed the shield away and grabbed Ennius' wrist in his left hand. He stepped to the side to avoid Ennius' right-hand dagger and drove the flat of his blade against Ennius' midsection. The taller man went down, and Lorcan danced back, watching. To his shock, quiet and sedate Ennius got to his feet crowing with laughter.

"You did it!" he shouted. "You did it!" Lorcan took his helmet off, and yelped as Ennius grabbed him around the waist and lifted him into the air. "Did you see that? He beat me!"

"Ennius, put me down!" Lorcan shouted, laughing. He stumbled as Ennius set him on the sand, turning to see the other gladiators had come out to congratulate him.

"You did well!" Yaroah proclaimed. "You did very well. Manius, didn't he?"

Manius snorted. "Sloppy. Ennius made a mistake, letting you get the net away from him. Your opponent in a real battle won't be so careless."

Lorcan nodded. "I know. It's a start. I'll be better tomorrow."

Manius narrowed his eyes. "You'd better be. You're debuting tomorrow."

All at once, the other gladiators exploded, startling Lorcan with the ferocity of their outrage. It was Yaroah who was the loudest. "It is too soon! He's not ready yet!"

"I say he's ready," Manius answered. "And I say he's fighting. Tomorrow. Practice is done. To the baths with you, and then to dinner. Lorcan, prepare your armor and your weapons."

Lorcan glanced at the others, then nodded to Manius. "Which armor?"

"You'll be fighting as a *murmillo*." Manius turned and walked out of the arena. "Prepare him!" he called over his shoulder.

"I think that means you're eating with us tonight," Nona said softly.

"I'll be glad of the company," Lorcan answered. "Come on. You can tell me why you're all so upset in the bath."

No one said anything until it became clear that Manius was not going to be joining them. Even then, Yaroah posted Nona to watch the door as they sat in the *tepidarium*.

Ennius gestured to the floor in front of him. "Come here," he said to Lorcan. "I'll braid your hair. I will keep it out of your face tomorrow."

Lorcan moved to sit on the ground between Ennius' feet, letting the other man comb out his long hair. "So why are you all upset?"

"Because something is not right about this," Yaroah answered. "Because for all of us, for our first real battles, we knew days in advance. There were preparations, and there was a feast. This?" He shook his head. "I worry. You have not even made your oath."

Lorcan frowned. "And you don't think I'm ready?"

"I think you could be more ready," Yaroah answered.

Lorcan sat quiet for a long time, thinking, ignoring the way his head was moving gently as Ennius made dozens of tiny braids. Why would Manius rush him into the arena? The answer seemed clear and terrifyingly obvious. At last, he looked up. "He's sending me out to die, isn't it?"

Ennius snorted. "It doubt it, even though it would solve his problems. Decus was here yesterday. Wanted to see you. Manius told him no."

"Decus?" Lorcan coughed. "Tavi's father?"

"They argued. Loudly." Ennius tugged on Lorcan's hair. "Turn a little. That's good. Decus wanted to know what your price was. Manius won't sell you."

"I think he will be wagering against you tomorrow," Yaroah said, his voice low. "Lorcan, you must win tomorrow."

"I know," Lorcan answered. "I know." He looked over at Yaroah. "Do you think Livia knows?"

"I doubt it," Yaroah said. "Or she'd have told one of us. Asked us to look after you."

"Which we'd do anyway," Ennius added. "You're our brother."

Lorcan tipped his head back. "Thank you."

"So, we should explain to him what tomorrow will bring," Nona said. "So he does us proud."

Yaroah nodded. "True. Lorcan, you will not fight here. We will go to the Coliseum."

"I know. Livia told me, and we went past it, when she took me to Apollo's temple," Lorcan answered. "That's not far. Are we going to walk, or take a cart?"

"Neither. There is a tunnel below the *ludus* that leads right there," Ennius said. "Once we're there, you will be put into a cell. We all will." He chuckled. "Armed slaves trained to fight make them nervous. They'll come get you when it's time to fight."

Lorcan nodded. "Will I know who I'm fighting before?"

"It won't matter yet," Yaroah answered. "You won't know any of them, and Manius hasn't let you come see when we fight. He should have." He frowned. "And I didn't give it any thought, but he should have, as part of your training."

"No matter," Lorcan said. "I go on the sands, and I fight."

"No, first you salute the Emperor. Or whoever of the Imperial family is in the box," Ennius said. "If it's not the Emperor, it'll be Gaius. The heir. Tavi might be there, too. Or maybe not. The Emperor is at the summer palace. Tavi might have gone to join him."

Lorcan felt a pang. He had been hoping to see a familiar face. He nodded. "Salute the box, and whoever is sitting there. And then?"

"Try not to die," Yaroah said, his voice dry. "When you beat your opponent, the Emperor decides his fate."

Lorcan stared at him. "What?"

"If you don't kill him by accident, the Emperor might decide he needs killing, and tell you to do it." Yaroah made a gesture with one hand. "You see that, you kill them. There's no arguing, either. You do it, or you die with him."

Lorcan nodded slowly. "I understand. And then?"

"Then?" Yaroah chuckled. "Then, Livia might get mad at you."

"Why?" Lorcan looked up at Ennius, who was… well, the only word was *giggling*.

"You know how they scrape the oil off of us?" Yaroah answered. "Do you know what they do with it?" Lorcan shook his head, and Yaroah grinned. "Gladiator sweat is in high demand among the high-born women, Lorcan. And if the gladiator wins, and wins well? So is he."

Lorcan frowned. "Sweat. They want sweat. Why?"

"It's an aphrodisiac," Ennius answered. Lorcan looked up at him. "I don't know that word."

"A sex potion, Lorcan," Yaroah explained. "They put it into their cosmetics, and they think it makes them… I don't know. Something."

Lorcan blinked. He looked up at Ennius, then shook his head. "You're making fun of me, aren't you?"

"No, they're not," Manius said, pushing past Nona. "There will be women who want your sweat, and once you win, there will be women who want you in their beds. Men, too."

Lorcan slowly got to his feet. "That won't be happening."

"Good. I'm glad you agree with me on that," Manius said, his voice mild. "Have you told him everything he needs to know?"

Yaroah looked at Ennius, then at Nona. He shrugged. "He is as informed as we can make him. I will not say he's prepared—"

"None of you were prepared the first time you fought," Manius interrupted. "And yet here you are."

"And if all the gods will it, we will all be here tomorrow," Yaroah said, standing up. He rested his hand on Lorcan's shoulder. "Is it time for Lorcan's feast?"

Manius scowled. "We will feast tomorrow, if he wins." He turned and left. Yaroah snarled something in his own language and spat.

"This will not end well," Nona grumbled. "He's defying all the traditions, and you a *semideus,* he has to know the gods will be watching."

"My gods are a long way away," Lorcan said. "I doubt the Roman gods will pay me any mind."

"Who can say, with gods?" Ennius said. "Come on. Let's go find Corvina and get something to eat."

Dinner was quiet, which Lorcan appreciated. His stomach felt like it was tied in knots. He didn't understand why Manius was turning on him, but he was determined to survive. Survive and win his freedom. He ate sparingly, slipping tidbits to Corvina, wondering where Livia was. She usually ate the evening meal with them, but tonight she was absent. Manius also did not attend the meal, until the house slaves cleared the last plate. Then he appeared in the doorway.

"Lorcan, to your cell. The rest of you, leave him be. He needs to rest."

Lorcan rose from his bench, lifting Corvina to her perch on his shoulder. As he stepped back away from his couch, the other gladiators rose and surrounded him. Yaroah put his hands on Lorcan's upper arms.

"Little brother," he said. "You're one of us. One of our family. Tomorrow, you'll do us all proud."

Lorcan smiled. "Thank you, Yaroah. I will do my best."

"They'll never know what hit them," Nona jibed, and the others laughed.

* * *

Lorcan stopped inside his cell when he saw that the oil lamp was already lit. He looked around the narrow space and saw the metal glinting on blanket-covered straw on the bed-shelf. The door closed behind him, and didn't need to turn to know that Manius had followed him in.

"You're chaining me?" he asked. "Why? I'm already locked in. Why chains?"

"It is part of what to expect tomorrow," Manius answered. "You will go to the arena in chains. All of you."

"No one mentioned that when they were preparing me." Lorcan turned. "I know you've gotten used to it by now, but you needn't lie to me anymore."

Manius chuckled, a dry sound that reminded Lorcan of old leaves. "But then I'll have no amusement at all," he teased, and his smile confused Lorcan. "However, this is not a lie. It's new, and I've not had to subject the others to it before. Now, though, by decree of the Senate, gladiators will go to the arena in chains. As Ennius said, armed slaves make Romans nervous."

Lorcan stared. "You were listening?"

"Of course I was listening," Manius scoffed. "I am always listening."

"Then why are you sending me out to die?" Lorcan demanded.

Manius looked startled. "Is that what you think?" he asked. Then he frowned. "I... I can see why you'd think so. I'm not. You've been distracted. Now you're not. Part of that is my fault—I've given you outrageous freedoms for a slave, and your training has suffered for it. You're good. You can be better. You need to be better. Now, you can believe me or not, but I promise you that I am not lying." He paused. "The truth is that I'm sending you out so you can get your revenge."

"Revenge," Lorcan repeated. Then he coughed. "Gnaeus. I'm fighting Gnaeus tomorrow? I thought you sold him to the mines in Elba!"

"Livia told you that?" Manius shrugged. "I did. But I've no control over what they do with him once he's left me. The trader who bought him from me sold him to another *ludus*. He fights tomorrow, and then his owner is taking him to Antioch. This will be your only chance to fight him."

Lorcan frowned. He turned and paced the length of the room, then came back. "Why didn't you explain that to me?"

"Because feuds and vendettas are forbidden to gladiators, but I know that revenging an insult is important to your people. I learned that from my wife," Manius answered. "I've been working for this since I found out that Gnaeus was fighting for the *Ludus Maximus*. I only just got confirmation today, and I came straight away to tell you that you were fighting tomorrow. There's no time for the usual niceties or rituals if you want Gnaeus' head."

Lorcan nodded. "I should thank you, I suppose."

"You should. We'll have your debut feast and all the rest of the ceremonies before your next fight. Which will be at the *Ludi Romani*, before the Emperor." Manius reached out and rested his hand on Lorcan's unoccupied shoulder. "You know that if I allow anything to happen to you, Livia will poison me."

"She would not!" Lorcan protested with a laugh.

Manius laughed with him. "Perhaps not. But she'll make me wish she had," he said. "I'm your owner, Lorcan. But I'm not your enemy. Now, you get to bed."

"Manius, how am I going to fight a *cestus*?" Lorcan asked as he sat on the bed-shelf. "And will he be fighting as a *cestus*?"

"He will. He knows no other way. And he does not know that you are a two-handed fighter now."

"A two-handed fighter who doesn't know how to fight a *cestus*," Lorcan pointed out. "You said that Yaroah was specially trained to fight him. That's training I don't have. What do I do? How do I fight him?"

Manius picked up the chains and stepped back. "He needs to be close to beat you, Lorcan. If you use your shield, you can ward him off that way. I know I told you that you would fight as a *murmillo*, but perhaps not. You could fight with two swords. If you use two swords, then you'll have to force him to defend. Don't let him close."

Lorcan nodded. "I need to drive him down and keep him down. What armor will he wear? I don't think I ever saw him armed for the arena."

Manius smiled. "You've seen what he wears in the arena. A *cestus* wears no armor. Finish him and finish him fast."

Lorcan brought Corvina down to her spot on the bed and frowned. "Will I have to kill him?"

"That's up to the Emperor," Manius said. "But accidents have been known to happen." Lorcan looked up sharply, but Manius only shrugged. "They have. Now, you need to sleep."

Lorcan nodded. "And the chain? Why are you chaining me tonight if we don't need it until tomorrow?"

Manius smiled. "I will give you a choice, Lorcan. I will chain you tonight… or I will lock your door. Which will it be?"

Lorcan blinked, then realized what Manius wasn't saying. "Oh. I… oh." He felt his face growing warm. "I… the chains."

"That's what I thought you would answer." Manius stepped forward and held out his hand. Lorcan offered his wrist, and Manius closed the manacle around it. He twisted the key, then looked at the wall over the bed-shelf. "I didn't realize that. The ring is gone."

"There was a ring?" Lorcan looked and saw a hole in the stone. "I was wondering what that was from. What will you do now?"

"Stand up and turn around."

Lorcan gaped at him. "Behind my back? How will I sleep?"

"The chain is long enough that you should be able to keep your arms to your sides. And if you need to use the pail, then pull one arm behind your back." Manius tugged on the chain. "It's this or a locked door." Lorcan scowled but stood up. He turned his back to Manius, who drew his other arm back and locked the manacle around it. He rested his hands on Lorcan's shoulders, guiding him back down to sit on the straw-covered shelf. "Lie back. If you end up lying on your hands, I'll take them off."

When Lorcan was flat on his back, his arms were trapped at his sides. He shifted, feeling the chain digging into his arse. "I don't like it."

"You'll live. Now sleep." Manius paused, then smiled at him. "Or don't sleep." He blew out the lamp and left, closing the door behind him. Lorcan waited, but there was no thump of a latch. The door was still unlocked. He closed his eyes, hearing Corvina shifting in the patch of uncovered straw next to his head. She gurgled at him, and he smiled.

"Good night, my friend," he murmured in Gaeilge, and felt her preening his hair.

He was drifting, almost asleep when he heard the creak of his door opening. He jerked, forgetting that he couldn't move, then gasped as a body covered his, pinning him to the bed. His yelp was smothered by a mouth, and he recognized Livia's scent and the feel of her. He strained against the chains and groaned.

"Am I hurting you?" she whispered against his mouth. "Are you all right?"

"You're not hurting me. I just can't move."

She chuckled. "I know. He told me what he'd done. I don't like it, but I'm grateful. I couldn't bear it not to be with you before you go into the arena."

Lorcan rubbed his cheek against her hair. "When he told me my choices, it wasn't even a choice. I've missed you." She kissed him again, and he moaned. "Gods, woman, I'm fair going to burst."

She laughed and kissed the tip of his nose. "Not yet. Not until I'm done with you." She shifted, moving off of him. Lorcan felt something press against his lips. "Bite this," she said. "Or you'll wake the entire hall."

"You like it when you make me yell," Lorcan grumbled.

"Yes, but no one is supposed to know I'm here," Livia answered. "You can yell all you want in my rooms because no one else is over there. We can't even go there, because we have to go past all the other doors to get there, and we might wake someone. So bite this."

Lorcan sighed and bit down on what turned out to be a thick pad of what he thought was cloth or leather.

"All right, now I need for you to sit up," Livia said. He felt her hands on his arms. "And turn, so your legs hang down."

Sit up? Turn? What was she doing? Lorcan did as he was bid, so that he sat on the edge of the bed-shelf. Livia moved to stand between his knees, gently tugging his tunic up to his armpits.

"I wish I could take this off," she murmured. "No matter. It won't get in the way." She ran her hands down his chest, then over his thighs. Lorcan heard rustling, felt her moving, and realized that she had gone to her knees. Then her mouth closed over his cock, and he understood the reason for the gag. He bit down hard, trying not to howl. Bran had enjoyed doing this to him, had loved it when Lorcan reciprocated, but he and Lorcan had learned what they knew from tavern tales and stable fumblings; Livia clearly knew far more about pleasuring a man this way than he or Bran had ever dreamed possible. And there was something else. Something… tingling? He squirmed, which only made Livia suck harder. She started to hum, and his cock started to tingle more intensely, a growing feeling halfway between hot and cold. He shifted again, reaching forward and coming up short as he forgot the chains binding his wrists. He couldn't move, he couldn't speak to stop her. He moaned, not sure if he'd have stopped her even if he had been able to speak. He felt her laugh, then one hand slipped between his legs and under him, and a single finger caressed his arse and *pressed*. Lorcan came with a muffled howl and felt Livia laughing around his cock. Dimly, he felt her bathing him clean with her tongue, rough lapping like one of her cats. Then she straddled his legs, took the gag from his mouth, and kissed him. He tasted himself on her lips, mingled with…

"*Cartal*?" he asked. "Am I tasting *cartal*?"

"*Mentha* leaves," she agreed. "I rinsed my mouth with a tincture of *mentha* leaves. Did you like it?"

"I think you noticed me liking it," Lorcan answered with a chuckle. He kissed her again. "What about you, love?"

"This was all for you tonight," she said, running her hands down his rucked-up tunic and over his bare belly. "You're not in my bed tonight, but I'm going to do my best to show you what you're fighting to come back to tomorrow."

"I'll be in your bed as soon as I can be, and every night after, my love," Lorcan said. "I promise you that." He closed his eyes, suddenly tired. "Can you stay?"

"Stay? Here?" Livia gasped. "I… I suppose I could. If I'm out before dawn, so no one knows I was here." She yawned. "Yes. Ah… let me move. Then lay down on your back."

"I'm not ready for anything else, Livia," Lorcan warned. She giggled and moved off his legs, helping him to shift around and lie down.

"Silly bird. I'm not looking for bed play now. I want to be held. Now, can you pull your knees up to your chest?"

Lorcan frowned into the darkness, then breathed, "Oh. Oh, I see. Yes." He pulled his knees up until he was curled into a ball, and then tried to bring his hands forward. Livia guided the chain over his heels, and Lorcan let his legs fall back down and stretched. "I wish I'd thought of that sooner."

"I'm glad you didn't," Livia said. "I liked having you like that. And having you like that."

"You liked having me chained up?" The idea was new to Lorcan. Would he mind being chained if it was for Livia's pleasure? Or, a small voice in his mind asked, for Tavi's?

He didn't think it would be so bad.

As if she was reading his thoughts, Livia answered him. "I do like it. Tavi taught me, and it can be a lot of fun." She curled up on the bed-shelf next to Lorcan, facing him. "Imagine it. Being all tied up with the pair of us doing all sorts of wonderful things to you."

Lorcan shifted so that his chained arms encircled Livia, pulling her to his chest. "I've never been with more than one person before. At a time, I mean."

"Oh, we have so much to show you," Livia giggled. She pillowed her head on Lorcan's arm and yawned.

"Will I get to chain you up?" Lorcan asked. Livia giggled again.

"If you're very, very good."

Chapter Eleven

The cock crowing outside Lorcan's window was usually a welcome sound. This morning, it was an annoyance. He didn't want to wake up. He wanted to stay in bed with Livia.

Livia?

He opened his eyes to see that his cell was filled with light. It was well past dawn. Cursing, he shook Livia's shoulder.

"Wake up!" he hissed. "It's late!"

She groaned, rolled to bury her face in his chest. "… back t' sleep."

"Livia, it's after dawn!"

She jerked, looked at him in alarm. "What?"

"You need to go!" Lorcan pushed himself up, untangling the chain from Livia's rumpled gown and tumbled-down hair so that she could get up. "Before we're caught."

Without warning, the door opened. Nona poked his head in, then grinned. "Thought so. You're lousy at being sneaky, Livia. Come on. You can hide in my cell until we're gone."

"You heard me?" Livia gasped, trying to twist her hair into something resembling respectability.

"It's not like you two were quiet," Nona said with a laugh. "And I sleep light. Hurry up, girl."

Livia turned and kissed Lorcan, then rushed out of the cell. Nona grinned, then closed the door again. Lorcan looked down at his hands, realized that he'd need to fix the oversight, and rolled onto his back. By the time Manius arrived, his hands were once more trapped behind him.

"Did you sleep well?" Manius asked, a knowing smirk on his face. Lorcan smiled.

"I slept just fine." He got to his feet. "Do I get unchained now?"

In answer, Manius held up the key. Lorcan turned his back and let Manius work; once his hands were free, he rubbed his wrists where the manacles had dug into his skin. Manius opened the door and gestured, chains swinging from his hand. "We've time before we need to go. You won't fight until after midday. You've plenty of time to bathe and eat, and there will be a massage for you in the *tepidarium*. The others are already on their way to the baths. Go meet them there."

"Yes, sir." Lorcan hurried down the hall, but he saw Livia peeking around Nona's door. She blew him a kiss, and he smiled.

The other gladiators were still in the *natatio* when Lorcan got to the baths. He waved to them, stripped off his tunic, and dove into the water to join them. He surfaced and was immediately splashed by Yaroah.

"After today, you will no longer be a *tiro*," Yaroah said. "You will be a full gladiator."

"And that's a reason to drown me?" Lorcan wiped water from his face and pushed back the multitude of tiny braids.

"Nervous?" Ennius asked. Lorcan considered, then shook his head.

"Not yet," he answered. "It's what I've been training for, after all. It's my next step on my road that leads home."

Yaroah scowled. "Lorcan—"

"I'll find a way, Yaroah," Lorcan said. "I'll do it." He looked around, then pitched his voice lower. "And keep your voices down. Manius listens to us."

Ennius swore softly. "How'd you find out?"

"He quoted you, what you told me about armed slaves making people nervous." Lorcan looked around again. "I accused him of listening, and he told me he's always listening."

"When was this?" Yaroah asked.

"Last night," Lorcan answered. "Before—" He stopped, glanced at Nona, who started laughing.

"Manius let Lorcan have his own feast last night," Nona told the others, keeping his own voice down. "He left the door unlocked, and Livia came to visit."

The other two men looked shocked. "He did what?" Ennius gasped.

"He came to me last night. Told me I could have chains or a locked door. Told me that we'd all be going to the arena in chains, too. Why didn't anyone mention that?" Lorcan looked around to see blank looks, then remembered that Manius had said that it was new, something he hadn't subjected the others to that before today.

"He's going to chain us?" Yaroah hissed. "No!"

"I told you! I've heard the rumors from other gladiators," Nona admitted. "Remember? I warned you all—"

"But why now?" Yaroah asked. He spread his hands, making waves in the water. "Yes, you told us about the rumors. But the rumors of a slave uprising have been whispered in all the *ludii* for years. We've all heard them, and nothing comes of it. Why take them seriously now?"

"Because," Manius said, coming out of the shadows and toward the edge of the pool. "Because the *Ludus Trivium* is no more. Because the gladiators there turned on their *lanista* and their *doctores*." He folded his arms over his chest.

"Trivium?" Nona gasped. "That's impossible!"

"Sixteen gladiators and 20 slaves were executed for that impossibility," Manius answered, his voice quiet. "Do you understand why now?"

"When?" Yaroah answered. "When did this happen?"

"Ten days ago," Manius answered. "The last executions were three days ago. It's why there have been no games until today."

"You didn't tell us. And you didn't make us watch them die," Ennius said. "I'd wager every other *ludii* in Rome witnessed the executions."

Manius shook his head. "I didn't think it was necessary to make you witness them. I know you."

"Who?" Yaroah asked. "Who was behind it?"

"That, I don't know," Manius answered. "None of them admitted to being the ringleader, nor did anyone confess and give a name."

Yaroah grunted. "Not good. And it is not good that we be discussing this in front of Lorcan, on the morning of his first battle."

"We'll discuss it further later. But now, you understand why?" Manius looked around. "It will only be temporary. Until things calm down." He turned and started back into the shadows. "Hurry with your baths," he called as he walked out of sight.

"Until things calm down," Nona repeated, and snorted. "That will never happen. Once a rule like this is in place, it never goes away." He glanced at Lorcan. "Did you follow any of that?"

"If you mean, did I understand what was said, yes," Lorcan said. "If you mean, did I understand what you meant? No."

"Don't burden him with it," Yaroah said. "Not now. He doesn't need to know this yet."

Lorcan swam to the edge of the pool, pulled himself out, then sat on the edge. "I can't not have heard what I already heard. Might as well tell me and let me decide if it's something to fret over."

"He's got a point," Ennius said. "Not telling him, he's going to worry about what it means. Let's go in, and we can tell him."

The others got out of the pool, and they walked into the *tepidarium*. Lorcan nodded at Bruno, who seemed unusually quiet. The bath slave served as attentively as he always did, but he never once smiled.

"Bruno?" Lorcan asked softly as the man readied his strigil. "Are you all right? Can I help?"

Bruno glanced at him, then shook his head. "Not your concern, Lorcan. Thank you, though." He did his job, then left. Lorcan took his spot on the bench, frowning.

"Bruno bothering you?" Nona asked.

"No," Lorcan answered. "There's something bothering him."

"He probably had someone at Trivium," Ennius said. "We're close enough to them that the slaves here had friends and relatives there."

Lorcan looked up at Ennius. "Will you explain now? What happened? Manius mentioned executions, and gladiators turning on their *lanista*. And now gladiators must be chained."

"That's pretty much it," Nona said. "Uprising. There are more slaves in this city than citizens. If every slave rose up against their masters—"

"Don't even say that," Yaroah growled. "Or it'll be the mines for you, if Manius is feeling generous."

"I like my head right where it is," Nona assured Yaroah. "But Lorcan needs to know."

Lorcan nodded slowly. "I understand now. Ennius, you said yesterday that armed slaves make people nervous. So, gladiators— why do they even have gladiators? Why train slaves to fight if it's only going to make them afraid of us?"

"Because watching people fight to the death is fun," Ennius answered, his voice flat. "For them that never have to do it."

"They love us because we entertain them," Nona added. "And because we're everything they want to be, or want in their beds, depending on who you ask. And they hate and fear us because of what they made us." He grinned. "The contradictory life of a gladiator."

Lorcan didn't join in the laughter. He sighed and leaned forward, resting his arms on his knees.

"I don't like complicated," he said. "Things were simpler at home."

"Simpler," Nona said. "Simpler, he said. Cousins trying to steal your inheritance by having you knocked over the head and stolen away by raiders is simple?" He shook his head. "I'll take the complicated I know, thank you. Which, I think, is what you're really saying, isn't it?"

"I suppose," Lorcan shook his head, feeling the multitude of braids swinging over his shoulders. He wiped sweat from his face and looked around. "Change the subject. I'm supposed to get a massage, Manius said. I've seen you all have them. What's it like? I've never done this before."

"You'll like it," Yaroah answered. "It's to relax you and make your muscles loose before the fight. He didn't do anything else special for you for your first fight, so Livia will probably do it."

"She's good, too," Ennius added. "She has strong hands."

Lorcan looked around to see the others nodding in agreement. "She's done massages for all of you?"

"On occasion," Yaroah answered. "And that's all, if that's your next question. None of us have been in her bed."

"I wasn't going to ask that!" Lorcan protested.

"You weren't worried about that? Not even a little?" Ennius asked. "Anyone else would think that she's had each of us. Possibly all at once."

"I'm not worried about that. I've never been worried about it," Lorcan answered. "I told her the truth. Who was in her bed before I met her is of no concern to me. And she's told me who was in her bed."

"She's told you?" Nona laughed. "Bedtime stories?"

Lorcan grinned. "That's what she called it. So, I know that you've none of you any reason to be jealous of us. Gnaeus was the only one who felt that way."

"Because she's our little sister, as much as you are our little brother," Yaroah said. "Our Livia has never shown any interest in any of us."

"Did I hear my name?" Livia called as she came into the *tepidarium*. Lorcan blinked at the sight of her—instead of her usual draped gowns, she wore only a breastband and a loincloth similar to what Lorcan himself wore when he fought. "Father says I'm to give you a massage, Lorcan."

"Yes," Lorcan said. He rose from his bench. "Where do you want me?"

"And... we're leaving," Nona announced. Livia burst out laughing.

"Stop that!" she protested. "You know that when I'm working, I don't play games." She pointed to a long, low wall that separated the room, a feature that Lorcan had not understood until he'd seen Yaroah get a massage there. As was usual before a massage, there was a long linen cloth draped over the top. "There, Lorcan. Face down. The rest of you, go sweat and see if that makes your brains work better."

More laughter, and the other gladiators headed for the *caldarium*. Lorcan went to the table and sat down, watching as Livia set bottles into bowls of water. "What are those?"

"Oil, in hot water to warm," Livia answered. "Have you never done this?"

"Massage? No. Will you teach me?"

"If we have time. Once you're debuted, you'll be training more, and you'll be in the arena no less than every 10 days or so if you're not hurt." She straightened and smiled at him. "You won't have a lot of time for healing arts. I told you to lie down."

Lorcan grinned and stretched out on his belly, pillowing his head on his arms. "Now what?"

"Now, you just lay there," Livia said from above him. He felt something warm poured onto his back, then Livia's hands were spreading it out. She started to knead his shoulders, and he groaned. She did have strong hands, and what she did as she worked was a combination of pleasure and discomfort that might have turned into pain if she'd continued. She always seemed to know just when to stop, though, and when to work harder until the muscles that Lorcan didn't even realize were tight released.

"Are you awake?" she asked. Lorcan smiled, realizing that he'd been half-asleep.

"Barely," he admitted.

"Roll over."

He did, and Livia went back to work, starting with his feet and working up his legs. As she reached his thighs, Lorcan suddenly found it harder to relax, harder to ignore his rising cock. Livia didn't seem to notice, which Lorcan found surprising. She stayed focused on her task, moving from his legs to his arms. Her touch lightened as she moved over his recently broken forearm.

"Any pain here?" she asked.

"None," Lorcan answered. He made a fist and flexed his arm. "It feels fine."

"Make sure you wear your braces in the arena." Livia reached under his shoulder with one hand and pushed down with the other. Lorcan shuddered as something popped. Livia smiled and nodded. "Good. That was too tight." She moved around the table and did the same manipulation, getting a similar pop. Then she rested her hand on his shoulder. "Almost done."

Lorcan thought about what she'd done. What hadn't she worked on? It felt as if she'd touched everything below his chin.

Well, almost everything.

"What else needs to be done?" he asked. She smiled, leaned down and kissed him. He closed his eyes and reached for her, then almost levitated off the table when her oiled hand closed around his cock. He groaned against her mouth and groaned again as her other hand pressed down gently on his throat, pinning him in place. He ran his hand up her bare thigh, sliding his fingers underneath the edge of her loincloth, skimming his fingertips over the cleft of her arse. Livia whimpered.

"Livia, I said I wanted him relaxed for the arena, not unconscious." Manius' voice cut through the lust-ridden steam like a knife. Lorcan and Livia both froze, and she pulled back slightly. Inches apart, so close their noses were touching, their eyes met, and the both of them started giggling. Livia straightened, her blush spreading down her throat and onto her chest.

"Yes, Father," she stammered. She ran one hand down Lorcan's chest, then stepped back. Lorcan sat up to see Manius standing in the *tepidarium* door. He looked amused, so Lorcan grinned at him.

"I'd apologize, but I didn't have much of a say in the matter," he said. He glanced at Livia, whose blush had intensified. "Not that I minded at all. Or I would have stopped it."

She moved closer to the table, close enough that Lorcan could put his arm around her shoulders and pull her to his side. She rested her head on his shoulder.

"Be careful out there, Lorcan," she said softly.

"I will, my Livia," he answered, and kissed her lightly on the forehead. "I will."

"Go and finish your bath," Manius said, coming over and draping a robe around Livia's shoulders. "I'd recommend spending a little more time in the *frigidarium* pool today." He left, leading Livia out of the *tepidarium*. She looked back over her shoulder at Lorcan, who smiled at her. Once they were gone, he went to join the others in the *caldarium*.

Surprisingly, none of the other gladiators commented on his obvious arousal, nor about what he and Livia might have been doing to cause it. They welcomed him into the *caldarium* pool, where Nona passed him a dipper of cold water and an unexpected question.

"You're fighting Gnaeus today, did you know that?"

Lorcan took the water, poured it over his head, then shook his head and sprayed water everywhere. "I knew," he admitted. "But how did you know?"

"Gossip," Ennius answered. "Nona has all the best sources."

Lorcan shook his head again, then nodded toward the door. Nona's eyes widened, and he nodded. He moved closer and took the dipper from Lorcan.

"Bruno," he said, his voice pitched very low. "His woman works in the kitchens. She heard about today's games in the market this morning. They were taking bets. Gnaeus is facing a *tiro*, an untried *murmillo*. Betting is pretty fierce."

"The odds?" Ennius asked. "What are the odds?"

"Considering that no one has ever seen Lorcan in the arena, odds are 50 to one for Gnaeus to win. The fight is considered an insult to him. People are wondering who he got mad at him." Nona dumped cold water over his own head. "If I had any coin to spare, I'd be betting on Lorcan."

"Fifty to one odds," Ennius repeated, and whistled. "That's… that's impressive."

"What does it mean?" Lorcan asked.

"It means that the man who bets on you to win will win 50 *aureii* for every one that he wagered," Yaroah answered. "It's a princely sum for our Prince Raven, if Manius bets the way he usually does. And then there's the prize money. Nona, what's the prize for this fight?"

Nona grinned. "Ten *aureii*."

Lorcan looked at him. "Is that a lot?"

Nona looked around. "We haven't taught you about money yet? Do you have coin money, where you come from?"

"Yes and no?" Lorcan said with a laugh. "I know we have coin, but I've never had any of my own. I've never needed it, and it's easier to trade."

"All right," Nona frowned. "One *aureus* is 25 *denarii* is 50 *quinarii* is 100 *sestertii*. That's really all you need to know. Ten *aureii* is 1,000 *sestertii*. That's a lot of money." He looked thoughtful. "Manius bought you for 7,000 *sestertii*, Lorcan."

"I didn't know that," Lorcan said. "And Manius gets all of that? The prize money, and whatever he wins if I win?"

"You get part of the prize money," Ennius answered.

"We each get a third of our prizes," Nona added. "You being a *tiro*, you'll probably get a quarter. It's still a lot of money, and you can spend it however you like. Buy things to make your cell more comfortable, for example."

"Or you can put it away," Ennius said. "Save it, for when you finally go home."

"To pay my way?" Lorcan asked.

"Exactly," Ennius said. He turned to Yaroah. "How much do you have saved now?"

"Enough to pay my passage back to Carthage twice," Yaroah answered. "Enough to buy a fine house, and a fine wife, and live the rest of my life like a king. Twice. If I should ever see my freedom."

"You have that much money saved, and you're still here?" Lorcan said. "You can't just buy yourself?"

"Not if Manius won't take the money," Yaroah answered. "I have offered it. He will not accept it. Come, let us finish. It's getting late."

The ebullient mood gone, they made their way to the *frigidarium* and the cold pool. Lorcan lowered himself into the plunge, tipping his head back against the edge of the pool.

"Why would Manius tell me that I needed to spend more time here?" he asked without looking at the others. Only to look up sharply when they all started hooting with laughter. "What?"

"He caught you and Livia playing around?" Nona asked. "And he didn't kill you right off?"

"He wouldn't!" Lorcan protested. "He says that Livia would poison him if he does anything to me."

Nona burst out laughing. Yaroah shifted around until he was next to Lorcan. "He was telling you to cool your head. The lower one."

Lorcan coughed. "Is that why?"

"You can't be that innocent," Nona scoffed. "You have to have noticed that cold water cools a man."

Lorcan looked down at the water, remembering a happier time with Bran, on the beaches near Dun Morrigan. "I've had sex in water this cold before," he said. "Colder."

"It's colder than this where you're from?" Yaroah said. "Is that why you're so pale?"

Lorcan smiled. "No. But it is colder in Eire. Someday, maybe you'll come and see."

Yaroah laughed. "Not me! I want to go home where it is never so cold!"

Lorcan grinned. "I understand. I want to go home where it's not so hot!" When Yaroah stopped laughing, Lorcan changed the subject. "Yaroah, Manius told me once that you were specially trained to fight a *cestus*. What do I need to know?"

Yaroah frowned. "Not just any *cestus*. Gnaeus. Which is good for you." He frowned, the way he did when he was thinking. It made him look fierce, but it was also when Yaroah offered the best advice. "How will you be fighting him?" he asked.

"Manius thought I should perhaps fight with two swords, because Gnaeus doesn't know I can do that."

"No," Yaroah said. "No, you need your shield. If he gets close enough to hit you, you will go down, and he will win. You need to have your shield to get close enough to hit him."

Lorcan nodded. "All right. Sword and shield."

"Bring both swords," Ennius said abruptly. "Onto the sands. Bring both."

Lorcan looked at him and was surprised to see Yaroah had turned as well. "Why?" Yaroah asked.

"Because remember the last time you fought Gnaeus?" Ennius said. "He cracked your shield. You said if he'd hit you again, he'd have put his fist through it. So, if he does that… throw the shield. The way you did to me, but don't throw it away. Throw it at him."

"Then draw my other sword while he's confused?" Lorcan considered it. Would it work? Maybe. "I'll need to finish him before he gets close enough to hit me. If he hits me—"

"You'll go down," Nona finished for him. "When a *cestus* hits you, you go down."

"Gnaeus has killed men before," Ennius said. "By accident, he said, but that doesn't change the fact that the men died."

Lorcan swallowed. He hadn't been nervous before. He'd been excited, looking forward to this next step on his way home. But now… "How do I fight him?" he asked. "He's basically unarmed—"

"No," Yaroah interrupted. "He is not. Do not think that because he does not carry a weapon that he is unarmed. He is better armed than you, and more skilled with them." He frowned. "Use your shield. Strike at his legs. If he breaks your shield…" His voice trailed off, and he looked at Nona. "The gossip says Gnaeus will fight a *murmillo*?"

Nona nodded. "Yes."

"Then perhaps Manius is right. Perhaps you should fight as a *dimachaeri*. If he is expecting a *murmillo*, then he won't know what to do with you."

Lorcan blinked. "There's a name for it?"

"Yes, and you're not really trained to it," Ennius said. "I imagine that you will be, once this is over. What Tavi said that day? About watching you fighting being like watching a dancer? With a *dimachaeri*, it's even more so."

"I'll worry about tomorrow when I wake up tomorrow," Lorcan said. "I need to know what to do so that I do wake up tomorrow."

"Win," Yaroah answered.

* * *

Over a light midday meal, the other gladiators told Lorcan what to expect. He'd put on his armor at the arena at the Colosseum, they told him. All they needed to do was finish eating and go. So, after the meal, Lorcan followed the others to the atrium. Manius and Livia were waiting there. Livia wore a draped veil over her gown, covering her head. Lorcan had never seen her wear something like that before and wondered why. She turned toward him, and to Lorcan's great pleasure, he saw Corvina was sitting on her shoulder. She croaked at him as he came into sight, and he smiled.

"There you are," he said. "I'd wondered where you were."

"She was waiting for me in the workroom when I got back from your massage, and she's been with me since. I've been explaining to her that she needs to stay with me when you fight today." Livia raised one hand, and Lorcan saw that she'd wrapped her wrist in strips of cloth. Corvina moved from her perch on Livia's shoulder onto her wrist, and from there launched herself toward Lorcan, landing on his forearm.

"Does she understand?" Nona asked. "Lorcan, do you know?"

"I don't," Lorcan admitted. "I think so. And she likes Livia."

"I like her, too," Livia said. She came over to take Lorcan's free hand. "How's the arm?"

"Fine. I'm fine," he answered. "When do we go?"

"Are you so eager?" Manius asked with a laugh. He stooped and picked up several sets of manacles. "Are you eager for this?"

"No. I'm just starting to get nervous," Lorcan said, bringing his arm to his chest and stroking Corvina's feathers. "I want to go so that I stop fretting."

Yaroah's hand was warm on his shoulder. "You'll do fine."

"I have to win, you said," Lorcan said. "I'm just—"

"Scared?" Nona asked. "We all were, our first time."

"After this, you'll be a full gladiator," Manius said. "Today, you become one of us fully."

"And you'll do magnificently," Livia assured him.

"I'm sure Lorcan told you. You're all to be chained until you reach your cells at the arena. Your weapons and armor have been sent on ahead." Manius moved from man to man, chaining their wrists with manacles that proved to have shorter chains than the ones he had used on Lorcan the previous night. When he was done, he looked around. "Now, let's be on our way." He picked up a lantern that had been sitting at his feet and led them to a barred door and unlocked it. Opening it revealed a stair leading down.

"Are you afraid of enclosed spaces?" Nona whispered.

"No," Lorcan answered. "Corvina might not like it, though."

"You could hood her, like a falcon," Ennius offered. "Nona could make one."

"Hood her?" Lorcan stared at Ennius in horror. "No!"

Ennius held up his hands, his chains clinking. "Only a suggestion. Maybe she could meet us there if you don't want to take her through the tunnel?"

"How would she know where to go?" Livia asked. "Will she come to me, do you think? She can hide under this." She lifted a fold of her veil. Corvina bated, and Lorcan looked down at her.

"All right," he said, and passed Corvina back to Livia, who took the raven on her wrist. She brought her arm to her chest and laid a fold of her veil over the raven. Corvina popped her head out, croaked at them, then pulled her head back in.

"Problem solved," Nona said. "Let's go. Livia, take the other lantern?"

The stairs were narrow, as was the tunnel. It was only wide enough for them to walk single file. Lorcan thought about it as they walked, and realized this was more of *armed slaves make people nervous*. If someone tried to bring an armed force down this tunnel, all it would take to defend it would be a single man with a bow.

They walked in silence, until they reached a second stair on the far end. Manius went up first, and banged on the door at the top. At first, nothing happened. Then Lorcan heard a bolt shoot back, and the door opened. There were armed guards waiting at the top. One of them had armor that seemed more ornate than the others. He nodded to Manius as they all came out into the corridor.

"Got a new boy, I hear," he said. "Any good?"

Manius laughed. "You'll see, Julius. You'll see. Lorcan, come here."

Lorcan stepped forward. "Sir?"

The guard chuckled. "He's polite. Lorcan is your name?"

"Yes… sir?" He glanced at Manius and asked in Gaeilge. "Is that the right honorific?"

"Sir is fine, Lorcan."

Lorcan turned back the guard. "Yes, sir."

"Follow me," he said, turning. Lorcan looked at the others.

Yaroah nodded and smiled. "Julius will take care of you," he said.

Lorcan smiled in response and met Livia's eyes. "I'll see you after the fight," he said. She bit her lip and nodded.

"Be careful," she said.

Lorcan nodded. He looked over his shoulder to where Julius was waiting, then kissed Livia's cheek. "Corvina, you mind Livia."

A muffled click came from inside Livia's veil, making Livia giggle. Lorcan smiled and turned, following Julius away from the others.

Chapter Twelve

The cell that Julius led Lorcan into was very similar to his own cell in the ludus. Lorcan saw his armor and weapons sitting on the bed-shelf.

"I'll be back when it's time for you to go fight," Julius said. "To help you armor up. You're awfully friendly with Livia Manila."

Lorcan looked up at him. "Is that a problem?"

"She goes through men like a flame through tinder," Julius said. "Give me your hands. I'll unlock you. Then you can change and wait."

Lorcan nodded, watching as Julius unlocked his chains. "I know her past. I don't care. I love her, and once I have my freedom, she's promised to come back to Eire with me."

Julius looked up. "You're marrying her?" He snorted, looking both amused and surprised. "She's agreed?"

"Yes."

Julius snorted again. "I think I underestimated you. If you've tamed that she-cat, you're something more than you seem. Right. I'll lock the door, and you change and wait for me to come back. Need anything? Food? Water?"

"Will I be waiting very long?"

Julius shook his head. "You're the third fight. So, it depends on how long it takes for the first one to end. I'll come back when the second fight starts."

"Then just some water, please," Lorcan answered. Julius left the cell, and Lorcan heard the bar fall into place. He turned and stripped his tunic off. He'd decided to wear his *subligaculum* and belt, so he just needed to put on his braces. He slid his right arm into the long glove and started to tighten the lacings. As he finished, he heard the roar of a crowd from somewhere overhead—he looked up and saw a tiny, barred window near the ceiling.

He had finished his left brace and was strapping the *ocrea* around his legs when the door opened. Julius walked in and blinked. "What are those?"

"My arm was broken," Lorcan answered. "Nona made these to help protect the bone."

Julius nodded. "Makes sense, and Nona's a good one. Second fight just started. Let's get you ready. Stand up." Once Lorcan was on his feet, Julius crouched, checking the straps on the *ocrea*. "You need more padding with these," he murmured. "Tell Manius I said so." He grabbed one of the shin-guards and shook it, then nodded. "You've got them tightened well enough. Let's get the *manica*."

Lorcan held out his right arm, letting Julius position and tighten the wool-stuffed padded sleeve, then the articulated armor that reminded him of fish-scales. Julius buckled and tied, checked the fit, then fastened the chest straps and stepped back. "See how you move."

Lorcan flexed his arm and rotated it. He nodded. "This is good. Thank you."

"You're small for a *murmillo*," Julius said. "Are you any good?"

Lorcan shifted once more, then picked up his *spatha* and his shield. He looked at Julius and grinned. "We'll see after the third fight?"

Julius looked at him and laughed. "Whatever else, you've got stones on you. I've got your helmet. Let's go."

Lorcan followed Julius out of the cell and through the halls, toward a gate through which he could see sunlight. The sound of the crowd was very loud.

"How many people are out there?" Lorcan asked.

"No idea. Too many to count," Julius answered. "Ignore them. Your opponent is the only one you need to worry about. Well, and the Emperor. Put your weapons down there. You won't need them until the gates open."

Lorcan stared at him. "I was told the Emperor wasn't here."

Julius shook his head. "He wasn't supposed to be. Came back last night. No one knows why, but he and the Imperial family are all in their places today. You know what to do?"

"Yaroah told me. Salute the box," Lorcan said. "Then try not to die."

Julius barked with laughter. "That sounds like Yaroah. Did he tell you anything else?"

Lorcan shook his head. The crowd noise outside the gate swelled into a loud roar. Julius glanced at it, then back at Lorcan.

"That's it for the fight. They'll open the gate for you in a few minutes. When you get out there, salute the box. There are men out there with white rods about so long—" he held his hands wide. "They're the officials. Listen to them."

Lorcan nodded. He licked his lips and looked out through the holes in the gate. He could see men raking the sand, and for a moment wondered why. Then he realized—it was to clean up the blood. He swallowed.

"If you need to puke, now is the time," Julius murmured. "There's a basin over there."

Lorcan looked at him, saw sympathy in his eyes. "Thank you," he said.

"If you need it later, there's one through the *Porta Triumphalis*."

"The what?" Lorcan frowned. "The Triumph Gate?"

"The Victory Gate, yes. When you win, they parade you out of the arena through the *Porta Triumphalis*. I'll meet you there."

"You're very sure of me," Lorcan murmured without turning away from the gate.

"Oh, I want you to win. I want to see Gnaeus taken down. He's a prick." Julius grinned. "I bet on you, too."

Lorcan coughed and looked at Julius. "I'll do my best to make sure you didn't waste your coin."

Outside, there was a sound of trumpets, and the gates opened. Julius handed Lorcan his helmet.

"Don't put it on yet," he said. "Let them see you."

Lorcan grimaced at the helmet. "I'd rather not put it on at all. I don't like it." He belted on his sword, tucked his helmet under his left arm, then picked up his shield. For a moment, he didn't want to go out the gate. But going through the gate was the only choice, the only road that would take him home; he took a deep breath and nodded once. Julius clapped him on the shoulder.

"May Victoria smile on you, Lorcan. Go kill the bastard."

Lorcan snorted and walked out onto the sand. As he made his way out into the sunlight, the crowd roared, the sound enough to make him jump. He looked up... and froze.

He'd never seen so *many* people in one place before in his life. Too many to count, Julius had said. He hadn't been exaggerating. Lorcan turned in a circle, looking up at the masses of people that seemed to climb up to the sky. They were all screaming and shouting. At him.

It was terrifying.

"Lorcan!"

Livia's voice cut through the din like a knife. He turned once more and saw her and Manius standing near the wall on the lowest level. She looked worried, so he forced a smile and, on impulse, threw her a kiss. He could see her blush from where he stood, and the crowd roared their approval. Oddly, it was enough to calm him, and Lorcan turned back to the center of the arena. Gnaeus was already there, as were the rod-bearing officials. Lorcan walked toward them and nodded at the men.

"Sorry," he said quietly. "I've never seen so many people before."

"It takes all the *tirones* like that," one of the officials said. "You didn't faint or run. That's good. You know what to do?"

"Salute the box," Lorcan answered. "Then beat him like the dog he is." He nodded at Gnaeus, who glowered at him. Both officials chuckled.

"He'll go far, this one," the first one said to the second.

"If he wins," the second added. "Salute. With your weapon, *tiro*."

Lorcan looked around and saw a covered balcony draped in purple. There were a number of people there, men and women both, but Lorcan saw only one of them. Tavi. He was sitting behind several other men, but Lorcan could clearly see his curls and his dark skin. And he could almost feel the weight of Tavi's eyes on him. He licked his lips, and drew his *spatha*, raising it in homage, seeing Gnaeus raising his arm similarly. The crowd cheered, and one of the officials tapped Lorcan's arm. "This way, *tiro*."

The official led Lorcan off a short distance. He pointed at the sand. "Plant your sword there," he said. "I'll hold your shield while you put your helmet on." As Lorcan stabbed his sword point down into the ground, he continued, "I suppose you don't know. This is a very irregular fight. Cestus against *murmillo*? Not a fight we usually see. Why did you ask for this fight?"

Lorcan stopped with his helmet in his hands. "Me? Ask for the fight? I didn't. I didn't even know I was fighting until yesterday."

The official frowned. "Very irregular," he repeated. "We were told that this fight, this pairing specifically, was requested."

"Perhaps by Manius," Lorcan suggested. He pulled the helmet on and took his shield back. Then he pulled his *spatha* from the sand and rolled his shoulders.

"Are you ready?" The official had to raise his voice before Lorcan could hear him clearly. Lorcan nodded, and the official led him back to the center of the arena. The other official and Gnaeus were already waiting. The official raised his rod, holding it at about waist-height between Lorcan and Gnaeus. From somewhere, Lorcan heard someone shouting, but couldn't make out the words.

"Are you ready?" the official shouted. Lorcan nodded, watching Gnaeus. Gnaeus dipped his head once. The rod moved up and away, and the official shouted, "Fight!"

The world went away. There was only Gnaeus, and for a long heartbeat, the *cestus* didn't move. Lorcan steeled himself for the first blow, watching as Gnaeus tensed. Then he sprung. Lorcan slapped away the blow with his shield and swung low, thinking to take out Gnaeus' legs and end this quickly. His blade scraped against Gnaeus' left hand *cestii* as the other man blocked and danced backwards out of range. Lorcan stepped back and panted. It was already ridiculously hot in his helmet, and he wondered how long he could go like this. Gnaeus came toward him, and Lorcan raised his shield. If he blocked Gnaeus again the way he just had, could he maybe stab forward and finish him that way? No, it would leave his entire right side open. For a moment, he remembered his fight against Cormac. Then he realized what he needed to do. He crouched, then rushed at Gnaeus, slamming into him with his shield and bowling the *cestus* over. Lorcan bounced to his feet, only to find his way blocked with a pair of white rods.

"You can't do that, *tiro*!" one of the officials said. "Did Manius teach you nothing?"

Lorcan backed up a step, stabbed his sword down into the sand and tugged off his helmet. "Didn't teach me how to fight a man with iron in his fists, no," he panted.

"Put that back on!" the official scolded. Lorcan shook his head.

"No. I can't breathe, and I can't see. And he's not wearing one." He tossed the helmet to the side. As it hit the sand and rolled, the crowd roared their approval. Lorcan looked up at the rows of people that rose higher than the cliffs of the cove at him. He waved, prompting another roar. Then he picked up his sword. "I'm ready. Anything else I can't do?"

The official stared at him, then shook his head. "You're insane."

"Probably," Lorcan agreed. "Can I finish this now? What can't I do?"

"No clinching, for one."

Lorcan frowned. "That means I can't run into him or grab him?"

"Manius didn't teach you a damned thing, did he?" the official scoffed. "This is gladiatorial combat, not wrestling."

Lorcan grinned. "Good. I'm a lousy wrestler."

He saw the official's lips twitch. "Go fight, you lunatic."

Lorcan nodded and trotted back toward the second official, who had his rod raised once more. Gnaeus was scowling on the other side.

"I am going to kill you, boy," Gnaeus growled. The official looked startled.

"You can try," Lorcan answered. "But even if you somehow manage it, my Livia will never come to your bed."

"A woman?" The first official came to stand by his partner. "This fight is over a woman?"

"And it ends now!" Gnaeus lashed out. Not at Lorcan—he struck the closer of the two officials, who dropped like a stone. Lorcan jumped between Gnaeus and the other official, seeing Gnaeus grab the fallen rod.

"Do you have a way out?" Lorcan said over his shoulder.

"Yes, but—"

"Do it. Get out of here." Lorcan raised his shield, never looking away from Gnaeus. "Get out of here." Gnaeus advanced, twirling the rod lazily. Lorcan had seen Ennius doing something similar with his trident while waiting for his opponent. He glanced back, saw the official still lingering behind him. "Move!" he roared as he moved to meet Gnaeus.

The *cestus* clearly knew nothing about using a weapon. He clutched the rod in both hands and swung wildly, smashing it against Lorcan's shield. It shattered, splinters flying everywhere. Lorcan raised his shield over his head and struck at Gnaeus' midriff. The edge of his blade glanced off of the cestus' heavy belt and slid upwards; Gnaeus howled as the blade sliced a gash in his abdomen, stumbling forward and dropping the short, jagged piece that was all that was left of the rod. Lorcan rushed forward, his shield ready, his *spatha* held low. Gnaeus spun to meet him, lashing out with his left arm, putting enough force behind the punch that his fist went clean through Lorcan's shield. Lorcan gasped in shock and moved, twisting away from the iron-clad fist. He didn't release his shield, and his momentum carried Gnaeus' arm to an impossible point. The sickening crack of a breaking bone was almost drowned out by Gnaeus' scream. Both were immediately muffled by the roar of the crowd.

Lorcan dropped the ruined shield and staggered back. He could see blood, and the jagged edge of bone protruding from Gnaeus' arm, just above the elbow. He saw movement and registered two things—a horde of guards rushing out onto the sand, and a black form streaking down toward him from the sky. He raised his fist, and Corvina landed there. She mantled and screamed defiance at the world, and the world answered her as the crowd roared its approval.

"*Tiro*? Are you unhurt?"

Lorcan turned and saw the remaining official. He brought his arm down and settled Corvina on his shoulder. "I'm fine. I'm sorry about your friend."

"You're not done." The official touched his arm, then pointed. Lorcan turned to see and realized that the official was pointing at the Emperor.

"Oh. The others said he'd decide the end." Lorcan walked toward the box, until he could see clearly the older man sitting there. Frowning. Lorcan planted his *spatha* in the sand, went to one knee and waited.

The answer came quickly, and Lorcan swallowed as he saw the gesture that Yaroah had said meant death. He understood it, though. Gnaeus hadn't followed the rules. He'd killed one of the officials. He was a mad dog, and mad dogs needed to be stopped. Lorcan bowed, then got back to his feet and picked up his sword. He turned and went back to where the guards had surrounded Gnaeus, who was still rolling on the sand in a growing pool of his own blood.

"Is there a way this is done?" Lorcan asked the official. "A proper way?"

"There is a way that this is done, but I doubt he will go through the ritual," the official answered. His eyes narrowed, and he looked at the closest guard. "Get him up. On his knees."

Lorcan stood and watched as the guards pulled Gnaeus up onto his knees. One of them stepped forward.

"*Cestus*, you have been defeated. And you have been condemned by the Emperor. You know the ritual."

Gnaeus moaned. Then he spat at Lorcan. "I will not kneel to this barbarian!"

"You have been beaten, *cestus*," the guard repeated. "The Emperor is giving you a chance to die with honor, though you had none in life. If you do not, you will be executed."

Lorcan looked up. "How am I to kill him?" he asked.

"Usually, it's by slitting his throat," the official answered.

Lorcan nodded. He stepped forward. "Gnaeus, I give you my word. I will make it quick and clean. Will an execution give you that much?"

Gnaeus glowered up at him. "You lie!"

"I swear to you, on my honor as a prince of Eire and a son of the Morrigan," Lorcan said. "I will do as I said."

Gnaeus looked away, then nodded, his face suddenly grey. "I... it will be quick?"

"Quick and clean," Lorcan repeated. "And more than you deserve."

Gnaeus swallowed, then bowed his head. "I will submit."

"Go to him," the official said. "He will grasp your thigh. Then you will slit his throat. Do you have a dagger?"

"No," Lorcan answered. He looked at the closest guard. "Have you a blade I might borrow?"

The guard looked startled, then drew a dagger and passed it to Lorcan. He tested the edge and frowned. "Has anyone a sharper blade?"

The guard's neighbor snickered. "Told you to sharpen that," he muttered, and drew his own dagger. "Here, *tiro*. Try mine."

"Thank you." Lorcan took the offered blade and nodded when he tested the edge. "Yes, this is fine." He moved over to stand in front of Gnaeus. The official stood at his side. Lorcan glanced at him. "Are there words you say before I do this?"

"None," the official answered. "He will grasp your thigh. You will take him by the hair and slit his throat. Then they will take him away."

Lorcan nodded. He looked down at Gnaeus, who seemed resigned. The *cestus* raised his good hand and rested it on Lorcan's thigh. Lorcan reached out, took a fistful of Gnaeus' sweat-soaked hair, and neatly slashed his throat. A gout of blood washed over him; he let Gnaeus fall to the ground and tried not to hear the blood-curdling screams of approval from all around him. He felt sick.

"This way, gladiator," the official murmured. "To the Victory Gate. Wave to them, son."

Lorcan waved as he walked. "You didn't call me *tiro*," he said.

"You're not. Not anymore."

Lorcan glanced at him. "My name is Lorcan."

The official sniffed. "Not according to them," he said, and nodded toward the throng. "Listen."

Lorcan did and realized that the cries of excitement and enthusiasm had changed to a chant. And they were chanting *Corax*.

"When they announce you in the arena from this point on, it will be as Corax."

Lorcan nodded, not sure if he was feeling overwhelmed, ill, or both. "What's your name?" he asked.

The official looked at him strangely. "Linus."

"And your partner?" Lorcan looked back, to see that the body of the other official had been taken away, as had Gnaeus. Now, there were only men with rakes, clearing away the blood. "I'm sorry I wasn't faster."

"It was hardly your fault, Lorcan," Linus said. "If you feel the need, make a sacrifice in his name. Which was Crispus."

Lorcan nodded. "I'll do that. Thank you, Linus."

Then they entered the Victory Gate, and Lorcan saw Julius. Julius looked at him and went pale, and Lorcan looked down at himself for the first time.

His belt, and the entire front of his *subligaculum* were dyed rusty brown and crimson. Dried blood was caked on his skin from his waist to his sandals.

"Julius," he said, his voice cracking.

"You did well, Lorcan," Julius murmured.

"You said there would be a basin. I need it."

* * *

Lorcan felt as if he vomited for days. When he was finally done, he was certain that there should have been bones and entrails in the basin, because there couldn't be anything left inside of him. Julius didn't tease or make rude comments. He took Lorcan's sword, offered Lorcan his arm, and brought him back to his cell. He helped Lorcan off with his armor, left a flagon of watered wine, and promised to return with a clean tunic and a basin of water so that Lorcan could wash. Lorcan sat down on the bed-shelf and shuddered.

This hadn't been what he'd expected. None of it. The others had made it seem like a game. But now...

Now he was coated in the blood of a man he'd known. He hadn't liked Gnaeus. But he'd known him.

He closed his eyes, feeling Corvina rubbing her beak against his cheek. He reached up and stroked her feathers.

"This is what gets me home," he murmured in Gaeilge. "Right?"

She croaked at him. He smiled and clicked in response, then sighed. "Knew you'd agree." He leaned against the wall and closed his eyes. The others were fighting today, he thought. That meant he'd be locked up here until it was time to go back to the *ludus*. As soon as he was cleaned up, he'd sleep.

The door opened. Lorcan opened his eyes, expecting to see Julius. Instead, there was a woman standing just inside the cell. Lorcan had learned a little about gems and jewelry from his uncle and aunt, and from Ronan. From the looks of this woman's jewelry, she was wealthy. Her gown and veil were of some fine cloth, and she looked as out of place in the cell as a rose in a dung-heap. Lorcan slowly got to his feet and bowed.

"You had an impressive debut, Corax" the woman said. Her voice was clear and melodious, and as she moved closer, Lorcan caught a whiff of her heavy perfume. He wanted to back up, but there was nowhere to go.

"Thank you, my lady," he said.

"And you have lovely manners," she continued. "That's quite charming." She paused. "You're younger than you seemed from above. I wonder…" She looked him up and down., then came closer. "I think you'll make for a delightful surprise."

Surprise? Surprise for who? All at once, Lorcan remembered what the others had told him in the baths, about the women who would want him in their beds. He licked his lips. "I'd stay back, my lady," he said softly. He raised his hand to Corvina. "She's not tame. I'd not see you hurt."

The warning didn't work. The woman smiled. "A protector? Is she sent by your gods?"

"My gods are a long way away, my lady," Lorcan answered. "I do not think they have power here."

She laughed. "Of course they do. They are gods." She stepped closer. "Who are your gods, Corax? From where do you come?"

"From Eire, my lady," Lorcan said. "Do you know of it?"

"Only in that it is a far-away place, and peopled by barbarians. Apparently, very comely barbarians." She took another step closer. Her perfume threatened to strangle Lorcan, and he cleared his throat.

"Lady—" Lorcan attempted to back up and hit the bed-shelf. She rested her hands lightly on his chest.

"You're so young. Are you an innocent, Corax? Do you understand the ways of men and women?" She smiled. "Are you interested in learning? There's quite a lot I could teach you."

The door opened, and Julius walked in, carrying a basin of water. He saw the woman and rolled his eyes. "Drucilla!"

She looked over her shoulder. "Oh. It's you. Go away until after the next fight, will you? Corax and I were having a discussion."

"I will not. His master says he's not to be manhandled. So out, woman! And take your stink with you!" He stepped out of the doorway, letting the woman storm out past him. The door closed behind her, and he sighed and shook his head as he set the basin on the bed-shelf. "I'll have to find out who she bribed to get in here. She manhandle you much?"

"No," Lorcan answered. "Who is she?"

Julius looked at him, clearly shocked. "You don't know? Lorcan, that fine, upstanding example of a Roman matron is the wife of the Emperor's oldest son. She'll be Empress someday, and you can bet that her family makes certain that everyone knows it."

"If she'll be Empress, what is she doing down here?" Lorcan asked.

Julius snorted, putting down a bundle that he'd had under his arm. "You know full well what she was doing down here, Lorcan," he said. "She likes gladiators. Her husband was one. I think that's how they met, actually." He looked at the door. "I don't know why Gaius tolerates her behavior, though. They've been married years now, and she's never given him an heir."

Lorcan shrugged, going to the basin. "My parents were married six years before I was born. My mother lost four before me."

Julius winced. "That's a terrible thing. Go ahead and wash. There's a cloth in the bowl. The bundle is a drying cloth and a fresh tunic. Do you want your shield?"

Lorcan frowned as he unfastened his belt. "I'm not sure. I don't know if it can be mended, and it won't be as strong. Will it?"

Julius looked thoughtful. "Maybe. Sometimes, you have to break something to figure out how to make it stronger. Ask Nona. He'll know." He started toward the door. "Think you can eat?"

"Something simple, maybe?"

"I'll send for something. And I'll guard the door, so you have privacy. If Manius and Livia come down, should I let them in?"

"Yes, please. Thank you, Julius." The door closed behind the guard, and Lorcan stripped off his *subligaculum,* which was now stiff and cracking. He let it fall to the ground and wrung the wet cloth out. He asked Julius to replace the water in the basin twice before he felt clean enough to put on the fresh tunic, and even then, he wanted the baths back at the *ludus* with almost the same deep-seated need that he felt for his cloak, or for Livia or Tavi.

He set the bowl of dirty water on the ground and stretched out on the bed. Corvina climbed onto his chest and settled down, and he chuckled.

"Guess I'm not moving, hm?" he asked. He ran one hand gently down her back. "Corvina, I don't know how I can do that again. That… that was vile. That's nothing my father or my uncles prepared me for when they taught me to fight." He stared up at the ceiling, hearing a distant roar. Was someone else dead? He didn't know, but he shuddered all the same. "I'm the Battle Raven's own blood. You'd think that would mean that killing wouldn't bother me. But it did. I killed him like I was slaughtering a pig." He sighed. "Now I feel as though I'll never be clean again."

He dozed, sleeping fitfully, unable to ignore the periodic roar of the crowd. Finally, the door opened again. Lorcan blinked and grimaced. He glanced over, then sat up and spilled a squawking Corvina onto his lap as Livia came into the cell. Behind her was Manius, who looked positively jubilant.

"That was a most entertaining debut, Lorcan!" he declared.

"And Gnaeus is dead," Lorcan answered. "He murdered a man, and I killed him."

"The Emperor killed him," Manius corrected. "You were the Emperor's tool. You were his blade, nothing more."

Lorcan frowned. "That doesn't make me feel any better."

"You'll get over it. And you're unhurt?"

Lorcan smiled slightly. "I'm fine. Apart from being handled by someone named Drucilla."

Livia gasped, a small sound of outrage. "I'll scratch her eyes out!"

"You'll do nothing of the sort," Manius chided. "And did you give the lady what she wanted?" he asked Lorcan.

"Julius interrupted and sent her away." Lorcan reached out for Livia's hand. "I didn't want her, Livia."

She scowled, then sighed. "I know, love. But what we want and what we have to do are often two different things."

Lorcan nodded and pulled her close, wrapping his arms around her. Her warmth did much to settle his shredded nerves. "When do we go back?" he asked.

"That's why we're here. To get you. We're going back to the *ludus*."

Julius was waiting outside the cell. He smiled and offered Lorcan his broken shield. "Here. I had to find it for you. They'd put it to be burned."

"Thank you, Julius." Lorcan said. He took the shield and studied it. "I don't know how this can be put right again."

"See what Nona says," Julius said. "And I'll see you when you fight again."

Lorcan smiled, and followed Manius back to the door into the tunnel where the other gladiators were waiting. None of them, Lorcan noticed, were chained, and no chains were brought forth before the door was open. The walk back to the *ludus* seemed to take hours, and Lorcan was glad to see the stairs at the end.

"I want a bath," he said as they came out into the atrium. "And I want to sleep."

"Off to the baths, all of you," Manius said. "There will be a feast waiting, as soon as you're done. We need to celebrate —" His voice trailed off. Lorcan looked and saw a stranger waiting in the atrium. Manius went to meet him and took a scroll that was offered to him. He opened it, and his face went pale.

"Father?"

"Well, this is… unexpected," Manius said. "But I probably should have expected it. Go bathe. All of you." He rolled the scroll up and nodded to the man, who nodded in response and left. "Lorcan, once you've bathed, come to Livia's workroom. I'll need to prepare you."

"Sir?" Lorcan asked.

"We've been summoned before the Emperor. He wants to see you tomorrow morning."

Chapter Thirteen

Lorcan had spent enough time in his uncle's *baile* that the idea of meeting the Emperor didn't bother him. In truth, it amused him. What *had* Tavi said or done to prompt the invitation? Lorcan couldn't even begin to guess, although trying to was enough to distract him from his first day in the arena and let him get a full night's sleep. He woke at dawn to find that the invitation had thrown the rest of the *ludus* into a frenzy. The gladiators, for the most part, seemed to be exempt from it, but Manius never stopped moving, and the house slaves ran around at his orders as if their lives depended on it. And it seemed that at every moment, Manius was calling Lorcan to do something or try something on, only to change what it was the next time he called. It was, Lorcan thought, equal parts fascinating and frustrating.

"You know, I am a prince in my own land," he reminded Livia as she worked to comb the multitude of braids out of his hair. Manius had ordered her to do that before the morning meal, sending Lorcan to her from the *triclinium*. "My uncle is the High King. I lived as a fosterling for years in his court. I know how to behave myself in front of royalty!"

"This is different," Livia assured him.

Lorcan winced as her comb tugged on his scalp. "Leave me a little, Livia! How is this different?"

"Your uncle is a barbarian. The Emperor is a god."

"He is not!" Lorcan said with a laugh.

"He will be."

Lorcan frowned. "So? I'm a god, too. *Semideus*, your father called me." Livia's hands stilled. "He did?"

"I thought I told you that?" Lorcan said. "And are we done? I'm hungry."

"Almost." Livia started combing again. "Stay still and stop talking. You'll distract me."

Lorcan fell silent and let her work, his eyes half-closed in pleasure

145

at the feeling of her fingers in his hair. The questions rose once more—Why did the Emperor want to see him? Was it because of Tavi, and if so, what had Tavi *done*?

Finally, Livia ran her fingers through Lorcan's loose hair. "There. It's like silk. Now, go bathe."

"Bathe?" Lorcan repeated, turning to face her. "I did bathe. Last night. I want to eat."

"Bathe again. Father said. I'll be in with pomade—"

"No. No pomade. No perfume." Lorcan stood up. "I am not going before the Emperor stinking like that Drucilla woman did. I'll bathe. But that's all. And I'm going to eat something first."

Livia scowled at the mention of Drucilla's name. "I suppose. Then off to bathe. I'll have a tunic laid out for you when you're done."

Lorcan crossed to stand in front of Livia. "I didn't want her, my love," he said. Then he grinned. "Truly told? She terrified me."

"Did she really?" Livia gasped.

"I thought she might chew me up and spit out my bones."

Livia giggled. "That's a horrible image."

Lorcan nodded. "Julius told me that she's the heir's wife. That she'll be Empress someday. And that she hasn't given him an heir."

"That's all true."

"And he hasn't put her aside?" Lorcan took Livia's hand and started toward the *triclinium*. "Doesn't he need an heir of his own?"

Livia looked around, then leaned in close, whispering for Lorcan's ears alone. "It's not her that's the problem. It's him. From what I know, he was ill as a child, and it appears to have unmanned him. None of his lovers has ever quickened. But there are rumors that Drucilla has done away with four pregnancies."

Lorcan stared at her. "That's horrible!"

"Rumor says that she does it because she knows that if she has a child, she'll be put aside," Livia said. "But I'm not sure how accurate that is. Gaius can't divorce her because her family is powerful. And he has an heir. Decus' second oldest son. One of Tavi's brothers."

"That will cause problems, won't it," Lorcan murmured. "If the heir isn't the oldest?"

"The oldest is Arcus, and it wouldn't be a problem with him," Livia said. "He trained here, too. I was a little girl then, though. He's very sweet. And he's in Alba. That's where he wants to be."

Lorcan sat down on his couch and waited for Livia to join him. "What is there to eat?"

"I'll find out. Are you going to sit, or recline?"

"If it's just us, I'll sit." Lorcan watched as she left, then looked at the couch. Reclining to eat still felt uncomfortable, but it was the way things were done here. But if he was given the choice, he'd sit properly. Livia came back in.

"Someone will bring food in a moment. Where's Corvina?"

"I haven't seen her since early this morning. She flew off when Manius woke me up, and I haven't seen her since. Lucky bird is staying out of the way." He held his hand out to Livia, who came and sat next to him on the couch. "Livia, I don't understand. Why would the Emperor want to see me?"

"I don't know," she answered. "Perhaps it has something to do with the fight."

"I keep wondering if it's something else," Lorcan said, keeping his voice quiet. He glanced at Livia and saw her nod.

"That could be." She stopped and looked at the door. A moment later, Manius appeared.

"What are you doing in here?" he asked. "Shouldn't you be in the baths?"

"Not until I eat something," Lorcan answered. "I don't want to disgrace anyone by fainting from hunger in front of the Emperor."

"You didn't eat?"

Lorcan blinked in surprise. Manius wasn't usually this distracted. "Manius, you came and got me before I even left my cell this morning, and I haven't stopped moving since. Every time I came toward the *triclinium*, you sent me somewhere else. No, I haven't eaten. And I don't think you have, either. You should sit down before you fall down." As he said the words, he regretted them. He could talk to his father like that, or any of his uncles. But to Manius? It was out of the question!

Manius, however, didn't seem to take it amiss. "I can't sit. There's too much to do. Eat, then bathe. We'll leave for the palace when you're ready." He wandered out, leaving Lorcan and Livia sitting in stunned silence behind him.

"He's never like this," Livia said. "Ever."

Before Lorcan could ask her why she thought Manius might be acting so strangely, slaves entered with trays and goblets. Ennius had warned Lorcan about speaking freely around the house slaves—all of them reported what they heard to Manius. So, he stayed silent until he and Livia were again alone.

"You said that Manius trained the Emperor's sons," he said as he tore a flat loaf of bread in half. He handed one half to Livia. "That means he knows the Emperor."

"Yes, that's right."

"So why is this causing so much upset?" Lorcan waved one arm. "If you all know the Emperor?"

"Because he's never done this before," Livia answered. She took a bite of bread and reached for a bowl of olives.

Lorcan nodded, slowly chewing his bread. He stole an olive from Livia and popped it into his mouth, then swallowed. "So why now? Did I do something wrong? Or did I do something right?"

"I think we'll find out after you get to the Palace."

* * *

When Lorcan was finished bathing, Livia brought him a tunic made of fine linen, trimmed with elaborate embroidery. She combed his hair out once more, then kissed him.

"For luck," she said. "Now go. Father is in the atrium."

"How are we getting to the palace?" Lorcan asked. He knew roughly where the Imperial palace was—he and Livia had passed it when they'd walked to Apollo's Temple.

"Father said something about transportation being arranged," Livia said. "I'll come with you to the atrium."

They walked out of the workroom, and Lorcan heard a rusty squawk. Corvina was sitting on a bench in the garden, her head cocked to the side as if she wasn't sure what to make of things. Lorcan understood the feeling entirely.

"There you are," he said. "I thought you were going to be late and miss everything."

The raven clicked at him, then launched herself off the bench, landing on Lorcan's outstretched arm. She sidled up to his shoulder and preened his hair.

"You're taking her?"

Lorcan shrugged his other shoulder. "How often will a common raven have the chance to see an emperor close up? And do you honestly think I'd be able to keep her from coming with me?"

Livia smiled. "Well, no. Corvina, keep him out of trouble, will you?"

Out of the corner of his eye, Lorcan saw Corvina's head bobbing. Livia giggled, and Lorcan burst out laughing. "Where did you learn that?" he demanded. Corvina tugged his hair.

"You need to go," Livia said. "Before Father starts roaring."

They walked out to the atrium, where Manius was pacing back and forth. He scowled at them as they came toward him.

"What took you so long?" he demanded. "We've got to leave."

"How are we going?" Lorcan asked. "Do we have horses? Or a cart?"

"The Emperor sent a *lectica*. It's a high honor," Manius gestured. "Livia, lock the doors behind us. The others are in their cells."

"Yes, Father."

Lorcan followed Manius out, wondering what a *lectica* was. Outside, surrounded by several burly men, was a construct the likes of which Lorcan had never seen before. It looked like a high-posted bed, hung with curtains and lush with cushions. Manius ducked underneath the top rail and moved into the bed, settling down to recline on the cushions. He looked out at Lorcan and frowned. "Come along."

"What is it?" Lorcan moved closer, crouching to look inside. "This is a *lectica*?"

"You've never seen one?" Manius shook his head. "Oh, of course you haven't. Yes. Come in and sit down. Close the curtain behind you."

Lorcan entered the lectica and sat down, closing the curtains behind him. The moment the curtains closed, the *lectica* lurched and tipped. Corvina squawked and bated; Lorcan grabbed at the cushions, then stared at Manius as the man laughed.

"What's happening?" he demanded.

"We're on our way," Manius answered. "A *lectica* is carried. Those men? Are taking us to see the Emperor."

"I'd rather walk," Lorcan grumbled. The *lectica* pitched and swayed like the ships that had brought him to Rome. He shifted uncomfortably, settling Corvina onto the cushions next to him. Manius frowned.

"Do you have to take the bird with you everywhere?"

Lorcan smiled. "Do you think I have a say in it? She goes where she goes. She's not tame, Manius." *Nor am I*, he added silently. Instead, he peered out the curtain. "This is too much like being on a ship. I don't like it."

"It won't take long," Manius answered. "Now, when you meet the Emperor, you say nothing unless he speaks to you directly. Remember your place."

"I understand," Lorcan said. "I'm a slave, or so you keep telling me. What does a slave have to say to the Emperor of Rome?" He glanced out the curtains again. "If I'm going before the Emperor as a slave only, why am I not chained?"

"You want to be?"

Lorcan snorted. "Of course not. But does he want to see the slave, or the gladiator who put down a minor rebellion in front of all of Rome?"

Manius' eyes widened. "What? What made you say that?"

"It's true, isn't it?" Lorcan asked. "You told us that there was a slave uprising brewing. That's why we went to the arena in chains. Then a gladiator turned on one of the officials and killed him. And I stopped that gladiator before anyone else could get hurt. Then you brought us back to the *ludus* unchained. Did I quash that slave rebellion you were worried about? And wouldn't that be why the Emperor wants to see me?"

"I don't know why the Emperor wants to see you. But that's a good reason. Perhaps yes." Manius looked thoughtful as he ran his hand over the breast of his tunic. "I hadn't given Gnaeus' rebellion any thought, other than his hatred of you had turned him mad. But perhaps there was more to him than that. You may be right. Why didn't you say anything about this before?"

"Well, you've hardly been standing still long enough to talk to since the messenger left," Lorcan pointed out, making Manius bark with laughter. "And I honestly only just thought of it."

"It's a good thought," Manius said. "And you may be right. We'll find out soon."

Lorcan rested his hands on his thighs and tried to convince his stomach to stay where it was supposed to be as the *lectica* continued to sway.

"You look green."

"Will we be able to walk back?" Lorcan replied. Manius, to his surprise, smiled in sympathy.

"You should have mentioned you get seasick. Yes, we'll walk back. Open the curtain a bit. Fresh air will help."

* * *

"Why use these blasted things?" Lorcan had asked as the *lectica* had thumped to the ground. "This is a horrible way to travel."

"It's an honor," Manius repeated. "You've just traveled the way one of the Emperor's own family would have."

"Then they clearly none of them get sick on a boat," Lorcan answered. Manius shook his head and gestured for Lorcan to open the curtains the rest of the way. They disembarked, and Lorcan stood on his own two feet. Normally, he would have wanted to stare at the white marble magnificence that was the Emperor's palace. But today, he was concentrating more on convincing himself that he was actually standing still in a courtyard, not still swaying in an over-rated and overwrought contraption that seemed to serve absolutely no real purpose. Corvina rubbed her beak on his cheek, making soft, comforting sounds in his ear.

"Better?" Manius asked, coming to stand in front of him. Lorcan looked back at the *lectica*, then frowned.

"I really don't understand the point," he said.

"Separation," Manius answered. "The Imperial blood is above all others. This is just one way to show it."

Lorcan snorted. "My bloodline is divine. I still muck out the stables."

Manius clapped Lorcan on his unoccupied shoulder. "That's because you're a barbarian. Come along. Remember what I said."

Lorcan followed after Manius and the guards that escorted them, finally feeling well enough to marvel at the way that Roman nobles lived. The palace was lavish and large, and yet still seemed crowded, filled to overflowing with slaves and men in togas. From a distance, Lorcan saw a woman that he thought might be Drucilla, and averted his eyes. Despite the heat of the day, the place felt cold, and he wasn't sure if that was temperature, or the lack of familial warmth. Then the guards led them into a smaller chamber, where a single, toga-clad man stood with his back to the door, looking down at something on a table. Lorcan saw Manius go still, his shoulders stiffening, and realized who this must be.

"The *lanista* Manius Glabrio," one of the guards announced. "And the gladiator Corax."

The man turned, and Lorcan saw him clearly for the first time. In the arena, he had saluted the box, but it had been far enough that he hadn't taken the time to make note of one face out of the sea of similar faces. Now, he could see that the Emperor was an older man, his face narrow and angular, his eyes bright blue and sparkling with good humor.

"Manius!" he declared and waved one hand. Lorcan saw the guards bow and back out of the room, closing the door behind them. As the heavy doors thumped shut, the Emperor came around the chairs that stood between them and greeted Manius warmly. "My good friend," he said. "It's a pleasure to see you. It's been too long."

"It has, Your Majesty."

"Manius…"

"Lucanus, it has been too long," Manius corrected. He gestured to Lorcan. "May I present my newest student?"

Lorcan bowed deeply, then went to one knee. "Your Majesty."

"They call you Corax," Lucanus said. "Stand up, my son. Let me look at you. Your given name is Lorcan, correct?"

"Yes, your Majesty," Lorcan answered, rising to his feet. Lucanus nodded, then smiled.

"And your friend?" he asked, pointing to Lorcan's shoulder.

"Is Corvina, your Majesty."

Lucanus smiled, looking as mischievous as Conor for a moment. "Will she come to me, do you think?"

"She isn't tame," Lorcan said. He offered his wrist to Corvina, then held her at eye level. "Behave yourself," he said in Gaeilge. "I like him."

Corvina bobbed her head again, then stepped from Lorcan's wrist to Lucanus' as delicately as any fine lady. Lucanus smiled broadly, running one finger over Corvina's breast feathers.

"I can't say I've ever seen a raven this close before," he said, almost as an aside. "You're quite the beauty, Lady Corvina."

Corvina croaked at him, and Lorcan smiled. "She likes you."

"I like her," Lucanus said. "Now, it seems odd to me that one of the Raven Goddess' blood should keep a raven as a pet, Lorcan."

Lorcan swallowed. "You know who I am?"

"Of course. Partially because of my son, partially because of my grandson, and partially because the stories of your family have made their way here. They are quite extraordinary. Are they true?"

"I don't know what stories you've heard, your Majesty. So, I can't say," Lorcan answered.

Lucanus nodded. He gestured to the chairs, then carried Corvina over to take a seat. "What does she eat?"

"She's a hunter. She likes meat, and egg. She very much likes cheese, but she shouldn't eat too much of it," Lorcan answered, and

Corvina clicked her annoyance at him. "You shouldn't," he told her. "You'll get fat, and you won't be able to fly."

Corvina clicked again, and Lucanus laughed. "She understands you?"

"I'm not sure how much, but yes."

"Wondrous," Lucanus murmured. He set Corvina down on the arm of his chair. "Now, Lorcan. Lucanus the Younger has told me how you came to be in Rome, and a slave. I'd like to hear the story from you."

Lucanus the Younger? It took Lorcan a moment to realize that the Emperor meant Tavi. "I had a difference of opinion with my oldest cousin," he said slowly. "He wanted to be my father's heir. I disagreed with him. So did everyone else in the family. He challenged me, and he lost. So he left the family *baile*. He allied himself with raiders, and they laid a trap for me, using my youngest cousin as bait. They murdered my companion, and I ended up being sold as a slave in Alba."

"So I've heard from my son. He told me of your uncles coming in search of you." Lucanus stroked Corvina's feathers. "I'm surprised your cousin didn't kill you outright."

"It would have risked our grandmother's wrath, and he's not that foolhardy," Lorcan answered.

Lucanus nodded. "It would never do, to court the wrath of a powerful goddess. And I'm certain that she is powerful, the Morrigan. In her own lands, at least." He smiled. "Now tell me. What will you do, Lorcan, once you're freed?"

Lorcan coughed. He tried not to look at Manius, who was sitting silently to his left. "I know I must return home. Cormac intends to move against the rest of my family, and against my King. He needs to be stopped."

"But then you would court the wrath of your patron goddess," Lucanus pointed out.

"To save my family? That's a chance I'm willing to take." He looked down at his lap. "I also thought to take a wife," he added.

Lucanus laughed. "The stories say that your family knows their mates on sight. Have you found her here?"

Lorcan nodded. "Livia Manila."

"Manius? Did you know this?"

Manius looked stunned. "I knew they were sharing a bed. I didn't know that there was marriage proposal."

"I would have spoken to you when I was free to do so," Lorcan said. "As you keep reminding me, I'm a slave. I can't marry."

Manius frowned. Then he nodded. "I understand. We'll discuss it."

"Do you object, Manius?" Lucanus asked. "Livia is a wonderful girl, but her status—" he shook his head. "This is an opportunity that she'd not otherwise have."

Manius looked at Lorcan. Then he smiled. "No. No objections. Lorcan is a good boy, and a good fighter. I'm going to start training him as a *dimachaeri*. After seeing him on the sands, I can tell that he's wasted as a *murmillo*."

Lucanus nodded slowly. "Then you don't intend to free him."

Manius went still. "At the end of the year—"

"So my grandson tells me," Lucanus said, his voice suddenly hard. "And don't think that I don't know you've been telling your Carthaginian slave the same story for nine years now."

Lorcan saw movement and turned to see a toga-clad figure in the shadows. He started to rise, then smiled. "Tavi?"

Tavi came out into the room. "Apologies for being late, Grandfather. I was in the stables."

"Accepted, Lucanus. Come and sit." The Emperor gestured to an empty chair at his left. "Have you met Lorcan's lovely friend?"

"Yes," Tavi answered. He took a seat and reached out to run the backs of his fingers over Corvina's wing. "Hello, Corvina. She's visited me, Lorcan. Did she tell you?"

Lorcan smiled. "She might have, but she seems to understand me better than I understand her. I had been wondering where she's been going. It's good to see you, Tavi." Silently, he added, *I missed you. I love you.*

Tavi smiled slightly. "I missed you. I've been practicing with the *dolabra*. The guard think I'm insane."

Lorcan laughed. "And that's new?"

Tavi and the Emperor both started laughing. "I see why you like him," Lucanus said. He turned toward a table next to his chair, where an ornate casket rested. "Now, Lorcan, I have something for you."

Manius sat straight up. "You're not!"

Lucanus went still in the middle of reaching for the casket. He fixed Manius with a steely look. "You have an objection? After this young man single-handedly put down what may have been the beginnings of a slave revolt?"

"I…" Manius stammered, then fell silent. "As you wish, Your Majesty."

Lucanus nodded, his smile small and cold. "Yes, it is as I wish." He opened the casket and took out a small wooden sword. He turned back to Lorcan. "Do you know what this is?"

Lorcan looked at the thing in the Emperor's hands—it looked like a toy. "No, Your Majesty."

"This is called a *rudis*," Lucanus explained. "By all the usual customs, I should have bestowed this on you in the arena, after your fight. But I'm afraid I wasn't expecting to have a revolt yesterday morning, so I didn't have one with me. Poor planning on my part."

Lorcan licked his lips, feeling as if he was out of his depths. "I don't mind waiting a day."

"It should have been done in public, before all of Rome. However, I don't want to wait until your next fight, because I'd hate to have it prepared, and then have you lose, or be gravely injured." The Emperor arched a brow. "Come here, young Prince Lorcan, and take this from my hand."

Lorcan rose, crossing to stand in front of Lucanus. He went to one knee and held his hands up as a supplicant. "Thank you, your Majesty, for your gift," he said as Lucanus laid the sword across his palms.

Lucanus smiled. "You have no idea what this is, what I've just given you. Manius has told you nothing."

Lorcan didn't look at Manius, although he was very much aware of the man behind him. "I don't know, your Majesty."

"The *rudis* is given to a gladiator who has proven himself worthy of it." Lucanus reached out and rested his hand on Lorcan's shoulder. "It grants him his freedom."

Lorcan's jaw dropped, and he stared at the old man in shock, his hands closing around the wooden blade that was suddenly more precious than gold. "Freedom?"

"And I will make sure that you are returned home, as soon as possible." Lucanus patted Lorcan's shoulder. "You and your bride."

"Bride?" Tavi gasped.

"To be. Bride-to-be," Lorcan said softly. "And… as soon as possible?" He shook his head. Then he frowned. "Tavi… what was that word? You told me once, for a free man who fought as a gladiator? You told me your father fought as one."

Tavi frowned. "You mean *auctoratus*?"

"Yes, that's it." Lorcan looked down at the *rudis*. "May I stay on, Manius? As an *auctoratus*? Until the spring and my year with you is up?"

Lucanus frowned and sat back. "I would have thought you would return home as soon as you could. You said your cousin is a threat to your family and to your king."

"And I can't challenge him. Not yet. If I challenge him now, I will lose. I am not a good enough fighter to beat him. I know that now. I promised Manius a year," Lorcan said. "And in return, he promised that he would make certain that I was good enough to take back what is mine. If that bargain is still on the table, Manius?" He looked back, to see Manius was staring at him in stunned silence.

"You could always stay here," Tavi offered. "And train with one of the cohorts."

"Yes," Manius croaked, speaking over Tavi. He cleared his throat. "Yes, I will honor that bargain. Lorcan, *why*? You know I was not going to free you. Why do you stay?"

Lorcan got to his feet and turned to face Manius. "You've taught me so much since I came here. I am better than I was. I know that. And I know I have so much more to learn. I want to learn from you, from Yaroah and Nona and Ennius. I will fight for you, for the *ludus*. I'll make us both rich, just as we said. And in the spring, I will take Livia and go home."

Manius rose. He crossed to stand in front of Lorcan, his face unreadable. Without warning, he smiled. "My boy. I underestimated you completely. Yes, I will accept this. And yes, I accept your proposal to my daughter. We'll arrange it, as soon as you like. You won't be an *auctoratus*, though. That's only for freeborn citizens. You're a *rudiarius*. A freed gladiator."

"Does it matter?" Lorcan asked.

Manius grinned. "No. Not in the slightest. I accept."

"Good. Very good!" Lucanus said, clapping his hands. The sound startled Corvina, who launched herself from the arm of the chair and perched on a marble statue. She scolded, and Lucanus laughed. "I apologize, Lady!" he said. "Lorcan, you should collect her."

Lorcan smiled and went to the statue, coaxing the raven down to his wrist and holding her close to his chest. When he turned back, Tavi was standing just out of arms reach, looking upset.

"Could we talk?" he asked, his voice low. "Alone?"

Chapter Fourteen

"Of course," Lorcan answered, wondering what had upset Tavi. He'd find out soon enough, he knew. Tavi nodded and turned to his grandfather.

"Sir, may I take Lorcan and show him the palace? We have things to discuss."

"Of course," Lucanus answered. He smiled. "Manius and I have a lot of catching up to do. And I'm certain that Gaius and Decus will both be eager to see you as well, Manius." He turned toward Lorcan. "I'm very pleased to have met you, Prince Lorcan."

Lorcan bowed. "And I am honored to have met you, sir," he answered. Then he followed Tavi out of the room.

They walked in silence for a while through corridors of white marble, lined with statues the likes of which Lorcan had never seen before. He was torn between wanting to stop and stare, and needing to know what was wrong. What had upset Tavi? He had an idea that it might have something to do with the announcement of his marriage to Livia. But surely he'd explained about his bloodline, and finding his mate? He couldn't remember. Not that it mattered. Tavi was as much his mate as Livia was.

They stopped near an indoor pool that was open to the sky. It wasn't a bathing pool like at the ludus. This one was only a few feet deep, and the bottom was made up of decorative tiles. Tavi stared at them for a moment, then glanced at Lorcan.

"You're marrying her?" he asked, his voice quiet. "Why? Is she pregnant?"

"What?" Lorcan gasped. "No. At least, not that I know of. She hasn't been in my bed since we last saw you, anyway. Manius took his annoyance at you and your father out on me."

"He what?" Tavi looked stunned. "Lorcan, I'm sorry! I never meant—"

157

"I know. If you'd known that he'd react the way he did, you'd never have done it," Lorcan said. "It's no matter. Is that what's bothering you? That I'm marrying Livia? Tavi, it won't change what I feel for you. I still want you. I want you both."

"But you can't have us both," Tavi insisted. Voices echoed from a corridor, and Tavi looked up. "We can't talk here. Come with me." He led Lorcan down another corridor, past more statues, past guards and slaves, and into a courtyard. There, Lorcan pulled him to a stop, staring in wonder.

The courtyard was full of birds, the like of which Lorcan had never seen before. They were majestic beasts with long necks, and the longest tail feathers he'd ever seen. Some of them were a glossy blue, with tails of brown, blue and green. The others were pure white, the same color of Lorcan's own feathers. As he watched, one of them fanned its tail up and out, forming a backdrop of iridescent blues and greens. "Tavi? What are they?" he asked.

Tavi followed his gaze and smiled. "Oh. My grandfather's pets. They're Persian birds, and sacred to Juno. The first of them were given to him as tribute when he was my age. He's kept them ever since. He likes birds."

"That explains why he took to Corvina so quickly. These, though... they're beautiful." Lorcan stepped down into the courtyard. "Are they different colors for male and female? Like ducks?"

"Careful," Tavi warned. "They're vicious little beasts. I've still got scars on my arms from where they attacked me when I was younger. And no. These are all male. The females are smaller, and brown. Over there, by the wall. See them?"

Lorcan looked and saw the smaller birds. "But... the white ones—"

"Sometimes, they're born that way," Tavi said with a shrug. "The flock doesn't seem to care."

"Because they're captive?" Lorcan asked.

"Because it's normal," Tavi answered. "The same way I have brown hair and you have—" He stopped, and his eyes widened. "White hair. You have white hair and blue eyes. Lorcan, I know that you're the Raven Prince of Hibernia. Your uncles told me what that means, and that you're a *semideus*. The stories say you can actually become a raven. Your uncle Petran's hair is as dark as Corvina's feathers. Does that mean you're a white raven, like the white Persians?"

Lorcan nodded. "And I'm the only one. The only one that I know of. But if some of these can be white, that means that there can be other white ravens, too. Real ones, not just the statue and the stories about Apollo's white raven."

Tavi grinned. "It's actually not that uncommon. I've seen white ravens before."

Lorcan gaped at him. "What?"

"In Britannia. I went out with surveyors last year. My father is considering defensive bulwarks in the north, to guard against the Picts, and we were looking for sites." He cocked his head to the side. "Three. Maybe four of them. You might be able to tell if I saw the same one twice. When we go to Britannia, if we have time, I'll take you north and show you." He nodded at the raven on Lorcan's shoulder. "Maybe you can find a friend for Corvina."

Lorcan raised his hand and ran a finger over Corvina's breast feathers. "You make her sound like a pet. She isn't."

"No?"

"She's a friend. Tavi, you wanted to talk to me. And you were upset about Livia. Why?"

Tavi frowned. "Oh. Yes. Not here, though. This is just a shortcut. Come on." They walked across the courtyard and into another corridor, passing through more marble halls until they reached a door that Tavi opened. "In here."

Lorcan entered the room, walking to the center of what appeared to be a nicely appointed living area. There was a rack of scrolls on one wall, next to a table piled with more scrolls, and what looked like inkpots and pens. Through an inner door, Lorcan saw a wide bed. Corvina croaked softly and launched herself from Lorcan's shoulder, flying out through an open door into what looked like a small garden.

"Where are we?" he asked, turning to see that Tavi had come up behind him.

"My rooms," Tavi answered. He leaned down and kissed Lorcan, then pulled him close. It was awkward—Tavi seemed to only be able to use his right arm, but Lorcan closed his eyes and groaned, wrapping his arms around Tavi. The taste that he'd had in the baths that one time hadn't been enough. He'd wanted this for months. Forever, it felt like. He wanted Tavi the same way he wanted Livia, and just as much. He tugged on the layers of wool that enveloped Tavi's long body.

"Off," he mumbled against Tavi's mouth. "This needs to come off. I want to see you."

Tavi laughed. He stepped back and lowered his left arm, shrugging his shoulder at the same time. The toga slipped from his shoulder and fell in soft folds around him, landing with a *flump* on the floor. Underneath, Tavi wore a simple tunic. He pulled the tunic off over his head, then smiled at Lorcan.

"Your turn," he said. "I want to see you."

Lorcan had his tunic off before Tavi finished speaking and was back in Tavi's arms.

"I've wanted you since the first time I saw you on the sands," Tavi whispered in his ear. Then he laughed. "Togas are good for something, you know. I was hard enough that my teeth hurt after watching you fight that first time."

"I had no idea!" Lorcan answered with a laugh. He ran his hands down Tavi's sides. "You said you wanted to bend me over a bench and make me scream. Do you still?"

Tavi groaned. "You have no idea how many nights I've put myself to sleep dreaming of just that!" He looked around. "But the screaming part… that will draw a crowd."

"So?" Lorcan tugged Tavi toward the bed. "If you want, you can gag me. Livia did."

"What?" Tavi pulled Lorcan to a stop. "Tell me!"

"Two nights ago. She snuck into my cell, and she gagged me so that no one would know she was there."

Tavi stared for a moment, then burst into giggles. "That's… that's just so very much something I'd expect her to do!"

Lorcan smiled. "We'll never be bored, the three of us."

"Three?" Tavi repeated. He stepped back and licked his lips. "Lorcan, why?"

"Why? Why what?" Lorcan asked. He looked around, then held his hand out to Tavi. "Come sit. We need to talk more than we need to fuck." He led Tavi into the bedroom and sat down on the bed. Tavi perched on the bed across from him, his hands folded in his lap.

"Why are you going back?" Tavi asked. "To the *ludus*. You know Manius never intended to free you."

"I know."

"Then why?"

"What I told your grandfather," Lorcan answered. "I'm going to have a fight ahead of me when I get back to Eire. My cousin did this to me so he could take my place. I need to be able to beat him, once and for all. Which means that I need to keep to Manius' original plan for me. I need to train, and I need to win in the arena."

Tavi nodded slowly. "I thought—" He paused, then sighed. "I thought you'd live here, with me."

"You never asked me."

"When did I have the chance?" Tavi pointed out. "I was hoping you would, actually. You should. It fits your status more than living in the *ludus*. You're a prince. You should be treated like one."

"But I still need to train," Lorcan replied. "And if I don't keep busy until my year is over, I'm likely to go insane."

"I can keep you busy in the palace," Tavi said. When Lorcan laughed, Tavi's dark skin went darker. "Not like that! Well… sometimes like that."

Lorcan leaned closer, resting his hand on Tavi's leg. "Tavi, what about Livia?"

"What about Livia?" Tavi repeated.

"It's easier for you to come to us, than her to come here," Lorcan answered. He studied Tavi for a moment, then murmured, "Oh. You… you expected me to live here and give her up?"

"I thought—"

"No, Tavi," Lorcan interrupted. "I love you, but I love her, too." He looked down. "My kind. What do you know about us? About how we choose our mates?"

Tavi frowned. "That you know them… oh. It's Livia?"

Lorcan nodded. "She's my mate. I knew that from the first. But… Tavi, I don't understand it, but I knew it from the first time I saw you, too. You're mine, too. I don't understand how, but you are my mate, as much as she is. I love you both, and I'm not choosing between you. I know she loves you. She told me she did, and that the only reason you were parted was that you went to Alba. Britannia. Is that true?"

"Yes, but—"

"So why do you want me to choose between my mates?" Lorcan asked. "I love you both. She loves us both. And you?"

"I want you for myself!" Tavi blurted. "I want you to come back to Britannia with me, and I want to go to Hibernia with you. And until then, I want you here. By my side. For myself."

"And what I want doesn't matter? What she wants?" Lorcan said. "Because we discussed it. And we both want you."

"The stories say you only mate once," Tavi snapped. "You can't have both of us, no matter what you think. It's not in your nature."

"And you know more about being one of the Morrigan's blood than I do?" Lorcan retorted. "I'll tell you this, Tavi. The white raven in the Temple and I have something in common—we're neither of us real ravens. I'm the white freak of Eire. I have to ride a horse because I can't fly. I've always been more man than raven, so maybe I can't do mates the right way, either. Because what I feel for you is the same as what I feel for her. I love you both. I need you both. I can't explain it, and I'm not choosing one of you over the other." He got up and walked out into the front room, picking up his tunic. He pulled it on, then turned to look at Tavi, standing naked in the doorway. "And I'm finished with letting other people decide for me. Your grandfather said it—I'm a free man now. It's time I started acting like it." He swallowed. "I do love you, Tavi. We both do. I love you, and I need you, as much as I love and need her. And if you want to come with us to Eire, then we'll welcome you. And we'll be happy, all three of us. But I'm not giving up a third of me so you can have what's left."

"But—" Tavi looked lost. Then he turned and walked back into the bedroom. He closed the door behind him. Lorcan started to follow him, then stopped. He sighed and turned, leaving the room and slowly retracing his steps, going back the way they'd come until he was once more in the room where Emperor Lucanus was chatting with Manius and two men who Lorcan assumed were Gaius and Decus. The conversation died as Lorcan came back in. The old man looked at him and frowned.

"Lorcan?" he said gently. "There's a cloud over you. What's my grandson done?"

Lorcan considered the words, then answered in careful Latin. "We've had a… a difference of opinion. He wants what he wants. And I… don't want what he wants."

"Ah. Perhaps an agreement will come, then." Lucanus smiled. "Shall I talk to him?"

"Thank you, but I think he needs to decide on his own," Lorcan answered. "I don't want him to think that I asked you to change his mind or his heart."

Lucanus nodded. "A wise choice, then. And you're returning to the *ludus*?"

"Yes, sir."

"Then I wish you well, Prince Lorcan. I will, I hope, see you before you leave for your home. And before you leave, I shall order the temples to make sacrifices to Mars and to Victoria, that they will aid you in your quest to overthrow the usurper and regain what is yours."

Lorcan smiled and bowed deeply. "Your Majesty, I would be honored to see you again. Thank you, for everything."

* * *

True to his word, Manius led Lorcan back to the *ludus* through the streets of Rome. Halfway back to the *ludus*, Lorcan heard cawing overhead, and held his free arm out so that Corvina could alight on his wrist. She scolded him.

"Don't take that tone with me," he said softly in Gaeilge. "I'm not going to let him dictate my heart."

"What did happen between you?" Manius asked in the same tongue. Lorcan started, then silently cursed himself. He'd forgotten that Manius spoke Gaeilge.

"Just what I said to the Emperor. Tavi wants what he wants, and he doesn't seem to care that it isn't what I want." Lorcan hesitated, then shifted the precious casket under his arm and added, "I'm not a slave anymore. I don't have to jump when someone orders me to do so."

Manius snorted. "You didn't jump as a slave even when I *did* order you."

Lorcan laughed. "Well, perhaps not. Manius, when do I start training as a two-handed fighter?"

"As a *dimachaeri?* Tomorrow, if you want. And you'll be learning from me—I was once a *dimachaeri.*"

Lorcan looked at him and smiled. "I didn't know that. I look forward to learning from you."

"I look forward to teaching you. You learn very quickly." Manius stopped and stepped out of the flow of traffic. "Now, you want to marry my daughter?"

Lorcan nodded. "Yes, sir. I'm not sure of the procedure here—"

"How would you marry at home in Hibernia?" Manius asked.

Lorcan thought of his cloak, and the way taking a mate usually worked for his family. That wasn't an option. Not now. Idly, he wondered what would happen when he finally could give Livia her own cloak of feathers. Would it be white, like his? Or would her feathers be black, like all the other ravens. He didn't know. He also didn't care. It didn't matter right now.

"I'll owe you a bride-price," he said. "Ah… the full purses of my next two fights?"

"And then I'd have to support you that long?" Manius replied with a laugh. "No, let's say half the purse of your next four fights instead. You need to start building your savings. And, since you're now a free man, I should be charging you for your lessons."

"You'd do that?" Lorcan gaped at him, and Manius burst out laughing.

"No," he wheezed. "No, I wouldn't. You're too profitable. And given how much you made for me yesterday, just in the wagers I laid? I would be fine with half the purse of a single fight. We'll decide on what's fair, but I think that might be the bride-price I set."

Lorcan licked his lips and considered what little he knew about Roman money. "Are you selling Livia short?" he asked. "Or did I make that much for you?"

"I won back twice your purchase price," Manius admitted. He sounded smug. "Now, we'll have to decide how this arrangement will work. None of the other *autocrati* I've trained lived in the *ludus*. You'll be living under my roof as a student." He frowned. "And as my daughter's husband. We'll have to discuss this."

"All three of us, please. Livia knows more about your money than I do," Lorcan said. "Are records kept in the temples here? Do your priests do that? At home, records are kept by druids and *brehons*. Agreements are witnessed before the gods. Is that how business is done here?"

"You want a contract?" Manius asked.

"You don't?" Lorcan asked in reply, confused.

"It's a simple agreement… but if a contract is what you're used to, then we'll have a contract drawn up." Manius gestured. "That way."

"I remember. This is the same street that goes to the Temple of Apollo." Lorcan looked around. "What is winter like here, Manius?"

"Rain, and lots of it. The Tiber floods, some years," Manius answered. "Cold, but possibly not what you're used to."

"Snow?"

"Not in my lifetime, no," Manius said.

Lorcan blinked. "No snow? Then how do you know it's winter?"

Manius laughed. "You'll know. When you can't sleep for the rain pounding on the roof, when your armor rusts the minute you finish cleaning it, and when the arena goes squish when you walk across the sands? That's winter."

Lorcan coughed. "That sounds horrible."

"It doesn't sound any worse than the stories I've heard about snow," Manius said. "Let's go tell Livia she's getting married." He walked up the to the *ludus* door and pounded on it three times. He waited, then did it again. A few minutes later, they heard Livia's voice through the door.

"State your business!"

"It's me!" Manius called back. Lorcan heard the bolts shoot back, and the door opened. They entered the atrium, and Livia closed the door behind them, locking it once more. Lorcan turned to face her, only to see the worry in her eyes.

"What's wrong?" he asked.

"I wasn't sure you were coming back," she admitted. She folded her hands together in front of her. "Tell me everything?"

Lorcan glanced at Manius and smiled. "Would you hold this for me?" he asked, holding the casket out to Manius. Once his hands were free, he shooed Corvina from his shoulder. Then he went to Livia, met her eyes, and cupped her face in his hands so that he could kiss her deeply. She squeaked in surprise as his lips met hers, only to melt against him, her arms slipping around his waist. When they finally parted, she smiled up at him.

"I like the way you say hello," she murmured.

"No, that was how I say I love you," he answered. "And how I say will you marry me?"

Her jaw dropped. "Marry? Lorcan!"

Lorcan stepped back and held his hands out for the casket. Manius handed it to him, and he held it out to Livia. "Open it."

Livia's eyes widened, and she shook her head. "Oh, no. No, Lorcan. It isn't—" She opened the casket and gave a little squeal of joy. "It is! A *rudis*!" She looked up at him. "Does that mean you're leaving? We're leaving?"

"Not until spring," Lorcan said. "I have too much to learn. I'll be staying on as a *rudiarius*." He looked down at his hands. "Do *rudiarii* get tattoos for their wins?"

"No," Livia answered. "Only slaves are tattooed."

"Oh." Lorcan was surprised to find himself disappointed. "Can I have them anyway? They're not a mark of shame at home."

"They're not a mark of shame here," Manius said, baring his own tattoos. "They're a mark of identification. And I don't see why not. Livia, if he wants them."

"Then I owe you for yesterday's win," Livia said. She took the casket, put it on a bench, then threw her arms around Lorcan's neck. "I'm so happy for you!"

Lorcan wrapped his arms around her and buried his face in her neck. Softly, he whispered, "I saw Tavi." She stiffened slightly. "I'll tell you later, when we're alone. He's upset with me."

She nodded, her hair brushing his ear. She kissed his cheek, then stepped back. "We need to tell the others. And a celebration."

"Arrange it," Manius said. "And start planning for the wedding feast, too. Tell the slaves to let the others out of their cells. Lorcan, come with me. We need to get you a second sword if you're going to fight as a *dimachaeri.*

Lorcan followed Manius to the armory, where Manius stood back and let Lorcan enter. Lorcan stopped just inside the door.

"If my first sword is my *spatha*, what should I be looking for in a second sword?" he asked. "The same? A *gladius*?"

"For most *dimachaerus,* neither," Manius answered. He moved past Lorcan and took a pair of curved swords from the wall. "These are the weapons of a *dimachaeri.* These are *siccae*. And as it happens, these were mine.*"

Lorcan stopped in the act of reaching for one. "Your swords?"

"Yes. You can use them until we get a set made that is balanced for your hand. Until we do, you'll continue to fight as a *murmillo* in the arena, and you'll practice here with a pair of *spathae*. I want you to be fast with a heavy sword, so you'll be faster with these. The secret of the *dimachaerus* is in their speed."

Lorcan nodded. "I understand. Are there any currently fighting? Anyone I can see how they look?"

"You want to observe?" Manius considered it, then nodded. "I'll look into it. I don't know that there are any other gladiators fighting this way. It's a fading form—most *lanistae* consider it to be a bit insidious. It's lighter and faster, so it's easier for a good fighter to get behind and through their opponent's armor." He dodged at Lorcan, moving much faster than Lorcan would have expected, and the curved blade he held snaked around Lorcan's shoulder. Lorcan felt the tap of the blade on his shoulder blade, and stared at Manius in disbelief.

"You see?" Manius said as he straightened. "Even as old as I am now, it's still a faster form. You'll be faster still. Now, we'll have to change your armor, and your helmet. You won't have a shield, obviously. You'll have much lighter armor."

"And no helmet?" Lorcan asked hopefully.

"And a smaller, open-faced helmet."

"I like that," Lorcan said with a grin.

Manius looked thoughtful. "We have 15 days before the *Ludi Romani*, which is your next fight. The Emperor's birthday games are 30 days after that. If we work hard, you can be ready to fight as a *dimachaeri* by then." He put the *siccae* back on their pegs. "If you're willing to do the work?"

Lorcan looked at the blades. He'd never seen anything like them before, and he was certain that this was the edge he would need against his cousin. "I'll do the work."

"Then we'll start tomorrow." Manius looked at the blades on their pegs. "I'll commission a new set for you for the games. We'll have to swear the smith to silence though. I want no one knowing how you'll fight until after the birthday games. We'll plan it, you, me and Yaroah. But I think I want to incorporate that little stunt you pulled yesterday, with throwing your helmet. That was showy. Makes for a good spectacle."

"If you don't want anyone to know, then perhaps you shouldn't commission the swords until after?" Lorcan suggested. He stepped out of the armory and walked next to Manius back toward the atrium. "If we want no one to know, then we shouldn't tell anyone, and we should tell Nona not to gossip."

Manius nodded. "A good point. We'll discuss keeping secrets at the feast. As for the swords, yes, you're right. I'll commission them once you've debuted as a *dimachaeri*. Assuming the other *lanistae* don't have my head for it." He snorted. "They won't know what to do with you, Lorcan."

"There they are!" Lorcan heard Nona's voice ringing down the corridor. "Come on, tell us! Livia won't tell us anything! Why did the Emperor want to see you?"

Lorcan glanced at Manius, who nodded. "Go and tell your brothers,"

Manius said. "Just… don't expect a hearty welcome to the news from Yaroah."

Lorcan hesitated. "Let him buy his freedom," he said quietly. "Let him go home."

"This is not a discussion I will have with you," Manius answered, equally quietly. "Do not mention it in my presence again."

Lorcan looked at him, saw the chill in Manius' eyes, and nodded. "Yes, sir."

"Good. Now, go and show them."

Lorcan went ahead into the atrium, to where the other gladiators were waiting with Livia. She nodded toward the bench, where a cloth had been thrown over the casket. Corvina sat on top of the cloth, clearly guarding its secrets. Lorcan smiled as he went to her, and she hopped to the side so that he could pick up the casket. He turned, and Ennius crowed with elation.

"I told you!" He reached out and smacked Nona's shoulder. "You owe me 10 *denarii*."

"He hasn't shown it yet," Nona protested. "Come on, Lorcan. Is it really—?"

Lorcan opened the casket, revealing the wooden *rudis*. Nona let out a long breath. "Oh. That's beautiful." He looked up at Lorcan. "So when do you leave?"

"Spring," Lorcan answered. "I'm staying to finish my training. I can't defeat Cormac. Not yet. By spring, I'll know enough." He glanced over at Livia, then closed the casket and tucked it under his arm. He held his hand out to her and drew her to his side. "And until then… my brothers, will you stand with me when I marry?"

For a moment, the only sound came from the street outside. Then Yaroah burst out laughing. "You—! I swear, by all the gods of my homeland, you would fall into a pile of shit and come up carrying gold!"

The peal of laughter did much to calm Lorcan's mind. He'd been worried that Yaroah would resent his good fortune. But the man seemed to be honestly pleased with it.

"When will the wedding be?" Nona asked.

Lorcan looked at Livia. "I don't know. I don't know the traditions here."

"We'll need to consult the augurs, pick an auspicious day," she said. "You will need to buy a ring."

"A ring?" Lorcan looked around. "With what money?"

"Your purse from yesterday," Nona answered. "How much of that did he get, Manius?"

"A third," Manius answered. "It was still a respectable amount."

Lorcan nodded. "All right. Tell me what I need to do, and when, and where I need to be. Someone will have to go with me to buy the ring, to tell me what I'm getting." He hugged Livia to his side. "Is there a ceremony? Do we need to consult priests?"

"With your status as a freed gladiator, you can't enter into a full marriage with a citizen of Rome," Manius said. "However, there's another way. An agreement purely between you, me, and Livia. It says that if you live together as man and wife for a year, then you are married."

"So, we say we're married, and we're married?" Lorcan asked. "That sounds simple."

"There's a contract involved. We'll have that drawn up, and sign it on the appointed day," Manius said. "It will be witnessed by priests, and we'll have the feast on that day. For now, we'll feast your good fortune, Lorcan. And... I think you have things to discuss with your bride?"

Lorcan nodded. "Thank you, Manius." He looked at Livia, who nodded and took his hand, leading him out of the atrium.

"Father," she called over her shoulder. "Lorcan is moving into the room next to mine."

"Oh, be honest about it, Livia. I know full well he's moving into your room," Manius called back. Livia giggled and squeezed Lorcan's hand.

Hand in hand, they walked to Livia's garden. She stopped and turned to Lorcan. "Here, or in the workroom?"

"We're private enough here," Lorcan said. He led Livia to a bench and sat down with her. "I saw Tavi. I think he and his father had something to do with the *rudis*, although I'm not sure. The Emperor said it was because of my stopping Gnaeus. Putting down a slave revolt, he called it. Can one person be a revolt?"

"I'm not sure about him being a revolt, but he was certainly revolting. Go on."

Lorcan glared at her for a moment, making her laugh. Then he continued. "The Emperor asked me what my plans were now that I'm free. I told him I wanted to stay and keep training. And I told him I wanted to take a wife. That's you, Wife. In case you'd missed it."

"I didn't think it was Tavi," Livia answered. "He'd make an awful wife."

Lorcan sighed. "I think he thought otherwise. He was expecting me to leave the *ludus* and move into the palace with him. He had everything planned—we'd live there, and then go to Alba before he came with me to Eire. He wanted me all to himself, and when I told him that I wasn't giving you up, he got upset." Lorcan looked down at his sandals. "I told him the truth. That I love him and want him as much as I love and want you. And that we both love him, and there's room for him with us." He looked at Livia, only to see her nodding.

"There is. But he didn't want that, did he?"

"No. He wanted me to leave you behind. And I told him I wouldn't do that. I need you both. And he got mad and closed the door on me. So I left." Lorcan sat up. "I realized something today, Livia."

"What?"

"That I've lived my entire life with other people making my decisions for me. I've never had any real responsibilities, any real authority of my own. I've never stood on my own feet as a man before today." I've always been under my father's wing. He looked at her and smiled. "I'm a free man now. And no one will ever decide what my life will be again. That's for me to do."

"So long as you remember to ask for advice," Livia said.

"Of course," Lorcan agreed. "Advice, yes. But the decision is mine. And right now? There's nothing I can do about Tavi. He's made his decision. If he changes his mind before spring, then we'll see where we are."

Livia nodded and leaned into his side, resting her head on his shoulder. "I love you, Lorcan. My husband."

Lorcan smiled and kissed the top of her head.

Chapter Fifteen

Lorcan was flying, soaring in a way that he never had before, over frost-kissed hills that he knew so well he could walk them blindfolded. Home. He was home. He crowed his delight to the skies and wheeled on the wind, taking flight toward home. But there was smoke rising over Dun Morrigan, and the gates hung crooked on their hinges. Lorcan circled, calling, looking for any of his family. Then he angled down, finally coming to rest on the roof of his father's hall. Something was definitely not right here—the urla was ragged and torn underneath the last vestiges of dirty snow. Some of the houses were scorched and falling down. And the smell of the place! His mother would never have allowed this! But where was she? Where was his father? He called again, and heard voices. Unfamiliar voices, in accents that he didn't recognize. Wary, Lorcan hopped to the smoke hole and peered down into the hall.

The hall was filled with men. All of them unfamiliar, all of them armed. They laughed and shouted, throwing dice and drinking from the silver goblets that his uncle Niall had made, ones that were once fine but were now tarnished and dented. A fight broke out in the center, and the spectators shouted encouragement as the two men wrestled and swore at each other.

Then Lorcan heard a voice that he did know, and he pulled back so that he wouldn't be seen as Cormac strode into view. He cursed and kicked the wrestlers, then crossed to the seat at the front of the hall. Diarmuid's seat. There was a dirty fur thrown over it, which didn't seem to bother Cormac as he slumped down and called for wine. Lorcan shifted around the smoke hole so that he could see better, and he saw two things that horrified him.

The woman bringing Cormac his wine was his sister, Niamh. Her gown was torn and stained, her cloak was gone, and her ankles were chained. The chains clattered, catching on the dirty rushes that littered

171

the floor as Niamh walked past a double row of small cages. She lingered next to one for a moment, looking sadly at the raven imprisoned inside...

Lorcan woke with a jerk, breathing heavily and trying not to scream. The *ludus* was quiet, the only sound was the rain drumming on the tile roof. Livia was asleep next to him, her head pillowed on his shoulder, her breathing soft and regular. Lorcan closed his eyes and tried to slow his breathing. The same dream. Was this his fourth time, or the fifth? Did it matter?

Was he having true dreams? Was this what was happening in Eire?

He heard Livia's breath catch, then she stirred. "Hmm?" Her voice was sleepy and thick. "Lorcan? Another dream?"

"Yes," he answered. "Go back to sleep, love."

"You know I can't sleep if you're upset." She sat up and pushed her hair out of her face. "Tell me?"

"The same dream," Lorcan answered. "Flying over Dun Morrigan, looking in through the smoke hole. Cages." He turned, sitting on the edge of the bed. "Livia, I'm not dreaming. I'm having visions. This is what is happening at home. I... am I too late?"

"No, love," Livia answered, coming to kneel behind him. "Visions don't work like that. They're a warning of what is to come."

"Are you sure?" Lorcan asked, looking over his shoulder.

"In your dream, what time of year was it?" she asked in reply. Lorcan frowned, thinking.

"I... spring. But that could have been last spring, after I was taken." He thought harder. "No... no, that's not right. It was early spring. Maybe late winter. There was still frost on the hills. Still snow on the *urla*. This is what's going to happen."

"And we can't stop it," Livia said gently. "Not from here. It's not safe to travel so far in the winter."

Lorcan took a long breath. "I know. I just—"

"You're not allowed to worry yourself, Lorcan," Livia interrupted. "Not today. You have to fight today."

Lorcan looked back over his shoulder at her. "I'm not worried about *that*," he told her. In truth, he wasn't. He'd been working with Manius since the day after he'd been granted his freedom, intensive training that revealed that Manius was still a frighteningly good fighter. At first, their practicing had consisted of Manius putting Lorcan on his ass, but Lorcan had quickly grown tired of that. He'd pushed, and he'd learned, and

172

Manius had finally pronounced him ready for the spectacle in the Emperor's birthday games.

Today.

"Lay down," Livia urged, tugging on his arm. "It's hours yet before you have to be awake."

"I don't think I'll sleep again tonight, love," Lorcan said. But he laid down, and Livia snuggled up against his side.

"I could help you to sleep," she purred. Lorcan smiled into the darkness.

"If you did it as well as you usually do, I'll sleep through the games," he said. She laughed and tickled his ribs. He caught her hand and kissed her fingers, then pressed her open palm to his chest. "Today the games, and tomorrow the wedding."

"Does that make you nervous?" she asked. "The wedding?"

Lorcan frowned. "Should it? Are you nervous?"

"Maybe I will be tonight, but only because you won't be here. You'll be on the other side of the *ludus*, and I don't know if I can sleep without you here anymore!"

Lorcan chuckled. Apparently, part of the wedding ceremony required the bride to travel to her future husband's home. But since Lorcan didn't have a home that they could easily get to, they'd compromised—he would sleep tonight on the other side of the house, and the bridal procession would be through the atrium to "his" side of the *ludus*.

"I can't wait until I can take you home in truth," he said. "My parents will adore you. And there's so much I want to share with you."

"And we'll fly?" Livia asked. Lorcan patted her hand.

"We'll touch the stars, my love," Lorcan murmured. He rolled onto his side to face her, pulling her against him. "Even if you do think I'm making that part up."

She groaned. "You knew that?"

"I figured it out, yes. I'll prove you wrong, once we get my cloak back." Lorcan ran his hand down her back. "Do you not want to fly?"

She hesitated, and Lorcan felt her shiver. "I'm not very happy about high places," she finally admitted.

"Ah," Lorcan breathed. He kissed her gently. "Then we'll start slowly. My uncle Turlach didn't like heights, either. Or so I'm told."

Livia pressed up against him, her head tucked underneath his chin. "Be careful today, Lorcan," she whispered against his chest.

"I will be. And Yaroah will watch my back." He closed his eyes, holding her and listening to her breathing growing softer, deeper. She grew heavier in his arms, and he let her warmth and the soft rhythm of her breathing lull him into a dreamless sleep. He woke again when the cock crowed outside the window, only to find himself alone in the bed.

"Livia?" he called. There was no answer, so he got up and pulled his tunic on over his head before going out into the workroom. She wasn't there, either. Puzzled, Lorcan walked out into the colonnade, and found Livia standing in the garden, soaked to the skin by the rain.

"What are you doing?" he called. She turned and smiled, her face flushing red.

"It's silly," she answered. "It's something my mother taught me when I was small. If you have worries that are too big for you to bear, let the rain wash them away."

"I've never heard that before," Lorcan said, walking out into the rain. He tipped his head back, eyes closed, letting the cold water wash over his face. "Does it help?" he asked, shaking his head.

"I think so," Livia answered. "And I've never had the plants die."

"What?" Lorcan burst out laughing.

"If the rain is washing my problems away, then my problems are going into the plants, and into the ground. Sometimes, I've expected there to be big dead spots in the garden after I've done this."

Lorcan nodded. "That… makes sense. I wonder if the druids know?" He held his hand out. "We can ask them. Are you washed clean now?"

She smiled and took his hand, moving in close to his side. "I think so. It'll be miserable on the sands today. Will you be able to fight like this?"

"In this sort of rain?" Lorcan looked up again. "I think so. I've been training in rain like this for weeks." He tugged her hand. "Let's go dry off and get something to eat."

In the *triclinium*, they found the other gladiators, sitting and talking in low voices. Voices that cut off the moment Lorcan and Livia entered. Lorcan frowned as he and Livia took their places on their couch.

"What's wrong?" he asked. "You all have a storm cloud over you, and not just from the rain. What is it?"

The others looked at Nona, who couldn't seem to meet Lorcan's eyes. "I… found out about the spectacle today. It's all over the streets."

Lorcan frowned. "What about it?"

"What they have planned," Nona said. He shook his head. "What do you know about battles, about the history of Rome?"

"Nothing," Lorcan answered. He reached over and picked up a flat loaf, tearing it in half. He handed a piece to Livia and took a bite from the other piece.

"So if I say Horatius—"

"What?" Livia sounded shriller than Lorcan had ever heard her.

"What... no, that's a name. Who is Horatius?" Lorcan asked. He slowly sat up, setting aside his bread. "Yaroah, what are we doing?"

"In some spectacles, they fight famous battles all over again," Yaroah said. "Apparently, today they wish you to do the same."

"Me?" Lorcan frowned. "I thought we were fighting together?"

"We are," Yaroah answered. "And then you will fight again. Alone."

"It's not Manius' idea, either," Nona added. "He's furious. That's where he is, off trying to figure out who set this up and why."

Lorcan licked his lips and took a sip of water. "Tell me about this battle."

Nona looked around, saw the others looking at him. He nodded. "Right. You've been to the Palace. If you kept going in that direction, you'd see the Tiber River. There's a bridge there. The *Pons Sublicius*. It's a wooden bridge, not very big. When Rome was attacked, Horatius and two others set out to hold that bridge long enough for his men to tear the bridge down to the pilings. The other two fell back and ran. Horatius didn't. He held them back until the bridge fell, then he swam back across to safety. He single-handedly saved Rome."

Lorcan stared at him. "So this fight... I'm facing an *army*?"

"More like a *triarius*. But yes," Nona scowled. "Someone does not like you, Lorcan. And no one seems to know who. But all of Rome is talking about the fact that Corax is fighting the battle of Horatius at the bridge."

"How many men in a *triarius*?" Lorcan asked.

"Sixty," Ennius answered. "Sixty men who haven't already fought."

Lorcan frowned. He considered it, then looked up, curious. "And what are my odds?" Livia smacked him on the shoulder, and he winced. "What? Maybe you should go place a bet!"

"I wouldn't." Manius came in, looking fierce. "The fight may not happen."

"Did you learn anything?" Yaroah asked.

"That this fight was scheduled as a special request from the Palace,"

Manius answered. He crossed to his couch and sat down. "I haven't learned anything else. Lorcan, Livia, I'm going to ask this in all seriousness, and I want neither of you to take offense. But do you think that Tavi did this?"

"No," Lorcan and Livia answered simultaneously. Lorcan looked at her, and she nodded. He turned back to Manius and continued, "This isn't in him. He would take no pleasure over watching me be hurt, or killed." He frowned, looked at Livia again, then at the others. "Has word of the wedding reached the Palace? That it's tomorrow?"

"I believe so, yes," Manius answered.

"That Drucilla woman, then. Look to her."

Manius arched a brow. "Have you had other dealings with Drucilla, since that first time?"

"No. Julius told me after my last bout that he spoke to her husband, and that she's been denied access to the gladiator cells."

"Oh," Manius murmured. "I'd missed that. Yes, that might very well be it, if she thinks you asked him to keep her out. I don't know how she'd have done this, though. It's nothing that could happen quickly. The plans must have been laid weeks ago., and she'd have had to hide it. I'm trying to have the fight canceled, but with all of Rome talking about it—"

"Go place bets," Lorcan said. "Bet on me."

"Lorcan!"

"Are you insane?" Nona demanded. "You can't fight so many!"

"What will happen, if they cancel the fight?" Lorcan asked. "Especially if all of Rome is talking about it?"

He wasn't entirely sure himself, but from the horrified expressions on the others, it wouldn't be something wonderful. Manius turned pale. Then he nodded.

"I...see," he said slowly. "But this is suicide, Lorcan!"

"Unless..." Lorcan frowned, thinking fast. "You said that the battle was *three* men, Nona."

"It started with three. But two of them retreated, and left Horatius alone."

Lorcan nodded. "If we're recreating the fight, then shouldn't we recreate the actual fight? And start with three?"

"You have a plan, Lorcan?" Manius asked.

"I have an idea, if Ennius and Nona will help me," Lorcan answered. "Neither of you are fighting today, are you?"

"No," Ennius answered. "You want us to fight with you?"

"If you'd be willing," Lorcan said.

Manius cleared his throat. "Nona, Ennius? I won't force this on either of you."

"You don't have to," Nona said. "Yes. Ennius? Yes?"

"Of course, yes!"

Lorcan smiled. "I have no brothers in Eire. But I have three fine ones here in Rome, don't I?"

"Then why didn't you ask me?" Yaroah grumbled. Then he grinned. "Because I will have fought, too? And you wish two fresh fighters at your side?"

"That was my thinking, yes."

"I cannot argue with that," Yaroah said with a nod. "I don't like this, Lorcan."

"There isn't a single one of us who likes this," Nona said. "All right. Who's betting on us?"

Without warning, Livia burst into tears. "I can't believe you're going into this so calm!" she cried. "They're going to kill you all!"

Lorcan put his arms around her and held her as she cried. "No, love, no. We'll walk off the sands today, you'll see. I'll still be here tomorrow. And all the tomorrows after."

Manius still looked as though there were storm clouds behind his eyes. "I have one word of advice, Lorcan, and you won't like it."

Lorcan looked at him, frowned, and said, "I'm not going to her bed, Manius."

"It will placate her."

"It will make things worse. If it is her, then she's doing this because I refused her, and because I'm going to marry. She's thinking that if she can't have me, no woman will. If I give in to her today, then the next time she wants me in her bed, what will she do to get me? Who will she threaten then?"

Manius swore softly. "You're right. I'll do my best to have this fight changed. And after, I'll have words with Gaius about her." He sighed. "Livia, you'll stay with me today."

Livia raised her head, her face tear-streaked and red. "Yes, Father."

Lorcan touched her cheek and made her look at him. "Think of tomorrow, love," he said. "I'll come through this, and we'll have tomorrow." He kissed her gently. "Now go on. We have to get ready, and your father needs you."

She kissed him with more heat, then threw her arms around him. "Don't make me a widow before I'm a wife!" she whispered fiercely.

"I won't. I promise."

* * *

It seemed as if it was all too soon before they assembled in the atrium and Manius unlocked the door to the tunnel. Lorcan wasn't sure if it was distraction or deliberate, but none of the gladiators were chained before leaving the *ludus*, something that he'd come to expect. The air in the tunnel was thick and damp, and water dripped from the low ceiling. Lorcan shivered in the chill as they walked.

"You all right?" Ennius asked from behind him.

"Damp and cold." Lorcan said over his shoulder. "I'm not used to it anymore."

"This is what to expect for the next three months or so," Ennius said. "When it gets very bad, the tunnel floods."

"That only happened once. No, twice," Nona protested from in front of Lorcan.

"Still, it was slosh through cold water up to your knees to get to the arena," Ennius said.

"Then wet sandals the rest of the day," Yaroah added from the rear. "Terrible weather, Rome has. Lorcan, you say your home gets colder?"

"Colder than this? Yes."

"Forgive me if I say I've no desire to see your home."

Lorcan grinned and looked over his shoulder. "Maybe in summer, when it's all the colors of green that exist in the world."

"Perhaps. Someday."

Lorcan turned back to see that they'd reached the far end of the tunnel. The door was open, and Julius was waiting for them. He didn't look happy to see them.

"Tell me this isn't your doing?" he demanded as they came up out of the tunnel. "Manius, tell me?"

"None of mine," Manius answered. "It came from the Palace."

Julius rolled his eyes and groaned. "And there's no stopping it."

"Julius, what can you tell us?" Lorcan asked.

"There's half a *triarius* waiting for this. A mock-up of the *Pons Sublicius* ready to go out onto the sand. And it's the last fight."

"Half?" Nona repeated. "Only half?"

"You want a full one?" Julius asked, sounding both shocked and annoyed. "I'm sure it could be arranged."

"It was arranged," Nona answered. "There was supposed to be a full *triarius*. If there's only half…."

"Then someone is trying to help us," Lorcan finished. "Half. Thirty men. Nona, Ennius?"

"We can do some damage there," Ennius said. "It's better than we thought."

Lorcan nodded. "It is. Julius, do you know how the field will be arranged?"

Julius just looked at him. "Aren't you supposed to be married tomorrow?" he asked.

"Yes."

"And yet you're looking forward to dying today?" Julius shook his head. "Lorcan, my friend—"

"We'll be all right, Julius. But we need to plan," Lorcan interrupted. "Do you know how the field will be arranged?"

"I can find out. You and Yaroah are fighting midway through. So there won't be much recovery time." He gestured, and they followed him through the corridors to the cells. Braziers were set up every few feet, in a vain attempt to ward off the chill. "How will it be working?"

"If they want Horatius at the bridge, then they get Horatius," Nona answered. "And his two friends, whose names I can't remember right now. But there were three to start, so we're going to be out there, too."

Julius' eyes widened. "That… just might work. If you do it right. All right. I'll find out and get the information to you. I'll put you all in one cell, so that you can plan. Manius?"

"Anything you can do to help them is fine by me," Manius said. He held his hand out Livia. "Come with me, Livia."

Livia looked up at her father, then went to Lorcan's side and kissed him. "Be careful."

He smiled and brushed the hair back off her forehead. "I'll see you after the fights."

Once she and Manius were gone, Lorcan leaned back against the wall and let out a long breath. "Julius, tell me the truth—"

"You're insane, and you're going to die," Julius replied. Lorcan grinned.

"The first, I won't argue. The second? Don't count me as dead yet, my friend."

179

Julius just shook his head. "Come on. I'll bring a brazier for your cell, so that you don't get chilled and stiff. And I'll try to find out how the field will be set."

"What about the other fighters?" Ennius asked as they started walking. "The *triarius*? What's their feeling on this?"

Julius frowned. "I don't know. I haven't seen them. I'll see what I can learn." He opened a door and gestured for them to enter. "I'll get the brazier and have your armor and things brought in."

Lorcan moved into the cell, hearing the others behind him, hearing the door close. He turned and faced the men he considered his brothers. "So, have I fooled everyone so far?"

"Into thinking you're not terrified?" Nona asked. "I think so."

Lorcan grinned. "Maybe if I keep it up, I can convince myself. This is… awfully elaborate revenge for spurning her."

"Maybe it's not her?" Yaroah suggested. "Maybe it's her husband?"

Ennius coughed. "That's much more likely, you know."

"We have an advantage, you know," Nona said, his voice barely over a whisper. "A big one. Lorcan, you have to go out to your fight with Yaroah as a *murmillo*."

Lorcan frowned. "I don't have that armor. Or my shield. I don't think."

Nona went to the door and shouted, "Julius!"

A few minutes later, Julius came in, carrying a brazier tucked under one arm, and a bucket of coals. "What is it?"

"We need Manius. Can you send someone for him?"

Julius looked alarmed. "Is everything all right?"

Nona smiled. "Better than all right. But we need him now."

"I'll send for him." Julius set the brazier down, tipped the coals into it, then left, locking the door behind him. Lorcan paced the width of the cell, counting his steps. Eight steps. Eight more steps, going back the other way. He rubbed his hands, trying to plan. Defending a bridge. Three men against 30. If they could form a funnel… He gasped as he walked into someone. Someone who had apparently stepped right in front of him.

"Lorcan, you're going to wear yourself out," Ennius said gently. "Sit."

"I'm thinking. Planning," Lorcan said. He stepped around Ennius and kept pacing. "Tactics."

"You don't have enough information to plan a battle," Nona said. "Ennius is right. Sit down."

This time, it was Yaroah who stepped in front of Lorcan. "You will sit now," he growled. Lorcan looked up at him, then poked him in the ribs. A most uncharacteristic giggle escaped the bigger man, and Lorcan burst out laughing.

"How did you know he was ticklish?" Ennius asked.

"I didn't," Lorcan admitted. "All right. I'll sit."

The door opened as he perched on the edge of the bed-shelf, and Manius came inside. "What's so important?" he asked.

"We forgot Lorcan's armor and shield," Nona said. "Or did you forget that we had both *murmillones* fighting today?"

"No, I—" Manius stopped. His eyes widened, and he looked at Nona. "*Murmillo*, you said?"

"Contrasting pair of *murmillones*," Nona agreed. "For the spectacle fight."

"I see. And for this recreated battle… yes. Yes, that's a wonderful idea. I'll take care of it. Whose idea?"

"Nona's," Lorcan answered.

Manius nodded. "I'll be back. We have time. Rest, all of you." He left, and Ennius looked around the cell.

"Rest, he says. There's not enough room for the four of us to sit on the bed, and the floor is cold."

"We can sit close," Lorcan suggested. "And it will keep us warmer." He moved all the way onto the bed, shifting into a corner. The others joined him, and they ended up sitting facing each other—Nona and Ennius at one end of the bed, Lorcan and Yaroah at the other.

"All the shades of green, you said," Ennius said abruptly. "Your home, in summer. Is it really?"

"I think so," Lorcan answered. He leaned against Yaroah's arm. "Green and warm, and smelling of gorse and heather and apple blossoms." He nudged Yaroah. "What about Carthage? What's it like in the summer?"

"Not green," Yaroah answered with a laugh. "At least, not green in the summer. It is hotter than it is here. And it is dry. Where I am from, it is very close to the desert. It rains there in the winters, the same as here. But in the summers, we have no rain."

Lorcan remembered his short time in Carthage, and the heat there. "I was there, very briefly."

Yaroah nodded slowly. "Someday."

Lorcan kept his voice low. "I asked Manius to let you buy your freedom. He forbade me to speak of it again."

"I thank you, for trying."

Lorcan nodded, looking across at Nona and Ennius. "How about you two?"

"I was born in Ostia," Nona answered. "That's on the coast. My folks are fishermen. I was the youngest of too damned many, and they sold me and my sisters."

"Your *parents* sold you?" Lorcan gasped.

"Not sure if it was my father who did, or if it was my grandmother. But yes. When you have 10 mouths to feed, and seven of them girls, you do what you must. They kept my two oldest brothers and sold the rest." Nona shrugged. "Could have been worse. The girls probably all went to brothels. That could have been me."

"You were never that pretty," Ennius muttered. Nona elbowed him.

"I've been around gladiators since I was 10 years old," Nona continued. "I was sold as a house slave in a *ludus*. When the *lanista* caught me sneaking out and trying what I was seeing the gladiators do, he made me a *tiro*." He nodded to his right. "When he died, and we were all sold off, that's when I met this waste of skin."

"Flatterer," Ennius growled. "Manius bought us both at the same time. Yaroah, it's been four years? Or five?"

"Five," Yaroah answered. "He'd had a bad year that year. I was all he had left."

Ennius nodded. "Wasn't battles that took his others. It was plague. Took my last master, too. And Nona's."

"Plague?" Lorcan looked around. "I hadn't thought about it. But with so many, living so close, it would go through the city like a wildfire, doesn't it?"

Ennius nodded, his face grim. "That's how I ended up a slave. As far as I know, I was born in Rome. I'm not sure who my family were— they died from plague before I knew them." He looked distant. "There was a woman. She called herself a priestess of Orbona. I don't know if that's true or not, but she took care of us, all of the street orphans. We lived right off the Via Sacra. You walked to Apollo's temple, didn't you, Lorcan?"

"A few times, yes."

"You went past where I grew up." He smiled. "Grew up fighting and fussing. When old Mother Orbona died about seven years ago, I took a look around and decided that since the only thing I knew was fighting, that's what I'd do. I guess you'd say I sold myself. Then the plague took my whole *ludus*, and I came to Manius." He tipped his head back against the wall. "Dunno how old I am. Dunno how much longer I'll live. But I've lived better this past seven years than I ever did with Mother Orbona. She tried, but there were a lot of us. There wasn't ever much. I still go make offerings to the *lares* for her."

"You're overdue, by the way," Nona commented.

"I know. After the wedding."

"*Lares.* Those are the little gods, aren't they?" Lorcan said.

"Something like that." Nona scratched his chin. "Household gods, gods of the crossroads. Yeah, little gods is a good way of describing it. You have little gods, in Hibernia?"

Before Lorcan could answer, the door opened. He heard Julius' voice from outside, "Be quick." Then Tavi slipped into the cell. Lorcan heard Yaroah growl, and Ennius sputtered, "What the *fuck*?"

Then Lorcan saw the dark bruise on Tavi's cheek, and the blackened eye, and there was nothing but rage.

"*Who hit you?*"

Chapter Sixteen

Tavi stepped back, clearly startled. "I… it's nothing. I don't have time—"

Lorcan clambered over Yaroah's legs, stalked over to Tavi and grabbed his toga in one hand. With the other, he took Tavi's chin and turned his head to better see the bruises. There was a cut along one high cheekbone, and Lorcan snarled, "It's not nothing. Who hurt you? Who do I kill?"

"You can't kill him," Tavi blurted. "You can't. Now stop fussing at me. I need to warn you."

"Warn us of what?" Yaroah asked from behind Lorcan. "Lorcan, let him go. You're scaring him." He paused, then sniffed. "You're scaring me."

Lorcan blinked, startled. He looked back at Yaroah, then at Tavi. "I'm scaring you?"

Tavi nodded slowly. "A little. I've never seen you like this."

Lorcan let go of Tavi's toga. "I'm sorry. What are you warning us about?"

"This fight, this battle recreation? It's a trap," Tavi said. He took a deep breath. "My uncle—"

"Told you," Yaroah said softly.

"He's leading the *triarius*," Tavi finished. "Lorcan, did you insult my Aunt Drucilla?"

"Is it an insult to not want to be in her bed?" Lorcan asked. Tavi nodded.

"It's being made it out to be something worse. I don't know where he got the idea—no one will tell me the specifics, but Uncle Gaius is treating this as a personal insult. He arranged everything for this recreation, and my grandfather has no idea."

"How can they keep this from him?" Nona asked.

"He never wants to know about his birthday games," Tavi answered.

184

"He wants to be surprised. Uncle Gaius arranges everything. But this year, Uncle Gaius will be on the sands."

Lorcan nodded. "And… did he do this to you?" He reached out and brushed his thumb over Tavi's cheek. Tavi winced.

"No. This was my brother," he admitted. "Antius bets heavily on the games. He wanted to know what I knew about how you were training, so he could bet on you. Or against you. I'm not sure. I told him I didn't know anything. How could I? I haven't been in the *ludus* in months!" He shook his head. "Antius doesn't take the word no very well. None of my brothers do."

"What's going on here?" Manius demanded as he came into the cell. Tavi turned toward him, and Manius gaped. "Jove! What happened?"

"His brother happened," Lorcan answered. "And we have confirmation. The heir is behind this, and he's leading the men against us with the bridge battle."

"Antius did this?" Manius came closer and looked at Tavi's face. "And you kept it from your grandfather how?"

"You honestly think he notices me in the throng?" Tavi asked, his voice wry. "It's easy to stay out of sight when there are so many of us. My own father hasn't even noticed."

"Oh, lad," Manius sighed. "Go see Livia. She'll put you to rights. You risked a great deal to come warn us."

"I had to," Tavi said. He turned toward Lorcan. "I'm sorry. I wish—"

"The offer still stands," Lorcan said softly. "Come with us."

"My offer still stands, too," Tavi replied. "Come with me. Now. He'll kill you."

"I'm not turning my back on Livia," Lorcan said. "I love you both. Why can't you see that?"

Tavi swallowed, then nodded. "Don't kill him, Lorcan. And don't let him kill you. And… be happy. Tomorrow, I mean. Congratulations." He turned and walked to the door.

"Tavi," Lorcan called. Tavi stopped, but didn't turn. "It would mean a lot to both of us if you were there."

Tavi nodded. He didn't answer. Then he left, and Lorcan sighed.

"Well," Manius said. "Now we know."

"We already figured it out, though," Nona said. "It's nothing we hadn't put together already."

"Tell me about him as a fighter, Manius," Lorcan said. "What do I expect?"

"He fought as a *murmillo*," Manius answered. "He's about Yaroah's size and height. And he's the dirtiest fighter I've ever trained. If he can play a dirty trick or cheat to win, he'll do it."

Lorcan snorted. "Wonderful. I'm fighting my cousin." He leaned against the bed-shelf. "He's Yaroah's size? What about speed? And has he been fighting, or is he out of practice?"

"He trains with the legion," Manius said. "So he's in practice. He relies on his strength more than his speed. You may have an advantage on him."

Lorcan nodded, thinking. "He's leading the men. But he wants me, because I apparently insulted his wife by rejecting her." At Manius' shocked expression, he grinned. "That's what Tavi said, anyway. So... would he lead from the rear? Wait until I'm run down before facing me himself?"

"That would make the most sense, yes," Manius answered. "Does it change what you're going to do?"

"I'm not sure. Julius is supposed to find out how the field will be arranged. Then I can plan. For now, I just have ideas made out of smoke."

Manius nodded. "I'm looking forward to seeing what you come up with," he said. "Your armor and Yaroah's is being prepared, and Julius will inspect it personally before you arm yourselves."

"Are we fighting soon?" Yaroah asked.

"I think so, yes." He sighed. "Let me go see to Tavi and Livia. I'll come back after the first fight to hear the plan."

He left, and Lorcan went back to the bed-shelf, turning and perching on the edge. He folded his arms over his chest and tucked his chin down to his chest. He closed his eyes, and wasn't overly surprised when he felt warmth against both arms. When he opened his eyes again, Yaroah was on one side, and Ennius on the other. Nona stood in front of him.

"He'll come around," Nona said quietly. "He's confused."

"I don't understand why," Lorcan said. "I thought asking him to come with us was pretty straight-forward."

"From his side? You're asking him to give up everything. And you're going to be a married man. That might be something that's accepted in Hibernia, but here in Rome? It's... different." Ennius nudged Lorcan's arm. "Give him some time."

"Well, he has until spring," Lorcan said, trying to keep his voice light. His chest was tight, though. What if Tavi couldn't make up his mind before spring? Would he be able to leave one of his mates behind?"

He didn't want to find out.

"I can't think about him now," Lorcan said, trying to be firm. "I can't be distracted. I've got fights—"

The door opened, and Julius looked inside. "Lorcan, Yaroah. Time."

* * *

Lorcan frowned as he looked out at the slaves raking the sand clean. It felt odd to be back in his heavy armor, and he glared at the helmet that Julius carried. Then he looked up at his partner. "Yaroah, I don't think anyone ever told me. Who are we fighting today?"

Yaroah opened his mouth. Then he closed it. He frowned. "Julius, no one has told us. Who or what are we fighting?"

Julius looked at them. "You don't know? Oh, but you've been thinking of the other fight, haven't you? You're fighting *thraeces* today. I don't even know where Gaius found *thraeces*!"

Lorcan looked at Yaroah. "I don't know that one. What's a *thraeces*?"

"One is *thraex*. Several are *thraeces*. And it is an old style," Yaroah answered. He frowned. "They fight with *siccae*."

Lorcan's brows rose. "*Siccae*? Like… like Manius showed me? The ones he used to fight with?

"Manius used *siccae*?" Julius asked. "I didn't know that."

Lorcan nodded, thinking fast. "I saw them on the wall of the armory, and asked about them," he said, opting for half of the truth. "I'd never seen blades like that. He told me he used two. A *thraex* uses how many?"

"One, and a small shield." Julius held his hands apart to indicate size.

"And what armor?" Lorcan asked.

The gates opened, and Yaroah looked at him. "You'll find out in a moment," he murmured. Lorcan nodded and walked out onto the sands. The screaming crowds still made Lorcan flinch, but he no longer froze the way he'd done his first time. He looked up and around, and realized something.

"Yaroah, are there *more* people here?"

"Probably," Yaroah answered. "They love Lucanus, and they love seeing us fight. Putting both together? If anyone sneezes up there, the entire arena will fall ill."

Lorcan shook his head, shifting his helmet under his arm. Looking around the arena had also revealed that he and Yaroah were the only gladiators in sight. "And these *thraeces*? Where are they?"

Yaroah looked around. "That, I do not know. They should have entered at the same time we did." He nodded toward the Emperor's box. "Let us do our duty."

Together, they marched to stand before the box. Now that Lorcan knew who to look for, he could see the Emperor at the front of the box. The older man looked as if he were having a wonderful time, and he waved as Lorcan and Yaroah raised their swords in tribute. Lorcan couldn't help it—he grinned in response. Then he scanned the other faces in the box, and the grin faded. Tavi wasn't there.

"He's probably with Livia," Yaroah murmured.

"Am I that obvious?"

"Right then? Yes." Yaroah nodded. "Here are the officials."

Lorcan turned and saw a familiar face. He smiled. "Hello, Linus!"

"Corax," Linus said. "It's good to see you today. Yaroah, hello."

"Linus, who are we fighting today?" Lorcan asked. "And where are they?"

"Our instructions are to have you prepare to fight," Linus answered. "Other than that, we've been told nothing."

Yaroah growled. "I do not like that."

"Nor do we," Linus answered. "Put your helmets on and get ready. And Lorcan?"

"Yes?" Lorcan said as he planted his spatha into the sand.

"Keep your helmet on. We don't know what's going on today, and I worry." Linus looked around. "Prepare yourself for anything."

"Julius told us that we were fighting *thraeces*." Yaroah said. Linus scowled.

"And there's another puzzle. There are no *thraeces* in Rome." Linus looked past them. "Helmets."

Lorcan glared at his helmet, then put it on. At least it wasn't overly hot today. He pulled his sword free from the sand and turned to see that Yaroah was ready as well. Lorcan turned slowly in a circle, seeing the officials walking a few steps away.

"Back-to-back!" he heard Yaroah's voice faintly. "Be ready!"

Lorcan shifted, standing with his back to Yaroah. He turned his head from side to side, looking for movement. He heard a shout, the roar of the crowd. Then—

"Horsemen?" he blurted out, seeing three men on horseback burst from three opened gates. He had no doubt that there were three more behind him. As they got closer, he saw one raise his arm. Immediately, Lorcan raised his shield, protecting himself and Yaroah's unprotected back. The javelin hit his shield with a thump and felt to the ground.

"Javelins?" he heard Yaroah's voice from behind him. "Blunted, but still… someone does not like you!"

"I don't like him either!" Lorcan shouted back.

"Protect my back and get me that javelin!"

Lorcan planted his sword, raised his shield, and ducked, grabbing the javelin from the sand. He passed it back to Yaroah and grabbed his sword again, just in time for another javelin to thump against his shield. "What are you doing?"

"These are my weapons," Yaroah answered. "I used to hunt with javelins!"

Lorcan heard Yaroah grunt, and the crowd roared. He didn't stop to look back, planting his sword once more and fumbling for javelins. Yaroah took them, throwing a second one before Lorcan took a chance to look around. Two horses down, one horseman stumbling on the ground, another not moving next to his fallen mount. A third horsemen bearing down on them, a raised club in one hand; Lorcan shouted and dodged in front of Yaroah, keeping his shield between the horseman and his partner. The force of the impact knocked him backward, and he sprawled out on the sand for a moment, feeling as if his bones were still rattling.

"Lorcan?"

"I'm fine!" Lorcan shouted, scrambling back to his feet. His helmet had shifted, and he couldn't see; he stripped it off and threw it, grabbing for another javelin. He passed it to Yaroah as he looked around. More attackers on foot than on horseback now, so he picked up his sword once more. He glanced at Yaroah, saw that the other man had also taken off his helmet, and was holding a javelin with casual ease. The others were stuck point down in the sand, waiting. Lorcan moved back into position at Yaroah's back, just in time to see another horseman kick his horse into a gallop. His arm was raised—a club? A short sword? Lorcan couldn't tell. He dropped his sword, grabbed one of Yaroah's javelin's and threw. It was heavier than the javelins he'd learned to throw from his uncle's chariot, but it flew true, catching the horseman in the chest. He fell, and the horse thundered on past them and away.

"You can use these?" Yaroah demanded.

"They're charioteer weapons at home," Lorcan panted. "Learned from my uncle, the charioteer."

Yaroah barked with laughter. He shifted until he and Lorcan were once more standing back-to-back. Lorcan took a deep breath, looking around. "Five on foot?"

"Five," Yaroah agreed. "One still mounted. I do not see that he has any more javelins, though."

"And we have how many javelins?"

"Three."

Lorcan nodded. "What are they waiting for?"

The answer came almost immediately—the four standing men drew their swords and rushed at Yaroah and Lorcan, screaming like *bean-sidhes*. Lorcan and Yaroah both grabbed javelins and threw, and two of the four fell. Lorcan grabbed his *spatha* and raised his shield. His training with Manius had prepared him to face someone using *siccae,* and he could see now that the man he was facing was barely wearing any armor at all. But what he lacked in armor, he made up for in speed—Lorcan found it hard to get through his guard. Finally, he saw an opening—he whirled, crouched, and slashed across the backs of the *thraex's* legs. The man howled and fell, and the crowd screamed their approval. The sound of their approval almost drowned out Yaroah's voice.

"Lorcan! Behind you!"

Lorcan spun, and saw the horseman bearing down on him. He threw himself to the side, losing his shield as he rolled. A streak of fire burned down his bare back, and he cried out. He heard Yaroah roar, followed by...

Nothing?

Slowly, Lorcan got back to his feet, picking up his *spatha*. He shook his head, grimacing, feeling blood running down his back. Then he saw Yaroah, face down on the sands. The horseman had ridden away, and was circling for another pass. Lorcan scrambled to Yaroah's side, fumbling at his throat. There! A pulse, still strong. He'd just been knocked out. Lorcan licked his lips and looked around. What did he have? The last javelin. His *spatha*. And Yaroah's *gladius*. Carefully, he picked up the weapons, stabbing the swords into the sand on either side of himself, and picking up the javelin. He'd have one chance to get that rider off his horse.

The rider saw him standing, and kicked his horse into a gallop.

Lorcan set himself, holding the javelin loose in one hand, waiting… waiting… In one smooth movement, he raised the javelin and threw…

And missed. Lorcan swore and grabbed both swords. Nothing he'd learned had prepared him to fight a man on horseback, but the tales his father had told him gave him guidance. But it also meant getting far too close to the weapon that had felled Yaroah. He'd have to time this just right. He watched, crouched and coiled to spring, holding his breath, until the horse thundered at him, close enough that Lorcan felt its sweat spraying. As it reached him, Lorcan spun, flowing into a block and strike pattern that Manius had made him practice until he could do it without losing his balance. His left-hand blade met the horseman's strike with a tooth-rattling impact.

His right-hand blade sank into the horse's right foreleg.

The beast screamed and fell, and Lorcan scrambled out of the way of flailing hooves. The horseman flew over his mount's head and lay in the sand, unmoving. Lorcan slowly walked over to him. He knelt, poked the man with the pommel of his sword, then rolled him over. He sighed and rose, looking around for the officials. Linus was coming toward him.

"He's dead," Lorcan called. "I didn't mean to kill him."

"Accidents happen," Linus said. He stopped in front of Lorcan, then took Lorcan by the wrist and raised his hand. The crowd screamed. Lorcan looked up at the multitude of faces, then at Linus.

"I need to see to Yaroah."

"Please, go ahead. I'll send for *medicos*."

Lorcan planted both swords in the sand and ran to where Yaroah was just starting to groan and move. He dropped to his knees next to the man and helped him to sit.

"Gently," he warned Yaroah. He turned Yaroah's head toward him and looked into his eyes. "How many of me do you see?"

"One," Yaroah grumbled. "But he won't stay still."

Lorcan snorted. "You'll be fine."

Yaroah nodded and groaned. Then he grabbed Lorcan's arm. "Did we win?"

Lorcan smiled. "Yes. We won."

Yaroah burst out laughing. "Good! Good." He frowned and looked around. "I want to lie down."

"The *medicos* are coming, Yaroah," Lorcan said. "Then you can lay down."

The *medicos* arrived, and Lorcan wasn't surprised to see Livia among them. She was all business, seeing to Yaroah, taking charge of his care, and the way that the older male *medicos* deferred to her made Lorcan flush with pride. She noticed him watching her, and he saw her blush. But that was her only reaction as she ordered attendants to bundle Yaroah onto a litter and carry him off. He waved one hand in the air, and the crowd began to chant his name.

"You did well," Linus said from behind Lorcan. "Tell me why you're going to be up here again in three fights?"

"Is it just three?" Lorcan asked. "I should go get something to drink and try to rest." He looked back over his shoulder, at the slaves who were starting to clean the arena. "Although it looks like this might take a while to clear. And the short answer to your question is that I don't sleep with wives that aren't mine."

Linus' laughter was like the braying of a donkey, and startled Lorcan enough that he jumped. He made a face at Linus, who laughed harder. Then he heard a raven's cry from above. He looked up to see Corvina, circling; he held his arm out, and she stooped and landed on his wrist, sending the crowd into a frenzy. The chanting changed—no longer were they chanting Yaroah's name. But they weren't chanting Corax, either.

Corax princeps!

"Prince Raven?" Lorcan murmured. "How did they know?"

"Everyone knows, Corax," Linus said. "Now, shall we?" Linus gestured toward the Victory Gate. Lorcan nodded, wanting to ask more, wanting to be off the sands even more. He waved to the crowds and walked off the sands.

* * *

To his surprise, Julius wasn't waiting inside the Victory Gate. A stranger came forward.

"Corax, you're to follow me."

Lorcan looked around. "Where's Julius?"

"He's with your wounded friend. This way, please."

It made sense, so Lorcan followed. But the corridors they walked down weren't familiar.

"Where are you taking me?" he asked. "I have another fight to prepare for."

"This will only be a moment. Someone wishes to have a talk with you."

"A talk?" Lorcan stopped in his tracks. "It's not Drucilla, is it?"

The man turned. "No, it isn't Drucilla." He started walking again, and stopped outside a door. Opening it, he gestured for Lorcan to enter. Inside the room was a man that Lorcan had only ever seen once before, on the day that the Emperor had presented him with the *rudis*.

"Come in, Corax," he said.

Lorcan stepped inside, and the door closed behind him. "Are you Gaius or Decus?" he asked. "I've seen you, but no one introduced us."

The man smiled. "I am Gaius. And you... you are a puzzle to me."

"A puzzle?" Lorcan frowned. "Because I won't sleep with your wife?"

Gaius looked startled. Then he laughed. "Is *that* the dire insult to us I've been hearing about? Is that what this is truly all about?"

"You didn't know?" Lorcan gasped. "All this, and you had no idea why?" He stopped as he realized what Gaius had said. "Insulted you both? I never did! I've never even spoken to you before!"

Gaius shook his head. "Given the uproar that was brought to me, I thought you'd done something... well, it doesn't matter. You didn't, and I should know better than to not look for the heart of the matter. If I'd know the truth of it, I'd not have taken things this far." He sniffed. "And it's gone too far, hasn't it?"

"I don't think we can even see too far anymore. Not from where we are now," Lorcan answered. Gaius laughed.

"True. Very true. And... I wonder, Corax—"

"Lorcan."

"I'd forgotten that was your name. Lorcan. I wonder... you're a *semideus*, I'm told. And you're a remarkable gladiator. And, if the stories are true, you're a prince in Hibernia?"

"That's true."

Gaius' smile was bitter. "If I give you my express permission, would you go to Drucilla's bed?"

Lorcan coughed. "Morrigan, why?" he demanded. "I'm to be married tomorrow. I don't want another woman. And to be honest, your wife scares me."

Gaius burst out laughing. "Scary? Drucilla? She's... the very opposite of scary." He shook his head, chuckling. "Why am I asking?

Because her family wants a child of her body as heir to the Empire. Even though we don't appear to be able to have a child, and I have an heir. My brother's second son. But to be honest, I don't like my brother's sons very much, except for his oldest and his youngest." He shrugged. "I'd accept a child of yours as my own. If you were willing. And if I can watch."

Lorcan stared at him for a moment. A surprise, she'd said. A surprise for... her husband? Did they do that in Rome? And if they did, then why was Tavi pushing back? He coughed, and stammered, "That's... not a decision I can make lightly."

"It's not one I'd ask you to make lightly. You're to leave Rome in the spring?"

"That's my plan, yes."

"Then let me know before Saturnalia. That's the winter solstice," Gaius said. "That will give us time to be sure that she's pregnant before you leave."

"And how would you explain it?" Lorcan asked.

Gaius just smiled. "The Gods work in mysterious ways," he answered. "If after all these years of sacrifice, Juno finally decides to bless us with a child, who is to say otherwise?"

Lorcan nodded slowly. "I see." He paused. "If you kill me today," he added, "it would make it difficult to sire a child."

Gaius burst out laughing. "We'll make the fight look good. To make my father happy. And then... well, we'll see what happens then. Go prepare. I'll see you on the sands."

Lorcan nodded. "You're not what I expected," he admitted.

"Manius told you I was a dirty fighter, hm?" Gaius said. "I was. I was also young and foolish. Now... well, I've an empire to think of."

"Lorcan nodded. You said you don't like your heir much. Do you know he tried to get information on me out of his brother?" Lorcan asked. Gaius frowned.

"Antius did what?" His frown deepened. "I... this shouldn't surprise me. Antius is the one who came to me with all the tales of injury and insult. Drucilla never said a word about it. I didn't even know she went into the cells until Julius told me. What did Antius do to Tavi?"

"You should go find him. See for yourself." Lorcan smiled. "This has been an interesting discussion. I'll see you on the sands."

* * *

"Where have you been?" Julius demanded as Lorcan was led back to the cells. "I got to the Victory Gate, and you were gone. No one could tell me where!"

"Someone wanted to have a private conversation," Lorcan answered. "I'm fine." He turned to Gaius' servant. "Thank you."

Julius watched as the man bowed and left, and turned to Lorcan. "I know who that was."

"I expect you do."

"You had a talk with his master?"

"I did," Lorcan answered.

"And...?"

"Private, Julius," Lorcan said. He entered the cell, and Nona jumped up.

"There you are!" he cried. "We were starting to worry. You did fantastic out there. And... there's blood on your back. You're hurt?"

Lorcan tried to look over his shoulder. "How badly, Nona? I forgot it happened when Yaroah went down."

He felt a warm hand on his shoulder, and breath on his skin as Nona leaned in. "Ennius, ask Julius for water and a cloth. We need to clean this up and bandage it before we go back out. Lorcan, how's Yaroah?"

"I'm not sure. I think he'll be all right. He got his brains rattled." Lorcan yawned. "Ennius, ask Julius for something to eat and drink, too? Light. We're going back out again in three fights."

"Three?" Nona gasped. "Then why aren't we off being armed?"

"Because I'm delaying as long as I can," Julius answered. He entered the cell, then stepped out of the way for a pair of slaves, one carrying a bowl of steaming water, the other a tray. Behind them came Manius and Livia. Nona breathed a sigh.

"Oh, good. You can take care of him, Livia. I'm nowhere near as good."

Livia brushed past him and rested one hand on Lorcan's waist. He shivered at her touch.

"Lorcan?"

"Your hands are cold," Lorcan answered the question, looking over his shoulder. "I got sand in it, didn't I?"

"It's not bad. Nor is it deep. It won't need stitching, I don't think. At least, not yet," Livia answered. "I'll clean it. I'm not sure how I can bandage it that won't restrict your movements."

"Leave it, then," Lorcan said. "It's only going to get worse in the next fight."

"Here," Manius said, coming to stand in front of Lorcan. He held two flasks. "Drink these."

"What am I drinking?" Lorcan asked, taking one of the flasks. That one held some sort of meat broth, rich and salty, and he drained it greedily. "Oh, that's good."

"There's more." Manius took the empty flask and handed Lorcan the other. Lorcan took a sip, and almost gagged at the sweet, thick syrup.

"What is that?"

"Syrup of *glacula*," Livia answered from behind him. "It's a stimulant, and I've made sure that this syrup is safe. Just don't drink too much." Livia started bathing his back. "Do you use *glacula* in Hibernia?"

Lorcan took another sip. "I don't know. I don't know the name. What is it in Gaeilge?"

"I couldn't tell you," Livia answered. "I only know the name here. It may not grow there." She started dabbing at the cut, using something that stung. Lorcan winced. He handed the flask of tonic back to Manius and took another flask of broth. He drank this one more slowly, closing his eyes. Now that the fight was over, he was tired. But he had another fight to come, and deep thoughts to follow.

"Do we know how the ground will be laid out?" he asked.

"There will be a bridge laid down on the sand," Ennius said. "It'll be between the Victory Gate and the rest of the arena. We have to hold that bridge—if even one of the attackers gets across, we've lost."

Lorcan nodded. He sipped the broth and frowned. Then he held his hand out for the flask of syrup. He took a long drink, and chased the sticky-sweet liquid down with broth.

"It sounds as though our best chance will be to have the three of us act as the points on a narrow triangle," Nona said. "Lorcan, you take the bridge. Ennius and I will try to cut down the front lines, keep them off you. The way we discussed earlier."

"I think that's the best way," Lorcan agreed. "Or at least, I can't think of a better one."

"And Gaius will be at the rear. Do you want him, Lorcan?" Ennius asked.

"Oh, I won't rob you the glory of taking down the heir to the Empire," Lorcan told him. "If you get him, good. If not, if he gets past you, then I'll take him."

"Be careful with him," Manius warned. "He won't hesitate to kill you, but you must not kill him."

Lorcan hesitated, then quietly said, "I just spoke to him."

"You what?" Manius blurted.

"He had me brought to him when I came off the sands. He'd been led to believe that I insulted both him and his wife. He says that he'd never have taken it this far if he knew the truth of it." Lorcan finished his broth. "We've come to an understanding, I think. And we'll make it a good fight. I don't think I'm in too much danger. And besides, I've killed enough people today." He glanced back. "How's Yaroah?"

"He'll be fine with some rest. His skull isn't broken." Livia came around to face him. "Apparently, it wasn't the rider. It was the horse. He tried to do what you did, and the horse kicked his shield. That's what hit him—the shield."

Lorcan winced. "He's lucky it didn't do worse."

"If he'd been wearing his helmet, he'd be fine," Manius added.

"You wanted showy," Lorcan replied. He closed his eyes and yawned. "How's my back?"

"As well as can be expected," Livia answered. "Try not to do too much more damage?"

"I'll do my best," Lorcan said. He opened his eyes and smiled at her. "Kiss for luck?"

"Always." She moved against him and kissed him, wrapping her arms around his neck. Lorcan slid one arm around her waist, and the fingers of his other hand into her hair. He didn't care that the others were watching him. He needed this moment. There might not be another one.

When he finally let Livia go, her face was flushed, and her eyes sparkling. She hugged him tightly, and whispered in his ear, "We'll continue that later."

"With that much luck, we can't possibly lose!" Nona proclaimed.

Chapter Seventeen

Armed and ready, feeling oddly calm, Lorcan stood waiting for the gates to open. He could feel Nona standing at his side, Ennius behind him. To his surprise, Ennius had armed himself as a *secutor* today.

"The net and trident are good against one man," he'd explained. "Against an army? Better to have a sword."

"How are you feeling?" Ennius asked. Lorcan looked back at him.

"I'm fine. I think whatever that tonic was is helping." He shifted, testing his range of movement. He could feel the scabs pulling, and knew that the wounds would most definitely open again while he fought. He'd just have to hope he didn't bleed too heavily.

Outside the gate, he could see the slaves raking the sands and setting up the battle ground. The bridge was nothing more than a series of planks set side by side on the ground, over what looked like a long piece of blue cloth.

"Is that supposed to be the Tiber?" Lorcan asked.

"Seems so," Nona answered. "They're making it easy for you."

Lorcan glanced at him. "How so?"

"Horatius swam to safety across the Tiber in full armor once his men pulled the bridge down." Nona grinned. "They could have arranged that, you know. They've had small scale sea battles in here."

Lorcan stared at him. "You're joking! Julius, is he joking?"

"Nope," Julius said. "You can seal these corridors tight as a drum, and divert water from the Tiber in here. Look at the walls. See where the stone changes color? That's how deep the water gets."

Lorcan peered out through the gate and nodded. "I see it. That's incredible. I wonder if I'll get a chance to see it?"

"They don't do them all that often," Julius answered. "Lorcan, are you sure you're up for this?"

"Do I have a choice?" Lorcan asked, his voice dry. "They're

expecting me out there. If I don't fight, what happens? I'm told that there will be riots."

Julius scowled. Then he nodded. "Probably. You're right."

"I'm not letting people get hurt. I can do this." Lorcan picked up his swords—paired *spathae*—and looked at the others. "Julius, do you think we'll have time before they start us to walk the ground and revise our strategy?"

"I'll make sure you do."

Lorcan smiled, then turned as the gates opened. Nona and Ennius looked at him, and Nona made an expansive gesture.

"After you, oh mighty *Corax princeps*."

"Get fucked, Nona," Lorcan grumbled. Julius hooted with laughter.

"You're picking up bad habits from these two," he said. "I'll walk out with you and talk to the officials. I think Linus will be out there. He insisted."

Lorcan looked at him, puzzled. "Why?"

"I asked him. He says that you're the first gladiator ever to ask him his name." Julius smiled. "You're a good man, Lorcan. And I think all of Rome knows your story by now, about your throne being stolen. They want you to win."

"All of Rome?" Lorcan repeated. Then he turned and looked at Nona. "Linus said something about that, but I didn't ask him more. How do they know? Nona, have you been gossiping about me?"

Nona looked sheepish. "Maybe a little." He grinned. "It's good for your image. Makes you sympathetic. The people want a hero to love. That's you."

Lorcan sniffed. "I'm not a hero."

"Maybe. Maybe not. But they think you are. And they're waiting."

Lorcan grimaced. Was that why Gaius had asked him? Because everyone thought he was a hero? He shook his head and walked out onto the sand. The screaming of the crowd seemed even louder than it had before, and he turned in a circle and waved. To his shock, flowers started to rain down from the seats. Nona burst out laughing.

"Told you!"

Lorcan shook his head and started forward, toward where he could see the officials waiting. Linus was at the front of the group, and he frowned as the trio walked up to him.

"Three?"

"Horatius had two companions, or so I'm told," Lorcan said.

"Two companions who turned coward and fled," Linus said.

"Little details," Nona grumbled. "Not important."

Linus looked as if he wanted to smile. "You're all here. So we'll let it stand." He studied Lorcan for a moment. "Two swords?"

"For this fight, yes."

"Thought you were a *murmillo*?"

Lorcan grinned. "I'm full of surprises."

Linus smiled. "So I see."

"Linus, they want a moment to look over the staging," Julius said.

"Of course," Linus agreed. "Take your time."

Lorcan looked at Julius, then at Linus. "This is very unusual, isn't it?"

"Extremely," Linus said. "This sort of fight, no. But to have a gladiator who has already fought return to the arena? It's unheard of." He nodded toward the bridge. "So we're going to help you. Go look around. Take your time. When you are ready, we'll begin."

Lorcan smiled and walked away from the group, toward the bridge. He stopped there and planted his swords in the ground before he turned and looked around. "Where will they be coming from?" he called.

Linus used his rod to point to a gate across the arena. "There. They'll form ranks and attack from that direction."

"You're certain?" Nona asked. "Not coming from any other gates, just to put us off? No reinforcements?"

Linus frowned. He turned to Julius and said something that Lorcan didn't hear. Julius trotted off toward the gate that Linus had indicated, then went to the other entrances to the arena. A few minutes later, he was back.

"They're where they're supposed to be," he said. "And there's no one else ready to go at the other gates."

"Good." Lorcan smiled and crouched, studying the ground, picturing angles, possible attack plans, defensive maneuvers.. They'd be coming from that direction, then the most direct attack would be just *so*. If he put Nona and Ennius *there*... wait...

"How many across?" he called. "When they form ranks, how many across?"

"Ten," Linus called back. "With the commander—"

"In the rear," Lorcan finished. "That I know." Yes. If he put Nona and Ennius *there*, then they'd worry at the men at the sides of an attacking wedge. If they dropped enough men quickly enough, the fallen would form a barrier. And anyone who got past Nona and Ennius would be expecting him to fight as a *murmillo*, or however a Roman solider would fight. They wouldn't know what to do with him. He hoped. He got up and walked a straight line perpendicular to the bridge, counting his steps. Then he scraped a line in the sand.. "Ennius, I'll want you here." He said. He walked back along the same line, and scraped another line. "Nona, here."

Once the two were in place, Lorcan walked out in front of them, frowning. Had he judged it right? Only one way to find out.

"I think we're ready, Linus," he said. "At least, I don't think there's any more preparation I can do."

"That sounds as close to ready as anything I've ever heard," Linus agreed. "Come and salute the Emperor."

Lorcan nodded to the official, then looked to see that Nona and Ennius had moved to flank him, standing one step behind him to either side. He smiled—he had a wedge of his own.

They stopped in front of the box, and Lorcan looked up to see Lucanus looking down at him. The change in the Emperor's demeanor was jarring—before, he'd looked almost joyous. Now? The Emperor looked furious, and Lorcan wondered if it had to do with the fight.

"He looks angry," Ennius murmured. "Really angry."

"I know," Lorcan agreed. He raised his fist and saw the Emperor nod and raise his hand in acknowledgment. The crowd cheered, and Lorcan turned to face Nona and Ennius.

"I'm expecting a wedge," he said as they walked back toward the bridge. "I've put you in positions so that you can take the sides of the wedge. Stop them however you can. The ones that get past you I'll deal with."

Nona nodded. "And we build a barricade with the bodies, hm? Good plan."

Lorcan swallowed. He didn't want to have to kill anyone today, but the chances of avoiding that were slim. "Take your places and get your helmets on. And may all of our gods smile on us." He went back to the bridge, watched as Nona and Ennius took their places. Linus waited for Lorcan to nod, then turned and shouted.

Across the arena, the gates opened. Men started to file out, forming ranks, and Lorcan started counting.

"I thought you said 30!" he called. "Half of a... what did you call it?"

"A *triarius*," Nona called back. "And yeah, 30."

"That's a lot more than 30," Lorcan muttered. He swore softly, seeing Linus striding across the sand toward the assembled forces. A big man walked to meet him—Gaius. Linus gestured broadly, clearly incensed. Gaius turned, frowned, then stalked back toward his men. His voice was loud, and it carried across the sands:

"…told you to send in half of the *triarius*! Who are these men? And what do you mean, making me look like a fool in front of my father and all of Rome? Get the rest of these men off the sands now! And go with them!"

Nona trotted over to Lorcan. "Someone made a big mistake?"

"Sounds like it," Lorcan agreed. "I wonder who?"

"Whoever is acting as Gaius' second, I imagine," Nona said.

"At least we know Gaius is going to play fair today," Lorcan said. "Half the *triarius*? That's almost sane."

"You have a funny idea of what's sane, Lorcan."

Lorcan grinned. "Go on back to your place."

Nona trotted back into position, and Lorcan licked his lips. The *triarius* had formed ranks—three rows of 10 across—and he finally had a good look at them. Their armor wasn't anything like what he was expecting. Nothing at all like what he'd seen in the arena, nor what he'd seen on soldiers in the city. This armor was very ornate, very fanciful— breastplates ornamented with colored enamel and helmets with ridiculous metal crests. They carried shields that were slightly rounded squares, and to Lorcan's surprise, they wore no leg protection at all.

"Nona, what are they wearing?" he called. "That's the most ridiculous armor I've ever seen!"

"Oh, they're supposed to be Etruscans," Nona called back. "That's the army that was attacking Horatius."

"Etruscans dressed like whores going to war?" Lorcan called back, incredulous. He'd forgotten that there were more than just his men that could hear him, and that his voice would carry to the first rows of spectators, who roared with laughter. The laughter spread like waves through the crowd, as his words were repeated from seat to seat.

"Oh, they'll be saying that for weeks," Ennius said. "That's a good one."

"Wonderful," Lorcan muttered. He checked his armor, planted one sword in the sand, and wiped his palm on his *subligaculum*. He switched his hand, and watched the ranks of men across from him. He could hear Gaius' voice bellowing orders.

Then came the final word: *Attack!*

The men facing them surged forward, forming the expected wedge as they rushed to engage. Time seemed to slow to a crawl as the point of the wedge approached Ennius and Nona. Lorcan had positioned them in just the right places, and they hit the men just behind the point of the wedge. The man at the front kept on coming, and Lorcan was ready. He didn't leave his place at the head of the bridge, letting the man come to him. Once the attacker was in striking distance, Lorcan sprang, darting forward and striking his shield, then dancing back a half step before spinning and sweeping the same *spatha* up underneath the edge of the shield, the blade slicing into the attacker's thigh. The man screamed, and Lorcan pulled the blade free, spun again, and sunk his left hand *spatha* into his opponent's unprotected calf. The man fell, screaming, and Lorcan moved on to the next attacker.

And the next one.

And the one after that.

He lost count somewhere between three and five, and just settled on holding the line, beating anyone who came at him, and trying not to fall over from exhaustion. Whatever benefits the tonic had given to him at the beginning of the fight were gone, and he knew that he was flagging. His lungs burned, and he ached in the places where attacks had gotten through his guard. But there were still men coming at him, and he wasn't going to allow himself to fail. How long had they been out here? He didn't even know.

There was a moment, a breath, and he stepped back and knelt down. Just for a moment. He heard a shout, and the crowd reacted, seeming abnormally loud. He looked from side to side, seeing Nona still standing. But he wasn't fighting. He was staring off across toward Ennius. Lorcan looked, and realized that he couldn't see the *retiarius* at all.

"Ennius?" Lorcan shouted. Where was he?

"He's down!" Nona shouted back.

Lorcan swore in Gaeilge, words that his mother would have blanched to hear from him. Then he switched back to Latin. "Nona! To me!"

"Ennius?"

"We can't help him now!"

Nona hesitated, then jumped over the bodies of the men closest to him and raced through the carnage to Lorcan's side. Lorcan got back to his feet and glanced at Nona. "Still in one piece?" he asked.

"More or less. A little battered, but I'll still get full price at the market. You?"

"Tired." Lorcan shook his head. "How many more are there?"

"I lost count," Nona said. "You, too?"

"Yes." Lorcan swallowed and looked around. The ground closest to them was littered with fallen men, liberally painted with blood. But there didn't seem to be anyone left standing except the officials "Where's Gaius?"

"I don't know," Nona said. "Have we won?"

"No idea. It's quiet. Go see to Ennius," Lorcan said. "I'll hold the bridge."

The moment Nona moved off, one of the men on the ground rose. Lorcan straightened, recognizing Gaius.

"You were playing dead?" Lorcan asked.

"Not playing, no," Gaius said. He winced and took his helmet off, turning it so that Lorcan could see the dent. He let it fall. "One of them got me a good one, knocked me off my feet."

"We're not done here, are we?" Lorcan asked.

"No," Gaius answered. He gestured away from the bridge. "Come out here, where it's clear. Winner takes all."

Lorcan licked his lips again, then nodded. He looked over at Nona. "How is he?"

"We need to get him to Livia."

Lorcan nodded. "Nona, hold the bridge." He walked toward Gaius, who fell in next to him. Side by side, they walked out onto the empty sands. On impulse, Lorcan turned and raised his sword to the Emperor. When he turned back, he saw that Gaius had done the same.

"You've very good," Gaius said. "I can see that Manius had been pushing you hard. This is going to be fun."

Despite himself, Lorcan laughed. "You don't get out much, do you?"

"Not like this, no."

"Then let's have you your fun so my friend can get to a healer." He saw movement, looked over to see Linus had come close. "We're going to finish this here, Linus."

"Very good." Linus nodded and raised his rode between them. "On your honor…"

Lorcan met Gaius' eyes; the bigger man smiled as he moved into position. Lorcan's world narrowed to the rod, the blades in his hands, and the man facing him.

"Lorcan!"

Lorcan jerked at the sound of Manius' voice. He turned and, to his shock, saw Julius, Manius and Yaroah running from the Victory Gate.

"What is this?" Linus demanded.

Manius stopped, panting. Julius looked grim, but Lorcan didn't pay him any mind. "Yaroah, what are you doing up?" he demanded.

"It is necessary," Yaroah answered. "It is bad below."

"Bad?" Linus said. "Bad how? What's happening?"

There was a loud crash behind them. Lorcan wheeled, seeing the gates were open, and armed men pouring out onto the sands. Some were dressed at Etruscans, others wore the *subligaculum* of a gladiator. All were armed, and Lorcan realized what was happening below and spilling out onto the sands.

The slave revolt.

Above him, he heard screaming—the wrong kind of screaming. He looked up and saw that the people in the stands were running, panicked. There was no one in the Imperial box except guards. Lorcan looked around. "Anyone who can hold arms and is loyal to Lucanus, to me!" There wasn't a lot of movement from the defeated. But then, he wasn't expecting it. Nona raced to his side.

"There might be others to support us," Julius offered. "Right now, they're locking down anyone who's not out here."

"They might do better in getting them armed and ready to fight," Nona said.

"Who would they be fighting for, though?" Gaius asked. Nona went pale.

"Right. Forget I said that." Nona looked at Lorcan. "It's us against the whole damned world, isn't it?"

"Looks like it," Lorcan said.

Next to him, Gaius swore. "Aulus, what are you doing?" he roared.

"Aulus?"

"My second, the one who brought too many men onto the field," Gaius answered. "He… oh, no. No! Aulus, damn your eyes!"

"Can they get to the Emperor from here?" Lorcan asked. "That's their goal, isn't it? Kill you, kill the rest of your family?"

"I… I don't know," Gaius looked at him. "What do we do?"

Lorcan stared at him. "You're asking me?" He turned, looked around. "Linus, if they get past us, can they get into the stands?" Lorcan demanded.

Linus nodded, his face pale. "If they get to the Victory Gate, they can get to the rest of the arena." Linus grimaced. "The access isn't well guarded from there. Not the way it is by the cells."

"Linus, you and the others get out of here. Tell them inside to seal the Victory Gate and not to open it again, and to seal the access to the rest of the arena. Julius said it could be made tight as a drum. Do it. Whatever you have to. And…" He looked at Gaius, who met his gaze with stony calm. "And if we go down, then do what happens when you make it tight as a drum. Understood?"

"Lorcan! I can't!" Linus stammered. "You and… and Gaius—"

"Don't argue! Go!" Lorcan roared. Linus blanched and ran, leading the other officials to safety. "All right. Manius, where's Livia?"

"When things started, Tavi spirited her off. She's probably with the Emperor now, and safer than anyone," Manius answered without looking away from the assembling men. "They're not all slaves. They're not all gladiators."

"No, some of them are legionnaires," Gaius said. "And some… I don't know them. Mercenaries?"

"Fuck," Nona breathed. "Where do we hold the line?"

Lorcan looked at Gaius, and as one they answered, "The bridge."

Quickly, they moved toward the makeshift bridge, picking their way through the bodies. Nona moved away, and Lorcan saw him helping Ennius to his feet. He could just hear Nona's voice, "Come on. I'm not leaving you out here to be stepped on. Let's go. All right, come on…"

"Take him to the gate," Lorcan called. "Then come back. He'll be safer there."

Nona nodded, and he started toward the Victory Gate. Yaroah moved off to help him, and the two carried Ennius off. They were back quickly, and Lorcan tried to ignore the blood on their hands.

"Now what?" Gaius asked. "Why aren't they attacking?"

Lorcan frowned. Then he coughed. "Gladiators, legionnaires, and mercenaries. None of them know what to do with the others. There's no one taking command over there!"

"Then… what do we do?" Julius asked.

Lorcan looked at him, then at Gaius. "You're taller than I am. How many do you think there are?"

Gaius' brow furrowed and his lips moved in silence as he counted. "Fifty?" he offered. "More or less?"

Lorcan turned and looked at the men surrounding him. "Yaroah, you're at the bridge. Nona, stay with him. Ah… Julius, how well do you fight?"

Julius looked embarrassed. "Not as well as you need. I'll hold the line. If it hits us, it's too late anyway and we're just waiting for the flood."

Lorcan nodded. "Fine. What do we so?" He grinned up at Gaius. "They're confused. Let's go make it worse and see how many we can kill before they take us down."

Gaius gaped at him. "You're insane!"

"You want to be a hero of Rome?" Lorcan asked. "Have your name be repeated for generations? Have gladiators fighting this battle for sport when we're all dust?"

Gaius blinked. Then he straightened. "How is it that you're a better son of Rome than I?" he demanded. "You're a barbarian, and a former slave. You shouldn't be willing to die for us!"

"I'm willing to die for your father, your nephew, and for a chance to see my wedding tomorrow," Lorcan answered. "Ready?"

Manius clapped him on the shoulder. "I wish your father could see this," he said. "He'd be proud enough to burst."

"One day, I'll tell him," Lorcan said. "For now? I'll settle for having you in that place."

Manius turned slightly pink, and he nodded. "I'm honored. Well, *Corax princeps*? Lead us."

Lorcan nodded. He moved forward slowly, picking his way through the bodies until his path was clear. He heard Gaius on his right, Manius on his left. And above him, screaming her defiance, was Corvina.

Lorcan took a deep breath, then took off running, echoing Corvina's attack cry as he threw himself into the throng.

Chapter Eighteen

There was something to be said for fighting a force that wasn't used to fighting as a group. The legionnaires clearly didn't care about either the gladiators or the mercenaries. The mercenaries looked to be at least three different groups, and each of them stayed together. The gladiators fought as individuals.

There were still too many of them.

Lorcan spun, cutting a man off at the knees, then jumped back to his feet and stepped back. He bumped into someone and whirled, only to realize it was Gaius.

"There are too many of them!" Gaius panted.

Lorcan nodded, turning to put his back to Gaius'. He rested for a moment against the larger man's broad back as he scanned the fighters. "Most of them are mercenaries!" he gasped. "Or am I wrong?"

"You're not wrong. So?"

"So hire them!" Lorcan said. "Offer them more!"

Gaius coughed, then turned and raised his voice, "Hear me, any of you hire-swords! Whatever you've been offered to fight against us, I will double it if you fight for Rome!"

The fighters went still all around them. One of the mercenaries walked forward, looked Gaius up and down, then spat in the sand. "Why do you think we'd fight for you?" he demanded in heavily accented Latin. Behind Lorcan, Manius coughed.

"You won't fight for Rome," he said in Gaeilge. "Will you fight for the Battle Raven, son of Eire?" Lorcan stared at Manius, who nodded, not looking away from the mercenary. "Well?"

"The Battle Raven?" the man repeated. "Who dares claim that bloodline?"

"I do," Lorcan said in Gaeilge. "I am Lorcan mac Diarmuid mic Morrigan, and I am a child of the Morrigan's blood. If you won't fight for Rome, will you fight for me?"

"What are you saying?" Gaius asked. "Manius, what are you two doing?"

"Saving your arse," Manius answered.

A man in Roman armor pressed forward, his sword bared. "Hibernian! What are you doing? Kill them!"

The mercenary scowled. He spun, his sword flashing, and the Roman fell. Then he turned back to Manius.

"You were saying?"

Lorcan walked forward. "What's your name?" he asked the mercenary.

"Tiernay."

"Tiernay," Lorcan said with a smile. "Will you fight for me? Now, and when I return to Eire? I've need of good men to help me take back what's mine."

"What's the offer?" Tiernay demanded.

Lorcan swallowed, his mouth suddenly dry. What did he have to offer? He looked at Manius. "How much do I have?"

Manius smiled. "Tiernay, what have you been promised?" Tiernay named a number that meant nothing to Lorcan. Manius, however, laughed. "Is that all? For treble that, will you follow the Raven?"

Tiernay snorted. "For treble that? I'll follow the Raven's own."

"Done." Manius nodded. "Prince Lorcan? Your army awaits."

Lorcan laughed. "Tiernay, let's clean up this mess."

Tiernay grinned, revealing discolored, broken teeth. "All right! We fight for the Raven!" He turned to Lorcan. "Who do you want to kill?"

"Whoever you were working for and with," Lorcan answered. Tiernay stared at him.

"You want Rome to win?"

"This time."

Tiernay scowled. Then he nodded. "All right. For triple pay, Rome can win. This time."

* * *

The final fight was short and bloody. Tiernay's band of mercenaries added an advantage to Lorcan's side. They were a surprisingly well-trained and cohesive group, and they went through their former companions like a rampaging storm. There were few survivors—the legionnaires and gladiators who rose against Rome refused to surrender when the chance was offered. Those who did survive were taken away in chains. Just where, Lorcan didn't ask. He didn't want to know. He slumped on the sand in the middle of the arena and tried his best to not fall asleep. His arms and legs both felt leaden, and he ached from dozens of small wounds and a few larger ones. In addition to the slice on his back, there was a long diagonal gash on his left thigh—he wasn't sure when he'd gotten that one, and it hurt enough to make walking painful.

Heavy footsteps came closer. Lorcan didn't turn, knowing that whoever it was would probably announce themselves. They did, by slumping down next to him and leaning into his shoulder. Lorcan looked over and grinned. Yaroah.

"So… is it always like this, as a gladiator?" he asked, his voice cracking.

Yaroah snorted. "No, not always. It is occasionally exciting."

Lorcan groaned. He'd known from the minute he'd asked the question that Yaroah was going to make a joke of it. But hearing Yaroah laugh was enough to make up for it. He leaned into Yaroah's solid bulk and yawned. "Now what?" he asked.

"I do not know," Yaroah said. "This… this is all new ground. This is more than a slave revolt. There were legionnaires involved, and mercenaries. There is more here than it seems."

More heavy footsteps. This time, Lorcan looked up to see Gaius and Manius. Gaius looked battered and bloody, and more than a little grim.

"Did you learn anything?" Lorcan asked as they stopped in front of him.

"Only that your Tiernay killed Aulus too quickly," Gaius answered. "None of the survivors know who was paying him. Nor does Tiernay."

"So we don't know who was behind this," Manius finished. "But whoever it was, we can hope that they've learned their lesson."

"Now let us hope the gods are listening," Yaroah said, He shifted away from Lorcan and got to his feet. Then he held his hand down. "Come on, Raven. Let's go home."

Lorcan got up, hopping a little as he tried not to put weight on his left leg. He saw Gaius' jaw drop, and turned to see a small group coming out through the Victory gate. Two figures ran from the group toward them. Lorcan staggered forward, almost falling, and was hit from two sides by the two people he wanted to see more than anything.—Livia and Tavi Both of them were laughing and crying and babbling in Latin, which Lorcan's mind stubbornly refused to translate. He clung to both of them, just letting their voices wash over him.

"I'm fine," he finally murmured in Gaeilge. "It's over. We're all safe."

"And you've lost Latin entirely, haven't you?" Tavi said with a laugh.

"I'm exhausted," Lorcan said. "I'm hungry. I need to eat, and sleep."

"You're coming back to the Palace," Tavi said. "All of you. Grandfather said." He looked over his shoulder. Lorcan looked past him, and saw that another reunion had apparently happened between Gaius and his father. Now, they were coming toward Lorcan, Gaius standing at his father's shoulder, Decus next to him, and a third man standing behind them. Lorcan straightened, leaning on Tavi for support, his other arm around Livia. The way it should be, he thought.

"Who's that other one?" Lorcan whispered.

Tavi hesitated, then answered, "My brother Antius."

Lucanus looked stern as he approached; he stopped in front of them and pointed at Lorcan. "Do not even *think* about kneeling!" he commanded. Then he smiled and closed the distance, embracing Lorcan tightly. "My son," he breathed, and Lorcan heard Tavi gasp. "Truly, the gods brought you to Rome." He stepped back, his hands still on Lorcan's shoulders. "Gaius told me that you took command, that it was all your doing that this revolt did not spread off the sands. He tells me that there has never been a truer son of Rome, and you not even born to the Empire."

Lorcan felt his face grow warm. He glanced at Gaius, only to see the man nodding. He looked back at the Emperor, "Your Majesty, Gaius…"

"If you're going to finish that with the word exaggerates, I most certainly do not," Gaius interrupted. "Now hush, Lorcan, and accept your reward."

"Reward?" Lorcan looked at Tavi, then at Livia. "Your Majesty, there's nothing I desire—"

"I've called you a true son of Rome. I meant it," Lucanus said. "From this day forth, you shall be known as Albus Corvus Torvus Victorinus. I name you as part of my household, and grant you all rights and privileges of the patrician caste."

"I'll… I'll be what?" Lorcan stammered.

"He's just made you a Roman citizen," Livia whispered, sliding her arm around his waist. "A noble Roman citizen."

"Albus Corvus… white raven?" Lorcan looked up at Tavi. "Am I translating that right? What does Torvus mean?"

"Fierce," Tavi answered. "I might have translated what Lorcan means for my grandfather. Now say thank you, Lorcan."

Lorcan stared at him for a moment. Say thank you? For what? For making him a nobleman of an Empire he couldn't wait to leave? For taking away his very *name*?

But… this was how they were trying to reward him. It wouldn't matter once he was gone. And he needed to be gracious. To be his father's son.

Lorcan turned to the Emperor and bowed from the waist. "Thank you, Your Majesty. I am honored."

"There will be a triumph," Lucanus added. "For you and for Gaius."

"Father," Gaius protested. "Is that necessary?"

Lucanus smiled. "A small triumph. An ovation. So that all of Rome knows of your victory, and at what odds."

"Your Majesty?" Lorcan said. "I've no objections to having whatever a triumph is, so long as it's not tomorrow." He smiled down at Livia. "I have other plans for tomorrow."

Lucanus looked at them, and his eyes widened. "I see," he said slowly. "Of course. We'll plan the triumph for—"

"Give them a few days, Father," Gaius murmured.

"A few days' time," Lucanus finished. "We'll consult the augurs for the proper day." He looked around. "Now, I've sent the injured on to the palace to be tended to, and Manius has gone with them. Except for this fine man," he nodded at Yaroah. "Who refused to leave you behind. You're fortunate in your friends, Albus."

Lorcan swallowed. "Sir, if I could still be called Lorcan?" he asked. He heard his voice wobble, and cursed silently.

Lucanus smiled gently. "You can be called whatever you want."

"Lorcan, there's still your mercenary to deal with before we go," Gaius added. "Get it done quickly. You need to be off your feet."

Lorcan nodded, then realized there was one other thing he needed to do. He turned and saw Antius looking at him. "You're Tavi's brother, I'm told?"

Antius frowned. "I am."

"And Gaius' heir?"

"Yes. So?"

"And… you wanted to know how I fight." Lorcan glanced at Tavi, who shook his head, looking alarmed. Lorcan nodded in response, shook off the supporting hands and stepped forward, only to see that Antius was coming closer. Good.

"He told you that?" Antius said, his voice quiet.

Lorcan struck the moment that Antius was in range—a jab to the gut that doubled Antius over, then a punch that would leave him with bruises that mirrored Tavi's. Antius landed hard on the sand, howling.

"Lorcan!" Lucanus gasped. "What are you doing?"

Lorcan ignored him. He hobbled closer, standing over Antius. "Never touch my Tavi again. Understand me?" He nudged Antius with one foot. "Understand?"

There was a wheeze, and a nod, which Lorcan figured was the only answer he was going to get. He turned back and saw Lucanus examining the bruises on Tavi's face.

"You've made an enemy in him," Gaius murmured.

"He can put his name on the list," Lorcan answered. "He's not to touch Tavi again."

"I understand. And I'll make sure he behaves." Gaius took his arm. "Now, Tiernay is waiting for you."

Lorcan nodded. "Where?"

Gaius nodded, and Lorcan turned to see Tiernay leaning against a wall. When the mercenary noticed that they were looking at him, he straightened and started toward them.

"Tiernay, thank you," Lorcan said as the man reached them. "If you'll come to the *Ludus Manius* the day after tomorrow, I'll see that you get your payment. And if you're still in Rome in the spring, then I will be in need of your services again for when I return to Eire."

Tiernay smiled. "You're going back? I heard them. You're a citizen of Rome now, and a favorite of the Emperor. Why go back?"

Lorcan stopped, surprised. "Because... because that's my home. And I might need help taking it back."

Tiernay nodded. He stepped forward, his hand outstretched. "Your hand on a promise of spring, then?"

Lorcan took Tiernay's hand, "To spring, and a return to Eire."

Tiernay laughed, his hand tight on Lorcan's. "Here's to Eire. And here's to my king." He tugged Lorcan closer, and something slammed into Lorcan's side. He heard Livia scream, and almost missed Tiernay's final words as he fell.

"Cormac sends his regards."

***

"Lorcan."

Lorcan opened his eyes at the sound of the woman's voice. He was lying on his back in the middle of a green meadow. He saw up slowly and looked around. This wasn't Rome. Where was he?

"You're in my domain. I can't keep you here for much longer, though.".

He turned, and saw a woman sitting on a rock nearby. She looked to be of an age with his mother, but somehow even more beautiful. Her raven-black braid was draped over one shoulder, and her skin was the ruddy tan of someone who enjoyed the sunshine. He'd never seen her before, but he somehow knew who she was.

"Grandmother?"

"I thought we'd talk before I sent you back." She smiled. "You're an intriguing one, Lorcan."

"Your domain, you said. How did I get here?"

"I pulled you here. With some effort, I'll admit—you're a long way from home, fledgling." She rose, coming over to sit in the grass next to him. "It's a kindness. You're were grievously hurt."

Lorcan remembered the gut punch, and met the Morrigan's eyes. "Tiernay stabbed me."

"And your new friend Gaius took his head off for it," she added. "Your woman is quite distraught."

Lorcan swallowed, running one hand over his side. "Will I die from it?"

"You'll wish it, probably. But .your time isn't done yet It was a poor strike—the blade glanced off your belt. You'll be in pain for a time, and you'll have a good scar. And I'm keeping you here through the worst of it."

Lorcan frowned. "Cormac sent him to kill me. How? Why? How does he even know I'm still alive?"

"He holds your cloak. He knows you live. And, I think, he fears you will return." Morrigan smiled. "As he should. You are a most worthy son of my line, Lorcan. You will be an excellent instrument of my wrath."

"Against Cormac?" Lorcan asked. She nodded. "And if I kill him?"

"He has already been cast out and declared outlaw," Morrigan said. "Do not fear my vengeance."

"Thank you, Grandmother." Lorcan shifted. "Are the dreams I've had true visions?"

"Visions are always true," Morrigan said. "Except for when they are not."

Lorcan burst out laughing. "That's not helpful!"

"The further ahead in time, the harder it is to say what will be and what will not be. You have seen what is possible."

Lorcan considered her words, then nodded. "I see. And the cages?"

Morrigan scowled. "That is true. He has caged his kin."

"Should I return home now?" Lorcan asked. "Not wait for spring?"

"No," Morrigan said. "You will wait until spring. You must heal, and you have more to learn."

"Oh. Right. I'm hurt." Lorcan looked down at himself. "I'd forgotten."

"I need to put you back now," Morrigan said. "You won't see me again, or hear from me. But I wanted to tell you that I am most pleased with you, my Lorcan."

Lorcan looked down. "Even though I'm a freak, and not a real raven," he asked, his voice quiet.

"You're not a freak, my dear grandson, and you are very much a real raven. You were made this way for a purpose."

"What purpose?" Lorcan asked.

She smiled. "You'll find out." She reached out and touched his forehead, and the meadow started to fade. "When you're finished."

* * *

Lorcan was getting very tired of opening his eyes. But, he reasoned, the alternatives were nothing he wanted to deal with. Not just yet. He had too much to do. So he opened his eyes. He way lying propped up on his left side, surrounded by cushions. From this position, he was looking out into a walled garden that he was certain he'd never seen before. It was raining outside, a light, soothing sound. There was another noise competing with it, an odd, repetitive buzzing sound coming from somewhere behind him. And he hurt. All over, and enough that he wondered just what his grandmother was saving him from if he still hurt this much after having been saved from the worst. *No, don't answer that. I don't want to know. At all. Thank you, Grandmother.*

Distantly, he thought he heard her laughter.

There was a weight on his calf. He looked toward the foot of the bed and smiled—curled up next to him on the wide bed was Livia, fast asleep with her cheek pillowed on one hand, and her other hand resting protectively on his leg. She was here. He'd be fine.

The buzzing was still there. He turned his head again, couldn't see that far, and shifted slowly onto his back. And immediately regretted it. There was a reason they'd left him on his side—he'd forgotten the wound on his back. He would have laughed if he wasn't sure it would hurt worse. Nona, sitting upright in a chair, his head slumped forward, sound asleep. The buzzing was coming from him. As Lorcan watched, he jerked, winced, and looked up. His eyes widened.

"You're awake?" Nona whispered.

"You snore," Lorcan answered, trying not to laugh. "I had no idea you snored."

"Of course not. I never slept with you," Nona answered crisply. "Now, are you going to live? Looks like it."

Lorcan grinned. "No choice. I'm not finished yet."

Nona stopped. He frowned slightly. Then he shook his head. "Not asking you to explain that. I don't want to know what you mean."

"How's Ennius?" Lorcan asked.

"Awake. And cranky," Nona answered. "He's tired of being abed."

"Tired... Nona, how long have I been asleep?"

"Four days," Livia answered, her voice sleepy. "Almost five. No... no, it's late. Five. We could get you to drink water and broth, but you wouldn't wake up."

Lorcan turned his head to see her sitting up. "Five days? Livia—"

"You don't need to apologize," she said. "It wasn't your fault. Nona, go tell the runner that he's awake."

Nona rose from his chair, and Lorcan noticed for the first time that the man was armed.

"We're in the palace, aren't we?" he asked as Nona left. "Why is Nona armed?"

"Yes, we're in the palace. And yes, Nona is armed. Because no one knows yet who was behind that plot," Livia answered. "All they managed to get out of the prisoners was that they were supposed to make sure that you were dead along with the Imperial family." She took Lorcan's hand, running her thumb over his fingers. "Gaius is beside himself that this got past him. Lucanus is just furious."

Lorcan frowned. "And Tavi?"

Livia hesitated, then sighed. "Tavi is... complicated. He's going back and forth between being worried over you and being angry with you for breaking his brother's nose."

Lorcan nodded. "Two questions."

"What?"

"Should I not have? And can I sit up?"

Livia smiled. "Silly bird—"

"Corvina!" Lorcan looked around. "Where is she?"

"She's been in and out," Livia said. "The last time I saw her, though… ah… she was sitting on Tiernay's head, and… well… he didn't have eyes anymore. I think she's furious, too."

Lorcan blinked. "Is his head on a pike somewhere? Where's the rest of him?"

"Probably thrown into a pit with the other conspirators. And you knew? That Gaius took his head."

Lorcan nodded. "The five days I was asleep was courtesy of my grandmother, who told me it was to save me the worst of the pain. She told me what happened."

"Did she tell you everything?" Livia asked.

"I don't think so. Just about Tiernay. He was sent, Livia. My cousin sent him."

"Was your cousin behind all of this?" Lorcan looked up to see Gaius in the doorway. The big man smiled. "I'm glad to see you awake. Was this sent from your cousin?"

"No," Lorcan answered. "Only Tiernay was sent for me. At least, that's what my grandmother says."

Gaius nodded, walking further into the room. Nona followed him and closed the door behind himself. Gaius took Nona's abandoned chair, pulled it closer to the bed, and sat down.

"So… now what?" Gaius asked.

"Now?" Lorcan looked at Livia. "I'm going to try to sit up."

Gaius barked with laughter. "All right. If that's what's next. Livia, how can I help?"

Between Gaius and Livia, they got Lorcan into a sitting position, propped up by cushions. It wasn't any less painful, but Lorcan felt a little better for it, especially when the door opened again. Lucanus and Manius entered together. Gaius offered his father the chair, which Lucanus drew right up next to the bed before he sat.

"Well, now," Lucanus said. "You gave us all a fright. And missed your own wedding!"

Lorcan swallowed. "I didn't mean to frighten anyone. And I am sorry, Livia."

"I already told you, it's hardly your fault," Livia said. "If it helps you feel better, the next morning I went out and threw rocks at Tiernay."

Lorcan giggled. Then he groaned. "Don't make me laugh!"

Lucanus looked amused. "And we'll take care of the wedding. Don't worry."

Lorcan nodded. "Thank you. How are you, Manius?"

"Getting too old for this sort of thing," Manius answered. "Feeling every one of my years, and have been for days."

"You fought brilliantly," Gaius said. "I can see how you turned out such an amazing fighter as Lorcan."

"That was only partially my doing," Manius demurred. "Now, has anyone brought Lorcan up to date?"

"He knew about Tiernay," Livia said.

"How?" Lucanus asked.

"My grandmother told me."

"Your grandmother, the goddess?" Lucanus breathed. "She spoke to you?"

"She's the reason I was asleep so long," Lorcan said. He explained what the Morrigan had told him. Gaius whistled softly.

"Well, that's not something I expected to hear," Lucanus said. "I don't think it helps us at all."

"And that's all I know," Lorcan added. "Except that I know that Nona is armed because no one knows who was behind things."

"Nona is also armed because he, Ennius and Yaroah are now *rudiarii*, and have been named as *doctores* of the *Ludus Manius*," Manius said. "I'll offer the same to you, although I know I'll lose you and Yaroah both come the spring."

"*Doctores*?" Lorcan frowned. "You mean, teachers?"

"That's exactly what I mean. Ennius is *Doctor Retiarii*, Nona is *Doctor Secutorum*. Yaroah is *Doctor Murmillones*, and you, my boy, will be *Doctor Dimachaeri*," Manius continued. "We'll have to bring in some new *tirones*."

"Slaves?" Lorcan asked slowly. Manius smiled.

"Not necessarily. We made it known that you would be one of the *doctores*, and I already have young freedmen clamoring to learn from you. But we'll worry about all of that when you all are healed and ready."

He chuckled. "And if you go back to the arena, you'll command purses like no other gladiator in the history of Rome!"

Lorcan nodded. "And in the spring?"

"If you decide that you're still going to leave in the spring, then you'll leave in the spring, and with my blessing," Manius said. "Yaroah is staying until spring, and says that he will take the same ship you do when and if you leave."

"If?" Lorcan looked at Livia. "When did it become an if?"

Lucanus reached out and rested his hand on Lorcan's. "I was rather hoping you might consider remaining in Rome," he said gently. "Think on it, Lorcan. You're a hero, and all of Rome knows your name. You have the highest regard of the Empire, and of the Emperor."

"And his heir," Gaius interjected.

Lucanus smiled. "You've a wife, and a future here. A very bright future, if I have anything to say on it."

Lorcan licked his lips and looked at Livia. "And I have the highest responsibility to my family. To my home. What is happening there, it's because my cousin couldn't accept that I am everything he ever wanted to be. Everything he thought he was supposed to be. And if I stay... if I turn my back on my family..." Unbidden, the image of a raven in a small cage came to mind. He swallowed. "I can't stay. I thank you for everything. But my road leads back to Eire."

Lucanus patted his hand. "That was what I thought you would say. But, I had to offer. Rest now, Lorcan. We'll consult the augurs when you wake, to see when best to hold the triumph and your wedding."

Lorcan nodded. "Thank you. For everything."

Lucanus rose, and he and Gaius left. Manius closed the door behind them, and took the abandoned chair.

"If I'd had any idea how upside-down you were going to turn my life," he started. Then he laughed. "I'd still not have changed a moment of it. Livia, do you think Lorcan could eat something?"

"He should. I'll go." Livia kissed Lorcan gently, then left the room, taking Nona with her.

Lorcan smiled. "You wanted to talk in private, I assume?"

"You assume correctly. Lorcan, someone tried to assassinate the Imperial family. And you. Why?"

Lorcan shook his head. "I don't know. I don't understand why anyone would want to hurt Lucanus. I like him. And Gaius—he reminds me of my cousin Ronan. My best friend. They're good men, the both of them. And Lucanus is a good ruler, isn't he?"

"Yes." Manius leaned back and laced his fingers together over his stomach. "None of this makes sense. It's too ridiculously complicated. It should be obvious who is behind it."

"Why?" Lorcan asked. "This is very different from how it would be at home. If someone was going to challenge Eogan for the throne, they'd just challenge him. It's happened two or three times since I was a boy. There wouldn't be assassins or any of this plotting."

"There's ruling, and then there's politics. Your uncle and your father, they rule. Politics is interesting, Lorcan. The more complicated a plot, the easier it is to find the source. Too many loose ends means that the tapestry unravels far easier."

Lorcan nodded. "I know enough of weaving to know that. But if you have a few strands, and ply them together..."

"You create something nigh unbreakable," Manius finished. "Which is why this is so frustrating. There are too many ends! And none of them show where they originated!"

"That's the other reason you want me to stay," Lorcan murmured. "You know I'm not part of it, because they want to kill me, too."

"And because you have absolutely nothing to gain from it," Manius added. "Who would benefit from this?"

Lorcan shrugged. Then he winced. "I don't know. You tell me. Who benefits?"

Manius shook his head. "I've talked with Lucanus over this. For hours. Who benefits, if the imperial family dies? And we don't know. It can't have been Antius—he was a target, too. The next youngest after him is in Thracia, and can't return to Rome. The rest of Tavi's brothers... they're satisfied with their lot, the whole pack of them."

"What about Tavi's oldest brother? The one in Alba?"

"Arcus? Impossible. He has no ambition at all, to the point that he abdicated his position as Gaius' heir some 10 years ago. And he's got a wife and eight children in Alba. He'll be provincial governor, and that's all he wants." Manius scratched his chin. "I don't know."

"So what do I do?" Lorcan asked.

"You rest. You heal. Then... we'll see what happens. And, in the spring, you go home."

Chapter Nineteen

It was 10 days before Livia deemed Lorcan healed enough for the ovation. The night before, he and Gaius moved to a tent erected near a small altar on what Gaius called the Fields of Mars.

"Now, what exactly are we doing?" Lorcan asked as he and Gaius shared breakfast the following dawn.

"No one told you?" Gaius shook his head. "It's a parade. We go from here to the Temple of Jupiter. Have you been to the temple yet?"

"No," Lorcan answered. "The only temple I've visited has been Apollo's."

"Ah. You've seen it, though. You must have. It's visible from everywhere in Rome."

"The big white temple on the hill?" Lorcan asked. "I saw it, but I didn't pay it much attention."

"That's it. We're going there. The captives first, to show who we defeated. There's some painting that depicts the fight, but I've not seen it yet. And then us. Behind us are the sacrifices. A pair of sheep for each of us. You can ride, I hope? Otherwise, it's a long walk."

"I can ride," Lorcan answered. "But… you want me to wear that?" He pointed to the pile of folded cloth that Gaius had brought in with him. "That's one of those draped toga things, isn't it?"

"Yes, and it's your right to wear one now. And yes, you can ride in one." Gaius smiled. "I'll show you what to do."

He picked up the cloth and shook it out. Lorcan came closer and touched the purple border. "Tavi wears one, but his is all white."

Gaius laughed. "You've seen him in a toga. I'm impressed. Getting Lucanus the Younger to wear a toga at all is like trying to sweep back the tide. He's lived in Alba for so long that he doesn't like them. But Father says he has to wear one. And Father says you have to wear one, too. It's a sign of your rank. Now, usually you'll wear the *toga alba*, like Lucanus. But for this, you wear the *toga praetexta*."

"All right," Lorcan sighed. "How do I do this?"

"Put this on, first," Gaius said. He handed Lorcan a tunic with two purple stripes that ran from the shoulder to the hem.. Lorcan slipped it over his head, smoothed it over his chest, then frowned.

"Gaius, how do you ride without trews?" he asked.

"What?"

"You want me to ride a horse. Without trews. I'm not sure what your plans are for this evening, but I've need of this later," Lorcan said. Then he had to wait until Gaius stopped laughing.

"We can walk," Gaius said, wiping his face. "It's a long walk, but we can walk. If you think you can?"

"I can walk," Lorcan said. "How do I put on the toga?"

Gaius showed him, draping the long semicircle of cloth over his left shoulder, gathering it until the edge hung to Lorcan's wrist. The brought the rest of the cloth up and around Lorcan's right side, across his front, and over his left shoulder once more. He repeated the gathering and wrapping, draping the loose end over Lorcan's right arm. Then he tugged a small section of the under layer up and out.

"This is the *umbo*," he said. "When you're out and about, you can use this to hold things." Gaius stepped back and nodded. "It suits you," he said. "And the gladiator tattoos make it look even more impressive. You know, this is really unheard of. Freedmen aren't usually allowed to wear the toga."

"I'm getting used to being the only one of my kind," Lorcan said as he looked down at himself, wondering what his mother would say if she saw him dressed like this. Would she think it suited him?

She might, he decided as he ran his fingers through his hair. He'd have to ask Livia what she thought when he saw her. She and Manius were at the *ludus*, preparing for the wedding that would immediately follow the ovation. He looked around.

"Now what?" Lorcan asked.

"Now… be glad it's not raining," Gaius said, and settled a crown woven of *myrtus* leaves on Lorcan's head. He put a similar one on his own, then took Lorcan's arm. "We've a long walk ahead of us. Just keep thinking about what you've got waiting at the end."

There were people lining the processional way, cheering and throwing flowers. At first, it had been interesting. Almost amusing, to see the women in their draped veils standing with their men. There had been children, marching alongside Lorcan and Gaius, playing at being gladiators and fighting mock battles armed with sticks in place of swords.

And there were *hills*. Lorcan hadn't realized just how many hills there were in Rome, nor how steep they were. The longer they walked, the more Lorcan realized that perhaps 10 days hadn't been long enough. His leg started to ache. Then his side. His back itched where the wool rubbed against the healing wound, and he was certain that something was going to open and start bleeding, ruining his tunic and toga.

"How much longer?" he whispered to Gaius as they crested another hill.

"We're about halfway," Gaius answered. He looked at Lorcan. "You're very pale. Are you all right?"

"Aching," Lorcan said. "But I'll make it."

"If you pass out, Livia and Tavi will take turns murdering me," Gaius said. "We can walk slower."

"I'd appreciate that."

They slowed their pace, and kept walking.

"Wave at them, Lorcan," Gaius had told him. "You're a hero, and they love you."

"Nona told me that in the arena," Lorcan said. "They don't even know me, and they love me. It's really very odd."

"It's Rome," Gaius answered, as if that explained everything. Lorcan looked at him, and he laughed. "It is! There's no other explanation I can offer. Now wave!"

Lorcan waved, and kept walking.

"How long have we been walking now?"

Gaius looked up. "Ah… an hour, give or take?"

"That short? It seems like it's been longer."

"I know," Gaius agreed. "I could normally walk this in less time, but we have to keep to the pace set by the prisoners. Who seem to have slowed down."

Lorcan nodded. "What happens to them, when they get to the end."

Gaius shrugged. "Depends. For the legionnaires? They'll be executed. The slaves, too. The mercenaries will be sold as slaves. They won't be sold in Rome, though. They'll be sent out to the colonies. Probably to the mines."

"So they're in no hurry. Having been on that side of the slave chain, I can't say I blame them."

Gaius winced. "I never thought about it that way."

"I never did, either. Until it happened."

Gaius didn't answer, and when Lorcan looked at him, he looked troubled. They kept walking.

"You're limping. Why are you limping?" Gaius asked, sounding worried.

Lorcan snorted. "I was wounded in the leg. That might be why. Am I limping, though? I hadn't noticed."

"You are definitely limping. We're almost there. Can you make it?"

Lorcan looked at him, smiling. "Do I have a choice?"

Gaius shook his head and sighed, offering his arm. "You're insane. Lean on me. We'll make it."

"We don't have much further, do we?" Lorcan asked, leaning on Gaius' arm.

"Not much farther. One more hill," Gaius assured him.

Leaning on Gaius, Lorcan looked at the road ahead. They kept walking.

"One more hill, you said," Lorcan said as they stopped at the bottom. "You didn't say it was the biggest hill!"

"It's actually not. It's the smallest of the seven hills. But it's the most central and defensible, and it was a sacred place before Rome was Rome. Where else would you put a temple to the Father of the Gods?"

"I don't know." Lorcan frowned. "We don't have temples like this to any of our gods. I don't think they'd like it."

"Really?" Gaius sounded both amused and shocked. "No temples? Then where do you sacrifice?"

"Stone circles. In the middle of flat areas."

Gaius snickered. "Someday, I'll come to Hibernia, and you can show me."

"Someday, when you come to Eire, I'll be happy to show you all the places. We're not getting up this hill if we don't start walking."

"The road isn't bad. It winds though, so it's longer than it looks. Think you can make it?" Gaius asked. "Your limp is worse."

"It's either walk, you carry me, or I ride the sheep," Lorcan answered. Gaius burst out laughing, and Lorcan chuckled.

"I'd pay good coin to see you ride the blasted sheep," Gaius said.

"So would I. Here we go." He heard a raven calling and looked up. "There she is!"

"Who?" Gaius looked up. "Oh, your raven? I was wondering where she was."

"So was I, to be honest. She flew off last night, and didn't come back. I think she may have spent the night with Livia." He held his arm out, and Corvina landed on his forearm. She cocked her head and looked at him, then clicked. Lorcan smiled and clicked back at her, then let her move to his shoulder.

"You missed the walk," he said to her as they started up the hill. "You're here for the hard part, though. Thank you."

She rubbed her beak against his cheek. He smiled, feeling suddenly warm. The pain seemed to ease, and he straightened, letting go of Gaius' arm.

"Lorcan?"

"I'm all right," Lorcan said. "I'll make it."

They walked slowly up the winding hill road, and the magnificent structure at the top grew larger and larger. There were six carved white marble columns at the front, and Lorcan wasn't sure how many more down the sides. Lorcan wondered what the inside looked like, if it was as grand as the outside. Would he get to see it?

"Do we do the sacrifices in the temple?" he asked.

"Outside. In the courtyard." Gaius nudged him gently. "Which you should be glad of."

"Why?" Lorcan asked, looking at Gaius.

"Stairs." Gaius looked as if he was trying to be serious, but the corners of his mouth kept twitching. Lorcan shook his head and sighed.

"You'd love that, wouldn't you?" he asked. Then he looked over his shoulder. "Or is it that you'd want to see a sheep climb stairs?"

"You riding a sheep climbing stairs, maybe."

Lorcan burst out laughing, which set Gaius to laughing, and the echoes of their mirth rang off the sides of the buildings. The people who lined the streets laughed with them, and a child ran out toward them. Gaius scooped the girl up and carried her back to her mother, then rejoined Lorcan.

"Almost there. One more turn," he said. "Let's go."

One more turn, and the road opened up into a wide courtyard. There were smaller versions of the large temple in places, which Lorcan imagined were outbuilding or possibly living quarters. In the center of the courtyard was a small pool of water, and a white marble altar that stood as high as Lorcan's waist, on which a fire burned in a large metal brazier. There were three men standing at the altar, and Lorcan realized with a frisson of pure panic that he had no idea of what to do now.

"Gaius!" He grabbed the bigger man's arm.

"What? What's wrong?"

"The… the priest?" Lorcan looked over to see the men coming toward them. "What do I call him? Them? Are they all priests?"

Gaius nodded. "I understand. Of course. Yes, those are all priests. The one wearing the toga like yours, and the apex—sorry, the hat with the spike. He's the Flamen Dialis. His name is Valerius, and he'll be overseeing the sacrifices."

"So is he the high priest of Jupiter?"

"Yes. The one on his left, with his head covered? That's Sulius, the Rex Sacrorum. He's the High Priest of High Priests, to put it in a way you'd understand."

"I don't think I do, but go on."

Gaius paused. "I'll explain more later. It's the other man you want to watch. That's the Pontifex Maximus. His name is Antonious, and he's the head of all religion in Rome. And he and Valerius be performing your wedding later."

"He…" Lorcan frowned. "I didn't think we had a priest doing anything for the wedding. Manius said it was something about living together for a year. That was before, though. Now I have two?"

"You're right. That was before. Now, you're marrying as a patrician, an honored citizen, and Father is honoring you by allowing you to marry your Livia in the highest rites." Gaius smiled. "Trust me on this, Lorcan. Just smile and nod, do what they tell you, and eat the bread when they hand it to you."

"I… right. Whatever you say." Lorcan straightened. "Proper honorific for the flaming—"

Gaius snickered. "Flamen. Flamen Dialis."

"Flamen Dialis. What do I call him? Or any of them? I don't want to offend them or your gods."

Gaius nodded. "Holiness. Just call them all Your Holiness. Wait. Wait a moment. I forgot." He stopped, took Lorcan by the shoulders, and turned him. He frowned, said, "Excuse me, Corvina," to the raven, and he reached over Lorcan's shoulder, pulling a fold of toga up over Lorcan's head like a hood. He did the same to himself. "We go before the gods with our heads covered."

Lorcan nodded. He reached up and touched Corvina's breast. "Should I send her off?"

"I don't know," Gaius admitted. "Ask them."

Lorcan nodded. He followed Gaius, bowing when the other man did.

"So, this is the upstart," he heard someone say. Startled, he straightened. He wasn't sure who said it.

"Holiness, if you've objections to my father honoring a hero—" Gaius said.

"I've spoken to the Emperor." It was the Pontifex Maximus. "I think it a poor precedent to raise a slave to the sacred ranks of patrician."

"The young man's deeds cannot be questioned, Antonious," the Flamen Dialis said. "And if anyone should hold sacred rank, it should be a *semideus*." He smiled at Lorcan. "Albus Corvus, it is a pleasure to meet you. I've been wanting to ask. Your raven. Is she an emissary of your goddess? I understand you are the child of a Raven Goddess."

"I am, Sir," Lorcan answered. "And… if she is an emissary of my grandmother, she hasn't told me so."

He smiled. "Would she? Regardless, she is welcome in the temple. Come now, I know we go from here to your wedding. I don't want to keep you."

***

Lorcan had seen sacrifices before, but he'd never been a participant. He'd never before been so intimately involved, and he wasn't sure it was something he wanted to do again. The Flamen Dialis Valerius had used a bronze knife to kill both sheep with easy familiarity, then butchered them and prepared the meat for the spit. Some of it would be burned to honor Jupiter, Gaius told him. The rest would be eaten.

"By who?" Lorcan asked.

"Given how green you look right now, I'm assuming not by you," Gaius teased. He handed Lorcan a flask. "Watered wine. Really, it bothered you?"

"I'm not certain why." Lorcan shook his head. "Other than it's not what I'm used to."

"I've heard what you barbarians do," Gaius said. "Complete immolation, isn't it? I'm not sure which is better. But doing it this way feeds the hungry."

"True." Lorcan smiled. He sipped from the flask and passed it back to Gaius. "Now what?"

"Do you want to try and eat? There's the wedding banquet to come."

"I'm not very hungry," Lorcan admitted. "A little nervous."

"I remember that feeling. I remember thinking that Drucilla was the most beautiful woman in the world, and that I was the luckiest man." Gaius looked at the flask, then took a long drink. "Now? Well, I'm jealous of you, Lorcan. You and Livia—have you given my request any thought?"

"I discussed it with Livia while I was healing," Lorcan answered, keeping his voice low. "And... I still haven't decided. But if I do, I have to sire my own heir first. If that's agreeable to you? And to her?"

Gaius looked distant for a moment, then nodded. "She'll agree to that."

"There's one thing, though," Lorcan added. "Siring a child... I don't know what that child will be."

Gaius' eyes widened. "What do you mean?"

"The stories your brother told you about my kin? About changing to become a raven? That's true. If this child is born with feathers, then there won't be a man in Rome who won't know that you didn't sire it."

"The shape changing is true?" Gaius gasped. "Then why don't you just fly home? Wait... you don't have feathers. Or do you, and I'm missing something?"

"My feathers were stolen by the cousin who sold me. I don't know if siring a child on a woman who isn't my mate would mean that the bloodline and my grandmother's gift would pass on that child."

"So... if the babe is born with a raven's feathers, I'll have to bring them to you in Hibernia, won't I?" Gaius said. "I can agree to that. And hope it doesn't happen. I'll just have to take special care to keep anything untoward from happening like the ones before." Gaius looked grim, and Lorcan gaped at him.

"You *knew*?"

"I knew. I won't ask how you know. I assume it has to do with Livia. I know she's a *medicae*. Yes, I know the rumors. Drucilla swears that she did nothing, that it just... happened. I don't know, but I regret each of them. I told you. Her family wants a child of her body to be my heir. I don't seem to be able to sire one, so I arranged it. Just as I arranged it with you. I want children of my own. I know they won't be of my blood, but I want a child to call me father." He blushed slightly. "Does that make me weak?"

"Hardly. I understand it. My parents waited years for me."

Gaius shook his head. "You don't understand it. You know what I mean, but until you're there… your father would understand of what I speak of. You can't. And I hope you never do." He offered Lorcan the flask again. "More?"

"No, thank you. And I think you've had enough."

Gaius snorted. "Hardly. Let's go, then. I can't wait to see Antonious trying to look down his nose at you without my father noticing." He gestured. "There's a chariot waiting."

Lorcan grinned. "Can I drive?"

"You know how?"

"Learned from my uncle, who is my father's charioteer." Lorcan followed Gaius around the side of the temple, to where he saw a chariot hitched to two beautiful brown horses.

"Maybe another day," Gaius said. "I'm to deliver you to your wedding in one piece. And I know my team. They're feisty." He took the reins from the slave waiting, waited until he was sure Lorcan was holding on. Then he snapped the reins—the chariot lurched forward.

"Now that we're alone, and I can be sure no one is listening," Gaius called as the chariot passed out of the Temple and onto an unpopulated road. "I understand what he sees in you. My nephew."

"Tavi?" Lorcan felt his face growing warmer. "I… I wish he understood. That he'd listen."

"What's the argument?" Gaius asked. "I won't say anything."

"He wants me for himself. But I won't give up Livia. I love them both. He's admitted that he loves us both, but he won't accept that I can't be with just him." Lorcan frowned.

"Oh. That's a thorny one," Gaius said. "Decus, he says you know your destined wife from the minute you meet them. Is that true?"

"Or husband. Yes." Lorcan looked around. "And it's both of them. Livia accepts that. Tavi doesn't."

"That would never be allowed in Rome. Two men? Not in a marriage. Lovers, so long as you're discreet, but never a marriage." Gaius glanced at Lorcan. "That might be why Tavi is having a hard time of it, you know. In Rome, a marriage is between a man and a woman. Not between two men, and not between more than two. Maybe he just can't see that it's possible."

"He has until spring to figure out that I don't live my life by Roman rules, and that he doesn't have to either."

229

Gaius nodded. "He'll come around. He does love you. We all know it."

Lorcan looked around at the buildings they were passing. "There are people up ahead. We'd best stop talking about this. And here's hoping your gods are listening, and one of them thumps him awake."

"Do your gods do that? Thump people to make them listen?"

"Well, Grandmother does. Sometimes. I've no experience with the rest of my relatives on that side." Lorcan looked at Gaius. "Yours don't?"

"I didn't think so, but now I'm starting to wonder," Gaius said.

"Wonder what?"

"If you're not here for just that purpose."

Chapter Twenty

Once they reached the palace, Lorcan was whisked away by slaves and taken off to the baths. There, he was pleased to find the other gladiators already in the *tepidarium*. Ennius was still very pale, but he was in a merry mood as he welcomed Lorcan.

"Behold, the bridegroom cometh!" he called as Lorcan came into the bath.

"Not yet, he doesn't," Nona jibed, then hooted with laughter. "Oh, you're too easy, Lorcan! You've gone bright red!"

Lorcan snorted, sitting down on the bench next to Yaroah. "Are you going to be like this all day? Because I've already had a day."

"How was the ovation?" Yaroah asked.

"Educational," Lorcan answered. He rubbed his thigh. "Annoying in places. And a very long walk. My leg aches. I want to go soak in the *caldarium*."

"You've barely been in here. Wait a bit. Have a drink." Nona passed a goblet to him. "Tell us about the ovation."

"Educational how?" Ennius asked.

Lorcan considered the question while he sipped his wine. "I like Gaius. A lot. He reminds me of my family. The high priest doesn't like me. He thinks I'm an upstart, and that I set a bad example."

"High Priest?" Yaroah asked.

"Something maximus? Named Antonious."

"The Pontifex Maximus?" Nona snorted. "Not surprising. He doesn't like anyone who doesn't meet his standards. And no one does. Well, Drucilla does."

Lorcan looked over at Nona. "Wait, why her?"

"She's his sister," Ennius explained.

Lorcan nodded. "Ah. Livia told me her family was powerful, and that's why Gaius won't divorce her."

"Her family is the most powerful in Rome, barring the Emperor." Nona took another goblet and took a drink. "What do you know about religion here?"

"Nothing. And I'll keep it that way, thank you," Lorcan said. "I don't want to get involved. I'm going to keep my head down, teach what I know, fight in the arena, and go home in the spring. It's already been far too exciting. Enough that Gaius told me he thinks the Roman gods brought me here to cause trouble." No one laughed. Instead, they all looked thoughtful. Lorcan groaned. "Not you, too?"

"It would explain things," Ennius said. "Why everything is happening now."

"No. I am not a tool of your gods." Lorcan set his goblet down.

"Would you be able to tell?" Yaroah asked. "And I am asking that to you as a child of the gods. Would you, a *semideus*, be able to tell if you were being used by another person's gods?"

Lorcan stared at him. "I... don't know."

"Then do not say you are not. Say rather that you cannot know. It might be so. Come, you need to be scraped, and we will go have that soak."

In the *caldarium*, Lorcan lowered himself into the pool, hissing as the hot water washed over still-healing wounds. He leaned back against the side and closed his eyes. Was he being used by the gods? He didn't like the idea. He'd known his grandmother watched him. She'd admitted to it herself. But using him? That was something else entirely. And to what end? Grandmother had said that he would be an instrument of her wrath. But could other gods use him, too?

Grandmother, he called silently. *Can you hear me?*

No answer. He wasn't expecting one. She said it would be a while before he heard from her again. There were no answers there.

But maybe there were answers somewhere else?

* * *

The palace slaves seemed happy to help him find the Flamen Dialis, leading him through the halls until Lorcan felt as if he'd never find his way back. They left him outside a door, and Lorcan knocked and waited. A woman opened the door, saw him there, and smiled at him.

"You must be Albus Corvus Torvus," she said. "My husband described you."

Lorcan bowed. "I am, my lady. Or… is it your Holiness? I don't want to offend."

She laughed. "I'm not easily offended. My name is Cordelia. I'm the Flamenica. Were you looking for Valerius?"

"If he's available," Lorcan said. She nodded and opened the door the rest of the way. Lorcan got a good look at her when she did—her hair was braided up in an odd, conical style, wound with a purple band. There were oak leaves in her hair, and her robe was unlike anything he'd seen a woman wearing before. Her robes of office, he assumed, and followed her inside.

"Valerius?" she called. "Albus Corvus Torvus has come, and would like to speak to you."

"A moment, my dear," he called back. A moment later, Valerius came out of an inner room. To Lorcan's surprise, he wasn't wearing the spiked hat.

"Welcome, welcome," he said, beaming at Lorcan. "Come, sit with me. You look as if you have heavy matters on your mind. That's not good for a man on his wedding day."

He led Lorcan to chairs and sat down, gesturing to another chair. Lorcan glanced at the chair before settling onto the ground to sit at Valerius' feet.

"My dear boy!" Valerius protested. "What are you doing?"

"At home, when one goes to learn from the *Ard Ollamh*, they sit at his feet," Lorcan said. "You're not a druid, but you are a high priest, and I'm here to learn. It seems… disrespectful to do otherwise."

"I see." Valerius nodded. "What are you here to learn, my son?"

"A few people today have said that they think I'm here because your gods brought me here. That I'm here to cause trouble. To… to thump people awake. How can I know if that's so?" Lorcan folded his hands in his lap. "My grandmother spoke to me while I was healing. She says I've a purpose—"

"We all have a purpose, my boy," Valerius interrupted. "We won't know it until our time is done, but we all have a purpose."

"That's what she told me," Lorcan said. "Is that mine? To be an instigator of trouble, in places I never even dreamed I would see in my lifetime?"

Valerius frowned. "That isn't a question I can answer, Albus—"

"Please," Lorcan interrupted. "My name is Lorcan. The Emperor renamed me, and I am grateful for what he's done, but… my name is Lorcan."

"Lorcan, then. Of course." Valerius looked up. "Cordelia, if you'd be so kind? Then, perhaps, you could join the conversation?"

She touched his shoulder, then moved away. When she came back, it was with a tray. She poured goblets of wine and handed them to Lorcan and to Valerius, then sat down. "What's the question?"

Lorcan repeated himself, and she looked thoughtful.

"That's a very old question," she said. "Very timeless." She smiled. "Man has been asking it since the gods created us, I think. Why me?"

Lorcan smiled. "That's not exactly the question," he said. "I think my questions is more 'is it me' than 'why.' I don't need to know why. I just want to know if I am."

"I can't say I've ever spoken directly to the gods," Valerius mused. "I've spoken to augurs who spoke on behalf of the gods, but directly? No. But then, how can I say that? Would I know the difference?"

"If you spoke directly to Jupiter," Cordelia said, "I doubt you'd survive the experience."

"True, my dear. True." Valerius nodded. He sipped his wine, then nodded again. "I think the answer is yes, young Lorcan. But perhaps not in the way you think."

"Yes, I'm an instrument of the gods?" Lorcan said.

"Yes, but aren't we all?" Valerius asked in response. "We're all put here to a purpose, yes? Your grandmother tells you this, so you have it on much better authority than I, who has never been assured of such by my patron god. That makes us all instruments of the gods, here to fulfill whatever that purpose might be. It may very well be that your purpose in Rome is to open our eyes to the possible." He nodded again. "Yes, I think that might be it."

Lorcan considered it. "That's a much more comfortable idea than me being here to cause problems."

Cordelia laughed. "My boy, who says that it's not the same thing?"

"Cordelia, stop. Lorcan needs the peace of mind that answers bring," Valerius chided gently. "I wish I could give you better answers."

"I don't think there's such a thing as a better answer when we're talking about the gods," Lorcan said. "They don't deal in absolutes."

Valerius burst out laughing. "In six weeks, I could make a priest out of you!" he declared. "Or a philosopher. Have you read much philosophy, Lorcan?"

"No, sir," Lorcan answered. "I've only just learned Latin, and I'm still learning. I'm not very good with reading it yet. And I've no Greek at all. Isn't philosophy written in Greek?"

"Some of it, yes," Valerius answered. "Some in Latin." He looked at Cordelia, then at Lorcan. "What are you planning on doing to keep yourself busy until you return to Hibernia?"

"You know I'm leaving?"

"Frankly, my boy, I'm surprised you're still here!" Valerius laughed.

"I promised Manius I would stay the year," Lorcan said. "I mean to keep that promise. Until I leave, I'll teach the new *tirones* at the *ludus*, fight in the arena, plan how I'm going to win back what's mine, and enjoy being married."

Valerius nodded. "Good plans, all of them. Especially the last." He smiled. "Add coming to visit me to your list. I'll teach you philosophy. And Greek, if you want." He got up out of his chair. "Now, I need to prepare myself for your wedding. And so do you."

* * *

"Stop pacing," Gaius said. "You'll limp. You can't limp at your own wedding. It's a bad omen."

"Is it? I didn't know that. I don't know anything. No one's told me anything," Lorcan answered. He stopped pacing, then looked around the decorated atrium. "I don't know what I'm supposed to do. And where is she?"

"Probably on her way. The procession will be here soon. The runner arrived a few minutes ago," Gaius said.

"And what do I do?" Lorcan asked.

"I will explain everything when the time comes, Lorcan," Valerius said, coming into the atrium. "Do we have our 10 men?"

"Yes, Holiness."

"The bride is here. Let us go meet her." He led Lorcan and Gaius out of the garden and into the hall, where a crowd of men were gathered. Lorcan saw the other gladiators and Gaius' brother in the crowd. He didn't recognize the others. And he didn't see Tavi at all.

"He didn't come," he said softly. Gaius rested his hand on Lorcan's shoulder.

"There's still time."

Lorcan nodded. But privately, he wasn't sure that Tavi would be one of the witnesses. He wasn't sure if he'd see Tavi ever again. He followed the Flamen Dialis through the halls and out to the palace steps. There, the entire world stopped.

Livia. She was veiled in flame, a bright orange-red length of some fine cloth covering her hair and face. But it was unmistakably her. Drucilla stood with her, smiling softly. Manius stood behind her, watching with pride as she did… what was she doing?

"Part of the ritual," Gaius whispered. "This is her role in it. Don't worry."

Lorcan nodded, and tried to remember to breathe. All at once, he wanted his parents. They should be here to see him marry. He hoped they'd forgive him.

Maybe they could have a wedding feast in Eire, once things were over and settled. Yes, that's what they'd do.

"Gaius, if you would bring the bride over the threshold?" Valerius asked. "Lorcan, once she is here, ask her for her forename."

Lorcan nodded, wondering what a forename was as he watched Gaius. He approached Livia, bowed to her, then scooped her up gently in his arms. He stepped carefully over the threshold, then deposited Livia on her feet in front of Lorcan. Lorcan could just see her features through the veil.

"You're so beautiful," he murmured. "What is your forename?"

She smiled. "Where you are Gaius, there shall I be Gaia," she answered.

Apparently, it was the right thing to say. The men all cheered, and Valerius stepped forward. He took Livia's right hand and placed it in Lorcan's. "Come with me, my children." He turned and led the way back to the garden. The Pontifex Maximus was there, and the Emperor. The other men ranged around the edges of the garden. An altar and brazier had been set up there, and the Flamen Dialis directed Lorcan to lead Livia around it three times.

"Now, stand here," Valerius said. He stepped back, and the Pontifex Maximus came forward to join him. Lorcan didn't follow much of what they did next, as fruit and flowers were burned to Jupiter, Juno, and to gods whose names he didn't recognize. A sheep was sacrificed, and the omens proclaimed favorable. Then someone handed him a branch, and whispered to hand it to Livia. In response, she handed one to him.

"Now, you will give your marriage vows," Valerius said. Lorcan bit his lip. Vows? Had anyone said anything about vows? Behind him, he heard someone—Gaius?—groan, and realized that he needed to come up with something quickly. He only half listened as Livia gave her vows and placed her branch into the brazier, his mind racing. By the time everyone was looking at him, he had an idea. He placed his branch into the brazier, then took both of Livia's hands in his. He met her eyes, took a deep breath, and began:

"You are the joy of all joyous things," he said in Gaeilge. "You are the light of the sun, the door of the chief of hospitality. You are the surpassing star of guidance. You are the step of the deer on the hill, the step of the steed on the plain. You are the grace of the swan of swimming. You are the loveliness of all lovely desires." He paused, and repeated his words in Latin, saw Valerius' broad smile and Antonious' glower. He grinned, and continued, once more in Gaeilge, "A shade are you in the heat, a shelter in the cold. Sight are you to the blind, a staff to the lame. A harbor are you at sea, a fortress on land. A well are you in the desert, and health to the ailing. I claim you as mine, as I am yours, and may anything that is evil to us, or that may witness against us be illumined to us, obscured to us, banished from us, forevermore."

He repeated the words in Latin, and as he finished, and he saw tears on Livia's cheeks. But she was smiling. Happy tears, his father would call them. He'd done well.

"Repeat after me," Valerius said softly. "To me, myself, as ever my fate endures to live."

Lorcan nodded. "To me, myself, as ever my fate endures to live."

"Well done," Valerius said. "Now come and sit. And whatever you do, Lorcan, do not stand or move from your seat."

Lorcan glanced back at Valerius, but knew better than to ask why. Later, he would ask. For now, he held Livia's hand and led her to a pair of chairs, set closely enough that they could both covered by a single sheepskin. A still raw sheepskin, Lorcan's nose told him as he took a seat. Then he realized that this was the skin of the sheep that had been sacrificed at the beginning. He shuddered, but didn't rise.

"Are you all right?" Livia whispered in Gaeilge.

"Be better once this thing is tanned," he answered back, and she giggled.

"It's tradition."

"Roman traditions are more than a little strange."

Livia giggled again, and Lorcan smiled, running his thumb over the back of her hand. Around them, the other guests took places on couches and chairs, and the Pontifex Maximus spoke. Lorcan tuned him out, wanting only to look at Livia. He didn't really care what the man had to say, and he didn't think there was anything else he needed to do. Then a slave appeared in front of them, carrying a tray. bearing a single loaf of bread She knelt, and offered it to them.

Eat the bread, Gaius had told him. He nodded his thanks to the slave and picked up the flat loaf. As has become habit, he tore it in half and offered a piece to Livia. She took it, looked impishly at him, then tore a piece of the bread off and held it to his lips. He laughed and ate it, licking the tips of her fingers. She blushed furiously. He smiled and offered her a piece of bread the same way.

She bit him.

He burst out laughing, and gave in to temptation, leaning over and kissing her. There was a smattering of applause, and more laughter, and Valerius came to stand in front of them. He gestured to a slave who carried another loaf, and the slave cast the bread into the brazier.

"Jupiter Farreus, we beg that you accept the offerings on behalf of this new-married couple. Smile down on Albus Corvus and his bride, that they might have a long and happy life together." He turned to face them. "My children, I can see already that your marriage will be a happy one, and that what I'm about to say isn't necessary. But I do have to say it. Marriage isn't just in happiness. There will be hardships that you will face, and you must face them together. Marriage is not an idle undertaking, especially not the bonds that you have forged today—by sharing the bread in this manner, you are bound one to the other in the most sacred manner, and all the gods of your people and ours witness that you are now one, as intermingled as the clouds above. Do you understand this?"

Lorcan looked at him, then at Livia. He smiled, reaching out to cup her cheek. "I understand. And I'd have it no other way."

"Then by the gods immortal, you are joined together in matrimony." Valerius folded his hands and stepped away from the altar, looking around at the others. "Assembled and honored guests, please welcome Albus Corvus Torvus Victorinus, called Lorcan, and his bride Livia Corvina." He looked down at Lorcan, smiled, and winked at him. "You can stand up now."

Lorcan rose, bringing Livia to her feet. He looked around. For a moment, there was a pang of loss—Tavi wasn't in the crowd. He hadn't come.

"Lorcan?" Livia murmured. "You stopped smiling."

He looked at her, met her eyes, and shook his head. Reluctant would-be mates could wait. Spring could wait. Cormac could wait. So could the rest of the guests. Right at this moment, he had something far more important to do. Ignoring the words of congratulations, putting all other thoughts out of his mind, he pulled Livia into his arms and kissed her.

Right at this moment, nothing else mattered.

We hope that you enjoyed book two of Blood of the Raven series, *Ravenfall*! Please, consider leaving a review on either Amazon or Goodreads. Reviews are the life's blood of the independent author and publisher and would be greatly appreciated.

Want to keep up with the latest from Elizabeth Schechter and Riverdale Avenue Books? Sign up to our newsletter where you can find free books, exclusive promo codes and latest news: https://preview.mailerlite.io/preview/1098983/sites/136486432257607665/0kJ9TD

Looking to be an ARC reader/reviewer? You can sign up to our Reviewer/ARC Program at the link provided here: https://preview.mailerlite.io/preview/1098983/sites/160569605411046909/pvCkb9?fresh=1

About the Author

Elizabeth Schechter has been writing award-winning Romantasy since before romantasy was a word. Her writing credits include the award-winning steampunk romance *House of Sable Locks*, the Celtic romantasy series Blood of the Raven, and 2021 VIVIAN finalist *Written in Water*.

She was born in New York at some point in the past. She is officially old enough to know better, but refuses to grow up. She lives in Central Florida with her husband and son.

Elizabeth can be found online at http://elizabethschechterwrites.com.

Subscribe to Elizabeth's newsletter at https://www.subscribepage.com/k4u7k2

Other Riverdale Avenue Books/Circlet You Might Like

Ravenborn: Book One of the Blood fo the Raven Series
By Elizabeth Schechter

House of Sable Locks
By Elizabeth Schechter

Like a Breath of Flame
Edited by Cosmin Alexander and Cecilia Tan

The Siren and the Sword: Book One of the Magic University Series
By Cecilia Tan

The Tower and the Tears: Book Two of the Magic University Series
By Cecilia Tan

The Incubus and the Angel: Book Three of the Magic University Series
By Cecilia Tan

The Prophecy and the Poet: Book Four of the Magic University Series
By Cecilia Tan

Spellbinding: Tales From Magic University
Edited by Cecilia Tan

www.ingramcontent.com/pod-product-compliance
Lightning Source LLC
Chambersburg PA
CBHW020559030726
47497CB00007B/2008